DARK ARENA

BOOKS BY JACK BEAUMONT

THE FRENCHMAN SERIES
The Frenchman
Dark Arena

DARK ARENA

THE FRENCHMAN RETURNS

JACK BEAUMONT

BLACK STONE
PUBLISHING

Printed in the United States of America

First edition: 2024
ISBN 979-8-212-63104-4
Fiction / Thrillers / Espionage

Version 1

Blackstone Publishing
31 Mistletoe Rd.
Ashland, OR 97520

www.BlackstonePublishing.com

Jack Beaumont is the pseudonym of a former operative in the clandestine operations branch of the French foreign secret service, the DGSE. He joined "The Company" after being an air force fighter pilot and later flying special operations and intelligence missions. In 2021, his debut book, *The Frenchman*, quickly became a bestseller and is now published internationally and in translation. *Dark Arena*, his second book, continues the story of French spy Alec de Payns. Beaumont's background gives his novels a level of authenticity that few other spy thrillers have been able to achieve. You can find him on Instagram at @jackbeaumont_official.

To my wife and children
And to my brothers in arms
Patriam Servando Victoriam Tulit

PAUL

Prague in early February wasn't all that bad, thought Paul Degarde, even for a southern Frenchman accustomed to the Mediterranean warmth. There was no snow on the ground in the Czech capital, but Degarde waited in the Jungmann Square Starbucks, where his toes wouldn't freeze. He'd been in his holding zone for forty minutes. He'd walked his safety route before arriving at the coffee shop; however, last night's insomnia and the seven coffees he'd drunk were not calming. For now, he focused on not fidgeting or looking impatient, both "tells" that watchers would look for.

At forty-four minutes, Degarde wrapped a plain scarf around his neck, covertly dismantled his phone, and poured the pieces into his jacket pocket. Standing, he picked up a tourist camera from the table in front of him, dropped it in his other pocket, and emerged into the afternoon. The cold air tightened his jaw as he moved through Jungmann Square, his gait relaxed but his mind a laundry list of actions and contingencies. Paul Degarde may have been a fully commissioned case officer—an *officier traitant*, or OT—of the DGSE, France's foreign secret service, but he was not from Operations. His academic background in Russian foreign policy, and his fluency in the Russian language, had seen him recruited as an analyst by the Company twenty years earlier. For analysts who worked with the DR—the Direction du Renseignement, the Intelligence Division of the Company—some basic training in clandestine liaison was required, which he'd used at his two embassy external posts in Greece and Turkey. There were rules for how he conducted himself in the field, even if his job was the relatively low risk processing of human sources.

He had six minutes between Starbucks and his contact point. He had to be nonchalant while detecting and memorizing everything on the route. He knew from his fieldwork that once he was back in Paris, someone from the DO—Direction des Operations—could gatecrash a debrief and start asking detailed questions about who and what was around him during a meeting or a route.

He walked across Františkánská Zahrada Park, through the Světozor passage with the tourist crowds and came out in Vodičkova Street, where he turned right to create a visual "loss" for potential followers. He walked fifty meters up the street before crossing it, giving him an excuse to look for traffic and determine followers.

He moved into a medieval walkway, past a line of eight advertising panels, and walked at a slight angle to them so as to remove a convenient line of sight for any followers. He advanced to a set of steps at the end of the lane where a luminous sign indicated Kino Lucerna. Inside the building's gallery, a horse was suspended upside down from the vaulted ceiling. He took a few photos, playing out his tourist legend and allowing a final check for followers. By the time he lowered his camera, he knew he was clean. If things went wrong, the camera shots would let the Company know his location before he disappeared. He pushed the thought of capture from his head. Unlike the DO operatives, he had his secret weapon, right against his heart in his jacket pocket: his diplomatic passport.

He climbed the stairs to the café, choosing a table located slightly back from the bay windows, with a view of the gallery and the stairs. Lotus was due to arrive at 3:00 p.m., which left Degarde fifteen minutes to sit and watch.

He ordered a coffee and prepared for the wolf to show the tip of his nose. The main operational security method he had to adhere to when managing clandestine "drops" was the *itinéraire de sécurité*—IS—which involved walking routes, finding angles, checking in reflections and creating *points de passage obligés*—zones that a follower had to commit to in order to maintain their "tail," and which made it obvious they were following. Besides the IS there was also a hygiene protocol called the "tourniquet," which involved a team of least two OTs, who would overwatch a security route and "clear" an operative out of their mission zone, ensuring no followers. He didn't have a team overwatching this operation, so he focused on his tradecraft and waited, controlling his breathing and refraining from fidgeting. If Lotus was a no-show after twenty-five minutes, he'd play it by the book: there was never a compelling need to wait more than ten minutes past the agreed meet time.

He'd arrived from Paris the previous morning, and at his hotel, the Old Royal Post, he'd asked to be moved to another room immediately after check-in. Then he'd walked to the French embassy, located west of the Vltava River. Degarde considered the Vltava to be the natural demarcation between his life and mission zones: in his mission zone, he was a spy whose every movement and interaction was controlled by the Company; in his life zone, he was a midlevel diplomat with declared duties, none of them controversial.

At the baroque palace that housed the French embassy, Degarde had met the chief of station, who worked under the cover of cultural attaché of the embassy. He'd briefed the local DGSE man on the real purpose of his visit and the backup he would need if the contact with his source did not go as planned. Contact with an already-recruited source did not usually necessitate a DO protection scheme, so Degarde was responsible for his own safety.

Now, as he sipped his coffee in the Café Lucerna, his Paris apartment in the thirteenth arrondissement, where his wife Katie and daughter, Louise, were waiting for him, seemed very far away. He tried not to think about Paris. Some operatives in the Company could spend weeks in the field under these conditions, somehow remaining calm and focused and keeping their families in a separate mental compartment. He didn't know how they did it. Instead, he turned his mind to the meeting with Lotus—the codename for Lado Devashvili, a former member of the Georgian government who'd branched into the business world in the early 1990s when the Soviet bloc fell. Devashvili spent very little time in Tbilisi with his family, given his job kept him so busy meeting prostitutes at luxury hotels. Lotus provided everything that might be required by a foreign government or its contractors: drugs, escorts, boats, planes, IDs, and weapons. What the DGSE required was hard-to-come-by intelligence. There was no collusion between the Company and Lotus, only an exchange of documents for cash. Degarde had spoken to him once, through the operational agent of the DO who had recruited Lotus and transitioned Degarde to become the handler. That three-way meeting in Vienna had been a memorable one for Degarde— not just because he'd met Lotus for the first time, but because he'd met the well-known Aguilar, from the DGSE's Y Division, the section responsible for clandestine operations. Lotus's face resembled a metal plate chiseled for many years by expensive vodka bottles, in the center of which sat two small, sunken eyes. Even Lotus had been wary around Aguilar, Degarde noted. After the meeting, Aguilar had warned Degarde to be particularly cautious around Lotus. "Avoid talking to him, and always be very careful to carry out your personal security measures. Imagine you're dealing with a cobra in a round room."

Since that initial encounter, Degarde had met Lotus clandestinely in the major cities of various European countries, always under the guise of business trips. Degarde contacted Lotus via the standard liaison plan, making an appointment and stating his needs, and the Georgian appeared miraculously to pass on information that was generally considered high quality. While impressed by the level of information, Degarde would have preferred not to come within five hundred kilometers of the man.

At 3:01 p.m., a tall, fat man wearing a long coat entered the Lucerna's gallery. Lotus was well within the Company's accepted −1/+2 minutes window for a contact. His tweed trilby hat was in his hand rather than on his head, indicating that he didn't think he'd been followed; however, Degarde's position gave him a view of everyone who came into the building behind the Georgian. Degarde took the green *Geo* magazine from his bag and put it on the table in front of him, indicating to Lotus that he'd detected no followers and the exchange could proceed.

Lotus crushed his cigarette beneath his heel and climbed the marble stairs to the café, where he sat at a free table between Degarde and the exit. He put his hat on the table, took a packet of cigarettes from his pocket, and put it next to the hat, then signaled to a waitress and ordered a whisky. Degarde paid his bill—keeping the receipt so he could charge his coffee to his

mission expenses—and stood up. Tucking his magazine under
his arm, he walked to the exit. As he passed Lotus's table, he let
his hand drag and retrieved the packet of cigarettes. Lotus did
not react. Everything happened so naturally that only a trained
observer would have seen the drop.

Degarde walked down the marble stairs to the foyer and left
through an exit that neither man had used when they arrived.
He turned right and headed toward the National Museum, pausing along the way to take tourist snaps. At the statue of Saint
Wenceslas, he entered the adjacent Metro station, turned left
at the bottom of the stairs, and walked with the crowd toward
the disabled toilet. After locking himself in, Degarde pulled
the packet of cigarettes from his pocket and opened it to reveal
four tightly folded A4 sheets. Three of them were printouts
of emails, containing the names and addresses of the senders.
Degarde skimmed them: in Russian, the writers of the emails
asked Lotus to set up various services for their benefit in the
Cypriot city of Larnaca, and also on the Lebanese and Syrian
coasts in the Mediterranean. Degarde felt his blood run cold
as he unfolded the fourth sheet and saw the letterhead. It was
a classified document from the Russian defense ministry indicating the appointment of specialist agents from the SVR, the
civil foreign intelligence agency, at the Russian military base
at Tartus in Syria, and the deployment of intelligence drones
at the Khmeimim Air Base, another Russian facility in Syria.
He wondered how such a significant document had fallen into
Lotus's hands, and decided it warranted staying an extra night
in Prague to play out his tourist legend. His training empha-
sized that if an OT had any doubts while in the field, or had
a sense of heightened risk, they should put any followers "to
sleep" by spending hours wandering a city in tourist mode, with
no hint of training.

He took his small camera out of his pocket and, after setting the sheets flat on the floor, photographed them twice each, making sure to erase each photo as soon as it was taken. His glasses slipped over his nose and his hand was shaking. The Company's Technical Division would retrieve data from the camera's memory card upon its return, and the numbers of the remaining photos would follow each other in the event of an inspection.

Having roughly verified the content of the drop, it was time to move to the second phase of his contact: remuneration. Degarde tore the sheets into tiny pieces and let them fall into the toilet. He would have liked to proudly exhibit the Russian classified document to colleagues at his intelligence desk, or "BER"—it was quite a coup—but he wasn't going to travel across Europe with such a dangerous prize in his possession. He flushed the toilet several times, removed an envelope from his bag which he placed in his jacket pocket, then he left the bathroom and took the westbound Metro line. No longer carrying compromising material, he began to feel calmer as the train picked up speed. But he would only breathe easily on the plane back to Paris, he knew, when this was all over.

He emerged from Mustek station and walked through the pretty streets of old Prague until he arrived at Svateho Jilji church, entering the building through the side door on Zlatá Street. Lotus sat alone in the first row of the left aisle, seemingly deep in prayer. Degarde wondered which saint would listen to him. Apart from a few tourists and a priest checking his candles, the church was otherwise empty. Degarde sat at the other end of Lotus's pew and, without turning his head from the transept, took the envelope from his pocket and placed it gently between them. Inside was ten thousand euros, which Lotus would probably spend on vodka and a girl. With this Christian thought,

Degarde stood and crossed himself, as Lotus put his hat on the envelope.

Degarde walked down the central aisle and stepped out onto Husova Street. He plunged into the small passage in front of the church, to the left of the beer museum, and set about exiting his mission zone.

He walked past the medieval torture museum and over the seven-hundred-year-old Charles Bridge, which was the point de passage obligé leading to his life zone. For followers to stay on his heels, they would have to reveal themselves on the bridge. He breathed out slowly when he reached the far bank and took some tourist snaps, turning to face the way he'd come. He was on the alert for someone he might have noticed earlier in the day, without announcing that he was looking. But he saw no faces he'd seen before and no "parasite gestures" that were supposed to look natural but were forced.

He took another photo, committing to the role of tourist now. He would spend the next twenty-four hours meandering the streets and visiting museums, taking a hundred shots of Prague. He wished he could show his wife and daughter this city, so beautiful under the late winter sun and so relaxing when you didn't have to retrieve secret documents from one of the Company's most dangerous sources.

Considering himself clean, he hurried up the stairs into the lobby of the Old Royal Post and asked to extend his stay for an extra night; there was just so much to see in this beautiful city, he told the woman on reception. Then he went up to his room and changed his flight.

After buying souvenirs in the airport's departures concourse, Degarde sat at the bar and ordered a whisky. He was exhausted. The extra day in Prague had been spent walking in his office shoes, and his feet ached. Easing back in his seat, he rummaged in his jacket pocket, took out the various pieces of his phone, put it together, and turned it on. He was pleased to see that there was no missed call from Katie. Even though he'd been away a night longer than planned, she would have understood that he couldn't break from his legend to call her. He sent a text to the embassy's "cultural attaché," thanking him for his time and his welcome, then pulled the battery from the phone again. The chief of station would understand that Degarde was at the airport and all was well.

Degarde took a sip of his drink, thinking of those documents he had briefly seen in the bathroom. Tartus and Khmeimim. Why would Moscow send more SVR men there? What were the Russians preparing in the Mediterranean?

The flight to Paris was announced. Degarde drained his whisky and joined the queue to board, thinking that James Bond could not have done better.

PARIS

It was 9:32 p.m. when Paul disembarked at Charles de Gaulle and headed for the RER to get lost in the crowds and complete his last safety route alone before returning home. At the boarding area for the Paris-bound RER, the information panel indicated that the next train had been delayed by forty-five minutes due to a signal failure. Degarde was tired and wanted to go home. Though he knew he should follow procedures, he considered that no opposing service was following him, so he returned to the terminal and went to the taxi stand. Putting a slight feeling of professional guilt to the back of his mind, he got into his assigned taxi and gave the driver his address, then he turned on his phone and texted his wife: *Just leaving the airport. I'll be home in 35 minutes.*

The following morning, Degarde ate breakfast with Katie and Louise and then took the Metro to Porte des Lilas, emerging in the twentieth arrondissement just before 9:00 a.m. It was still cold enough to warrant gloves and his black woolen beanie as he walked toward the Company's headquarters. He wasn't too concerned with his "hygiene"—he'd walked his security routes the previous day in Prague before going to the airport, and he didn't feel the need to do another before entering the Centre Administratif des Tourelles, known colloquially as the Cat, even though he knew many OTs did. Instead, he was anticipating his debriefing with sector manager Marie Lafont at 3:00 p.m. He'd have time to drop the camera's SD card with the Technical Division—the DT—before writing his report. He was eager to get the photos of the documents before lunch so he could analyze them before the debriefing. Lafont could be forensic about source materials.

He entered the DGSE building on Boulevard Mortier, known as La Piscine by many employees because it was beside an indoor swimming pool where so many of them exercised. He passed through the many security points. A hotchpotch of Napoleonic and late 1960s architecture, with a modern American overlay, the headquarters of France's foreign intelligence service looked like it had been constructed to completely confuse an outsider.

He walked downstairs to the DT's basement level, which was vast and ran under Boulevard Mortier into the building over the road. In the administrative area, he dropped the SD card with a techie who sported a Flock of Seagulls haircut and a t-shirt with a picture of an audio cassette, and asked for the "prod" to be sent to his office.

Degarde went back upstairs to the cafeteria to grab a coffee and *pain au chocolat*, and seeing four of his colleagues on the velvet benches at one of the round tables, he wandered over to join them.

"Haven't seen you for a couple of days, Paul," said Stefan, a DR analyst on Degarde's floor who worked at the Africa section. "You been on a trip?"

"Yes," said Degarde, unable to repress a proud smile. "But I can't tell you more than that. You don't have the need to know."

His colleagues laughed.

"James Bond for a day," said Romain Precheur, the Counter-Proliferation analyst.

"Well, he'd better learn to drink a martini," said Stefan. "Last time I saw Paul drinking gin, he threw up on himself."

"Bond drinks vodka martinis," said Romain.

"Even worse," said Stefan. "Paul passes out with vodka."

"Okay, okay," said Degarde, smiling as he stirred sugar into his coffee. "The only thing I can tell you is that the quality of the prod is as good as the girls in the country I visited."

"Let's hope you weren't in Pakistan then, *mon pote*," said Stefan, which triggered more laughter.

He walked the stairs up into the main building and entered his office by inputting the week's digital code. In front of him were various files containing information grabbed by sources over the previous months. He was expected to take in strands of information and synthesize pieces of a puzzle. He had barely closed the door behind him when there was a knock. He opened it to find an internal courier, who handed him a sealed envelope containing the printed documents retrieved from his SD card. Closing the door again, he perused the contents closely. One of the documents Lotus had supplied was an email in Russian about an event scheduled for two weeks' time in Monaco, aboard a yacht called *Azzam*. Degarde couldn't remember this email from his quick verification in Prague. The Russian term for "making a deal" was used in the email, and the language suggested a very high level of discussion. There was also a phone number listed for an unidentified person who seemed to be a person of interest, a POI, for the Russians.

Degarde knew immediately that Lafont would want more

detail, so he left his office and walked down to the department that generated intelligence from Open Sources. He asked them to research *Azzam* and have the information for him by 2:00 p.m. Back in his office he called the DT, thanked them for the SD images, and asked for a "phone environment" on the phone number in the email; if they succeeded, it would tell him where the phone was being used. Then he opened the reports section of the DGSE computer system and wrote two reports. One was for the analysts, an "O" report written objectively that did not allow the reader to see the identity of the writer or the sources of the intelligence, and the other one was called "R" and explained how the contact with Lotus was done and the security measures he took around it.

As Degarde filed the reports, the internal courier knocked at his door and dropped off a file that contained pictures, specifications, and ownership details of *Azzam*. It was an eighty-two-meter, ten-stateroom motor yacht, Degarde learned, built in the Netherlands in 2017 at a cost of seventy-eight million euros. It was owned by a UAE shell company, and its home port was Port Vell, Barcelona. It didn't feature in any social pages, and it didn't appear to be owned by a movie star or a Silicon Valley billionaire. There wasn't much on *Azzam*, but that wouldn't stop Lafont asking for more.

At 2:58 p.m., Degarde dropped his iPhone in the box outside the E sector briefing room on the third floor and took a seat at the large oval meeting table, across from the current head of BER–Europe, Lars Magnus. Magnus was tall and youngish and seemed a little spooked by the presence of his immediate predecessor in the role, Marie Lafont, who sat beside him. Marie Lafont was a well-dressed brunette in her early forties. She was smart and driven and had field experience, which set her apart from many of the careerists at the Company. Now a sector manager, she was running this operation. She didn't acknowledge Degarde's arrival; she was on the phone, asking someone to join them. After a quick conversation, she hung up and turned to Degarde. "Based on the prod I received this morning, I asked Briffaut to sit in. He should be here soon."

Degarde nodded and smiled but his stomach clenched. Dominic Briffaut was the head of Y Division; he didn't often leave the Bunker, as the headquarters of clandestine operations was known, to come for idle chats at the Cat.

"We need to know what they're planning on that boat," said Lafont. "And we need a phone environment to locate this number in the email."

"It's done, boss," Degarde said, relieved he'd taken the initiative.

The bearish form of Dominic Briffaut entered the room, mug of coffee in his hand. He threw his coat on one of the spare chairs before taking a seat. "I have twenty minutes," he said. "Tell me what you've got."

Lafont took Briffaut through the document drop in Prague and the information gained from it, including the intelligence drones being staged in Khmeimim Air Base, the new SVR intelligence postings at Tartus, and the meeting in Monaco aboard *Azzam*; so far, there was nothing to connect the phone number of the POI to the meeting on the yacht, she added.

Briffaut nodded through the briefing, asking only a few clarifying questions. The two senior people were economical with their words, Degarde noticed. And Magnus—despite being the head of BER–E—stayed out of it.

When Lafont had finished, Briffaut turned to Degarde, focusing on him. "You've dealt with Lotus more than anyone. Was there anything different about our Georgian friend in Prague?"

"I don't think so," said Degarde. "I never talk to him. I collect the prod and I give him the money."

"Sometimes a man doesn't speak with words," said Lafont, with a very faint smile.

"Was there more eye contact than you're used to?" Briffaut pushed. "Did he try to start a conversation?"

Degarde shook his head. "It was business as usual."

The Y Division chief stared at Degarde in silence for a few seconds, then he stood, grabbed his coat, and, talking to Lafont, said, "I'll leave you to find out more about that phone number, and I'll investigate a way on to the boat. Let's talk tomorrow."

And then he was gone.

Back in his office, Degarde found a message from the DT: the phone number on the Lotus prod had been used in Genoa several times in the past twenty-four hours. He sent an internal email to Lafont to let her know, then put all the material he'd amassed in his office safe, shut down his computer, and headed to the Metro. He mulled over the debriefing as he traveled home. It had not gone terribly—after all, he'd retrieved the documents without screwing up the mission—but the prod had delivered more questions than answers. The Russians were increasing their presence on the Syrian coast, and the Palais de l'Élysée would expect the French security services to tell them why. And it was important that the Company get the information to the President before the Americans or the British could do it.

It was a little before 7:00 p.m. when he turned the key in the door to the mid-nineteenth-century apartment in the thirteenth—the rent was subsidized, thanks to Katie's connections—and let himself in. No murmur of a TV or squawk from an Xbox. That meant Louise might be reading, which made Degarde happy; he was tired of nagging her about screen time.

He hung up his coat, walked past the kitchen, and froze at the tableau before him.

Three men in black balaclavas. His child on the sofa, crying. His wife on her knees, hands tied behind her back, a hand holding her blonde hair in a gloved fist.

"Who are you?" Degarde demanded, but instead of answering, the man closest to him took one step toward him and swung a black handgun that caught Degarde in front of the right ear. Degarde staggered sideways into the sideboard, and a vase toppled from it and smashed on the floor.

"Dad!" screamed Louise, and the third masked man slapped the child hard with the back of his hand. Her mother screamed before a big hand was clamped over her mouth.

As Degarde pushed himself off the sideboard, he could see his wife's blue panties on the Persian rug beside the television screen, ripped at the sides. As he tried to stand, his vision swimming, his assailant kicked him in the balls. Degarde sagged to his knees, retching from the pain.

"So," said the man holding his struggling wife. "Our friend lives like a king in beautiful Paris, eh boys?"

His French was good but heavily accented. Russian.

"What do you want?" gasped Degarde, switching to Russian. "My family have no part in this."

"So why bring them into it?" asked the Russian, his grip on Katie's face tightening. "You make another country your business and then claim you are immune? The French have such a sense of humor."

Louise stirred on the floor. Degarde could see she was crying, tears running down her bruised face onto her Paris Saint-Germain shirt. She didn't have Katie's blonde hair but the dark curls of

Degarde's mother. They framed a face full of fear and despair, and this hurt Degarde more than his aching testicles.

"Let them go," he said. "I'll tell you what you want to know."

The lead man chuckled. "You hear that, boys? He's offering to talk."

The man who'd assaulted Degarde also laughed. He grabbed the collar of Degarde's woolen jumper and leaned in. "You'll talk, all right, Comrade. You'll *beg* to do it."

Degarde tried to reply but the handgun slammed into his face again, and the scene before him went black.

CHAPTER
ONE

Alec de Payns walked in the morning sunlight across the Pont des Bergues, spanning the Rhone, aiming for Geneva's *rive droit*. He'd been walking for sixteen minutes, which had given him time to relax into his legend of a design student named Guillaume Roger, while also checking for followers. Geneva gave the surface impression of a wealthy, civilized city; however, it was also a historic crossroads of national interest and money, and de Payns was always careful in this city of spies.

He stepped onto the Quai des Bergues, turned right, and walked along the river to where it opened into Lac de Geneve, a haven for cruise boats and waterside bars and restaurants. He crossed onto the Quai du Mont-Blanc, where the buildings became grand. One of them was the Ritz-Carlton Hotel, where he was due to meet his new friend Nikolai, a fellow student at the HEAD design academy, and his father.

De Payns walked past two black Mercedes-Benz SUVs parked on the Ritz-Carlton apron and entered the impressive white marble foyer with its black-and-white marble-tiled floor.

There were two military-looking men in the lobby, dressed in black suits and tactical boots. De Payns had been expecting to see them, just as he was expecting to see the tall blond student standing by the marble staircase, his red woolen scarf a raffish contrast to his expensive sand-colored suit.

"Guillaume!" Nikolai waved flamboyantly, his Russian accent echoing around the huge room. "Over here."

Nikolai moved in for a hug, and de Payns could sense the security people watching them.

"I hope you're not freaked out by these apes," said Nikolai, cocky and rude and eminently likable. "My father only visits once a year, and he travels with this zoo. Is it okay?"

"I hardly noticed," said de Payns, with a smile. "Thought maybe Putin was in town."

Nikolai laughed then, suddenly serious, said, "Dad has to have these people around him when he travels because of his work. Please don't be scared."

"Thanks for the warning—I'll try to look brave," said de Payns. He started to walk away, but Nikolai grasped his bicep to stop him.

"Dad and I love each other," he explained earnestly, "but he thinks that the Russian climate is not good for me right now." Nikolai bit his lip and looked away. "It just doesn't . . . agree with me."

De Payns felt for him. Their friendship hadn't touched on the subject of Nikolai's sexuality. Now Nikolai was trying to find a way to warn his French friend that the Russian military and intelligence worlds did not accept gays. Even the sons and daughters of senior officers could find themselves sent to rehabilitation camps, to be physically and psychologically broken down, and turned into *real* Russians.

"I understand, my friend," said de Payns. "I guess you are

much better off in Geneva, especially for the arts."

They moved into Fred by Fiskebar, a pricey bar favored by Nikolai. De Payns usually avoided drinking there; Geneva had much better taverns. But his social manipulation had succeeded, and Nikolai now wanted his father to meet his new friend. Nikolai was not aware that also dotted around the hotel was de Payns's mission team, consisting of Templar, positioned in the hotel for threats, and Danny, who was in the van controlling the comms. They'd both cover de Payns when he left the hotel, doing counter-tailing, and if necessary, they'd run a tourniquet. Aline, a petite blonde who worked for the Company, was sitting alone in the Fiskebar, drinking a Coke. She'd been recording audio and HD video of the bar with a hidden device for ten minutes before de Payns arrived, and she'd clandestinely record the meeting from her table.

Nikolai's father was already seated at his table when the two students arrived. De Payns flashed his big smile, in keeping with the youthful student persona he'd cultivated. "So pleased to meet you, Mr. Beshivsky," he said, using the surname assumed by Nikolai. "Welcome to Geneva."

As they made small talk, de Payns assessed the man in front of him: he was around fifty, with pale, cold eyes, a full head of salt-and-pepper hair, and a strong body. De Payns could feel the other man's eyes scrutinizing him in return, the father trying to work out if Nikolai and de Payns were lovers. After all, that was why Nikolai had been exiled to Geneva under a false name.

When Nikolai rose to go to the bathroom, de Payns was left alone with his new acquaintance, whose real name was Lazar Suburov, a full colonel in the Russian FSB, the country's federal security service. Suburov was the number two ranking officer in the Intelligence Directorate for Chechnya. The Company had codenamed him Keratine, and he was of value to France, which was why de Payns was going to try to turn a senior FSB officer while armed Russian henchmen stood guard outside.

"So," said Keratine, "Nikolai tells me you share a passion for art and for partying? I'm glad to hear he has found a like-minded friend, given he doesn't see his family much anymore."

"Well, actually," said de Payns, letting his expression harden, "I'm not your son's friend. I work for the French services—and from now on you'll work for us too."

The blood drained from Keratine's face. De Payns recognized real fear in his eyes.

"You could refuse," continued de Payns, "but I guess you know what happens if your colleagues discover that your son is not dead, like you told them, but hiding out in Switzerland because he's gay?"

Keratine cleared his throat, his pupils dilating. "Exiling a gay son isn't so unusual . . ."

"Even if he's in contact with a foreign intelligence service?"

"Fuck," mumbled Keratine. He slumped in his seat, rubbing his face as if trying to make the conversation go away.

"I understand the Russians like to *reeducate* homosexuals," said de Payns, keeping his voice flat but strong. "The Chechens in particular. It's not pretty, but highly effective, I hear."

Keratine winced. "Look, I love my son. He's not here because I'm ashamed."

"I don't doubt it," said de Payns, seeing that Nikolai had moved to the bar and was ordering drinks. "Nikolai is an impressive young man."

Keratine sat up, seeming unsure whether to be sad or angry. "I knew this moment would come one day. Please don't do this. There is no need."

De Payns kept talking, knowing the entire interaction was being recorded by Aline from the bag on her table. "You will be contacted in Russia by a man named Guy. He'll introduce himself as a friend from Geneva. I suggest you respond positively to his requests, for the survival of your son—and perhaps to also stop your career from submerging?"

Nikolai returned with the drinks and resumed his seat. "So, have you got acquainted?" he asked, a boyish quality evident now he was less nervous. "How do you like my friend, Dad? I told you he was fun."

"Your friend is very nice," said Keratine, eyeballing the Frenchman.

De Payns stood. "Well, I know how much you have missed each other, so I'll leave you to have some quality family time." He turned to Keratine. "Sir, it was very nice meeting you. Maybe we'll meet again?"

"I don't think so," said Keratine, with a brief hate-filled glance, "but you never know."

De Payns passed the Russian thugs in the lobby and stepped out into the street. He crossed the road and walked north along the Quai de Mont-Blanc, finding some shade from the trees that separated the famous street from the lake. He now had to conduct a tourniquet overseen by the three-person mission team, ending at a *plan de support*—an advertising poster at a bus stop on the Rue des Pâquis, which would feature a sticker, or *gommette*. If the sticker was red, he was being followed and he'd move to an exfiltration plan.

The route took sixteen minutes, his team detecting if he had followers and communicating with one another over the radio net. He walked to a Coca-Cola ad on a bus stop and saw the red gommette. Yet just because there was a tail, it didn't mean he could break from his legend and start acting like a spy.

He kept walking and entered Geneva's central railway station, walking to a magazine stand where he pretended to be interested in a publication. He waited for a train to arrive, and when there was a crowd pouring down the main concourse, he joined them. After ten seconds, he took a sudden turn to the right and walked out a side passage into the sunshine and onto the grounds of the art and design school. He walked out the other side of the campus, leaped onto a tram, and rode it four blocks west before jumping off and treating himself to a browse through a three-story department store. When de Payns was sure he no longer had a follower, he moved to the dead mailbox that had been set up along with the tourniquet and had now been "armed" with a white gommette at the end of a street called Rue Jean-Gutenberg. He followed the street for twenty seconds before seeing a red bicycle with a wicker basket parked outside a bakery. From the basket he grabbed a white envelope—left there by Aline—and quickly dropped his French ID card in the name of Guillaume Roger in another envelope in the basket. De Payns kept walking, and at the end of the street put the sticker he was carrying on a concrete lamppost, which told Aline he'd made the exchange and she could return for the envelope.

De Payns walked to the Crowne Plaza, where a room had been booked under the name on the new ID card he'd just picked up, Benoît Droulez. The booking had been made by Renan, an infrastructure Honorable Correspondent—HC—working in the hotel. An HC arranged important matériel and services for visiting OTs. Renan worked in the Crowne Plaza and would ensure no bank details were needed and there was no trace for the Russians.

In his room, de Payns lay on the hotel bed, cycling his breathing. He felt safe in this hotel because Renan was a clan member, one of a secret group that included Shrek, Templar, Rocket, and himself, who were sworn to support one another. That's how de Payns worked, and it was what he relied on for

his sanity. He visualized every step of the morning and the tourniquet. He thought about faces he'd seen in the hotel and on
the tram, and what he might have missed. He thought about
Nikolai, and about Nikolai's father's face when de Payns had
given him the facts, the *dévoilement*. He thought about how the
scenario could be turned on his own family and quickly pushed
that thought down as far as it would go.

CHAPTER

TWO

De Payns flew into Orly on Friday morning and rode the Orly-val shuttle to the Place de la Bastille, where he sat down in the Hippopotamus café at 10:29 a.m. Before he could pick up his menu, a man ten meters away took a blue cap from his table, put it on his head, and walked onto the street.

De Payns followed the man for six minutes, into a quiet side street, where the man took off his cap and de Payns heard a silver VW Golf starting beside him. The man walked on, and de Payns got in the car.

"Good morning," said de Payns to the driver, who was his colleague and friend, Jéjé. He didn't know the woman in the passenger seat, so he didn't use names.

They drove east across Paris to the suburb of Noisy, and after clearing the security gate—which de Payns had to do without Company ID—Jéjé pulled up outside the side entrance of the Bunker. The headquarters of the Y Division was an old fort, set in parklands and surrounded by a castle wall that had somehow stayed erect through the centuries. Known as the Bunker, the fort was the home of the Company's Operations section, the Y Division. It was physically separated from the other DGSE divisions—Intelligence, Technical, and Administration—which were situated at Boulevard Mortier in central Paris.

"The boss wants to see you," said Jéjé with a smile as de Payns climbed from the car. "No pressure, mon pote."

De Payns entered through the secret employees' entrance, ran up the stairs to the first floor, and walked the squeaking floorboards to his small office with its eastward views over the leafier part of Paris. The office was plain and government-issue, with a nondescript desk, a basic safe on the floor in the corner, and a keyboard and screen with no port for a thumb drive or any accessories. His French rugby team coffee mug was the only personal item on his desk.

Around him he could hear other *officiers traitants* banging on their keyboards. The French secret service was capable of interesting adventures, but the whole show ran on reports and briefs. Grabbing his mug, he made for the kitchenette and made himself a capsule coffee. He was reaching for the sugar when a throat was cleared behind him. He turned to see Margot, Dominic Briffaut's middle-aged executive assistant, who stalked the halls of the Bunker doing the work of a sergeant-at-arms.

"The boss is waiting for you," she said without preamble.

He thanked her but she was already walking away.

He followed her up the stairs to the top floor and through the antechamber to Briffaut's office.

"Go right in," said Margot.

De Payns shut the door behind him as he entered.

At the desk, with a view of Paris behind him, was Dominic Briffaut, head of the Y Division. He was a solidly built man of West African heritage who had been recruited from French special forces. Even in his early fifties, he looked as though he could operate in the field.

"So," said Briffaut, polishing an apple on his shirt. "How did it go?"

De Payns took a seat. "I think we won the first round. He wasn't expecting it."

"Do we have a reliable source?"

De Payns nodded. "I think it'll hold for a while, but Jim will have to be careful. Even if Keratine loves his son, he might still declare the approach to save his career."

Briffaut looked at de Payns. "I know how you feel about Jim, but you'll have to get over it." He bit into the apple.

De Payns felt his nostrils flare. Jim Valley, the Company's OT who would handle Keratine in Russia, had worked for Philippe Manerie, a corrupt director of the DGS—the Company's internal affairs directorate. It was Jim who had recently taken de Payns's wife, Romy, and his two sons on an abduction simulation, designed to leverage de Payns's silence.

Briffaut continued. "Jim is pretty good at what he does. And the investigation showed that he was just obeying Manerie's orders; he had no idea he was betraying the Company."

De Payns made a face—the Cat would rather redeploy a wayward employee than risk dirty laundry finding its way into the newspapers. "I guess putting him in the DR is what they had to do."

"And I guess I had to agree to it," said Briffaut flatly.

De Payns wondered what Romy would say if she found out her husband now worked with the man who'd abducted her and their children.

"We've received an urgent request from the DR," said Briffaut, tapping a file on his desk. "A source produced some serious stuff. Looks like the Russians are deploying those new observation drones at Khmeimim in Syria."

"Okay," said de Payns, intrigued. The Russians' new DA42NG drone was used by their intelligence service, the FSB, in areas where it was up to no good: Mali, Libya, Chechnya. It wasn't a general surveillance aircraft. Deploying it at Khmeimim—the Russian air base on Syria's Mediterranean coast—indicated Russian escalation.

"The documents suggest the SVR are also beefing up operations at their Tartus navy base."

"Shit," said de Payns.

"One of the documents the source supplied mentions a deal between the Russians and another party. It's due to go down on a UAE-owned boat called *Azzam* in two weeks' time."

"Where's the boat?" asked de Payns.

"It will be in Monaco," said Briffaut. "In a separate email, there's mention of a person with an associated phone number. The phone was just located in Genoa."

De Payns repressed a sigh. No doubt this meant more travel, the possible sabotage of his weekend plans, and almost definitely a fight with his wife, Romy.

"I want you to leave for Genoa on Monday," said Briffaut, as if reading de Payns's mind. "Take a technician with a spinner and put a face and an ID on this number and the person operating it. We're calling him Starkand—operation is Bellbird."

The boss pushed a file across the desk. This was a DAO, a *demande d'aval d'opération*—the official tasking by the DR for the Y Division to go to work. De Payns opened it and looked at the attached printout with the phone number of Starkand's phone.

"On your way to Genoa, you can stop in Monaco and get us access to *Azzam*," Briffaut added. "We need someone on board, or we need to bug it in advance. We have to know who's talking and what they're saying."

De Payns stared at him. "Do I look like Harry Houdini to you? How do you want me to set this up in two weeks?"

"We have an HC in Monaco," said Briffaut. "An old-timer. His name's Johnny. He's been asleep for ten years."

"*Ten years?*" echoed de Payns. "I'll have to blow the cobwebs off him."

"Save your judgment for the meeting," said Briffaut, pushing a second file across the desk. "Here's his file. The *plan de liaison* to wake him up is inside. If he replies, go see him. If not, we'll find something else."

De Payns breathed out and avoided Briffaut's stare.

"You'll have to go Monday, at the latest."

De Payns hissed. "That means goodbye to my weekend. I was away this week."

"Life is tough," said Briffaut, trying to smile. "But so are you."

"Yeah, right," said de Payns. "In that case, I'll take next Friday off and spend a long weekend with the family."

Briffaut shrugged acceptance. "And let me know if you're meeting Johnny."

De Payns nodded. "Can I take Lolo as the technician?"

"If you want, but make sure he uses his brain this time, otherwise he's out."

"What do you mean?" asked de Payns, chuckling.

"When he gets in the field, he goes all James Bond and thinks with his underpants."

"Understood, Boss," said de Payns. "I'll make sure he doesn't jump on anyone."

Briffaut nodded his approval, his attention already on another set of files.

There was a knock on the door.

"That'll be Shrek," said Briffaut. "You can let him in on your way out."

CHAPTER
THREE

Shrek stood back from Briffaut's door and muttered a quick hello to Aguilar as his friend left the boss's office.

"Come in, Shrek," the boss called.

Shrek shut the door behind him, and the head of Y Division waved him to a seat.

"What I'm about to tell you doesn't leave this room, understand?" ordered Briffaut. "At least, not before Monday."

Shrek nodded. "Got it."

"You know Paul Degarde?"

"From the Russian desk? Sure, but not well."

"Two days ago he had a nasty surprise, after returning from a foreign trip."

Shrek sat up. "In Paris?"

"Yep," said Briffaut, balling his big fists on the desk. "His wife and daughter were pretty shaken up, but Degarde didn't make it."

"Fuck," said Shrek, before he could stop himself.

"That was my reaction. DGS have taken the wife and child out of harm's way."

"What happened?" asked Shrek.

"DGS checked his last text messages, and he was well clear after seeing his source and leaving the country."

Shrek's mind whirled: OTs were constantly reminded to be especially careful when they landed back in Paris—*back from the moon*. That's when they were at their most vulnerable: tired from the mission and wanting to get home. That's when they were tempted to take shortcuts, which was why the importance of being clean for the "last mile" was hammered into them so forcefully.

Briffaut continued. "He was clean into Charles de Gaulle, but he took a taxi straight home from the airport."

Shrek almost felt sick. "*Quel con*, what an idiot!"

"It's done now. Our job is to work back and find who did this. I want you to go see Degarde's wife, make her talk. We need her to spit out all her memories."

"DGS are finished?" asked Shrek, aware that the Company's internal affairs officers sealed off such scenarios as if the entire organization was leaky.

"Not officially, but I'll get you a window of a couple of hours, and you have my authority to use all your skills."

Shrek nodded. He was known for an interview style that got results without the need for raised voices or threats. A lot of manipulation, yes, but no threats.

"And just so you know, the source Degarde was handling was Lotus. You see what I mean?"

"I see," said Shrek. In other words, Paul Degarde had probably dragged a bunch of Russians into Paris.

"I'll give you the address on Monday," said Briffaut.

Briffaut hit his intercom and was talking to Margot as Shrek left.

De Payns flipped through the file Briffaut had given him; the picture of Johnny must have been at least twenty years old. He wondered why the Corsican had been put to sleep for a decade and whether it had to do with his reliability. He found Johnny's contact phone number and the "wake up" authentication script in the back of the thin file. Smiling at the old-school script, which was reminiscent of the clandestine liaison tools they were taught at Cercottes, the DGSE training facility outside of Orléans, he picked up the phone and dialed.

A voice answered after two rings; a gravelly male voice, wheezy like the Godfather's. With authentic Corsican manners, the voice simply said, "Yes?"

"Can I rent a house in the countryside, behind Nice?" asked de Payns.

"The holidays are over, so it's a good time right now," the Corsican replied without hesitation. "Tell me what you need."

"I need fresh air," said de Payns.

"Let's meet on Monday at the Hotel de Paris—the Bar Américain, six p.m."

De Payns agreed and put down the phone. The entire interaction had taken twenty seconds, and at the end of it he had a meeting with Johnny, and he knew the man was a professional.

It was midafternoon when de Payns reached the "safe house," which in the Company was called an OCP, or Operational Clandestine Premises. It was located in an anonymous building in the eleventh arrondissement. He entered the week's numerical code into the number pad at the building's portico and pushed through the door as the bolts slid back. He now stood in an internal antechamber, with a closed security door in front of him, and listened to the security bolts slide home in the door behind him. He waited for thirty seconds; then, when the green light was illuminated on the number pad for the next door, he input the DGSE's daily code and entered. He wanted to make this quick. With his reports on Geneva written, he was able to leave work early, and now he had a good shot at making it home for dinner with Romy and his sons, six-year-old Oliver and eight-year-old Patrick. It could be a struggle to make time for his family, while at the same time having to put them in a sealed compartment when he was operational. He intended to make the most of these few precious hours he had stolen before he had to leave for Monaco and Genoa.

He walked past one bedroom—made up for agents on the move—and glanced into another room consisting of servers and a desk with a computer. He continued on through the kitchen to his locker, where he located a manila envelope labeled *Benoît Droulez*. Taking off his watch and emptying his pockets of wallet and phone, de Payns stripped himself of his false identity and placed the items in the envelope. He changed his brown leather loafers for a pair of Asics sneakers and switched his blue sports coat for a windbreaker. Then he opened the envelope labeled *Home*. He put on his own watch, checked his wallet, and put his phone in his jeans pocket. Then he left via the secret rear door, emerging in a service lane, and headed for the Metro.

It was just before five o'clock when he reached the second-floor landing of his apartment building and paused at the Napoleon-era door. The address he'd secured for his family was well above what he and Romy could afford in the private housing market, but after a recent security scare, when Philippe Manerie was revealed as a mole in the Company, the de Payns family had been relocated to a beautiful apartment in the thirteenth arrondissement, reserved for well-connected military and intelligence officers.

He pushed through the door and out of habit deadlocked it behind him. From down the hall, he could smell fish baking and the sounds of SpongeBob making sense of his world. He emerged in the large kitchen and living area and saw his sons lying in front of the television.

"Hi, Dad," called out Patrick, who had a mouth full of orange. Oliver rolled a Lego machine-of-war across the carpet, oblivious to his surrounds.

De Payns wandered back down the hall and found Romy at her computer in the spare bedroom. She had changed from her professional clothes into jeans and a tight-fitting tank top. De Payns had a quick flash of *what if* and put on his best smile, but her expression when she looked up from the screen put an end to that idea.

"I have to rewrite a report," she said. "Can you take care of dinner and deal with the boys?"

Before de Payns could answer, she added, "And you'll need to do the shopping—there's nothing for breakfast."

"Can I have a shower first?" he replied, being sure to wipe any sarcasm from his tone. Her policy job at the Tirol Council environmental think tank was demanding, and even if it was a little lefty, it gave Romy a chance to make a difference in green energy, and he was trying to support her.

Romy eyeballed him. "I've dealt with the boys on my own for the last two days, and I work too, remember?"

"Okay, I've got it covered," said de Payns. He'd been hoping for a pleasant evening but decided he might as well rip off the Band-Aid now since they were already sniping at each other. "I'm off on Monday for three days or so."

Romy gave him a look. "Do they do this on purpose? They know you have a family, right?"

"Yes, they know."

"So, they want you to lose that family?"

De Payns shifted his stance. "Is that a threat?"

"It's not a threat, it's fucking exhausting, that's what it is."

In de Payns's experience, once Romy started swearing, she was digging in for a fight.

"It's important," he said.

"Oh, it's *important*, is it?" she said, slapping her hands on the desk either side of the keyboard. "You're out there playing cowboys and Indians while there are people working on real plans for the planet."

"Cowboys and Indians?" echoed de Payns, a little shocked. "That's what you think I do?"

She shook her head, the anger going out of her. "We have different views on how to save the world, that's all. You and your friends use violence while the people I work with are about ideas and collaboration, trying to build a better world for our kids."

"And who protects the kids?" he asked, the words escaping before he could stop them. "An economist with a TED Talk?"

De Payns stood in the shower, seething; angry with Romy for her intellectual snobbery and furious with himself for rising to the bait. His wife was smart and so were her colleagues, but that didn't make him a caveman with a club. And it didn't make her idealism a shield against some of the monsters he'd met. Truth was, he wished Romy and the Tirol Council were right, that clean energy and aggressive wealth-redistribution policies would solve the world's evils. Unfortunately, human beings tended toward power and personal gain, and as long as human nature prevailed, the common good would never be the objective of all. There were people out there so greedy and disrespectful of their fellow humans that they would not be stopped until someone like Templar held them by the throat and squeezed the life out of them. Templar did not do TED Talks or go to cocktail parties. But Templar was prepared to walk in the dark and protect those who couldn't. De Payns avoided telling Romy that her husband was also prepared to fight in the dark arena so that civilians could live in peace. But he wasn't going to win an argument with Romy by spelling out what he and his colleagues did to keep her kids safe.

He thought about his mission to Monaco as the warm water ran down him, and he worked hard to push thoughts of the mission and Johnny out of his head.

Stepping out of the shower, he dried and dressed quickly and returned to Romy in the spare room. Hugging her and reading what she was typing on her computer, he said into her ear, "Sorry, honey, I went too far. Thank you for trying to save the world. Next weekend, I'll take Friday off, and we'll go to Deauville."

He sensed a smile as he kissed her earlobe. "I'm off to do the shopping," he said.

CHAPTER
FOUR

De Payns flipped breakfast pancakes and pointed to the coffee he'd made for Romy.

"Drink your coffee," he said, as she drifted around the apartment loudly looking for a favored hairclip.

"I said no TV before school," de Payns growled as Patrick hit the remote and the screen came to life.

It was 7:28 a.m. on Monday, and de Payns was playing his part in the weekday morning routine, painfully aware that he'd soon be heading for Monaco and leaving Romy to cope on her own with the kids. De Payns and the boys had enjoyed the weekend, kicking the soccer ball, practicing some karate, and eating at a Japanese restaurant where the boys had food thrown into their bowls by a chef who played ABBA on his little speaker. He'd drunk wine and gone to bed early with his wife. Not a bad result for a cowboy.

Romy returned to the kitchen, her hair up and her heels sounding harsh on the polished wooden boards.

"I have a new rule for the males in this house," she said,

sipping her coffee carefully so as not to ruin her lipstick or splash the white shirt she wore under her blazer. "Don't touch my stuff."

"Where was it?" asked de Payns, pointing to the tortoise-shell hairclip now in her hair.

"On the Lego box," she said. "The boys are going to Ana's after school, and she's taking them to karate. I'm picking them up from there."

"Okay," said de Payns.

He deposited the pancakes on a plate, then walked her to the door.

She kissed him. "Be careful," she said. "And what I said about you playing cowboys and Indians? I only say things like that because I can't bear to think about what you actually do."

"I know," he said, accepting a kiss.

She pushed away from his arms. "And remind the boys that Ana's getting them from school."

"Okay," said de Payns.

She walked across the foyer, her shoes clicking on marble, echoing against the vaulted ceilings.

"Eat up, boys," he yelled as he strode down the hallway. "We leave in nine minutes."

Their walk to school involved a detailed discussion on Paris Saint-Germain soccer club and a teacher called Mr. Simmons, who was from England and taught music. He apparently had a terrible sense of humor and liked to play "Deutschlandlied" to see the looks on the French kids' faces.

"Tell him that a German wrote the music to 'God Save the Queen,'" said de Payns.

"Is that true?" asked Patrick as they emerged on Avenue du Maine.

"Maybe not," said de Payns, as they waited at a pedestrian crossing. "But we just want to see the look on his silly English face, *non*?"

The boys were still laughing as they crossed the street toward the school. He said goodbye, all the parents quickly putting on their COVID masks to prove they were responsible. One of them—a well-dressed Parisienne—walked toward de Payns and his boys, dropping her mask as she did.

"Hi, Ana," said de Payns, as her son Charles ran to play-punch Oliver.

Ana Homsi smiled, a flash of teeth beneath intelligent dark eyes and a high forehead. "You have the idea, Alec," she said, pointing at de Payns's face. "I should do that."

"Dad never wears one," said Patrick. "We tell him, but he never remembers."

De Payns cottoned on. "Oh, this thing," he said, touching the mask that usually sat at his throat. "Do I have to wear one outside?"

Ana laughed. "Who knows?"

"No one knows," said Oliver.

"So many laws and rules that you can't obey them all," said Ana, with a smile. "But the government always has something to arrest you for."

"Too many rules—maybe that's why PSG keeps losing," said Patrick, and Ana laughed.

De Payns found himself laughing along with this charming woman, Syrian by descent but with no Arab accent. He had a flash of insight into his boys, accepting the care and affection of an adult outside their immediate family. He wondered where he had been during this transition in which Romy and Ana had stitched together a series of arrangements in order to pursue their own careers. It relied on a child's trust and a parent's authority, which in this group was Ana. De Payns felt like a bystander, and Ana's attempts to make him seem less like one just made it more obvious.

The boys moved toward the school gate. "Ana's getting you from school," de Payns reminded the boys as he hugged them goodbye.

"We know," said Oliver, following his older brother into the school grounds. "It's Monday."

After two Metro journeys and a bus, de Payns arrived at the Bunker and went straight to his office, where he took his small backpack from the safe in the corner.

A soft rap on the door behind him announced Margot's presence. "Aguilar, boss wants to see you. He's in the park."

He descended the stairs past the Y Division gym, emerging into the cool morning sunshine of the fort's parklands. Thirty meters away Dominic Briffaut gesticulated with his cigarette at a woman in her midthirties, Greta, who appeared to be listening but, judging by the expression on her face, not agreeing. De Payns stood off, waiting for his boss to call him over. Greta stalked away from Briffaut and gave de Payns an annoyed look as she passed—no doubt another OT who'd been told, "*Thanks for your opinion, now do as you're told.*"

Briffaut extended a pack of Camels and lighter as de Payns approached. "We all set for Genoa?"

De Payns took a smoke and lit it. "We'll be out of here by nine-thirty."

"Lolo's using the big head?" asked Briffaut.

De Payns shrugged. "I'm told Lolo's sharp, he'll find that phone."

"What about Monaco? You contacted Johnny?"

"Yep," said de Payns. "We're on for tonight."

"Be careful with him," said Briffaut. "His job is to get us on a boat. Don't get lured into his bullshit."

De Payns nodded and took a drag on his cigarette.

Briffaut's gaze shifted to another OT who was waiting to talk to the boss. "Don't linger down there. I need you back in Paris."

CHAPTER
FIVE

De Payns keyed in through a security door to the Bunker's basement level, housing both the Y Division car park and the Y-9 group, which provided cyber and technology support for operations. De Payns walked past the mechanics' bay to where the tall, shaven-headed figure of Lolo Suquet stood beside a silver Renault Megane.

"This is us?" asked de Payns as he approached the car and slipped off his pack.

"Sure is, boss," said Lolo. He was dressed in a brown biker's jacket, black shirt, and black jeans. In his late twenties, Lolo had been recruited out of the Université Paris Nanterre where he was a junior lecturer in electrical engineering. He was smart but he'd had limited time in the field—certainly nothing approaching de Payns's experience.

"Everything ready?" asked de Payns, placing his pack on the back seat.

"Whisky and cigarettes," said Lolo with a smile. "Condoms too."

"Think with the big head, Lolo," said de Payns. "We got our matos?"

The Y-9 group usually worked on cyber operations in the bowels of the Bunker, or in operations vans—'subs'—supporting missions with high-powered listening posts and data hacks. The chance to travel with a field operative to Monaco and Genoa might sound like shaken martinis for the tech people, but de Payns treated the trip as routine, and his priority was to ensure he had his materials—matos—in the car.

"The plates and papers are in the spare tire well," said Lolo, referring to the change of number plates and registration papers carried by OTs traveling out of Paris. "The spinning laptop and camera are loaded and fully charged, plus we've got backup batteries and a stack of clean SD cards."

"Tracker?" asked de Payns.

"Two of them, also fully charged," said Lolo, giving the thumbs-up.

"ID?" asked de Payns, meaning did Lolo have the basics to pass as someone else while in Italy.

"Yep, did some gardening on the weekend," said Lolo, referring to the small actions in and around an OT's false address that firmed up the assumed ID.

De Payns nodded and pointed to the dangling silver earring Lolo wore in his left lobe. "That'll have to go."

"Just a couple of square guys, huh?" replied Lolo, reaching for the earring.

"Something like that," said de Payns, opening the driver's door.

They made fast time on the A6 out of Paris, which went through Auxerre and bypassed Dijon, where de Payns had been based as a fighter pilot during the Kosovo conflict. It was a part of his life that had been so important at the time, but the great pride he'd once felt was fading with the years. De Payns had been cleared to fly combat, in Mirage 2000 fighters, at the age of twenty-one, and he remembered every sortie over the Balkans. But a back injury and spinal surgery had meant he could no longer fly fighter jets, and he found it easier these days not to dwell on it. Easier, perhaps, because the early days with Romy occurred when de Payns flew, and it was that version of him she remembered so fondly.

They stopped for lunch at a Total roadhouse just north of Villefranche, and de Payns opted for one of the outdoor tables so he could sneak a smoke after his baguette. He was aware of his senior role at the Bunker, and the fact that early-career people like Lolo were hungry for insights and wisdom. He didn't mind talking about tradecraft and some of the lessons he'd learned, but he also lived in a world of information compartments, so being interrogated by a younger OT could be exhausting. He wiped his fingers and put a cigarette to his lips. "So, Lolo," he said, lighting the smoke as Lolo played with his tuna salad, "you're fairly new to the Bunker. What's your story?"

Lolo smiled. "I did electrical engineering at the Université Paris Nanterre, and then I became a junior lecturer in telecoms engineering. I worked briefly at Vodafone, and now . . ." He shrugged.

"What did you do at Vodafone?"

"Tower testing, network commissioning. You know: propagation delay, latency, basic fix-it algorithms and some code overwrites."

De Payns smiled. "Basic, huh?"

Lolo looked away. "Some people can sing, some can hit a golf ball. This is my thing."

"I'm told you're the best we have on a spinner," said de Payns. "We're looking for a phone number currently being used in Genoa, and with a spinner in place, we hope to identify the user. You been in the field before?"

"I passed the basic courses at Cercottes," said Lolo. "I've been in the sub"—referring to the vehicles used by the Company for observation —"but nothing like this."

"Where have you operated?"

Lolo went to answer, then stopped himself. "Actually, no comment."

"Good answer," said de Payns, glancing at his watch. "Enjoying the job?"

Lolo shrugged. "I'm loving it, but this is the part that I really want to do."

"In the field?" asked de Payns, subtly watching a couple at the neighboring table who looked stilted in their interaction.

"For sure," said Lolo. "It would be great to see how to do it properly."

At the next table, the woman shook her head and looked away from the man. They were having a domestic; they weren't watchers.

"Doing it properly takes a lot of anxiety," said de Payns. "You'll get the hang of it."

They sat on the speed limit as they motored south, and de Payns used the time to bring Lolo up to speed on their first liaison in Monaco.

"I'll be meeting someone at the Bar Américain in the Hotel de Paris," said de Payns. "His name is Johnny, and you won't come with me. I need you sitting in a corner, looking like you belong there, but keeping an eye on things. You'll cover the contact."

"An eye on things?"

De Payns turned down the radio. "You'll get out of the car a few blocks from the Monte Carlo casino and take a stroll, checking your hygiene, then you'll enter the bar."

Lolo looked at his map.

"Have the directions clear in your head," said de Payns. "In the Américain, you sit at a table, not at the bar, and this table will give you a view of the entrance and an overview of the room."

Lolo folded the map and listened.

"You'll be in the bar twenty minutes before me, and you'll just observe. You're looking for anything special before I get there."

"For instance?" asked Lolo.

"For instance, a couple of guys like us, taking positions. Maybe a man and a woman operating as a couple. When you see me come in at minus one/plus two, I will sit at the bar counter. You'll check if anyone enters just after me. Keep an eye on where these people sit, but don't stare at them. You'll have to memorize everyone you see there."

Lolo nodded.

De Payns overtook a truck. "Hopefully, you'll see Johnny come in and approach me. When the meeting happens, your job is to check if he looks at anyone in the bar, or if anyone looks Johnny in the eye. You wait for me to finish my chat and leave, and you'll observe if anyone follows me out. After five minutes, leave the bar. We'll meet at the car one hour after I leave."

"Okay," said Lolo, serious.

"Please try to be natural," said de Payns. "And remember, don't catch anyone's eye. People who stare are conspicuous. Use your peripheral vision to observe."

Lolo beamed. "It's very kind of you to send me in like that. But I'm just a technician, remember?"

"When you work with me, there's no such thing as *just*," said de Payns. "You'll be fine; nothing can happen to you if there is no collusion between us."

"I don't know if I can do this."

"It's what you've always wanted, remember?"

"I don't want to screw it up," said Lolo.

De Payns turned to him. "Sorry Lolo, but it's an order, if that's what you need."

De Payns gave Lolo a potted history of Johnny, a former SAC man who was now retained by the Company as an Honorable Correspondent in Monaco. Johnny would be asked to arrange access to a superyacht called *Azzam*, which would be berthed at the principality's Port Hercules in ten days' time.

"SAC?" asked Lolo.

"Service d'Action Civique," said de Payns. "The French intelligence organization that answered only to de Gaulle."

De Payns could see his colleague trying to remember. "The SAC was very right-wing, very violent, wasn't it?"

"True believers: '*God without the clergy*,' I think was the phrase," said de Payns. "They were anti-Communists, from the Resistance."

For several minutes, there was silence in the car, broken by Lolo. "So, this Johnny, he just lives in Monaco, waiting to help the Company infiltrate a Russian party? Doesn't sound too good for his health."

De Payns smiled, knowing he'd got Lolo focused on the evening ahead. "Did I tell you he's Corsican?"

"Oh, I see," said Lolo nodding slowly.

"Yes, it's not Johnny's health that's in question. But you don't have to deal with him, and you won't. I want you just to sit in a corner of the bar and keep an eye on things, okay?"

"Sure," said Lolo bravely. "Do we leave the guns in the car?"

De Payns laughed. "Of course. Johnny's one of the good guys."

CHAPTER
SIX

They pulled into a truck layover on a rise just east of Cannes. It was late afternoon, and the sun was low in the sky. Lolo fished the sealed packet from the spare tire well of the Megane. He replaced the Paris "75" number plates with "06" plates that indicated a vehicle registered in the Nice area. De Payns watched his junior partner work smoothly, switching the rego papers in the glove box for the ones matched to the Nice number plates, and then sealing the Paris plates and papers in the plastic bag which he then replaced in the tire well. The entire procedure took him around eighty seconds.

They continued on the A8 freeway around Nice, taking the Monaco off-ramp and pulling into the streets of Monte Carlo as the sun hit the horizon. They cruised along the Avenue de Monte-Carlo, the sight of women in fur coats emerging from Bentleys and playboys leaping out of Lamborghinis eliciting a torrent of comments from Lolo.

"I need one of them," he said, as they slid past a gullwing Mercedes. "That Merc would change everything."

De Payns pulled up to the curb and checked the time: 6:14 p.m. "Leave the gear here, and that includes the biker jacket."

Lolo exited the car, and de Payns drove further east, where he parked, slipped on a dark sports jacket, and walked for several blocks, past jewelry stores and lavish apartment buildings.

He did some basic hygiene routes to see if he had watchers and paused at a D&G storefront window, checking in the reflection. Turning left on the Avenue de Monte-Carlo, he walked a block south to the front steps of the Hotel de Paris, passing through the foyer and heading upstairs to the Bar Américain. Checking his watch as he entered the lush tribute to 1920s American speakeasies, de Payns saw it was 6:29, inside the −1/+2 margin for the 6:30 p.m. meeting. He leaned against the leather-padded bar and waited for a middle-aged English couple to give their orders. Turning slowly to the room, he spied the view to the bar's terrace and clocked Lolo at a corner table but didn't look at him.

"I think the fish is good today," came a voice close to de Payns's right ear. The gravelly whisper spoke in Corsican-accented French.

De Payns turned to face the source of the comment, a tanned, bald man who looked to be in his late sixties, although his shoulders and chest still filled out his brown leather sports coat and his neck was bullish. He had all-knowing eyes and a weathered face that looked like it had been carved from granite. The bio on Johnny had mentioned his black belt in judo and his stint instructing unarmed combat in the SAC. Despite his age, he stood like a man who wasn't about to fall over.

"The morning catch is always the best," said de Payns.

The man held his gaze. "Alec?"

"Johnny?"

Johnny nodded and smiled. "What would you like to drink? It's on me."

De Payns glanced into his Perrier, the only thing he could afford in the Bar Américain. "I'll have a Jack Daniel's."

Johnny turned to the waitress. "Give me a bottle of Jack Daniel's and three glasses."

Johnny turned to the room. "Let's find a quiet place to have a chat and tell your young friend to join us."

De Payns followed and nodded to Lolo as he passed him.

Lolo looked petrified at the change in plans but joined de Payns and Johnny at their table, remaining silent after the introductions.

Having poured the whisky, Johnny leaned back in his chair with the air of a man who controlled the city. "So, what can I do for you?"

De Payns explained what the Company needed: access to *Azzam*.

"Is this an infiltration?" asked Johnny. "You want people on the boat or are we inserting electronic surveillance?"

"Aim for infiltration but settle for audio and video," said de Payns. "We'll take what we can get. We want to see who's in the meetings and what they talk about."

Johnny nodded slowly and looked into his drink. "Superyachts mean heavy security on the boat, and if the Company is so interested, I'd say there'll be overwatch around it."

De Payns couldn't argue with his reasoning. "It's not an easy one," he conceded.

"It might be impossible," said Johnny, chuckling. "But I guess that's why the Company wants to do it."

When Johnny had the details he needed, he told de Payns that he'd look into it and suggested they meet for lunch on Thursday at the Monkey in Kimono café, on the secondary road from Nice to Cannes. Then he produced a hotel swipe card and placed it in front of de Payns.

"You know, I miss those days with the Service," said Johnny. "You're doing a hell of a job—and I know what I'm talking about."

"I don't doubt it," said de Payns, eyeing the swipe card.

Johnny said, "I know the Company doesn't always look after you guys, so that's the key to a room upstairs. Have a good night in Monaco, on the house. Enjoy yourselves."

Before de Payns could respond, the Corsican stood, adding, "See you on Thursday at the Monkey."

When Johnny had gone, leaving the bottle of Jack Daniel's, Lolo was almost jumping out of his skin with enthusiasm.

"Look at this," he said with a smile, picking up the swipe card. "A free night at the Hotel de Paris!"

The Company's financial comptrollers were notoriously tight and demanded receipts for even the smallest claim, which they often challenged. Now Lolo was seeing the land of Aston Martins opening up to him.

De Payns smiled. "You think anything is really for free?"

Lolo wasn't listening. "We've got the whisky, we've got the room. Let's get some girls and party!"

De Payns pushed his glass away. "Go and have a look at the room, tell me what you see up there."

"What do you mean?" asked Lolo.

De Payns gave him a cold look. "I mean, put down your glass and shift your brain into work mode, then go up to the room, check it out, and come back down to describe it to me precisely."

When Lolo was gone, de Payns helped himself to a glass of the complimentary water and thought about the next stop on their tour. They would be in Genoa the next morning and looking for Starkand, their person of interest. Not the most exciting gig, but the job was often like that. Even though de Payns was trained for the most difficult and dangerous type of spy work—personal infiltration, where he pretended to be someone else—most of his operations hinged on surveillance and reconnaissance: the collection of information at a distance with the POI never being aware of it. Recruits at the DGSE were sometimes frustrated when they saw how much of their training was in following, photography, and audio recording. That's what constituted A-level product at the Company. When intelligence was being graded for its strength, personal contact could only ever achieve a B ranking, no matter how explosive the revelations.

Lolo reentered the bar, smiling like a child. "My God, we hit the jackpot."

"Tell me."

Lolo was wide-eyed. "It's the Princess Grace Suite. It must take up most of the top floor. My monthly paycheck wouldn't cover even a night up there."

"Views?"

"Across the harbor and marina."

"And let me guess," said de Payns, "a bottle of champagne on ice?"

"Yes!" said Lolo. "It's amazing."

"I'm sure it is," said de Payns. "You know the corner I dropped you on?"

"Yes."

"Be there in fifteen minutes."

Lolo frowned. "What, outside?"

"Yes."

"But we have a room for the night. We can stay here and go to Genoa tomorrow. It's perfect."

"Fifteen minutes," said de Payns.

Lolo looked at de Payns to check he wasn't joking and then slowly stood. "Okay. But can we keep the whisky, at least?"

"Of course," said de Payns, as he watched his colleague get back into character and walk out of the bar.

They sat at a picnic table at one of the entries to the Parco del Beigua, drinking the Jack Daniel's and putting Italian plates on the car. The lights of Genoa twinkled in the distance, and they both wore jackets against the cold breeze whistling down from the Alps. Lolo had recovered from his disappointment and now wanted to know why they'd had to leave the hotel.

"It doesn't matter what they teach you at Cercottes," said de Payns. "Your first job is to stay alive."

"Okay," said Lolo.

"That's fairly simple when you're single, but when you have a family, and you want to stay in the field, your job is to ensure that no one ever connects you back to your life zone."

"What's that got to do with the hotel? Johnny's on our side, non?"

"Says who?" growled de Payns, lighting a cigarette.

"Well, the Company. The boss."

De Payns smiled. "Let me give you the rule for all spies, throughout all of history: it's your life, so the responsibility for its security is yours too. If you bring the wolf to your door, it's your fault. So, you live by this rule: *la confiance n'exclut-pas le contrôle*. Trust doesn't exclude checking."

"Fair enough," said Lolo. "So what did you see at the hotel?"

"A man I've never met, who offers me a bottle of whisky when I asked for a glass, and who offers me a suite at the Hotel de Paris, accommodation he knows I can't afford. He's probably looking for leverage."

"But how?"

"We'd be up there drinking our whisky, and then there'd be a knock at the door around midnight, and she'd be tall and blonde, and her friend would be pretty with big tits, and maybe there'd be drugs, and maybe there's recording equipment somewhere in the suite . . . you get the picture?"

Lolo nodded. "Okay, it's a setup. But what does Johnny do with the pictures?"

"Maybe nothing, or maybe he works out I'm married, and one day I get some very interesting pictures in the mail, and I have a choice: do some favors for Johnny or blow up my marriage. Or: I can walk away from the Princess Grace Suite at the Hotel de Paris and sleep in the car with my colleague."

Lolo laughed out loud. "So, it's not like it is in the movies?"

"Only the paranoia about getting caught."

CHAPTER
SEVEN

They booked into a three-star hotel with "light" business IDs, which for de Payns was Benoît Droulez, consultant. The hotel was four blocks inland from the horseshoe-shaped Port of Genoa, in the center of the old town. Starkand's phone activity had initially been identified at a cell tower in the business and tourist hotel district, which was where they would start their search.

Having showered and changed and grabbed breakfast at a café, they set up the Toshiba laptop that ran the spinning machine and positioned it on a table in the hotel room. Spinning machines were not as powerful as often portrayed. It was almost impossible to simply put someone's cell-phone number into a computer and determine its location, unless the phone itself was being tracked or was transmitting location data from a phone app. The aim was to use the spinner to first establish the tower that the target's phone IMSI—the unique identifier located on the SIM card—was connecting to. Having established this location "bubble," Lolo would trick the target's phone into connecting with the spinner, which operated as if it were a cell-phone tower. Phones connected to Lolo's spinning machine would have their IMSI numbers displayed on the Toshiba's screen, slipping off as they moved away and found another tower. By confining the target's IMSI to the bubble created by the spinner, the target could eventually be identified.

Lolo activated the main screen of the spinner, and after one minute, there were twenty numbers connected to their closest tower. Some numbers moved off the tower, and others stayed connected. The phone number they were waiting for would appear in red when it connected to their local tower.

"We're up," said Lolo, confirming that the spinner was operational.

De Payns made coffees and they got comfortable, waiting for Starkand's red IMSI number to show.

This finally happened just after midday. Lolo called de Payns over, and they watched Starkand's IMSI connecting on a single tower. For the next thirty seconds, other numbers on the screen changed as they came into contact with the tower and moved off, but Starkand's number remained.

"Where's that tower?" asked de Payns.

Lolo turned to another laptop and identified the Genoa tower number on a map. "North of here, nine blocks."

De Payns stood. "Let's have a look."

They drove north, through tight streets, meandering pedestrians and unruly traffic. The old town of Genoa was five hundred years old in places, and it seemed to work better for pedestrians and scooters than for cars and vans.

"You think he has a job?" asked Lolo, as de Payns negotiated the traffic. "Or is he just walking around?"

"Genoa is not used by arms dealers or terrorists," said de

Payns. "I'm thinking he's a working professional, but it's just an assumption."

"We know it's a he?" asked Lolo.

"No," said de Payns, eyes fixed on the pedestrian traffic.

They came to a major crossroad, with a museum on their right and a library on the left. There was a town square and the imposing lines of one of Genoa's palaces.

"We're in the Big Bubble," said Lolo. "Starkand's phone is pinging."

They slowed and pulled to the right to allow a delivery van through.

"Grab a table at that café," said de Payns, nodding at the outdoor tables beside the car. "I'll be across the road."

Lolo pulled on a dark green cap and walked to a table at the café, as de Payns pulled back into the slow traffic and drove. It was early afternoon in Genoa, and the young scooter riders couldn't get off their horns.

He parked and took a table at a café across the road from the car. He keyed his burner phone and Lolo answered immediately.

"We have him," said Lolo. "He's moved onto the spinner, so he's nearby."

"When he moves off it, let me know," said de Payns, as a waitress came to his table.

The Company had a rule against OTs waiting in cars, so de Payns sat in the café's shadows, sipped on his black coffee, and wondered how all the threads would tie together. Johnny from the old days; a yacht called *Azzam*; a POI in Genoa mentioned in an adjacent piece of prod but not necessarily connected to the yacht . . . He'd been rushed into the field, and he looked forward to Briffaut explaining what this was all about.

His phone beeped: Lolo telling him the Starkand phone

had moved off the spinner, meaning he was moving out of their vicinity.

He left money on his table, strode back to the car, and picked up Lolo on a nearby corner.

"We'll know in about twenty seconds if he's on foot or in a car," said Lolo, referring to the typical cell-tower coverage in European cities.

De Payns drove north and Lolo said, "He's on foot."

De Payns took a right and drove off the main road and onto a side street, the light dim because of the medieval houses pushed up to the street. As they reached the end of the lane, Lolo sat up. "Got him again."

They looked and saw several pedestrians walking in the street. Lolo nodded through the windscreen. "Could be that guy, the overcoat."

About thirty meters in front of them was a dark-haired man around six foot tall, wearing a taupe coat over a navy-blue suit.

They idled slowly until the car behind them sat on the horn and de Payns pulled to the right again. The other driver revved through with a stream of Ligurian invective.

When they reentered the flow of traffic, de Payns scanned the pedestrians but there was no sign of the overcoat man.

"Out you get," said de Payns. "Find him and keep visual. Call me on the burner."

Lolo left the car and started walking.

De Payns avoided angry Italian drivers for two minutes, and then his burner phone rang.

Lolo said, "He's crossed the square, going into a side street."

De Payns swung left, swooped to a bus stop, and Lolo clambered into the car. Across the square they watched the man in the overcoat walking into a street that joined the square. He had dark hair with touches of silver, cut short, late forties, walking with no obvious injuries. There was a black leather briefcase in his left hand.

"Get close to him with the IMEI machine and confirm if you can," said de Payns. "I'll keep driving."

Lolo slipped out of the car once more with his IMEI identifier in his pocket, and de Payns searched for a café. His burner beeped: Lolo wanting to be picked up again.

He stopped at a corner at the bottom of San Siro, and Lolo got in the car with a satisfied thump on the dashboard. "It's him," he said, holding up his IMEI device. "He's carrying the phone identified in the phone environment."

"Where is he now?" asked de Payns, accelerating into traffic.

"I followed him to the Al Basilisco, it's a private hotel on San Siro," he said, picking up his laptop and opening the spinner screen. "He grabbed something from a Fiat parked outside before he went into the hotel."

"Is he still moving?" asked de Payns.

Lolo shook his head as he focused on the spinner screen. "He's staying put."

"Time to eat and have a drink," said de Payns. "But before we go, you can put a tracker on that Fiat."

Lolo shut the laptop and fished in his computer bag, pulling out a black plastic box the size of a USB memory stick. It had a powerful adhesive on the back of it. Lolo's task was to attach it to the underside of the car, in one of the wheel arches.

"You saw that café on Cairoli, the Gatto Bianco?"

"Sure."

"I'll meet you there in fifteen minutes," de Payns said. "And take the long way around."

Lolo slipped out of the car and mingled with the shadows. De Payns put the car into gear and drove away.

CHAPTER
EIGHT

Next morning, they drove to the Al Basilisco, reaching the street at 6:18 a.m. Lolo opened the Toshiba and activated the tracking program that would place the Fiat on a map and give them its exact location.

"I guess I don't have to know this either way," said Lolo, shining an apple he'd taken from the hotel lobby's fruit bowl. "But is the target a good guy or a baddie?"

"We don't know," said de Payns, who'd scored a banana from the same bowl. "Let's just say he's implicated in some interesting meetings, and because we're nosy, we'd like to know who he is."

De Payns dropped Lolo at the Gatto Bianco and parked up the street from Starkand's hotel. Then he walked past the hotel to a café at the intersection. It was a quiet street, and cats wandered around as if they owned the place.

De Payns ordered a coffee and sat outside with a view of the hotel, wearing a padded jacket against the early morning cold.

At 7:34 a.m. Starkand left his hotel. As he walked toward the Fiat, de Payns tried for some pictures, which he knew would not be good enough. Starkand drove past the café, and de Payns walked to the car, calling Lolo as he did. Picking up Lolo, they drove south for eight blocks, following the red dot of the tracker on Lolo's screen. They closed in on the Fiat in time to see Starkand take a left into an old alleyway. De Payns paused at the alley's entry, and they watched Starkand emerge from the Fiat carrying his briefcase. He veered into a building and disappeared.

De Payns couldn't see the street numbers of the buildings, so he asked Lolo to go for a walk. As his colleague got out of the car, de Payns lit a smoke and also alighted from the car, crossing the road and setting himself up at a stack of t-shirts outside a tourist knickknack store. He made a mental note to himself: if he operated in Genoa's old town again, he'd perhaps try a scooter instead of a car.

Starkand left the building two hours later, and de Payns found Lolo at a bus shelter.

"Twenty-six Falamonica," said Lolo, clambering into the car and giving de Payns the address he'd been sent to find. De Payns pulled the Renault into traffic to tail Starkand.

"There's a brass plaque beside the front door that says 'Istituto Ligure.'"

"Ligurian Institute," said de Payns. "Have a look—let's see what he's up to."

Lolo pulled up the website on his laptop as Starkand drove north, up the valley behind Genoa. Lolo read out what he could find: the Ligurian Institute was a think tank focused on European economic policy. It held conferences and published reports that were forwarded to European governments and corporations. Subject specialties included monetary policy, immigration, fiscal policy, and energy.

"In their publications section, they list a document called

'*Connecting Europe: the argument for natural gas pipelines to support renewables*,'" said Lolo.

"So, they're realists," said de Payns, fairly sure he'd trigger his young colleague.

"I agree," said Lolo.

They swapped a look and Lolo smiled. "Not all young people are Marxist degrowthers," he said. "I mean, I want to reduce our use of fossil fuels, but I'm not going to live in a cave."

De Payns laughed. "Okay, you pass the sanity test. Now you're ready for the secret handshake."

They followed the black Fiat up into the hills behind Genoa, past the Staglieno Cemetery with its acres of statues and monuments, and then swung around the massive spiral where the A12 freeway crossed over itself and subsequently aimed south. The Mediterranean sparkled under a cold haze to their right, and it seemed likely that Starkand was heading for Portofino.

They kept behind the Fiat for the next forty minutes, sometimes relying on the tracker's signal, sometimes on sight. De Payns pulled closer as they came into the cramped surrounds of Portofino, but to his surprise Starkand didn't stop but kept driving south, through Portofino and out onto the *penisola*.

"Dammit," said de Payns, under his breath.

"What's the problem?" asked Lolo, looking around at the lush greenery and medieval mansions abutting the seafront. "This is beautiful."

"Yes, but on the peninsula, you can't see the cafés from the road, and parking is a bitch," said de Payns. "You thought Genoa was a pain? Wait till we get to the end of this road."

They drove down the peninsula coast road, through postcard scenery, and came to the superyacht marina at the end of the spit, looked over by Brown Castle on the headland. The yachts were even larger than those they'd seen in Monaco, some of them akin to small cruise ships, sitting in the blue waters of Portofino like jewels set in lapis. Cafés, bars, and luxury-goods shops populated the waterfront road, but the quay itself was invisible from the road.

Starkand's Fiat slowed and stopped in front of an old building with an awning that said *Winterose Wine Bar.*

A parking valet greeted Starkand and took his car. De Payns checked his watch and saw it was 11:28. De Payns assumed Starkand was early for an 11:30 meeting.

"You'll have to go in," he said, looking around for parks and seeing none.

"Photographs?" asked Lolo, watching Starkand enter the wine bar.

"Not yet," said de Payns. "I want you to do a look-see."

Lolo nodded, understanding. His job was to go into the wine bar, ask for a menu, and look around, see who the target was meeting with. He'd assess other details that they couldn't see from the road, too, such as whether the wine bar had rear access or an al fresco section.

As Lolo crossed the road to the Winterose entrance, de Payns idled along with the other cars and the pedestrians and then pulled over at the Italian Yacht Club, making a U-turn that brought him back to the Winterose. He looked for vehicles that had tried to follow his U-turn, and seeing none he drove back up the peninsula, waited for two minutes on the shoulder of the road, and pulled another U-turn. As he drove past the Winterose again, Lolo emerged from the restaurant and saw the Renault.

"He's with a woman, brunette," said Lolo, slipping into the passenger seat. "She sounds American but is comfortable with Italian. And I think Starkand might be German, but with very good English."

"You heard them speak?"

"Snippets. They spoke in English, and they won't be there for long. She ordered coffees only."

"Rear access?"

"All of these restaurants and bars connect to the terrace along the waterfront. She can leave on foot or by boat, or maybe her car."

The valet glared at them, and de Payns found another parking perch further down the road.

"Tell me about the woman," said de Payns.

"Midthirties, athletic build, classy dresser, and a Jackie Kennedy haircut."

"Does she have a phone?"

Lolo paused, remembering. "Not on the table."

De Payns nodded. "Bring the spinner. We'll try our luck when she leaves the meeting, see if we can grab a number."

"Okay," said Lolo, pulling his laptop up from the footwell.

They ordered coffees at a café that looked on to the Winterose entrance and waited.

"What's she wearing?" asked de Payns.

"Orange silk top, sleeveless, and white cotton shorts. Brown leather loafers, suede."

"Who ran the meeting? What was the body language?"

"Woman seemed to have the authority," said Lolo. "She spoke and he listened."

Twenty minutes later, Starkand left the Winterose.

"He's alone," said de Payns. "We tracking the target's car?"

"It's being driven to the wine bar," said Lolo, looking at his Toshiba screen.

"Wait here," said de Payns, standing and picking up his backpack. "Call me if the woman leaves by the front door."

He crossed to the harbor side of the street, walked west for thirty paces, and took a right into the apron of the Portofino

Coast Guard building. The side alley connected to the water-front terrace that ran to the marina's main piazza. He walked toward it with a tourist's gait but keeping a good pace. He clocked middle-aged Germans and cashed-up Americans in their early thirties sitting on the terraces behind the restaurants. Tender boats pulled up and departed, disgorging visitors to spend their cash on the world's most overpriced coffee and wine.

He saw the orange silk top about thirty meters in front of him, walking away. She lifted a phone to her ear.

De Payns keyed his burner phone and called Lolo. "She's just taken a call," he said, and hung up, hoping Lolo would capture the number.

He stayed twenty meters behind the woman, noticing she walked confidently and that, as she spoke into the phone, she made gestures with her free hand that indicated she was giving orders. De Payns closed in on her as she paused in front of a building called the Royal Apartments, a yellow-painted build-ing with green shutters. He pulled back and tucked in behind a group of Germans who loudly asked one another where Detlev had got to. "*Still drunk from last night*," said one of them, and they laughed at a volume guaranteed to annoy other European nationalities.

De Payns got a line of sight; she was fifteen meters from him and trying to get off the phone call while holding up her hand to a man who was keeping a speedboat idling alongside the wharf. De Payns slipped the Canon 5D camera from his pack, powered it up, and acted like a tourist taking photographs. As the woman disconnected, de Payns nailed three direct front-on shots. She climbed onto the idling white-and-blue speedboat, which imme-diately pulled away from the quay. De Payns grabbed shots of the boat's transom, and the name *Melissa* written in black script. Bringing out his burner phone, he called Lolo. "The woman just

hung up ten seconds ago, and now she's on a speedboat heading out of the bay. Could you isolate an IMSI?"

He stowed the camera and retraced his steps, looking for
watchers while keeping an eye on the *Melissa*. It hit top speed,
skating across the blue-green harbor toward open waters, slowing beside a glossy black superyacht. He took out the Canon
again and raised it to his eye, moved to his right eight paces to
get a better line of sight, and looked through the telephoto lens.
The superyacht was also called *Melissa*, and off the back of the
transom, it flew a Cypriot flag.

When de Payns got back to the café, the images he'd taken
now deleted from the card for retrieval at the Bunker later, Lolo
was already moving toward the hastily parked car, which was
being eyed by a policewoman.

"It's my fault, *scusa*," said de Payns, starting the car. The
cop wasn't impressed, but the two Frenchmen kept smiles on
their faces as de Payns injected the Renault into the traffic and
pulled away.

They stayed twenty cars back from Starkand on the westbound A12. Lolo was able to track the Fiat when they lost
visual contact as they sped in and out of a series of tunnels cut
into the hills. They passed the huge road spiral above Genoa
and continued west, toward the junction where traffic could go
north for Milan or south toward Marseille. They followed the
Fiat south into the Genoa Airport precinct, which turned into
the Hertz drop-off car park. De Payns kept going to the main
departure apron.

"You drive," said de Payns, as he alighted with his backpack.
"Get that tracker off our friend's car, and circle back where I
can see you."

There was a party of Chinese travelers whose bags were
being unloaded from a small tour bus and onto several large

baggage trolleys. De Payns stood between the bags and the terminal windows and fished his Canon from the pack. It had a 135mm EF lens on it, which was not the strongest telephoto lens but, because of its compact shape, was the lens least likely to announce itself as professional equipment.

He waited for Starkand to show, and after six minutes saw him walking with other travelers along a pedestrian path toward the terminal. When he filled the viewfinder, de Payns took five quick shots, then deleted the images before returning the camera to his bag. Starkand swept by, carrying a leather carryall, and de Payns followed him into the departure hall. While Starkand punched in his numbers at the check-in kiosk and got a boarding pass for his flight, de Payns pretended to be engrossed in the magazines at the newsagent.

Starkand moved toward the security screening gates, but detoured to the Poste Italiane box, pausing at it briefly. He walked past de Payns at ten meters' distance, and de Payns could now see Starkand was midfifties and well kept. The target glanced at his watch as he put his bag on the security screening conveyor, as if concerned about making his flight.

There was an announcement in Italian, and Starkand hurried away to his gate on the other side of the security screening. De Payns walked to the departures board and looked from the top down: the only flight currently boarding was LH6921— Lufthansa, to Munich.

CHAPTER
NINE

De Payns and Lolo motored west, the sprawl of Nice to their left and the blue of the Med beyond it. Lolo had found a local radio station that played hits of the 1980s and 90s, and de Payns was discovering that being a telecoms genius did nothing for a man's pitch, at least not when trying to sing to Cyndi Lauper. De Payns flicked his cigarette out the window and looked at his watch: 11:49 a.m. "We should be right on time for our lunch date."

They'd enjoyed a few drinks the night before in Genoa and had eaten early before hitting the road for the lunch meeting with Johnny. Lolo had found some information on the *Melissa*. It was owned by a Cypriot company named Red Ocean Holdings Ltd., with the shareholders represented by nominees in the Cayman Islands. De Payns wondered about the connection with Lotus and Starkand.

To their right, a large backlit sign featuring a monkey in a kimono loomed two hundred meters from the highway, and de Payns steered for the off-ramp. They drove up a lane lined with old olive trees and emerged in a car park in front of the café. The elevation caught the breeze, and he smelled the salty fragrance from the sea as he stood and looked around. There were five other cars in the car park and a kids play area in front of the building.

They walked into the restaurant, and, before the maître d' could seat them, de Payns saw Johnny sitting at a window table, looking at the view.

De Payns took a seat in front of Johnny, and Lolo sat beside him. When they'd ordered two coffees, Johnny looked at his watch and smiled. "You are well trained in the Company."

De Payns smiled back. "So, Johnny, what time were the prostitutes meant to turn up?"

"Around two," said Johnny, looking at his hands.

"You know," said de Payns, "if you have something to ask me, you could do it directly instead of trying to leverage me with blackmail. It would be much better for our relationship."

Johnny nodded his acceptance. "Okay, point taken. So let me be direct—I have this new business partner I'm not so sure about. Would it be possible for you to check his file at the Company?"

"You either don't trust him or you don't know him?"

Johnny shrugged. "If I could know in advance, it would avoid a bad partnership for me and a bad ending for him."

"No problem," said de Payns. "That's what friends are for, right? Helping each other. You give me his name, and I'll check him out."

The waitress delivered coffees, and de Payns noticed that Lolo avoided catching her eye.

"And *Azzam*?" asked de Payns.

Johnny breathed out. "Well, it's not a piece of cake. She's owned by the UAE, so it's impossible to bug her before the meeting, and we can't really recruit crew members—the current crew are well paid and have been thoroughly vetted by the security people."

De Payns made a face. It was what he'd been expecting.

Johnny smiled. "But the good news is they need temporary staff for two days at sea next week. Seems there's an event onboard."

"How is that good news?" asked de Payns.

"The company providing the extra staff is based in Nice, and it's owned by someone who owes me."

"You mean you can get someone on *Azzam* as a waiter or waitress?"

"If you can come up with a steward with a good résumé," said Johnny, "I can make sure they're hired."

De Payns had to keep the Renault under the speed limit as they negotiated the heavier traffic on the periphery road north of Marseille. He lit a cigarette, cracked the window slightly, then fished out the phone hidden under the driver's seat and powered it up.

"Boss, it's me," said de Payns, as Briffaut picked up. "I'll debrief when I get back, we're looking at around nine p.m."

"I'll be here," said Briffaut.

"And a heads-up. To get on the boat, we'll have to find a waitress or waiter, and quickly."

"Thanks," said Briffaut. "Drive carefully."

The traffic thinned out as they headed northwest away from Marseilles, and as they headed north on the E15 for Dijon and Paris, de Payns settled at a cruising speed of 135 kilometers per hour.

"So, Lolo," said de Payns, relaxing slightly. "How was that for fieldwork?"

"I liked it," said Lolo, reclining his seat. "But, shit, Johnny was a wake-up call."

De Payns nodded. "Yes, they're not made like that anymore."

"I mean, did he really say, '*bad ending*'?"

De Payns laughed. "And you know what? I think he was serious."

They arrived at the Bunker just before 9:00 p.m. after dumping the burner phones and completing a series of vehicle self-checks, looking for tails. When they'd decided they were clean, they drove in the security gate, and de Payns told Lolo he could unpack the car and go home.

De Payns walked through to the techies in Y-9 and dropped the SD cards with the OT doing night duty, then he climbed the stairs to his office and picked up his personal belongings from his safe. He wandered down the hallway, saw that a few people were working late. The light was on in Briffaut's office, and the boss was sitting at his desk smoking a cigarette—which was forbidden in the DGSE—and drinking a glass of whisky, which was authorized.

"Want a drink?" asked Briffaut, and de Payns took a glass from the top of the filing cabinet and poured himself a short measure of Briffaut's Glenfiddich before taking a seat and debriefing on the trip to Monaco and Genoa.

Briffaut nodded at the information and asked if Johnny was as reliable as he was legendary.

"He's a professional, which is a start."

"By the way," said Briffaut, "you've got tomorrow off. That's official."

"Thanks," said de Payns, thinking the family could catch the 3:00 p.m. train and be in Deauville for dinner.

Briffaut looked out his window at the night and sucked hard on his cigarette. "Remember Paul Degarde?"

"DR guy, running Lotus," said de Payns, as he helped himself to one of Briffaut's smokes. "I did the handover in Vienna."

"We lost him."

De Payns paused. "He's off the net?"

"He's dead," said Briffaut, crushing his smoke in the ashtray. "Fucking Russians."

They stared at one another. A death in the Company was keenly felt.

"Where was he operating?"

Briffaut shook his head. "They got him in Paris. Waiting at his apartment. Raped his wife but let her live. Kid watched it."

De Payns's stomach seized into a fist, and he let out a small moan: the spy's nightmare of bringing the wolf to the family home.

Briffaut sighed. "It gets worse. I sent Shrek down to talk to her. Read this."

De Payns picked up the report that Briffaut pushed across his desk. It was open at the third page, and de Payns scanned it quickly. He froze as he read the second paragraph:

OT's wife does not speak Russian but heard the word #AZZAM# mentioned by OT and by the Russian who raped her. The word AZZAM was used many times by both parties before OT could no longer speak. OT's wife does not know what AZZAM means. She did not disclose AZZAM to DGS investigators. She has not conducted subsequent inquiries into the meaning of AZZAM.

"Shit," said de Payns, pushing the report back across the desk, paranoia rising.

Briffaut turned away from the window. "So, there's a few knots to untangle."

"How is Lotus connected to Starkand?" asked de Payns.

"There's that," said Briffaut. "But we also have a security

problem in Paris, along with this headache: if Degarde talked about *Azzam* with the Russians, maybe he talked about the rest of the Lotus documents he brought back from Prague."

"Fucking Lotus," said de Payns, shaking his head. "I told Degarde to be careful. How is his family doing?"

"In isolation and in shock. His wife can't call anyone—not even her mother—and the daughter will be enrolled in a new school under a new name."

De Payns wished he hadn't asked: their lives were ruined. It was what he feared might happen to his own family someday.

He changed the subject. "Lotus might have thrown him under the bus, or perhaps Degarde fucked up somewhere."

"He did fuck up," said Briffaut. "He took a taxi home from Charles de Gaulle. We think there was a reception team checking diplomats at arrivals."

Briffaut changed tone. "So, we have Lotus dropping documents about *Azzam*, and we have Russian thugs killing one of our own over a conversation that centers on *Azzam*. I had a meeting today with the Europe section at DR, and we don't understand the link between Lotus and the Russians. We need to be on that boat, so I guess you'll be learning a new job."

"*Me?*" replied de Payns, surprised.

"Yes, you," said Briffaut, who was accustomed to OTs pushing back. "You have that ID of the barman, so after your relaxing long weekend, you'll have two days' training in a Paris hotel learning how to be a waiter."

"Why aren't we using Aline?" asked de Payns; he was already overstretched on his various identities and operations. "She usually does the hospitality jobs."

"Given the people we expect aboard *Azzam*, she'd attract the wrong kind of attention, if you see what I mean."

De Payns did see. A shapely blonde French girl would be

very conspicuous on a boat filled with Arabs and Russians. There'd be no blending into the scenery.

He sighed. "Thanks a lot, boss. Thanks to Degarde mentioning *Azzam* to the Russians, I can expect a spy hunt onboard."

Briffaut lit another cigarette. "We have to at least try. I mean, one of our own died over this."

"I'll do my Genoa report on Monday," said de Payns, moving for the door. "If I have the time between carrying plates and writing my last will and testament."

Briffaut smirked. "Enjoy your long weekend. And close the door on your way out—I can't get caught smoking."

CHAPTER
TEN

When de Payns got up to the room he'd booked in Le Trophée, he took one look at the big double bed and was tempted to collapse onto it and sleep for a week. But the sight of the famous Deauville beach through the windows was too much for Patrick and Oliver, and the next thing he knew, de Payns was following them across the road and the boardwalk and onto the beach to kick a soccer ball around. Romy sat on the edge of the board-walk, and when de Payns turned to see if she wanted to join them—she was rather competitive around a soccer ball—he saw her glowing in the late afternoon light of the Normandy coast, wrapped in a woolen fisherman's jumper.

"You playing?" asked de Payns, tearing off his shoes and socks, as Oliver insisted he was Messi.

"I'm enjoying watching my men," she said.

De Payns turned back to his boys to hear Patrick announce he was Ronaldo.

"In that case, I'm Platini," said de Payns, swooping in and stealing the ball from Patrick's feet.

"Who's Platini?" demanded Oliver, as de Payns dribbled around him and nutmegged Patrick.

"You'll find out," said de Payns, whooping with laughter as his boys gave chase across the sand.

They ate great seafood at the Bar du Soleil, pulling on jumpers and jackets as the sun reached the horizon and the beach glowed bronze in the cold. They wandered along the boardwalk toward the amusement park, dodging other Parisian families trying hard to relax, until they reached a waterfront carousel in front of the Hôtel de Ville. The boys wouldn't allow de Payns to avoid the amusement ride, so he bought tickets for Romy and himself and rose to the trot on a wooden horse while music from a century ago clanged out of the old machine. He was transported back in time to his childhood, when he and his sister were taken on holiday to Bournemouth—not because their mother was English but because of their French father's connections with the Moran family. The two families had been tight in de Gaulle's inner circle while the Free French movement assumed the role of government-in-exile in London in the early 1940s. Free French Forces was akin to a secret society, with de Gaulle as the grand master and its members swearing lifelong oaths of loyalty; members of the Order of Liberation, as it was called, received the specially struck Cross of Lorraine with the inscription *Patriam Servando Victoriam Tulit*—By serving the Fatherland, he achieved victory. When the war was won, Eymeric de Payns—Alec's grandfather—went back to France to manage forestry assets for de Gaulle, and François Moran married into landed nobility in England and raised a family there. Alec de Payns and his sister had spent their holidays in Bournemouth—and sometimes Wimbledon, Twicken-ham, and Royal Ascot—getting to know the Moran clan as if they were family. One of François Moran's grandchildren was Mike Moran, sworn officer of the British secret service, and Alec de Payns's friend. De Payns sometimes wondered about the duality of his Anglo-French makeup and if it helped or hindered him in his profession.

By the time they hauled themselves up to their room at Le Trophée hotel, de Payns was so tired and happy that he didn't even reach in his pocket for a cigarette.

The weekend was a blur for de Payns, who'd forgotten how energetic his boys were. They went on a coastal walk north of the town, they ate in trendy cafés, and in the midafternoon, Romy hired a beach hut called Frances McDormand and bought a sixpack of Heineken. It was relatively warm for winter, so the boys briefly braved the cold of the sea and dried off in front of their hut. Romy and de Payns lounged in the sun while the boys kicked their ball in the sand.

"Why are we called Frances McDormand?" asked de Payns, looking along the row of little huts.

"Haven't you seen all the posters for the film festival?" replied Romy, looking like she was designed to have her feet in the sand and a bottle of beer to her lips. "It's very famous. They'll have all the movie stars wandering around here later this year. They'll probably stay at our hotel."

"I don't know," said de Payns, with a mock frown. "Could be a KGB front."

She laughed and slapped him on the arm. "Don't tell me—just like Greenpeace, right?"

"Well, now you mention it . . ."

They teased one another as they had done when they first met: de Payns a dashing air force fighter pilot and Romy a graduate in economics with first-class honors doing contract research work for OECD and NGO think tanks in Paris. She found his distrust of anything that smacked of communism funny, and it had been a running joke between them for many years. But having graduated from the Sorbonne with a PhD and now with a full-time position at the Tirol Council, he'd noticed she was less playful when it came to economic theory.

"I'm loving Tirol," she said, as if reading his mind. "I love working with people who have such a strong faith in what they are doing."

"I'm happy for you," said de Payns, taking a sip of beer, eyes fixed on the boys. "It's great to find something you love doing."

"Really?" she asked. "You're okay with it?"

"Of course," he said, surprised. "It's what you wanted. Why wouldn't I be happy?"

She sighed and looked away. "Sometimes I feel the Company changed you. I'm having a hard time recognizing you."

"Recognizing me?" he repeated, trying to gage if they were embarking on an official fight or if there was room for a three-point turn.

"Everything is dark to you," she continued. "You're totally paranoid. I talked about it the other day with Ana, and—"

"You did what?" de Payns interrupted, now knowing it was going to be a fight. "You've told her what I do?"

"No, of course not," said Romy dismissively. "But, well, she's not stupid, you know."

De Payns heard a roaring in his ears and, despite his effort to maintain self-control, shook his head slightly.

Romy continued. "You never talk about your job. It's all just, '*I work at the Ministry*', and, '*Logistics is such an important part of the military*', but you're always away, and when you are you don't contact me. Women notice these things, Alec."

"Maybe they notice, but that doesn't mean you have to talk about it."

"I don't talk about it, that's the problem—and someone like Ana sees that very clearly."

De Payns was becoming flustered. When Ana and her husband, Rafi, first befriended the de Payns, he'd had her checked with the DGS and found no flags on her. Ana was very sharp and very beautiful, and he'd initially been suspicious of how close she'd grown to his wife. "I told you, just tell her I work for the Ministry and I get called away a lot."

"Other couples aren't like us, Alec," Romy said, voice even. "In normal marriages, you don't just *tell* people to think a certain way and it comes to pass."

"I don't see why Ana would be so interested in what I do," said de Payns.

"She doesn't care about what you do; it's what you *don't* do that gets her attention," said Romy. "If Ana wants Rafi to pick up a loaf of bread or get the boys from karate, she just rings him and it's no problem. That never happens with us. Ana has noticed that, and she can see I'm not happy about it."

Alec's head was spinning; he had a vivid mental image in his head of Paul Degarde killed, his wife raped. He needed to feel safe with Romy, but she was pushing all the buttons he'd warned her about.

"You told her I don't contact you?" he asked, hearing a professional edge coming into his voice.

"No, of course not," she said, still calm. "But like I said, she's noticed."

"What does she ask about?"

"The same thing any friend would want to know," she said, her voice hardening. "'*Is Alec away? Can Alec get the boys from karate?*' But I act like I don't know what she's asking."

"What the hell do you think she's asking?"

"Why we are two wives but only one of us has a husband," said Romy.

There was an icy silence between them as they assessed the line that had been crossed. De Payns slugged on his beer and looked to the horizon, feeling lonely and wishing Romy would take back her words. He knew that was unlikely, though—those words had been years in the making, by the sounds of it. And if she'd meant them to hurt, she'd succeeded.

After a long silence, Romy cleared her throat. "Do you realize what it's like for me not to be able to talk to anyone?" she asked in a low voice. "You disappear for days, the boys can't talk to you, I can't get a lousy loaf of bread out of you, and when you do come home, you're useless."

"I'm exhausted," said de Payns.

Romy shook her head. "You're useless to me, useless to the boys. All the best of you is given to France."

De Payns looked at the sand, the fight not in him. "I'm trying . . ."

"Where is my fun pilot husband and his constant jokes?" asked Romy. "God, you used to make me laugh. These days I get my laughs with my friends and colleagues. I have more fun at one lunch with David and Kris than I do with my own husband."

"David and Kris?" De Payns shrugged. "Who are they?"

"Exactly," said Romy. "Why would you know who my boss is? Or who my colleagues are?"

"I didn't know you were going out to lunch," said de Payns. "Or who with."

"David is my boss," said Romy. "He's a really inspirational thinker about energy economics, and he's also really funny. And yes, we go to lunch. Colleagues do that."

It had been a long time since de Payns had been compared to another man, and he was caught off guard. "That's nice for David, but my life isn't exactly funny these days."

"You've become a porcupine," she snapped. "I can't talk to you anymore. And it's no use blaming Ana; she's just the friend who got close enough to notice."

"I'm trying to be a good father," de Payns protested. He lit a cigarette, blinking back tears, and avoided his wife's gaze. Then he rose and moved a few steps away. He was alone, solitary, even as he was surrounded by his family.

The train from Deauville arrived at Gare Saint-Lazare just before seven on Sunday evening. De Payns had been lost in his thoughts during the two-hour journey into Paris, thinking about Paul Degarde's family and wondering at his own fate aboard *Azzam*. Once he was on that boat, he was trapped and at the mercy of fortune, with only some tradecraft to balance the odds.

De Payns walked in front of his family with the luggage, aiming for the Metro platform to take them home. Romy followed, holding the boys' hands. As he came off the escalator and onto the Metro platform, he passed two drunk men in their midtwenties leaning against the tiled wall. As he turned to see if Romy was okay, the drunk in the NY Giants hoodie rose to his feet and circled discreetly behind Romy, pretending to hit her in the neck. De Payns reacted without thinking. Dropping the bags, he ran toward Romy, who was unaware of the action behind her. His adrenaline surged as he punched the hoodie-wearing drunk in the face and then, as the man was reeling from the punch, kneed him in the stomach. The other, larger drunk leaped on him, and de Payns hip-threw his assailant to the ground judo-style, the man's head smashed into the concrete. Grabbing him by the jacket collar, de Payns dragged the semiconscious man along

the ground until his head dangled over the edge of the platform and punched him repeatedly.

There was a squeal as a train approached, and then Romy was
hitting his back, yelling in his ear, "*Stop, Alec! Stop! Please, stop!*"

Becoming aware of her voice, de Payns emerged from his
psychosis. He stared into the scared eyes of the drunk, gasping for breath, then dragged him back onto the platform as the
train's headlight grew larger.

De Payns stood, blood dripping off his knuckles.

He turned to his family and saw two small faces filled with fear.

His wife's face was filled with disgust.

CHAPTER
ELEVEN

Jéjé pulled into a car park beneath a tree, about seventy meters from the black Mercedes-Benz SUV.

"Doesn't look like he's parking," said Templar, pulling fold-out binoculars from the inside pocket of his insulated windbreaker. "Passenger door is opening."

Jéjé got out of the Toyota Camry that they'd bought from a youth hostel in Batumi two days earlier, and he relieved himself in the trees that surrounded Tbilisi's Lokomotivi Stadium. He and Templar had been tasked with discovering what Lotus was doing and who he was speaking to. They'd spent two nights in the Las Vegas of the Black Sea—Batumi—watching Lotus gamble on the blackjack tables, become drunk, and then disappear upstairs to the casino's hotel with a prostitute in tow. Then they'd followed his chauffeured car, the black Mercedes, from Batumi to the capital of Georgia, Tbilisi.

"Lotus is getting out of the vehicle," said Templar, binoculars still at his eyes. "He's heading for the gardens."

"I'll take it," said Jéjé, zipping up. "He might make you from the casino."

Jéjé grabbed a Canon D5 SLR camera from the back seat of the Camry and checked the burner phone he'd bought at Batumi International, to ensure it had charge. He aimed for a secondary gate into the park that skirted the stadium and fell in with a group of Georgian families enjoying the winter sunshine. He wandered like a tourist down the western side of the park, taking a few shots of the gardens and the substantial fountains. The gardens had a north–south rectangular layout ending in a World War II memorial, and Jéjé walked along a hedgerow that gave him a view to the imposing monument. Fifty meters away, he saw the tall but wide form of Lotus emerge from the trees on the western boundary and cross the park's central avenue. He was wearing a black naval pea jacket over a pale blue woolen jumper, and his signature tweed trilby hat.

Jéjé took shots of the trees and fountains, and from the corner of his eye watched Lotus make for a park bench by a line of topiary, where a younger man in a beige windbreaker was sitting. Jéjé moved to the avenue of topiary and sat at another bench, where he pretended to be sorting through shots on his camera. He was now eighty meters diagonally from Lotus, and when he looked up, he watched the beige-windbreaker man's hand drop to the park bench and Lotus's hand reaching for the same spot.

Jéjé angled the display screen on the back of the camera, so he could see where it was pointed even as it sat on his lap, and took some shots of Lotus and his friend.

The meeting ended, and Lotus and his friend walked in opposite directions: Lotus away from the entrance he'd arrived through, and the windbreaker man away from the memorial end of Vake Park.

Jéjé deleted his shots and fished the burner phone from his pocket to call Templar. "He met with someone. European male, late thirties, dark blond hair, wearing a beige windbreaker. He's moving away from the memorial, Lotus is walking to the other side of the park."

"We have Lotus covered—there's a tracker on his Mercedes," said Templar. "Let me know where the POI is going."

The windbreaker man turned abruptly right from the central avenue and walked down a side path. Jéjé stayed back, building his legend as a tourist, and kept within fifty meters of the man as they moved toward the northwest end of the park.

Jéjé texted Templar: *Heading for lion statue.*

Templar's reply was immediate: *Copy.*

The man in the beige windbreaker walked briskly, and Jéjé evaluated his posture as being military or intelligence. Before reaching the lion statue, the person of interest veered to the left, through a small forest. They walked past the Caucasus French School and emerged on a street, where the man in the beige windbreaker walked straight to an idling silver BMW and slid into the back seat.

Jéjé keyed the phone. "Our POI just got in a silver BMW X7, heading east. He's a passenger."

"Across from you," said Templar.

Jéjé looked across the nature strip and saw Templar sitting in the Camry on the other side of the road.

Walking to the Camry, Jéjé got in and said, "He's going the other way."

"Not anymore he's not," Templar replied, looking in the side mirror.

The silver BMW accelerated past them, having just done a U-turn, and Templar pulled into traffic behind it.

As they formed a tail, Jéjé reached for the laptop on the back seat and opened it at the screen they'd been watching since the previous night: a map with a blinking red light, showing the whereabouts of Lotus's black Mercedes.

"Lotus heading east," said Jéjé, aware that the tracker they'd attached to the Mercedes in Batumi would transmit for another twelve hours.

"He's not going home," said Templar; the men knew that Lotus's family lived in a mansion on the west side of Tbilisi.

"Airport?" suggested Jéjé.

"Or a brothel," said Templar.

As he said it, the BMW they were tailing slowed and turned right opposite Lokomotivi Stadium, and Templar followed suit.

"He didn't go far from home," said Jéjé, as the BMW abruptly turned left across the side street and stopped in front of a security gate, the driver thrusting a swipe card out the window as the French team swept past.

"That's the Russian embassy," said Templar, laughing as he accelerated past.

Jéjé shook his head. "If these people didn't exist, we'd have to invent them."

They followed the tracker and arrived at Tbilisi International Airport two minutes before 5:00 p.m.

Templar took his turn tailing Lotus, leaving Jéjé in the car.

Lotus was not in the departures hall, so Templar pulled on his blue baseball cap and wandered to the security screening area and looked through to the airside section. It was a midsized single-terminal airport with only five gates. He moved away from the security screening zone and checked the departures board: two flights imminent, one to Ankara at 17:35, the other to Kiev at 17:45. Templar thought about pushing through the security screening section, but he didn't want the attention when he tried to get out of the locked-down area. Maybe he could find a service door and leave inconspicuously—he'd done it before—but there was a high chance he'd be caught, and this operation had to remain clandestine.

He was about to move back to the screening desks when he saw a movement from the left of his vision. Someone was leaving the male toilets, putting on his tweed trilby as he walked.

Lotus.

Templar put his eyes back on the departure board and let Lotus pass him. The Georgian walked to the screening gates, laid his briefcase on the conveyor belt, and held his arms out as the security woman waved her detector wand. Then he sauntered into the airside section, and Templar took up a position where he could see Lotus's disappearing back. He lost sight of him briefly while a family group stood and argued, and then caught a glimpse of Lotus taking a seat at the lounge in front of Gate 2.

Templar looked up at the departures board as he walked out of the terminal. Lotus had just been handed something by the Russian and now he was going to Kiev.

CHAPTER

TWELVE

The SD printouts and research packets from Genoa were dropped at de Payns's office at 9:16 a.m., as he sat down with his coffee and started his computer. He was planning to bury himself in his work; he owed Briffaut those reports, and he had to be at a steward training session at the George V Hotel at 2:00 p.m. Mostly, though, he was trying to shake the previous evening from his mind. The looks on the faces of his family haunted him. It was enough to make de Payns wonder about resigning. Which he would, if he wasn't so busy, as the joke went among his colleagues.

Reaching for his coffee, he saw the skinned knuckles of his right hand and could feel the small cut on his face tightening as he pursed his lips to drink. The violence was a blur, but he remembered hitting the first assailant with a straight right in the mouth and the sickening crunching sound when he judo-threw the second man onto the concrete. He should have left it when the second man hit the deck, but no: instead, he'd escalated. If Romy hadn't broken through the haze, de Payns would probably be in a police cell now, picking lice out of his hair. He didn't know what he was going to do. For the first time in their relationship, Romy had insisted he sleep in the guest bedroom, while the boys had slept in their bed with her. He felt so alone and scared that if he didn't manage to distract himself with work, he'd probably have to find a bar and start with whisky.

Opening the packet from the Y-9 people in the basement, he found a set of color prints with a white sticker on the bottom right of each with a location and date. He sifted through them, looking at the shots of Starkand walking toward Genoa Airport terminal, the photograph he'd taken in Portofino of the woman in the orange silk top, and the shots of the *Melissa* speedboat and superyacht. There were no "hits" on Starkand or the woman in the orange top; their identities remained a mystery.

The phone environment had picked up two "possibles" for Orange Top: one a number registered on Telecom Italia, and the other a Netherlands Vodafone number which looked like a burner phone. Neither of them showed much activity, and they'd called no numbers that were of interest to the Company.

The first research sheet from the DR team covered the Liguria Institute, but de Payns couldn't see Starkand's picture listed among the employees or consultants. Included in the pack was economic modeling work the Institute had completed on the benefit of Nord Stream 2, the natural gas pipeline running from Russia into Germany, versus the proposed EastMed pipeline that would pipe gas from the Israeli and Egyptian gas fields, through Cyprus and Greece and into Europe via Italy. The gas fields closest to Israel were named Leviathan and Tamar, the fields closer to Cyprus's southern economic zone were Aphrodite and Calypso, and the Egyptian blocks were Noor and Zohr. According to the Ligurian Institute, Nord Stream 2 meant Russian control and German benefits, whereas EastMed gave control to Israel, Egypt,

and southern Europe through a governmental framework called
the East Mediterranean Gas Forum. The Institute's report—
written in early 2020—labeled EastMed "politically challenged"
because Turkey, which was not included in the forum, opposed it.

The second sheet covered *Melissa*, owned by Red Ocean
Holdings with its home port being Larnaca in Cyprus. The
only attachments to the file were pictures of the vessel in various Mediterranean marinas.

De Payns finished his O and R reports on Operation Bellbird and wrote a memo to Briffaut on the Johnny meeting. By
now it was 11:48, which meant he'd have time to eat before he
traveled across the city for his steward training.

"You're still here," came Briffaut's voice. He was standing in
the doorway, wallet in his hand. "You hungry?"

They walked to the cafeteria, bought sandwiches, and sat at
a table in the adjacent park inside the Bunker grounds.

"You going on a superyacht with a face like that?" asked
Briffaut, mouth filled with bread and salami.

"It's healing," said de Payns, tearing the tab off his Coke.
"Just a scratch."

"Want to talk about it?"

"No."

"How about a simple statement: '*It's okay, boss, I'm not falling apart, and I'm fit for the field.*'"

De Payns watched an OT jogging across the park. "I got
in a fight last night at Saint-Lazare station. A couple of drunks
were giving Romy a hard time, and I didn't exactly use my
verbal skills."

"Someone fought back?"

"A dude who didn't want his head held over the edge of the
platform as a train approached," said de Payns, knowing from
experience not to bullshit this man.

Briffaut nodded. "Cops?"

"Well, the train arrived two seconds after I pulled his head back, so we jumped on and went home," said de Payns. "No cops."

"Romy?"

"Hates me," said de Payns, the words catching in his throat.

"She's a strong one."

"Yeah, I know," said de Payns. "But it's more than she bargained for. The boys are getting older, and now Romy's got a real job, a career."

"And you're dealing with the boys, but Romy's really managing them, right?"

De Payns shrugged. For security reasons, OTs were supposed to avoid hiring au pairs, and Romy's parents weren't in Paris. Wives were expected to pick up the slack, and de Payns noted that female DGSE careerists such as Marie Lafont remained steadfastly unmarried.

"It's bad enough when your wife's not working," said Briffaut. "But when she is, and needs support in the home, you're trapped here with work you can't walk away from."

De Payns shook his head. "So, it doesn't get any easier?"

"Only a handful of people have done our job, *mon cher*," said Briffaut. "We don't look for easy."

"You're twice divorced," de Payns observed mildly. "But you're still here."

"Married to the Company now," said Briffaut, his eyes suddenly narrowing. "I want you to see Dr. Marlene."

"No," said de Payns.

"Somehow you heard a question?"

"Okay, it's your call," said de Payns, knowing that arguments with Briffaut always ended in the older man's favor. "But look at me, boss—she'll put me on medical leave."

"No, she won't."

"She will," de Payns said. "Last time I saw her, I was a smart-arse."

"She won't," said Briffaut, standing and draining his coffee. "Do this for Romy."

"If I do it for Romy, I'll have to resign."

"I don't want you on medical—I want you well." Briffaut's phone sounded, and he made a face as he saw the screen. "Go see the doctor. That's an order," he said, and took the call as he turned away.

CHAPTER
THIRTEEN

De Payns sat up fully awake and checked the bedside clock: 2:09 a.m. His heart was racing, banging in his chest, and he knew from his dry throat and the sweat on his brow that he'd been panting in his sleep again. Romy had complained about it; apparently it was unnerving to lie beside a person who sounded like they were running the 1500 meters.

He slipped silently from the bed that Romy had readmitted him to and crept into the hall. The sounds of nothingness roared in his ears, and he noticed he was holding his breath. Forcing himself to breathe evenly—just like he'd been taught as a fighter pilot almost twenty years ago—he reverted to panting and had to steady himself against the wall as he swooned.

"Jesus," he whispered.

He couldn't access his dreams, which wasn't unusual for these turns. Whatever triggered him into such a state was buried deep and never revealed itself, much to the annoyance of Romy, who wanted the details of his nightmares. "*There can't ever be details,*" he'd told her. "*My career is over if anyone finds out about this.*" He knew she didn't accept that position; Romy held the view that being wife and mother gave her a status in his life every bit the equal of France; if anyone should have access to her husband's dreams, it should be her.

As he slowly got his breathing under control, snapshots cycled through his mind: the drunks at Saint-Lazare, the Metro platform lighting, Oliver's wide-eyed astonishment as he stared at his father. His wife's revulsion. As he focused on Romy's appraisal, a damp, low-level fear took hold. He tried some self-talking, telling himself that everyone was safe, his kids were unharmed, but the paranoia rose in him like milk on the boil. Pushing off the wall, he tiptoed to the end of the hallway where there was a small vestibule with a dresser that contained car keys and phone chargers. De Payns reached down behind the oak dresser cabinet and pulled out a black CZ 9mm handgun taped behind the cabinet and checked it for load and safety as his eyes adapted to the dark. He had never kept a handgun in the house until his run-in with Manerie. He'd been required to do a session with Dr. Marlene afterward because a person had died in front of him: a Dutch activist named Heidi Winnen. But he'd foxed the doctor, and any deeper benefit he might have gleaned from the woman was lost as de Payns concentrated on ensuring he'd not be placed on medical leave.

He was on autopilot as he held the CZ vertically beside his right cheekbone, not even acting consciously. He peered closely at the two deadbolt latches on the front door and slowly put his ear to the doorjamb, white noise rushing through his head, pulse banging in his temples. The door seemed okay, and he moved away, creeping down the hall to the boys' room. When they'd moved into the apartment, there were enough rooms for the boys to have one each, but they'd elected to sleep together in the large bedroom that had its own balcony and French doors that looked over the internal courtyard.

They were both sleeping, Patrick under his PSG quilt and Oliver still sleeping with the Wiggles. He checked the French doors and then had a quick look inside their wardrobe. Then he checked on Romy and padded to the kitchen.

He put his pistol on the counter by the sink and ran tap water into his hands, burying his face in the coolness, splashing his hair and feeling the liquid run down his back and hit the floor. Turning off the tap, he saw himself reflected in the window above the sink. He took stock of what he saw: a man still fit enough to run and fight, and in good shape for someone who was no longer young. But his face—usually an effective tool in charming and influencing people—was a mask of worry, his eyes sunken and his cheekbones more pronounced than usual. The scratch running vertically under his left eye was small but noticeable. He looked hideous.

Turning away from the sight of himself, he grabbed the CZ and padded across the large living room with its high ceilings, checking on the two banks of French doors that opened onto a balcony overlooking the street. He selected the sofa against the wall—the one that faced the TV screen—and sat on it carefully, his gun on his lap, his breathing becoming calmer but his mind still racing. He thought about how quickly Briffaut had twigged to what was going on in his family; that suggested it was a common theme of Company marriages. But de Payns didn't want to be a useless husband and absent father. He didn't want to be a danger to his family, or look dangerous to them, as he had at Saint-Lazare. Didn't want to make a mistake. Didn't want to bring the Russians into his life zone. Didn't want Romy and the boys confined to an anonymous house in the provinces, enrolled at schools under new names.

He didn't want to be Paul Degarde.

Romy appeared to his right, moving through the darkness in a white calico nightdress, her blonde hair tousled and her athletic body moving efficiently across the polished boards.

"It's me, it's me, it's me," she said, quite firmly and loudly as she approached and sat beside him, knowing not to spook him.

"Hi," he said.

She reached slowly for the pistol and took it from his hand, placing it on the other side of her. "We all safe?"

"Yep," he said, croaking slightly.

"Want to talk about it?"

"No," he said.

"Want to come to bed?"

"No," he said.

She put an arm around him and brought her face close to his. "That nightmare again?"

He shrugged. "Can't remember."

"Something happen at work?"

"No, I guess I just couldn't sleep," he said, his facial muscles hardening so he couldn't smile it off as he so often did.

Romy's eyes looked huge and dark in her oval face. "Are you okay?" she asked. She turned slightly and he could see her tears welling, and he realized what she was thinking.

"I'd never do that," he said.

She looked at him.

"*Never*," he said.

CHAPTER

FOURTEEN

Just before the lunch break on Tuesday, de Payns's second day of steward training, the door to the hotel dining room opened slightly, and Jéjé's head looked in.

"What's up?" asked de Payns, as he slipped out the door. "Day release for good behavior?"

Jéjé laughed. "Boss wants to see you, mon pote, not me."

Jéjé drove him across Paris, and when de Payns entered the antechamber to Briffaut's office, Margot told him they were waiting in the SCIF, the sensitive compartmented information facility. She walked him around the corner, took his phone, and shut the door behind him. Briffaut sat at the head of the oval table, Marie Lafont to his right and Lars Magnus, the head of BER–Europe, to his left.

As de Payns took a seat, Lafont pushed a file across to him.

"Lotus is still ours, until we know otherwise," said Briffaut, the file open in front of him but his eyes fixed on de Payns. "I want him active, so I need you to hand over to Jim."

"I'm in Monaco on Monday next week," de Payns reminded him. "I'm still in steward training."

"Where are you up to?" asked Briffaut.

"Silver service. Serving green beans without dripping butter on the guest."

"Okay, you passed with flying colors," said Briffaut, looking at his watch. "I need you in St. Petersburg before the weekend."

De Payns nodded, holding his tongue.

"I know it's short notice," said Lafont, peering at him over her half-glasses, "but given the way this is coming together, we need to keep Lotus productive."

"I'm sure," said de Payns. "You've tested him?"

"He responds to the LICLAN protocols," said Briffaut, referring to the maintenance of the *liaisons clandestines* protocols that allowed the Company to communicate with its sources and OTs. "There's no indication he was part of the Degarde murder."

"So, Lotus thinks it's business as usual?"

"We'd like that answered," said Briffaut. "Marie's people have gone over the product, and the realistic scenario is that Lotus wasn't aware of what was in the last package."

De Payns frowned. "Are you saying that he didn't understand what he was dropping to us?"

Briffaut shrugged. "Or he didn't look?"

"Lotus is a pure mercenary," said de Payns. "I assume he looks at everything he traffics and ensures the best stuff goes to whoever pays the most."

"Which would be France," said Briffaut, causing the others to laugh. The daily meal allowance for OTs in the field was 15.20 euros, and reimbursement required physical receipts.

"Let's say that Lotus is a useful idiot," said Lafont, "but we still want to maintain the channel to whoever is feeding him the product, because there's been a development."

De Payns cocked an eyebrow.

"Templar and Jéjé just got back from Georgia," said Briffaut.

"I see," said de Payns, leaning back in his chair. "Following Lotus?"

"And Andrei Lermatov," said Lafont, pushing another file across the table to de Payns. "He's a second secretary of cultural affairs, Russian embassy in Tbilisi."

In other words, Lermatov was SVR, Russia's foreign intelligence service.

De Payns flipped open the folder and scanned the file and the photo. "What did they see over there?"

"Clandestine meeting between Lotus and Lermatov in Vake Park, behind the big soccer stadium in Tbilisi," said Briffaut.

"Who made the drop?"

"Lermatov handed Lotus something, then was driven to the Russian embassy," Lafont said. "Lotus went to the airport and took a flight to Kiev."

De Payns nodded. "So, Lotus is feeding us great product, but it's coming from the Russian services?"

"We're trying to work out what it means," said Lafont. "It could be nothing, because Lotus takes from many sources and he sells to various clients. An SVR officer in Tbilisi could simply be another one of his sources."

This was plausible, de Payns thought. SVR midlevel employees trying to augment their meager salaries were the source of a lot of product to the Occidental services.

"Of course," continued Lafont, "there are factions in the Russian services, and one of them might want us to know what's going on in the Med."

"Factions?" echoed de Payns.

"Some of the general staff are locked into the Putin ecosystem; others are sworn to Mother Russia," said Lafont. "Even our own armed forces have groupings based on a world view."

"There could also be an economic angle, perhaps competing

oligarchs," said Magnus, whose background was economic analysis. "If you look at Lermatov's sheet, he came from the energy desk, and his previous postings were at embassies in Riyadh and UAE."

"Meaning?" asked de Payns.

"That's what we have to establish," said Lafont.

"And you want Jim Valley running Lotus?" asked de Payns.

Lafont nodded. "You did the original Lotus handover to Degarde. We'd like you to do it the same way with Jim."

"Why St. Petersburg?"

"Jim is in Moscow," Briffaut explained. "Given Lotus operates in Eastern Europe, St. Petersburg makes sense for everyone."

De Payns didn't like the rush. "Does Lotus know about Degarde?"

Briffaut shrugged. "That's your bag."

"And you want me in there on Friday?"

"At the latest," said Lafont.

"The Homsis are coming over Saturday night," said Romy, sipping at her Riesling as she leaned against the kitchen counter. "We're bringing Charles back here after Oliver's soccer game, and then Ana and Rafi will come over for dinner around five-thirty."

Romy knew her husband hated having guests in the house, but they were both still tense after the Saint-Lazare incident, so in the interests of fostering a normal family life, de Payns swallowed his objection.

"That sounds great," he said.

"They won't stay long—just a quick meal and a glass of wine," said Romy, shifting her weight. "Ana is so good with the school run, we have to return the favor where we can."

De Payns nodded. "Of course, it's fine."

"You'll be with Patrick's team at Université Paris Cité, and I'll take Oliver and Charles for their game at Charenton."

De Payns smiled. The idea of Oliver suiting up and running onto the soccer field was a thrill. He would have liked to take Oliver to buy his first pair of boots, but Romy had seen a sale on when she was shopping with the boys a couple of weeks ago, so she'd bought them then.

There was an awkward silence between them, and de Payns cleared his throat. "I'm going to see the doctor at work."

Romy looked at him, a neutral face. "Briffaut's orders?"

"His strong suggestion," said de Payns. "Which is sort of the same thing."

He looked past her, trying to avoid landmines, but Romy kept her eyes on him.

"I thought the doctor could end your career?"

"She can advise medical leave," said de Payns, "which means no more fieldwork. I'd return as a manager."

Romy's face shifted from neutral to positive. "You should take it."

"I'm not ready for that yet."

"*I* am."

They stared at one another, and then de Payns turned to the stove, where a pot of water was boiling under a colander, awaiting a pile of broccoli. "I'm going to see her, take it from there."

Romy pushed past him, scraped the chopped broccoli into the colander in one motion, and adjusted the heat. "Are you asking my opinion, or are you making an announcement?"

"Your opinion," said de Payns.

"Sort yourself out," she said. "That's my opinion."

"I'll try."

"The boys are growing up, Alec," she said. "What will you say to Oliver when he sees you creeping around the apartment with a gun? He's a light sleeper, you know that."

De Payns looked away. He'd grown up in an unhappy

household, with a French father who didn't know how to love his English mother. He wanted to be so much more for his own boys, and his wife. "I'll see the doctor."

"When?" she asked, with a challenge in her voice.

"Well, I'm away Thursday and Friday," he said. "And all of next week, so—"

"*Fuck*, Alec!" she said, the landmine fully detonated.

"I'm doing my best," he said.

"Get the boys out of the bath," she said, no longer looking at him. "Pajamas on, devices off."

CHAPTER
FIFTEEN

De Payns had a day before heading for St. Petersburg, so he used the time to do some gardening on the false identity he'd be using on *Azzam*. At all times he maintained five IDs, mainly presenting himself as a consultant or adviser when he went abroad under a cover. One of his IDs was for a film director, but on *Azzam* he'd be Frédéric Ruesche, a Parisian hospitality worker with various employers, including hotels and ski resorts. Having established the false ID, de Payns had to nurture it, which entailed regular visits to Ruesche's neighborhood to ensure that he was known to the community in the area. When the agents of the Iranian or Russian services came knocking to verify Ruesche's bona fides, there had to be shop owners saying, "*Yeah, I know Frédéric—he was in here having a beer last week.*"

He was dressed in jeans and sneakers and a down-lined windbreaker when he emerged from Riquet station in the nineteenth arrondissement. He turned right onto Rue Riquet, walking toward the canal, and paused at a small convenience store at the base of a building where he bought a carton of milk, a loaf of bread, and the latest edition of *L'Équipe*. He continued on toward the canal where there was a modernish apartment building to his right. He loitered outside the foyer until he saw a tenant walk toward the glass doors. De Payns held the door for her, smiled as she passed, and then stepped inside. A letterbox with the number 412 bore the name *Ruesche*, and he jiggled the cheap lock until it opened and removed his mail: low-rate credit cards, phone offers, and a letter from the building manager about parking.

He rode the elevator to the fourth floor and let himself into apartment 12 with the key he'd had cut a year ago. The Company's OTs were discouraged from renting apartments for their IDs. They had to find one that was uninhabited and use it as an address. In Paris, the level of verification required for a residential tenancy was heavy, and it was easier to be a glorified squatter. It allowed the OT to dismantle the premises within twenty-four hours, if the need arose.

Before pushing back the door, he checked the *bouletage*, a small needle jammed into the space between the door and the jamb. The bouletage was still stuck in the door, meaning it was highly unlikely anyone had been in the apartment.

Inside the small apartment, he paused and looked around after the door closed behind him. In a room with floorboards, he'd look at an angle of the sunlight and see if there were footprints in the dust on the floor. On the carpeted floor of 412, he instead checked for anything out of place. It looked okay: there was a small galley kitchen to his right and a sofa and TV set in the main room. He walked to a point beside the coffee table in the middle of the room and checked his three-point alignment: this was three items at the points of a three-pointed star. One was a landline phone that sat on a small table against the wall next to the main door. It was still aligned to point to where de Payns was standing. The second point of the star was a copy of *Time Out*, sitting on the sofa and lined up to point to his current position. The last point was a pen on a pad, sitting on the small counter in front of the galley kitchen. It was still pointing at de Payns.

No one had disturbed the three-point alignment, suggesting no unwanted visitors.

He entered the tiny bedroom, where he opened a sock drawer, then pulled a shirt from the wardrobe, placing it on the bed. In the bathroom he ran the shower for one minute and brushed his teeth, and then went to the refrigerator. He took out the old milk and bread and threw it in the garbage and put his fresh milk and bread in the fridge, which still contained two Heinekens and an orange.

He placed the copy of *L'Équipe* on the coffee table and threw the aging *Time Out* in the rubbish. Then he tied off the rubbish bag and picked it up, replaced the bouletage in the door, and threw the rubbish in the disposal chute before leaving the building.

Two minutes' walk along the Avenue de Flandre was a series of bars and cafés—not the most fashionable watering holes in Paris but good places to be seen and known. He dropped into Le Bastringue, a cozy neighborhood bar near the canal.

"Back from St. Moritz already, Fred?" asked the barmaid Yvette, while she chopped lemons. "No snow?"

"There's plenty of snow," said de Payns, smiling as he pointed to the Kronenbourg handle and reached for his wallet. "I was only at the hotel for the peak season; they let thirty of us go as it got quieter."

Yvette poured the beer and rolled her eyes slightly as a male voice in a back room demanded to know who had hidden the key to the cellar. "On the hook beside the desk," she shouted over her shoulder. "Where it always is."

De Payns paid and sipped the beer. "Anyway," he said, "I've got a gig on a yacht in Monte Carlo. Should be fun."

"Hobnobbing with the rich and famous, huh?" she teased. "You'll have to send me a photo."

Thirty-five minutes later, de Payns bought a packet of smokes from the Tamil lady in the news agency, and they had a laugh about the ongoing mask requirements of the pandemic response, and by 1:30 p.m. he was seated at a small outdoor table at a neighborhood café, making small talk with the waiter and ordering the ham omelet—"with extra peppers," said the waiter, before de Payns could finish his sentence.

By the time he'd used two trains and a bus to get back to the Bunker, his face and presence would be fresh in the minds of his local community if another service started sniffing around. No assumed ID was perfect, but Frédéric Ruesche was looking pretty solid.

CHAPTER
SIXTEEN

The winter winds whipped off the Arctic north and straight down the back of de Payns's neck. He cursed himself for not bringing a scarf as he walked his premeeting security route in an insulated Timberland rancher's jacket. But even as he felt the cold on his neck, he did not contemplate jumping in a St. Petersburg taxi to become the plaything of the Russian intelligence services.

Having played the part of Benoît Droulez, marketing consultant, who was wandering around St. Petersburg taking in the sights, he now meandered across the Dvortsoviy Bridge, slowing at two points to take photographs of the Neva River and the Hermitage Museum which dominated the skyline on the opposite bank.

He detected no sign of followers, and on the other side of the bridge he veered right and walked south along the riverfront. Glancing at his watch, he saw it was 9:26 a.m., putting him on time for his prehandover chat with Jim Valley before the meeting with Lotus.

Joining a gaggle of tourists, he crossed the Admiralty boulevard in front of a huge collection of buildings that had once
housed Catherine the Great's naval brains trust. He stepped into
the Hotel Katyusha and passed through the lobby as if a guest,
then took a side exit into a gentrified laneway. He walked to
the end of the lane, where there was a fork, took the left option,
and entered a smaller building that was used for conferences
and business-oriented events at the hotel.

At the top of a flight of stairs was a corridor and a door
marked *Baltic Room*. He glanced at his watch—9:30 a.m.—
then he knocked.

The bolt slid back and the door opened. Jim Valley stood
in front of him, over six feet tall and solidly built, although de
Payns noticed he'd grown out his dark gray hair now that his
special-forces days were officially behind him.

"Morning," said Valley, standing back to allow de Payns to
enter, and locking the door behind him.

There was a bank of windows along the wall of a large, white
room, with partial views of the Neva but mostly the back of
the Hotel Katyusha.

"I got the machine working," said Valley, moving in his outdoor
wear to a self-serve area that contained a capsule coffee maker.

"Black with one sugar," said de Payns, unbuttoning his
jacket and taking a seat at a white trestle table. "How're we
looking?"

"We're clean," said Valley, the machine grinding out a cup
of coffee. "I watched you come off the bridge, and there were
no followers."

De Payns hadn't asked for overwatch, but he was quietly
impressed with Valley's attention to security.

Valley put a mug of coffee in front of de Payns and a packet
of Russian-labeled biscuits.

"I think they're what the English call 'shortcake.'"

"Shortbread," said de Payns, whose mother had kept tins of the stuff in the cupboard above her tea-making gear. "And I think it's Scottish."

"Yes, of course," said Valley sitting with his own mug of coffee and staring at it too long. "I guess we should clear the air?"

"First things first," said de Payns. "Lotus is a Georgian fixer who sells us information gleaned primarily from the Russians, but occasionally from the Ukrainians and Turks too. And once from the Iranians, but that turned out to be Mossad bullshit."

"Okay," said Valley, nodding his large head.

"You've been sent the protocol for the drops, and I suggest you stick to it to the letter of it," said de Payns. "Lotus is promiscuous, which in my view increases the chances of him being leveraged by another service. So if he calls for the slightest variation in the protocol, reject it and let us know, all right?"

Valley nodded. "Got it."

"Are you aware of recent history regarding Lotus?"

"Are you talking about Paul Degarde?"

"Perhaps," said de Payns.

"I believe he used to do this job, and is now deceased," said Valley.

The two men looked at each other.

"The working assumption is that he was caught in his own home because he neglected his security hygiene when he landed in Paris."

"I didn't know that part," said Valley.

"Caught by Russians, we believe," said de Payns. "That isn't widely known, and I expect your discretion."

"Thanks for telling me," said Valley, his expression somber. "I'll keep it to myself."

"The drops have been nonverbal for more than a year, at my

insistence—that's because I consider Lotus dangerous," continued de Payns. "I'd like you to remain nonverbal."

"Sure, boss," said Valley, with no hint of sarcasm.

"As for clearing the air . . ."

"Can I go first?"

Jim Valley apologized for abducting Romy and the boys
a year earlier, adding that when Templar had ambushed him
at the farmhouse where he was holding them, he had already
decided to pull the pin on the kidnapping. It was an operation
ordered by his superior, Philippe Manerie, the disgraced former
director of internal affairs for French intelligence, the DGS. De
Payns knew some of the story was true: one of the other agents
who'd held the de Payns family at a farm in northern France for
thirty-six hours had told investigators that Valley was ending
the operation because he thought there was something off about
it. There had been no indication that Jim Valley benefited from
Manerie's dealings with a Pakistani terror cell that had attempted
to poison the Paris water supply; he was merely the muscle,
made loyal by old military ties.

"Must have been hard to turn on Manerie," de Payns
commented. "He was your commanding officer in the Marines?"

Valley nodded. "We served in Africa together, in the RPIMa.
He was a captain, and he was a damn good operator. The local
Marxists steered around him. So, yes it was hard to turn on him."

"But?"

"But I got a bad feeling about him toward the end there,"
said Valley. "And I draw the line at kids."

De Payns sensed the man was genuine. "Briffaut thinks
highly of you, and that's a rare accolade."

"Briffaut allowed me to live," Valley replied. "That's accolade enough."

De Payns checked his watch. "I won't be telling Lotus about

the Degarde murder. Let's hold that back and see if he offers anything."

"Got it, boss."

Lotus arrived at 10:01 a.m., and de Payns kept the conversation very short and simple; agents had been shuffled, but the payments stayed the same, and the protocol was unchanged. The new contact was Pierre, said de Payns, gesturing to Valley.

"Any questions?"

"Is there a reason why we are in Russia?" asked Lotus, who had kept his tweed trilby on his head.

"No," said de Payns.

"Then I request we not meet in this country again," said Lotus. "May I remind you of who Pierre and I are betraying? You might trick the wolf once or twice, but in his own den he still has the advantage."

"That's up to Pierre," said de Payns. "He's running the show now."

Lotus looked from de Payns to Valley and licked his bottom lip. "So, no pay raise?"

"The fee is the fee," said de Payns.

"You don't think the quality has improved, perhaps?"

"It's been good product," de Payns conceded. "A new source, huh?"

Lotus grinned and wagged his finger at de Payns jokingly. "Wouldn't the Company like to know that?"

"I'd never ask," said de Payns, returning the smile. "But if there is something you'd like to share . . ."

"Well," said Lotus, shrugging, "I didn't know I had a new handler, so I brought something very interesting."

Lotus reached inside his black pea jacket, drew out a packet of Rothmans cigarettes, and placed them in front of Valley.

"Not today," said de Payns. "When I leave, you can arrange your first meeting with Pierre and make the drop."

The Georgian made a face. "But I am here now."

De Payns looked at his colleague.

"We'll stick to the protocol," said Valley.

Lotus replaced the packet in his coat pocket, seeming to accept the arrangement. "So, where is my former contact? Promoted to a nice embassy in America or Southeast Asia?"

"What makes you think he was from the embassy?"

Lotus shrugged. "He is not like you and Pierre. You two are wild animals, right on the edge."

De Payns smiled. Lotus had used the present tense—"*he is*"—which suggested he did not know of Paul Degarde's demise. Standing, he nodded to Jim Valley and headed for the door.

"Good to see you again, my friend," said Lotus. "You should think about that pay raise."

"I should do many things," said de Payns, closing the door behind him.

CHAPTER
SEVENTEEN

Shrek had spent most of Friday morning following a low-level Hungarian diplomat to his twice-weekly visits to the Champ de Mars, and he'd still seen no meeting or handoff. Now back at the Bunker, he was tired, his feet hurt, and the surveillance work seemed endless and fruitless. He pushed off his Adidas sneakers and flexed his feet under his desk. His office, on the first floor of the Bunker, looked west across Paris, and as he stared out the window he thought through his next moves: write his surveillance report, catch the Metro home, and give his sore feet a rest with the aid of a quiet drink. He might even get in the door before five o'clock for once and be home before his wife.

He opened his DGSE account to write the report and remembered back to his university days and how his colleagues in the history department used to complain about being over-worked and underpaid. It seemed a lifetime removed from his visit to Katie Degarde earlier in the week. He hadn't known Paul well, but he felt an intense affinity with the Degarde family. Not only were the wife and daughter suffering the loss of a husband

and father, but they had the additional agony of relocation, a new school, and being prohibited to breathe a word of the grief to anyone.

He shook it out of his head, selected the "Surveillance" template in the computer system, and was about to type his first word when the landline buzzed beside him. Briffaut's assistant, Margot, calling him to the boss's office.

He went straight up. Margot waved him in, and as the door closed behind him, the boss rubbed his face, and Shrek noticed that the most indefatigable person in the Bunker was tired.

"Before I forget," said Briffaut, not bothering with a greeting, "Degarde's memorial is to be held at the Cat this afternoon. I'd like you to be there."

Shrek had seen the internal email and then forgotten. "Of course. Four, was it?"

"Five. And drag Aguilar along. Templar, if you can find him. Degarde might have been DR, but he was working with a source that we created and transmitted." He leaned forward and looked at a file on his desk. "Speaking of Paul Degarde, I've just been with Marie Lafont—she had an update."

"From DGS?" asked Shrek, as Briffaut handed him a stapled sheaf of papers which looked like printed photographs.

"Yep," said Briffaut. "They have a possible lead on a vehicle that might be connected to the Degarde murder. See the rego number?"

Shrek looked at the first sheet of paper, saw a "75" series number plate, meaning it was Parisian.

"Final page," said Briffaut.

Shrek flipped to the photograph on the final page. It was a dimly lit picture, taken at a distance, in poor light. He could make out what looked like a black van, maybe a Renault or Iveco. On the penultimate page of the document was a blown-up and enhanced picture of the van's rego plate. It looked heavily pixelated. "Is this plate accurate or guesswork?" he asked.

"It's the best we have, is what it is," said Briffaut. "This is potentially the only evidence of Degarde's killers. The footage comes from a garbage truck, taken around 4:51 a.m."

"It came from a video?"

"Dashcam, from inside the truck," Briffaut elaborated. "It's a still from the footage."

"Why is the van of interest?" asked Shrek. "It's a common model."

"Because it matches the time that the DGS investigators think Degarde died. It was just around the corner from the Degarde house, and they didn't turn on their lights."

"We know who owns it?"

"Monsieur Hertz, with fake ID," said Briffaut. "DGS think they've hit a dead end, but I'd like a second opinion."

"I'm on it," said Shrek.

"Put another way," said Briffaut, "you have forty-eight hours."

De Payns sat between Shrek and Briffaut at the rear of the hall that was tucked away in the oldest part of the Cat building on Boulevard Mortier. The large room's ornate ceilings and polished wood gave the affair a sense of ceremony, while its location inside the DGSE headquarters meant the Company's events could be conducted with some candor, with no need for speakers to censor themselves as they would if they spoke in public.

It was obvious that the men and women of the DR department of the Company liked Paul Degarde, judging by the funny stories they told about the Russian-speaking analyst.

"Paul was not a classic spy," said a teary CP analyst named

Romain, nodding at the large photo of Degarde mounted on an easel. "Hotel rooms made him lonely, so the field was not so good for him . . ."

The crowd erupted in laughter at this characterization of their former colleague, and de Payns laughed himself, understanding too well the human dimension of the work which was a million miles from what the movies portrayed. You could use a false name and build a credible legend, but despite all the training, an OT was still a man making his way in life. There was still the core of the real person, having to negotiate with himself, around fears and around family sacrifice.

A woman walked to the front of the room and talked about Degarde's encyclopedic knowledge of Russian novelists. "He was proud to go into the field if he was asked," she said. "He knew he wasn't one of those macho DO guys, he was realistic about who he was, but he would do his bit for France."

De Payns shrunk into his seat, praying that his career didn't end with one of these memorials. The thought of Romy and the boys being exiled from their own lives and not even allowed to hear the colleagues' stories about his job made him queasy.

When it was over, the three DGSE men moved to the rear door and found Templar leaning against the doorjamb. He'd been a Marines paratrooper before he joined the Company, and he still carried an aura of menace that eight years of intelligence training had not fully eliminated. They watched the DR employees congregate around the makeshift bar, and it didn't seem right to join in with Degarde's core crowd.

"I'm good for one round," said Briffaut, looking at his watch. "Then I have a meeting."

They adjourned to a bar a couple of blocks south of the Cat, and Briffaut ordered two rounds of whisky. "To Paul," he said, raising his glass.

"To Paul," the other men chorused, and downed their drinks.

Briffaut reached for his second glass. "It isn't your fault," he said, nodding at de Payns. "Lotus was cleared by the system. It wasn't your call alone."

"But I knew Lotus was dangerous," de Payns replied. "Enough that I told Paul to keep it nonverbal." He sipped at his second Scotch, slowly scanning the bar.

"But he was trained for it," Templar pointed out. "If we think too much about what might happen, we'd never do what has to be done."

Silence fell around the table, and Briffaut looked at Templar. "You hungover?"

Laughter seized the group, and Templar's poker face finally broke. "Shit, boss. It's that obvious?"

"Only when you're profound," said Briffaut, standing and draining his glass. "Don't get too drunk."

Templar, Shrek, and de Payns—three members of the clan, de Payns's crew—leaned into their table in the semi-dark of the Croix de Rosey, Paris's least-salubrious bar. It was an anonymous drinking hole on a long-forgotten lane in Le Marais, run by Tomas, a Franco-Austrian soldier who had fought for the Legion in the worst parts of Africa. The interior looked jumbled together, with faded 1970s beer mirrors, low-wattage light bulbs, and threadbare carpets from an era of landlines and typewriters. Still, this was the clan's safety zone, and Tomas didn't water his whisky or put a surcharge on the Jack Daniel's—which was handy because when Templar wanted to drink, it was red wine and Jack Daniel's all night long.

"We'll have to get these bastards," said Templar as the resident singer—a middle-aged woman—walked past them and took a seat beside the accordion player in the darkest corner of the bar. "Can't let them come into Paris and kill one of our own."

"We're working on it," said Shrek, who was the least gregarious of the trio, but probably the smartest given he'd been a university lecturer before joining the Company. His black belt in Wing Chun kung fu was also handy. "But I'd like to get an idea of what we're looking for."

De Payns noticed both men were staring at him. "Early days yet," he said.

Shrek nodded, looking into his drink. "So Degarde was handling Lotus," he said. "Any idea what he was carrying, and if it got him killed?"

De Payns couldn't divulge details, and Shrek knew it. "I think it was more about what he knew."

They were both aware that this had some connection with *Azzam*, but Shrek didn't let on.

"Perhaps I'm overthinking it, but do you reckon Lotus was dropping breadcrumbs?" asked Shrek.

"Or his source was feeding him breadcrumbs," said de Payns, watching the singer take a slug of wine and tune her guitar. "You're saying this could be a manipulation?"

Shrek shrugged. "Maybe one group of Russians feeds a story to Lotus, and another group comes into Paris to work out where that story is going?"

The singer greeted the dozen or so patrons and took a request from a table of drunks near the window.

"So, you're sad, mon cher?" said the singer, with a smile. "Time for a sad song."

She tapped three times on her guitar and launched into "There's a Tear in My Beer," which snapped the clan out of their grim moods. As Templar sang along to the song, de Payns felt a smile form on his lips. He was sitting with the two men he trusted most in the world, and even though they'd just left a memorial service for a deceased colleague, he felt a sense of security in the overwatch they provided for one another. As the singer switched to a verse of the song in French, de Payns decided that Shrek was right: they might be overthinking the mail drops.

Templar was right too: they'd have to get the bastards who killed Paul Degarde.

CHAPTER
EIGHTEEN

De Payns sat beside Patrick, on the RER traveling north from the university ground where his oldest son's soccer team had just played. He was hungover, but he'd kept his phone in his jacket pocket, noticing how many of the other parents stared into their screens on the sidelines while their children were playing soccer. It annoyed him, and despite the low parenting rating he'd received from Romy recently, he at least wasn't going to ignore his sons so he could read platitudes on LinkedIn.

"How come Sophie's so fast?" asked Patrick, sipping a Burger King lemonade, the Whopper long gone. "I mean, she sprints away from everyone and still has the ball."

De Payns nodded. "She's pretty good, but I bet she does extra training."

"She's also bigger than the rest of us," said Patrick, flicking his sandy blond hair off his brow. "That would help."

"You think because she's taller than you that she has more skills?"

"Hmmm," said Patrick, a smile starting at the corner of his mouth.

"What?" asked de Payns. "You still have to train—doesn't matter how big you are."

"Like that drunk at the Metro station?"

De Payns paused. "What about it?"

"The first one, the one you punched in the mouth," said Patrick, matter-of-fact. "He was bigger than you, but he didn't have the fighting skills."

Warning lights flashed for de Payns. "You shouldn't have seen that. It was my mistake."

Patrick shrugged. "It's all right," he said. "Violence is never okay until it's necessary, right?"

"Well, it might be true, when you say it like that," de Payns prevaricated, "but—"

"Sensei John told us they have a saying in Africa."

"What's that?" asked de Payns, regretting the turn the conversation was taking.

"The only thing worse than a violent man is an unprepared man," said Patrick. "Having superior manners is no defense against a fist."

De Payns chuckled, couldn't help himself. "Well, you listen to Sensei John, he's obviously experienced and smart. But perhaps don't mention his ideas to your mother?"

"No way," said Patrick, drink straw in his mouth.

The evening meal wasn't the waste of time de Payns had expected. Romy dished up homemade pizzas for the boys and a roast leg of lamb for the adults, and Rafi and Ana were good company. The wine flowed, and when de Payns had cleared the table, Oliver and Charles jumped on the Xbox while Rafi sat on the carpet and showed Patrick some moves on the chessboard.

"I love this new apartment, Alec," said Ana, as de Payns took a seat beside Romy. "That Ministry job is good for real estate, non? You must be doing well."

De Payns smiled, knowing that just about everyone in the Defense Ministry missed out on the famous subsidized apartments in the nice streets. They were reserved for the people who played politics rather than operated in the field. "We got lucky."

"Don't be so modest," said Ana, smiling. "And Romy's doing so well in her career too. I bet you're excited about this energy seminar."

There was an expectant pause, while de Payns tried to remember if Romy had said something about it.

"The Tirol Council seminar?" added Ana. "Europe in a Post-Carbon Era?"

"Umm . . ." said de Payns, confused. He looked at Romy helplessly.

"Didn't I tell you?" asked Romy. "We're invited to the big gala for the opening of the conference. We'll all have plus-ones—it should be fun."

"All of us?" said de Payns.

"You know, David and Kris and me—the team!"

De Payns smiled and tried to make a joke of his ignorance. "Just as well I love surprises."

"Oops, sorry," said Ana, laughing and reaching for the Riesling bottle. "Foot in my mouth. I thought you knew."

"Tell me about the conference," said de Payns, turning to his wife.

"We have some important speakers, actually," said Romy, avoiding his gaze. "David pulled some strings, and we'll have Tony Blair and maybe Bill Clinton at the gala night."

"I always liked Tony Blair," said de Payns. "I like the way he wrings his hands when he talks."

Ana spurted wine as she repressed a laugh.

"And Bill once gave me a copy of *Leaves of Grass*, but he doesn't phone, he doesn't write . . ."

Ana whacked him on the arm. "You're terrible, Alec."

"Actually, it would be quite a coup to get both Clinton and Blair at the conference," said Romy tersely. "David's doing a wonderful job."

"David sounds like a great guy," said de Payns.

"He is, actually," said Romy, sounding furious now.

"You got a smoker's window?" asked Ana, easing herself out of the argument she'd started.

"It's the middle door," said Romy, pointing at the French doors that opened onto the Juliet balcony. "But Alec doesn't smoke in front of the kids."

"Neither do you," said Rafi, not looking up from the chessboard.

"Yes, she does," said Charles, not looking away from the Xbox game.

CHAPTER
NINETEEN

De Payns listened to the soft purrs of the heating system and the small groans of the old building. Romy was deep in sleep beside him, barely making a sound. It was shortly before 3:00 a.m. and he was not going to stalk around the apartment with his handgun. His ritual was to make mental laundry lists before he went into the field, not unlike the checklists he'd been trained to make as a pilot. Mechanical failure and acts of God such as the weather were certainly real risks. But as all pilots were told, the most likely cause of a crash was human error.

Reduce the errors, decrease your risk.

He thought through the operational aspects of the *Azzam* infiltration. The overwatch team at Port Hercules marina were solid professionals, and not only did they have the best video and audio equipment to capture the guests boarding the yacht, but Danny and Jéjé were the core of the mission team, and they were capable people with special-forces backgrounds. He thought about the product-drop protocol, if one was needed while he was aboard: Danny and Jéjé would be following *Azzam* on a small cruiser, and for the period of an hour around midnight, they'd close in on the superyacht and wait for three long flashes of an infrared torch that de Payns carried disguised as a key ring. Having flashed the light, de Payns would drop the prod in waterproof canisters that looked like cigar tubes and emitted an infrared light beacon. In order to see the infrared light, the mission team would wear night-vision goggles. There was also a protocol if de Payns found himself in danger, but he didn't dwell on it.

His main concern was spending two days on *Azzam* with a strong enough ID to survive a spy hunt. Frédéric Ruesche was an identity he'd used before, but it didn't give him access to persons of interest in the way that his "consultant" personas did. When presenting himself as a service professional who worked at ski resorts and major hotels, his access became one of proximity and eavesdropping, which in many regards was riskier than making himself the "star" of the show. Under the Ruesche cover, he'd have to be dominant enough to get close to the POIs, while remaining insignificant enough that no one suspected him of absorbing their conversations.

Most importantly, he'd have to "be" Frédéric Ruesche by the time he fronted up at the labor hire office in Nice in six and a half hours' time. He'd stepped into Ruesche's world a few days earlier when he did his gardening, but by the time he walked onto that superyacht, he'd have to have all the mannerisms absolutely nailed because once on the boat, it was a totally immersive mission zone for two days.

He slipped out of bed and padded to the kitchen, where he poured a glass of water from the tap and made himself breathe properly. In through the nose, out through the mouth. He could do this, he told himself; he had the skills, and he had the background. He thought back to the Kosovo conflict in the late 1990s, when he was a special operations pilot ferrying generals, spies, and paratroopers around the Balkans. Most flights were conducted in violation of at least one rule of aviation and international airspace. He flew with transponders off, false tail numbers, no flight plan, and no landing lights. He landed on closed runways and took off against the demands of the air traffic controllers. Dangerous, illegal flying conducted under great secrecy.

One night, he was transporting a senior French official known as Saber into the former Yugoslavia, for a crucial meeting. The flight was initially delayed because there was a monster storm front moving across the Adriatic, and Sarajevo tower had closed the airport. However, Saber insisted on making the meeting, so de Payns flew the anonymous TBM 700 over the Alps and across the Adriatic and hit the storm at the Olympic mountain ranges that surround Sarajevo. The plane was thrown around like a balsawood toy as they entered the storm, and de Payns took radio updates from Bologna advising there were twenty centimeters of snow on the Sarajevo runways, the runway lights were off, and visibility was one hundred feet.

Using the only electronic aid operating at Sarajevo—the VOR, or VHF omnidirectional range signal system—de Payns conducted a K navigation which relied on a radio-beacon signal from Sarajevo airport called TACAN that gave the pilot direction and distance to the transmitter, and nothing else. De Payns calculated a rate of descent, which would have to be manually controlled. The lengthy flight had pushed the plane to the limits, and they'd have only two attempts at the landing and still have enough fuel to fly to Mostar for a refuel that would get them back to France.

De Payns adjusted his approach for wind, then let the TBM drop through the storm for what might have been the most frightening five minutes of his life. Sometimes diving, other times thrown sideways, he held his nerve as they plunged through the darkness, unable to look at anything except his TACAN numbers and his rate of descent. There was nothing else to see.

When the altimeter reached fifteen hundred feet, and he was committed to the flight path, he let down the landing gear and heard a sound from behind: Saber was vomiting, the violent motion of the aircraft proving too much. At two hundred feet he flared the TBM, hoping to have the plane ready for landing, if he was over the runway. They broke through at one hundred and fifty feet into a sea of white, with the only visible feature through the blizzard the red light of the Sarajevo tower to their left and several lights to their right, which would be the hangars of the airport's military section. He lined up with what looked like a runway under the snow, and as they touched down, he reversed the props to slow their speed, throwing up clouds of snow which blinded him even further. As he slowed the plane to a stop, two Audi SUVs, blue lights flashing, drove to the TBM and ordered de Payns to follow. He complied, Saber green with motion sickness and de Payns's flight suit soaked in sweat, both of them panting from the stress and adrenaline.

Saber made his meeting, and de Payns was noticed by DGSE. He'd subsequently been approached to join the Company.

De Payns walked across the living room with his glass of water and looked down onto the street. He had spent his career engaging in dangerous activities. But it wasn't the danger that was important, he realized; what saved him was the de-risking and the attention to detail. The key was his own mental preparation. That was how he'd endured high-risk situations in the sky and in his intelligence career. He reminded himself that he'd put in the work and he could trust his own process. He'd prepared for *Azzam*, and now he was ready to do his job.

CHAPTER
TWENTY

The hospitality company was called Hibiscus Hire, and it was tucked away in a block of two-story office suites a kilometer back from the Nice waterfront. De Payns climbed the stairs and walked into the lobby of the business at 8:30 a.m., as arranged via email.

"Frédéric Ruesche," he said, handing his French ID card to the woman at the reception desk.

The woman looked at the card, ticked off his name on a clipboard, and led him through to a meeting room where a man and two women were standing. All were in their mid- to late twenties and wore casual clothes.

"Let's go," said the woman from reception.

The five of them walked down a flight of fire stairs to the car park and climbed into a minibus.

De Payns sat next to a friendly man from Marseille named Jacques, and they swapped greetings as they merged onto the coastal road to Monaco.

"You know anything about this gig?" asked de Payns.

"Pays well and I don't have to buy groceries for a while," said Jacques, with a shrug. "Could be fun, as long as none of the guests is gay."

De Payns nodded.

"I'll take the brunette," said Jacques.

"I'm sorry?"

Jacques nodded to the two young women who were poring over their social media accounts, oblivious to their surrounds and each other. The brunette had introduced herself as Claire, the other woman was Simone.

"You can have the blonde," said Jacques.

"Oh, okay," said de Payns, smiling. "Bet she'll be delighted to hear that."

Jacques turned and gave de Payns a wink. "Don't worry, mon pote. Stick with me and you'll score."

The minibus stopped at Monaco's marina, and the woman from Hibiscus Hire led the foursome to a security gate, where she handed some paperwork to a security guard, who checked their IDs.

"I'll be here at the end of the cruise," said the Hibiscus woman. "You've read and signed our code of conduct, so please stick to it."

At the far end of the quay, a huge vessel loomed with the name *Azzam* stenciled on the side. Somewhere on the yachts and buildings around the quay, de Payns knew, a crew of three people from the Company were waiting to see the guests arrive and capturing them with high-powered lenses and sound-amplification dishes. From the surveillance material, the team would build a *trombinoscope*, a gallery of images, names, associates, and habits of the main players and locations in an operation. It was one thing to say that Russians were being hosted on a UAE yacht, but it was useless without the identities and their backgrounds.

De Payns marveled as he walked beside *Azzam*. He'd researched the boat but hadn't appreciated the true size of eighty-two meters. They walked into the yacht through a crew gangplank near the stern and were greeted by a middle-aged man called Tom, wearing whites. He led them down two flights of stairs, all the while chatting about the crew facilities, including the galley and mess area, which looked like the workers' mess in a mining camp.

"Ladies," he said, pointing to one side of the dark, cramped passageway, "and gentlemen," pointing to a mahogany door on his right. "Get unpacked, reserve a bed for yourselves, and meet upstairs in five minutes. Susan would like a word."

De Payns put his bag on the top bunk because Jacques got in first with the bottom. The quarters were like a coin slot, with a set of double bunks on one wall of the cabin, a louvered wardrobe on the other wall, and barely enough space to turn between them. Jacques lay on his bed and checked his phone while de Payns ducked out to look for the toilet. The layout of the yacht essentially put the crew in the area where the engines, diesel tanks, and sewerage was located, and judging by the crew entrance, the quarters were underneath the massive hangar that held speedboats, jet skis, and a small helicopter.

He checked the toilet and shower cabinets, then continued along the low-ceilinged passageway. There was a hum all around him with the occasional raised voice as the vessel was readied for sea. He reached the foot of a companionway and looked up. At the top of the stairs, two men looked down on him: one was Tom, the other a thickset Middle Eastern man, midthirties, in a black polo shirt.

"Hello, umm . . ." said Tom, searching for a name.

"It's Fred," said de Payns. "I'm a steward. I was just looking around."

"Ah, right. It's Susan you'll be looking for," Tom said. "And she'll be on this deck, but give her five minutes, okay?"

De Payns smiled his acquiescence but found his eyes locking with those of the Middle Eastern gentleman, who stared into his face silently, his thick neck straining as he chewed gum.

"Sure—I'll see you later," said de Payns, pulling back and returning down the passageway to his cabin. He wasn't going to be able to fade into the background on this journey; the onboard security had made that very clear.

An Englishwoman in her early forties, Susan addressed the four new stewards in front of the bar in an entertainment area that included a dancefloor with a disco ball and a nightclub lounge area. The marina was visible through the opened doors at the far side of the dancefloor. She told them that they'd been selected for their expertise and that their discretion would be appreciated.

"You'll be signing NDAs," she said, "but that's just a piece of paper. The rule on these yachts is that whatever happens here, stays here. Don't get into conversations with the guests, don't make passes at the guests, don't say yes to sex with the guests, and this is a dry tour, so no drinking. Clear?"

Susan noticed a lack of response. "I'm serious, ladies," she snapped. "Some of these people think an unmarried woman is a prostitute, so get this straight: no flirting, no batting eyelids, no sex. Got it?"

They all murmured their comprehension, and Susan moved on to who would be working in which sector of the vessel. They'd have specific tasks when entertaining, and each of them had a sector they were responsible for cleaning and maintaining, including guests' cabins. De Payns was assigned as backup barman on the main and upper decks, due to his experience as a sommelier in Paris hotels. His general duties section was stateroom three and the library and cinema above and below it.

They signed their NDAs and then peeled off into groups. De Payns and Simone were paired with Otis, the taciturn head barman of Malian extraction, who told them the guests were likely to be from the Gulf States and Eastern Europe, which meant the drinks orders would be predominantly champagne and vodka, and they'd have to keep a constant supply of caviar flowing.

They were given white shirts with gold trim and the word *Azzam* stitched on the left breast. The crew was segregated from the owners and the guests, so de Payns spent the morning and most of the afternoon with no view of the areas reserved for the playboys and their "companions," but he was asked to develop a detailed knowledge of the booze storage areas and the intricate rabbit warren of companionways and service passageways that allowed the crew to move around *Azzam* without being seen by the VIPs. He spent almost an hour with Otis and Simone, familiarizing himself with the cellar, which was located one deck below and held what de Payns estimated to be around two million euros worth of wine and port, in an area the size of a squash court. After stocking the upper deck bar and the owner's lounge—where it was obvious the meetings were going to be held—Simone and de Payns were sent back to the entertainment area to polish champagne glasses.

"The answer's no, by the way," said Simone, who was closer to thirty than twenty. "We're not sleeping together."

"Gee," said de Payns, holding a glass to the light to check for smears. "I didn't even get the thrill of asking."

She laughed.

"Or the adrenaline rush of being refused."

Simone shook her head. "Claire wants to swap cabins, but it's up to me apparently."

De Payns made a face.

"You know how this works, don't you?" she asked. "Crew pair-off—it's a thing. So, Claire and Jacques . . ."

"I like my bed," said de Payns.

"You didn't organize this with Jacques?" she asked.

"Jacques is precisely the kind of person I don't organize things with," said de Payns.

Simone chuckled, relieved. "Well, he's organized *something* with Claire."

"He can be his guest," said de Payns. "I encourage creative thinking."

The yacht left its berth just after 4:00 p.m., and de Payns and Simone were summoned to one of the upper decks, where the guests stood around a swimming pool while a Parisian jazz quartet played in the corner. The deck's glass barrier stopped the winter chill, but the Riviera had also served up a still afternoon, making for pleasant cruising. De Payns served half-filled champagne glasses from a silver tray, noting faces and groupings as he went. When he'd delivered drinks, he'd return to fetch platters of crusty bread with caviar spread on top, with shaved radish as a palate cleanser. As Otis had predicted, there was a UAE group—none of them in traditional robes—and also an Eastern European group in silk shirts and expensive jeans. He counted four security people, in black polo shirts and black pants, positioned around the sides of the deck. Their shirts weren't tucked in, and the bulges on their right hips demonstrated they were armed. It wasn't the sort of protection that was used in Paris; this was so conspicuous as to be almost a challenge.

"Who's our owner?" asked de Payns, as he returned to the bar and handed a tray to Otis.

"Blue jacket, silver hair," said Otis, doing his best to not look at the guests. "He's got a long Prince Something name, but he's called Jamal."

"I call him Monsieur Jamal?" asked de Payns, corking a bottle of Cristal he'd lifted from a silver ice bucket.

"You won't call him anything, Fred," said Otis, smirking. "We don't speak to Prince Jamal. We speak to Susan, and she speaks to him."

"I see," said de Payns. "And what happens if Jamal wants to tell us something?"

"He sends Ahmed," said Otis, angling his head slightly toward the security guard that de Payns had met earlier with Tom. Ahmed now wore a black windbreaker and leaned on the fold-back door that separated the pool deck from the bar. "But you don't want that because if Ahmed starts a conversation with you, you're probably in trouble."

"Tough guy?" asked de Payns lightly, fishing for information.

"And smart," said Otis. "He was a spy or secret police, something like that, back in Abu Dhabi. Stay away from him."

De Payns nodded and made a beeline for Jamal, a tanned, good-looking man in his early fifties, who wore his authority lightly. He was speaking to a younger, more intense Arab man with a tightly curated goatee and aviator sunglasses.

De Payns made to pour, and Jamal turned to stare at him with intelligent, ruthless eyes. "No, thank you," said Jamal in French, his accent neutral.

De Payns turned his body to the goatee man, who didn't wait for the bottle to be presented.

"Go on," said the man, jerking his thumb over his shoulder. "Piss off."

De Payns smiled and continued his rounds, pouring

champagne, eventually returning to the bar, where Otis was smothering a laugh.

"What's so funny?" asked de Payns, picking up a fresh bottle of champagne.

"I see you met Nasir," said Otis.

"Meet would be stretching it," said de Payns. "What's his problem?"

Otis lowered his voice. "His biggest problem is his excellent hearing, you understand, mon pote?"

De Payns did.

The full party of VIPs, as far as de Payns could make out, comprised Jamal and Nasir, and a tall Russian in a black silk shirt who kept his eyes on Simone. The other Arabs and Eastern Europeans looked like hangers-on. There didn't seem to be a meeting of the size suggested in the Lotus document drop. Given that most of the people around the pool were either heavies or lackeys, de Payns wondered if he was even on the right vessel.

De Payns asked Otis, "It's a small party we've got here—how come they needed extra stewards?"

Otis shrugged. "We're about half full. The real VIPs are here when the helicopters have landed."

The sun reached the horizon, giving the central Mediterranean a golden-rose light as *Azzam* sailed for the north of Corsica in light seas. The receding Cote d'Azur was transitioning into twilight, and guests reached for jackets and polar fleeces. De Payns was topping up glasses with Cristal when he saw a dark shape in the sky approaching the stern. By the time he'd retreated into the bar, a black EC-135 Eurocopter was flaring for landing at the helicopter deck which was two decks below and aft of the pool deck. This landing was followed shortly by two more.

The first of the new guests arrived poolside a few minutes

after the third helicopter landed. A trim man in his early forties, dressed in dark sports coat and a deep red shirt, emerged from the VIP companionway beside the pool deck and walked to the pool's edge, where he did what every military man did in such a situation: assessed his placement on the yacht and every single person around him and above him. Behind him, three heavies in slate-gray windbreakers and black ripstop pants fanned out around the pool deck, openly assessing the other guests as well as the security. De Payns saw small wires emerging from their left ears and observed bull necks and tactical boots. The tall man in the black silk shirt approached the new arrival and shook his hand. A torrent of Russian poured between the two men as de Payns approached with a bottle of champagne; he was dismissed in favor of Simone and her silver tray of chilled vodka shots.

De Payns lingered, on the pretext of topping up other glasses, and heard the tall Russian call his red-shirted compatriot "Boris."

Another party emerged on the pool deck. In the lead was a compact man in his late thirties—Arab, de Payns thought— who strutted to the pool surrounded by thugs. Behind him was a lean man with a small hunchback, in his forties, who looked like his security detail.

Jamal, the *Azzam*'s owner, approached the younger of the two and called over Boris and his Russian friend. The new group formed in the middle of the pool deck, circled by backup people and hangers-on, then an outer circle of security.

De Payns loaded up with canapés, and Simone followed him with a tray of vodka shots. Jamal shouldered de Payns out of the way, ushering Simone into the midst of the group, where hands reached for shot glasses. Holding his aloft, Jamal— speaking in English, which appeared to be the group's lingua franca—proposed a toast to the younger of the Arab men, whom he called Faisal, and then to Boris, welcoming them aboard his yacht.

The temperature dropped as the sun did, and the guests were called through to the mahogany-paneled owner's dining room, located forward of the pool deck. De Payns switched to sommelier duties, thankful that his mentors at the George V had prepped him for complicated wine lists and rich people showing off about vintages. He and Simone worked around the waiters, which included Jacques, whom de Payns noticed had left a small silver ring in his left earlobe despite being told by Susan to remove all jewelry.

The sommelier's station was set back from the dining room in its own little wine room, and as de Payns corked a 2010 Chateau Lafite, Ahmed entered, close-up and observing his movements.

"You're new," the security man observed, as de Payns placed the bottle on the sommelier's trolley and readied his napkins.

"I guess that depends on who is talking to me," said de Payns, smiling.

Ahmed didn't return the smile or take his eyes off de Payns. He was the same height and build as de Payns, but he'd spent more time in the gym.

"You're new to this boat," said Ahmed, his clean-shaven face impassive. "Where are you from?"

"Paris," said de Payns. "The George V, and in the winter sometimes I'm in St. Moritz."

"Monaco is a long way from Paris," said Ahmed, in Syrian-accented French.

"It's not a bad place for a working holiday," de Payns said, with a shrug. "I like the beaches and the girls, and the money is good when you get these kinds of gigs."

Ahmed nodded slowly, contemplating. "Girls and money. What else could you want?"

Seeming satisfied, he turned and left.

After the dinner, Otis called de Payns back to the main bar. "Get the owner's bar ready," he instructed. "They're going up there for a private meeting."

De Payns scooted up the companionway and let himself into the owner's bar. It had been decorated like a 1920s London club, with dark green Chesterfield chairs, wood paneling, a card table, a conference table, and even a bookcase. The bar itself looked like it belonged in *The Great Gatsby*. De Payns checked the wines and the cocktail equipment and then walked around the large room, turning on the wall lighting and the green-shaded lamps on small side tables.

He walked around the conference table, a great oval slab of oak; it was obvious this was where the VIPs were going to sit during the meeting. He wondered if he would have another chance as good as this one. He quickly turned off the lights he'd switched on because if he was going to plant a bug in this room, he didn't want to be watched on CCTV by security as he did so. He hurried for the crew companionway, went down three flights, and then moved aft along the narrow passageway that led to the crew quarters in the stern of the yacht. The engine sounds became louder as he entered the crew zone, and he was more aware of the movement of the boat as it surged through the Med.

Aware of the hostile security teams currently stalking the boat, he tried to tamp down his nerves as he ducked into his cabin and rummaged in the secret lining of his bag, pulling out a small, black plastic recording device the size of a thumb drive. Pushing back out through the cabin door, he emerged into the passageway and moved forward, feeling the surge of the vessel push him slightly into the right wall.

"You lost?" came the voice he now knew. French with a Syrian accent.

De Payns turned, acting like a man who'd been called by nature, as he faced Ahmed. "I can't find the toilet. I didn't know if I was allowed to use the one up there."

Ahmed got in close to him, and de Payns wondered if he'd been followed, or if the crew quarters was a standard security beat. "They're just up there," said the Syrian, neutral, looking for tells in de Payns's expression. "You were shown this morning."

"Oh, of course," said de Payns. "But it's like a rabbit warren in here. I got lost."

"Okay." Ahmed smiled and gestured for de Payns to walk in front of him. "The party is maybe ten minutes away from their after-dinner drink, so don't take too long."

De Payns stood in the tiny toilet stall, too nervous to take a piss. His hands were clammy, and he could feel cold sweat on his forehead. He had flashes of Romy and the boys, Paul Degarde and his wife, and his unexplained overreaction to the drunks at Saint-Lazare. He took a deep breath and brought his focus back to the present and his environment. He washed his hands and walked quickly back toward the owner's bar, pausing at the foot of the companionway that would take him up to it, when he almost ran into Simone.

"It's going to be a long night," she said, rolling her eyes. "The tall Russian—they call him Lenny?—has already checked to see how tight my pants are."

"That's nice of him."

"It would help if they'd given me the right-sized shirt."

De Payns nodded his agreement. The women wore V-necked shirts, and the one Simone had been given was a size too small.

"I'd swap you," said de Payns, tugging on his shirt, "but I don't want him checking my pants. I'm shy."

Simone giggled. "Let's get the bar ready, they're coming up."

"Would you mind going back for the corkscrews?" he asked, hoping for an opportunity to plant the listening device. "There's none up there."

"Ahead of you," she said, holding up a corkscrew and heading up the companionway.

As they entered the owner's bar, she asked, "Why have you been walking around here in the dark? Were you a ghost in another life?"

"I was enjoying the lights," de Payns explained, pointing through the glass doors that faced aft and back to the sparkling wonderland of Monaco and Nice, which blazed like Christmas trees in the darkening coast.

"I see," she said, placing the corkscrew on the bar counter. "We have a romantic."

"Well, it's not every day you're on a boat like this, watching a sight like that."

"You're right," she said. "But there'll be plenty more memorable sights before this cruise is over, and they won't be of Monte Carlo."

CHAPTER
TWENTY-ONE

There were six of them at the conference table: Boris and the tall Russian, Lenny; Jamal and Nasir, who were from the UAE according to Otis; and Faisal and his middle-aged sidekick from the pool deck.

Around the edges of the room sat the support people, and through the windows de Payns could see the small army of security thugs standing out in the cold, staring in at their bosses. The only security person inside the owner's bar was Ahmed, who sat on a stool beside the beer taps.

It was a heavily monitored table, and de Payns was measured in how often he approached. Jamal smoked cigars and Faisal cigarettes, giving de Payns an opportunity to change ashtrays as well as charge drinks.

"Tripoli could be ours again with a big surge," Faisal was saying as de Payns replaced his ashtray. "We need the airport and the treasury building, and the west is ours very quickly."

De Payns moved around the table, ears twitching at the references to Libya.

"You mean Bouri and El Sharara are yours very quickly?" quipped Boris with a smile, referring to two large oil-and-gas projects controlled by the western Libya government, the GNA.

"If the deal still stands, they'd be *our* fields," said Faisal. "And most importantly, we'd control Mellitah. Our royalty deal gives us a joint interest, no?"

De Payns had heard Mellitah mentioned at briefings in Paris. It was the compression station and main interconnector for the Greenstream pipeline that carried Libyan gas into Europe via Sicily. Most of Libya's petroleum revenues were generated from the west of the country, which was controlled by the US-backed GNA. The east of Libya was controlled by General Khalifa Haftar's LNA coalition with the support of his ally, Russia. The UAE supplied armaments to Haftar, who paid with Russian money. Vladimir Putin's primary goal was to control the petroleum assets.

"It's a joint venture all the way," said Boris, nodding. "The deal's still good. What do you need from us?"

De Payns moved to the bar and emptied the ashtray, his mind spinning at what he was hearing. It seemed the meeting on *Azzam* was about Russia and Haftar making plans to take the west of Libya and choke the natural gas supply into Europe. He grabbed a bottle of single malt Scotch and a jug of water and walked around the advisers, some of whom were drinking whisky.

". . . training and support . . ." said Boris.

Faisal: ". . . your special-forces people, for some lightning actions in . . . can't win a war in North Africa, only from the air . . . tell Dimitry we need some of those special operations people he holds back—the whole point of going private is so we can get things done . . ."

De Payns returned to the bar and prepared a tray with

replacement drinks. The Libyans were asking the Russians for special forces, but Russia didn't have an official contingent operating in Libya. Putin used a mercenary force called Wagner Group. The reference to "Dimitry" had to be Dimitry Utkin, the CEO of Wagner Group. Regardless of the fear levels that were rising in him, there was no way de Payns could go back to Briffaut empty-handed. He needed to take something solid back to Paris.

He faced the room and looked at his black Garmin sports watch. Angling it slightly, he hit the *back-lap* button twice in fast succession, setting off five hi-res camera shots. The principals had flown in on helicopters, circumventing the surveillance team around the superyacht marina, and de Payns needed a photograph of these people.

". . . but not in Chad," Lenny was saying, as de Payns returned with martinis and gin and tonics.

Faisal laughed and took a martini from the tray. "My uncle met his worst defeats in Chad. I don't think you have to worry about that."

"Not what we hear," said the tall Russian. "There's a lot of bad blood on that border, and your uncle has teams operating on the other side."

"Those are operations against Muslim Brotherhood terrorists," said Faisal, annoyed at the Russian. "Just like you had to act in Chechnya. It's not a war; it's a policing action."

"What my colleague is saying," said Boris flatly, "is that we can assist in training and troops, but we won't fight a grudge match that General Haftar lost in Chad years ago."

"But Niger's no problem?" sneered Faisal. This must be Faisal al-Mismari, de Payns realized: General Haftar's Western-educated nephew. "You'll fight those terrorists because Russia will get to control Niger's uranium, right?"

From the corner of his eye, de Payns saw Boris eyeball Faisal; his expression was dangerous.

The Libyan, oblivious, torched a new cigarette. "What about weapons?"

"What about them?" replied Boris. "You have what you need, no?"

"What about this new drone?"

Boris paused. "What about it?"

De Payns ran out of tasks at the table and retreated to the bar, from where he could still overhear snatches of the conversation.

". . . what use is a surveillance drone?"

". . . maritime tracking . . . Turkish weapons deliveries . . . intelligence is a weapon."

De Payns delivered a Scotch to the man sitting almost directly behind Boris, and heard Boris say, "Be patient. If we directly supply attack drones to Haftar, the Americans will supply their own to the GNA. You want that? Or you can keep it as weapons from UAE, input from Wagner."

"The Turks have used strike drones against us," said Faisal. "That's how we lost Al-Watiya Air Base."

"Yes, and an S-one system from UAE brought down those drones," said Boris.

"Not until we'd lost all of our gains," said Faisal. "The Turkish drones are defeating the S-one systems."

"Actually," said Lenny, smiling, "the Turkish operators are defeating the Libyan operators."

De Payns returned to the bar, where he noticed Ahmed's attention had switched from the table to him. "Let the girl serve the table—you get the help something to drink."

"Sure, boss," said de Payns.

"And Frenchie," said Ahmed, beckoning his attention. "You

tell those meatheads that if there's one cigarette butt on the deck of this yacht, someone's going overboard. Got it?"

"Sure, boss," said de Payns again.

He made his rounds of the security people, handing out small bottles of water, the Med twinkling in the moonlight and a cold breeze wafting across the deck. He showed them the crew toilets and he delivered Ahmed's standing order about the cigarettes, which was greeted with great mirth once the translations were made.

"He can fight me for it," chuckled a bearish Wagner soldier, who took his bottle of water and then offered de Payns a stick of gum. De Payns knew better than to refuse a gift from a Russian. It was always easier to take the damn thing and avoid the social arm wrestle.

"Nice," said de Payns, the horrible taste of peppery cinnamon bursting in his mouth.

"Mikhail," said the hulking Russian, offering his hand.

"Fred," said de Payns, shaking it. "Let me know if you need anything."

Back at the bar, de Payns stood off from the meeting as Lenny made eyes at Simone, and Nasir ogled her derrière, miming a bite.

"Worried about your girlfriend, are you, Frenchie?" asked Ahmed.

"She's not my girlfriend."

"Then stop clenching your fists. Go and be useful."

De Payns made a circuit around the edge of the room, collecting glasses. As he paused for an ashtray, there was a lull in the meeting, and Boris's voice cut through.

"We can revisit the question of weapons, but tell me, have you considered the document delivered to you last week?"

"Vulcan?" replied Faisal al-Mismari.

"That's right," said Boris. "You have an answer for us?"

Faisal chuckled. "Okay, so this is quid pro quo? A bunch of Libyans pull off a terror act under a false flag in—"

The table went silent, and when de Payns turned to look, Jamal's cigar hand was raised in a gesture of silence, and those around the table were staring at the Frenchman.

"I believe you're needed downstairs," said Jamal.

CHAPTER
TWENTY-TWO

He woke from a deep sleep as light poured in from the open cabin door.

"Sorry, Fred," came Simone's whisper, as the cabin returned to blackness. "Those two are in my cabin. Do you mind?"

"No," said de Payns, drifting back to sleep as Simone settled into the bottom bunk.

De Payns dozed, his vague concerns about Romy and the Tirol Council gnawing at his mind. He'd been facetious with Romy about loving surprises; he actually hated them for the simple reason that in his social world—his life zone—he needed a good idea of who he was speaking to before he spoke to them. It wasn't controlling or manipulative, as Romy had once accused him: it was an essential filter through which he decided who received which level of candor and allowed him to curate conversations away from anything revealing. Springing a surprise on him, such as the opening night of a Tirol Council conference, was not his worst nightmare, but it was close. He knew he'd embarrassed Romy by making

jokes about Tony Blair and Bill Clinton, and getting Ana
to laugh. But such deflections were natural reactions. What
was he supposed to say? *"Don't ambush me with openly political cocktail parties because they are the events that people like
me frequent in order to get people drunk and talking."* And he
shouldn't have been snide about this colleague of hers, David;
it was beneath him. But perhaps he'd have to remind her to
be careful when playing the jealousy game, because jealousy
might be exactly what you get.

He wondered about his increasing paranoia. The two people
whose opinions he respected more than any others, Romy and
Briffaut, had both asked him to see somebody about his condition. His natural reaction was to resist, but he wondered if it
could be all that bad . . .

He was deep in sleep when the lights came on, and he was
hurled by his t-shirt onto the floor. Stunned and winded, he
moved cautiously on the carpet, aware of two sets of black tactical boots near his face.

"What's going on?" asked Simone, hand over her eyes at
the blast of light.

"You're in the wrong cabin," said Ahmed. "Where's the
waiter, the earring guy?"

Simone dragged herself out of the bunk, tugging her t-shirt
down over her panties. "He's in my bunk."

"Get him," said Ahmed to his sidekick. "Frenchie, you stand
there," he said to de Payns.

De Payns, wearing nothing but his underwear and t-shirt,
backed up against the bulkhead as Simone left the cabin. Ahmed
opened the shuttered wardrobe where Jacques and de Payns
stored their bags. "Which one is yours?"

Squinting against the light, de Payns pointed to the black
Lacoste sports bag. "What are you looking for?"

"Who said I was looking for something?" asked Ahmed, positioning his body so de Payns had no path to his handgun. "And who said you could speak?"

De Payns nodded as Jacques was led into the cabin, rubbing his eyes and holding a shirt against his groin for modesty. "What the fuck?" he exclaimed, and the sidekick punched him in the kidneys from behind with a savage right hook, bringing Jacques to his knees, gasping for breath.

"In through the nose, out though the mouth," de Payns advised.

"Shut it," Ahmed told him, finger in de Payns's face, before addressing Jacques. "You swear at me again and you're over the rail, got it?"

Jacques gulped and nodded, his face in a wince.

"Now we're all here, let's see what you've brought onboard," said Ahmed.

"It's not mine," gasped Jacques. "This dude on the train asked me to hold it for his wife, and I—"

"What are you talking about?" Ahmed demanded.

"The cocaine," whispered Jacques, still clutching his side. "It's not what it looks like."

"What does it look like?"

Jacques grimaced. "There's quite a bit there, but I'm not a dealer or anything . . ."

"Shut up," said Ahmed. "I don't care about your drugs." He picked up de Payns's Lacoste bag and turned it over, watching the contents fall to the carpet, then he threw the empty bag to his sidekick, who searched it.

"Open that," said Ahmed, pointing at de Payns's toiletry bag.

De Payns collected the bag from the carpet and showed Ahmed the toothpaste, shaving gear, and a stick of Brut 33 deodorant.

"No condoms," said Ahmed, enjoying himself. "Not a gay, are you, Frenchie?"

"Only my right hand," said de Payns, and the two Syrians laughed.

"You're a funny guy," said Ahmed, smiling but trying to be serious. "What are these?" he asked, kicking three aluminum cigar tubes at de Payns. "You have cigars?"

"No," said de Payns, picking up the tubes carefully. He opened one and tapped out a cigarette. "My smokes."

"Why are they in a cigar tube?" asked Ahmed, gesturing to see one.

"On a yacht I have to smoke outside, and I want to keep my smokes dry. I hate damp cigarettes."

Ahmed made a face as he unscrewed a lid and confirmed they were cigarettes. "Show me the camera."

De Payns picked up the shiny waterproof Olympus from a pile of clothes and switched it on, handed it to Ahmed, who scrolled through the pictures. They were all of beaches on the Cote d'Azur and walking trails in the hills behind. There were several of the double carousel in Nice.

"No pictures of *Azzam*?" asked Ahmed. "Why not?"

De Payns shrugged, more nervous the longer the chat went on. He'd suspected there was going to be a spy hunt, but that didn't make it any easier when the trap started to close. "You think I should?"

"Everyone gets a shot of themselves on this yacht," said Ahmed, eyes boring into him. "But you have pictures of wooden horses and a tree?"

Before de Payns could answer, Ahmed was distracted by a black USB key he'd spotted in the clothes pile. "What's that?"

De Payns bent over and picked it up. "It's a hard drive—you know, with pictures, music, backups."

Ahmed nodded, took it from him, and handed it to the sidekick, who left the room. "Where's your phone?"

De Payns reached under his pillow and brought out Frédéric Ruesche's phone. He keyed in the password and handed it over.

Ahmed went through it expertly, like de Payns would go through a phone.

"These are pictures of your workmates in Paris?" asked Ahmed, flicking through galleries of people at parties and in restaurants listed in his legend. He stopped on the picture of a girl in a bikini at the beach. "She your girlfriend?" he said, showing the photo to de Payns.

"No," said de Payns. "Just a friend."

"You are definitely a gay," said Ahmed, shaking his head. "No real man can be just friends with a girl like that."

Ahmed handed back the camera, and the sidekick came back to the cabin with a laptop, with de Payns's hard drive plugged in. Ahmed sat on the lower bunk and scrolled through the data storage device.

"Toto *and* the Eagles?" said Ahmed, bemused. "That's a lot."

"I like easy-listening music."

"So, you have insomnia?" asked Ahmed, standing and handing back the hard drive. "That, or you're deaf. Tidy this up."

Ahmed opened Jacques's blue pack and upended it on the carpet. The bag of coke and a box of condoms were evident, but so was a black plastic device that bounced free and landed beside Ahmed's boot. Ahmed picked it up, inspected it, and looked at Jacques, who was on his knees, confused.

"What is this?" asked Ahmed.

"I don't know."

"Well, then it's lucky I can tell you what this is," said Ahmed, his face like stone. "This is a voice-activated audio recording device. It has a ten-hour battery and sticks onto surfaces like the underside of a table or a car dashboard."

Jacques shook his head. "I don't—"

"We've got our spy," the Syrian said, nodding at the sidekick, who bent and grabbed Jacques under the armpits.

"Spy?" echoed Jacques, struggling. "What am I spying on?"

"So, you're asking me the questions, now?"

"That thing's not mine."

"Just like the coke isn't yours, right?" replied Ahmed. "Remind me. Someone on a train has a wife with a recording device and just needs you to hold it? Sounds credible."

"I don't spy," said Jacques, his face white with fear. "I'm a ski instructor."

"Don't bother bullshitting," said Ahmed, as Jacques was dragged backward. "You can talk to me, or you can talk to the Libyans. I'll give you that choice, at least."

CHAPTER
TWENTY-THREE

The next morning, de Payns was kept away from the VIPs. As he served breakfast to the ten escorts who'd been helicoptered in from Monaco, he mulled over what he'd learned the night before. He was on the boat with two Wagner Group commanders—Boris and Lenny—and General Haftar's nephew, Faisal al-Mismari. The latter had uttered the word "Vulcan" and referred to it as a false flag, before Jamal had cut him off. What did it mean? De Payns knew he needed more.

After breakfast, Susan assigned him to cleaning cabins with Gretel, a permanent crew member.

"You start on the cinema, and I'll do the stateroom," she said, but de Payns told her, "Susan said I should go with you to the stateroom, so you can show me what to do."

Gretel was a no-nonsense Austrian in her late thirties, and she didn't like the change to her routine, but she shrugged and led the way. De Payns was put to work in the marble bathroom of stateroom three while Gretel did the bedroom. After a few minutes, he heard her saying something and stuck his head out of the bathroom to ask what she'd said.

"I'm just taking these to the laundry," she said, gesturing with her chin to the armful of sheets she was holding.

"Sure."

Alone in the bedroom, he checked the windows to see if anyone was outside and saw a glass door opening onto a small promenade deck.

No one was around, so he began a hurried search through the bags and the drawers. He came up empty. He turned to the walk-in wardrobe. Inside was a small hotel-style safe, and a burnished aluminum Zero Halliburton briefcase was lying flat on the high shelf where the iron was kept. Among the clothes on the coat hangers, he spotted a deep red shirt and a dark sports jacket: he was in Boris's stateroom.

Pulling down the smooth metal case, he tried opening it, but the latch was locked with a three-wheel combination. He turned the case toward the light and looked closely: the three nickel wheels had black number inlays. He slid the release bar sideways, and the case stayed locked. He took note of the random numbers of the wheels—0-8-5—because for many people in military and intelligence, the "locked" numbers on a combination lock were not random at all; they were their own code and could be a handy indicator of someone trying to get into their case.

He focused on breathing through his nose and calming himself, listening for the sounds of people approaching. He could hear Gretel's voice; she must be talking with someone in the passageway on her way to the laundry. From his pocket, he pulled a key ring which held a miniature black flashlight. The knob on the end of it could be clicked to produce a light for looking around in a car. But de Payns held the knob down for three seconds, and the device emitted a laser light. Shining the red beam sideways through the first wheel of the combination lock until he could see the locking mechanism, he slowly turned the wheel, waiting for the gap to appear that would signal the correct number. He found it at seven. He had turned the case around to begin the same procedure on the opposite wheel when he heard a noise by the stateroom door. He froze, his pulse loud in his head, then replaced the briefcase on the top shelf of the wardrobe and tiptoed from the bedroom back into the bathroom and from there entered the living area, where Ahmed was speaking to Gretel.

"It's our French chambermaid," said Ahmed, smiling. "Susan needs Gretel for a few minutes. You need to be shown how to use a vacuum cleaner, or do you Frenchies have a natural feel for it?"

"I can handle it," said de Payns.

As the security man and Gretel walked away, he realized he'd been holding his breath. He'd infiltrated boats before, but always as a guest or a contractor of some sort. Working in the bowels of a yacht and being treated like a serf by angry sociopaths was unnerving, not least because his hosts had already found one "spy" and de Payns had no doubt that the young roué was either in a cell being worked over, or he'd already been disposed of. He slowed his breathing to calm himself and returned to the wardrobe. He felt slightly guilty about putting the listening device in Jacques's bag when he realized he wouldn't have a chance to place it. It was an act of self-preservation, but it came with a price tag of guilt, and he had to consciously remove the feeling from his mind and get back to work.

He wiped his sweaty hands on his pants, then lifted the Zero case from the shelf and set it on the carpet. Turning on his laser light, he found the correct angle and turned the wheel until the gap lined up with the first wheel he'd cracked, listening for footsteps all the while. Now he turned his attention to the inside wheel, which was harder to gain an angle on. He turned the inside wheel one click and tried the locking slide; nothing. He moved the wheel forward by one click three more times without success, but on the fourth click the slide moved all the way to the right, and he opened the case, revealing a black MacBook. Pulling the USB stick that Ahmed had tested the night before from his right pocket, he plugged it directly into the laptop. He double-clicked a tiny button in the stick, and a small red light emanated for twenty-eight seconds, before it went off again, indicating a full download. Pulling out the USB stick, he shoved it in his pocket, returned the MacBook to the aluminum case, and rolled the three combination wheels back to 0-8-5, before replacing the case on the top shelf. He emerged into the bedroom and grabbed the vacuum cleaner beside the bed, hitting the power as Gretel walked into the room.

"You're slow," she said in French, dumping clean linens on the bed. "Did you take a nap?"

"No," he said. "I've been quite busy."

Together they finished the stateroom and moved on to the cinema. Gretel finally released him an hour later, and de Payns headed off to lunch in the crew mess, carrying the contents of Boris's MacBook in his pocket.

CHAPTER
TWENTY-FOUR

De Payns was kept at the pool deck bar and the main dining rooms for the evening shift, while the female crew were sent up to the owner's bar. It meant de Payns was not entirely trusted, but it also gave him access to the best information gatherers: the escorts.

While serving the women drinks before they went upstairs to perform their roles, he got talking to an English brunette named Lucy. She was pretty and smart, and laughed about the Libyan who'd had to pray for forgiveness before having sex.

"Faisal?" asked de Payns. "The dashing one?"

"If you like that sort of thing," she said, laughing. "One of those Arabs who can't switch off the serious stuff, you know?"

"Like what?" asked de Payns. "What serious stuff would you speak about in the bedroom?"

She rolled her eyes. "Oh, you know, '*The Russians are screwing us, everything is an angle with Ivan*'—that kind of thing."

"It must be quite a meeting they have going on here," said de Payns. "It sounds like it's all politics—talk about boring."

"Maybe something more than politics . . ." Lucy said, sipping her champagne.

"Oh yeah?" replied de Payns, keeping his tone casual.

"He kept muttering about this thing." She shrugged. "It's probably not as big a deal as it sounded. He's an intense dude."

"What kind of muttering?"

"Can I smoke in here?"

"Are you a guest or the help?" asked de Payns, smiling.

"A bit of both, actually. Shall we?" She pointed outside.

De Payns lit up for both of them, sheltering the flame from the breeze off the sea. He guessed they were south of Sardinia and perhaps west of Sicily.

"Sorry, I couldn't speak in there," Lucy said. "You see Carrie? The big Black girl?"

De Payns nodded. He'd noticed the tall African-American woman in a fuchsia dress.

"Well, she runs us," said Lucy. "She doesn't like us gossiping about the johns. Sorry, I mean the guests."

De Payns chuckled. "So, what's with Faisal and the muttering?"

"Oh, he was annoyed about having to go to Europe," she said, trying to flick ash over the side without success. "Said the fucking Russians should do their own dirty work."

"Dirty work sounds like a good job for the Russians," said de Payns, deliberately steering her away from the information he craved. He had to massage Lucy's communication, mindful of who else she was likely to talk to. One of those other people might be an interrogator, and when that happened, he didn't want Lucy connecting the forbidden information with this conversation.

"I don't know the details," said Lucy, "but Faisal is very nervous about it."

De Payns decided she needed to be shut down. "Well, I'd

advise you to stay uninformed about Monsieur Faisal's troubles. It's dangerous to be too curious with this kind of guy."

"You think?" she asked, lowering her voice.

"Actually, it puts *us* in a situation, now you've shared this with me," said de Payns, looking around him. "Thank you very much."

Her pretty face changed, concern creasing her forehead. "Sorry, Fred. I don't want to get you in trouble."

"It's fine," he replied, while making a face that said he was annoyed.

She moved closer, and he could smell the Joy perfume. "Please don't tell anyone that I spoke about him. I shouldn't have. Can I trust you?"

"Well, trust goes both ways, right?" replied de Payns, flicking his butt over the side. "I'm happy not to mention it to anyone if you never admit you spoke to me. It would be our secret. Deal?"

"Deal," said Lucy, her face relaxing. "I should go."

"You got your disco shoes on?"

Lucy laughed. "Faisal thinks the party's at stateroom five—not much disco in there."

Shortly after 8:30 p.m., the escorts left for the owner's bar. De Payns worked with the other stewards to clear the tables and glasses, and then weaved through the internal maze of passageways that would take him to the crew's section of *Azzam*. In the crew mess, he found Gretel, nursing a cup of hot chocolate and watching an Italian game show that featured people in the grip of either manic happiness or hysterical disappointment with no twilight between.

"Hi, Gretel," he said, using his basic German. "I accidentally locked myself out of the cabin, and I need my asthma inhaler. Could I borrow your key? I'll just be a few minutes."

Gretel barely took her eyes off the crazed game show host as she pulled her retractable keychain and unclipped the master key.

"No one else touches this," she said. "I'm trusting you, Fred. Be quick."

De Payns hurried to his cabin, dug his camera from the Lacoste bag, and checked it for battery charge and a MicroSD. Master key in hand, he moved quickly along the crew passageways and climbed forward and upward until he was in the section of the yacht that contained the VIP staterooms. He reached a corner where the carpet turned to an azure blue color and knew that around it was the double-wide passageway that housed stateroom five—Faisal al-Mismari's home away from home. Sticking his head around the corner for a peek, he pulled back quickly. "Shit," he hissed, his nostrils flaring with stress. At the end of the passageway was one of Faisal's bodyguards, sitting on a chair. He had to hand it to the Libyans: he would have done the same thing if his boss was on a superyacht surrounded by Wagner thugs and Emirati arms dealers. But time was running out; Gretel would blow the whistle if he didn't return her key in the next few minutes. He was scheduled to drop his product overboard at midnight if he had something, and he wanted the drop to include anything he could find in Faisal al-Mismari's room—preferably something relating to Vulcan, the "false flag" that the Libyan had mentioned the previous night, or this "dirty work" Lucy had said he'd been asked to do for the Russians in Europe.

He dropped down to a lower level, where food and wine were stored, moved aft, and ascended back to the stateroom level. He now approached the guard from the opposite direction. De Payns stuck his head around the corner. The guard was an athletic man in his late twenties, in the typical bodyguard dress of black polo shirt and gray ripstop pants. De Payns pulled back from the corner and looked for some props to work with. Behind him was a cleaner's cupboard. And halfway down the passageway, just before a companionway entrance, was a glass-fronted cabinet containing a fire extinguisher and a fire blanket. He grabbed the red fire extinguisher, banged his cigarette lighter against it so it rang like a bell, and then threw the extinguisher down the passageway, where it bounced and skittled into a bulkhead with a dull bang. Slipping into the cleaner's cupboard, he watched the guard come around the corner and head down the passageway, pistol in hand and eyes focused on the fire extinguisher. De Payns slipped out of the cupboard, retraced the guard's footsteps, and let himself into stateroom five, shutting the door behind him as the guard returned. De Payns fastened the lock and backed away from the door. The handle of the door moved and jiggled and then stopped; like any good guard, he was checking to see if the door was still locked and not forced.

Standing in the dimly lit room, de Payns felt like a rat in a trap. He turned his mind to the job lest he become lost in his fear. He looked around: there was nothing of interest on the bedside cabinet or anywhere conspicuous. He went through the main suitcase—the contents of which had largely been unpacked into the wardrobe—and then opened every cupboard and lifted up the bed mattress and all the cushions on the armchairs and sofas, working methodically; he couldn't do it too quickly or Faisal al-Mismari would suspect his room had been tossed. There was no briefcase, no laptop, and no files. Whatever Faisal al-Mismari had been asked to do by the Russians, de Payns suspected it would be written down. Wagner Group was a commercial enterprise working under a service contract with General Haftar's LNA government, and there had to be a reference to it.

De Payns expelled a big breath. He'd been a clandestine OT

for longer than most, and he wondered if his nerves were still up to this work. Perhaps Romy was right; maybe it was time to give up the field and move into management. He shook his head to clear his mind and focused on the question at hand: if he was Faisal, where would he hide his laptop?

He entered the glitzy bathroom—heavy in marble and gold plate—and kneeled to look in the commode cabinet beneath the marble countertop. As he did, bolts slid in the stateroom door and a man's voice sounded—Faisal. De Payns froze: he was caught with nowhere to hide.

"Okay," said a woman's voice, which de Payns recognized as Lucy's. "Where's the Charlie?"

"Let's not hurry," said Faisal, in the unmistakable tone of a man who finds himself irresistible. "Join me."

"I was joining you for a line," said Lucy. "And then we're hitting the dancefloor, remember?"

"We can dance here," said Faisal, and there was a respite from talk while something else started.

De Payns felt cold sweat on his forehead, his neck over-heating. He stuck his head out of the bathroom, where he was unsighted from the bedroom. He saw the walk-in wardrobe in the passage to the main stateroom and slipped quietly into its darkness. There was no way out of the cabin except by seriously harming Faisal al-Mismari, which would set off more than a spy hunt. The lovers came up for breath, and Lucy said, "Come on, let's do some Charlie and go back to the party."

"Okay, okay," said the Libyan. "Wait here."

De Payns stood, his back to the side bulkhead of the walk-in, beside al-Mismari's hangered clothes, praying the man wouldn't decide to change his shirt. But Faisal walked past the wardrobe into the bathroom and emerged again, talking as he went. De Payns listened to the sound of people snorting, and then Lucy said, "Come on, take me dancing," and Faisal made a comment about bossy Englishwomen.

The door to the stateroom opened and then closed, and de Payns released his breath. He could feel the fatigue in his bones, and he knew it was time to get out of there.

Walking to the windows of the stateroom, he unlocked the door that led onto the VIPs' promenade deck and stuck his head out. The sea whooshed by below, and the breeze was cold. The deck was partially lit but empty, and the sounds of a disco could be heard. De Payns slipped through the door and moved down the promenade deck, aware it was a no-go zone for the crew. At the aft end of the deck, there was a security gate, locked. He climbed onto the railing and eased around the gate, the sea foaming thirty meters below him. Landing on the other side, he saw the rear helicopter deck and descended a companionway to the level of the hangar and the speedboats.

"You lost?" The voice was South African, and de Payns smiled as Josey, a mechanic he'd met in the mess, walked out of the hangar.

"Actually, I am," said de Payns. "I'm trying to get back to the crew mess."

Josey sniggered. "You're two levels too high, mate. Above your station."

"I'm working on knowing my place," said de Payns, and the Saffa laughed.

De Payns descended two flights of the crew companionway and walked into the mess, where Gretel was still glued to the Italian game show.

"I'm sorry, Gretel—" he started, but she cut him off.

"Sshh," said the Austrian, as a contestant yelled with what could have been pain or joy. "This is the good bit."

De Payns dropped the key in front of her and made to go.

"Ahmed wants you," she said, without looking up. "They're at the disco."

The disco dancefloor was in the covered section that led on to the pool deck, and it was pumping with Rod Stewart's "Da Ya Think I'm Sexy?", the Russians and Libyans swamped for choice of dance partners.

Ahmed walked toward de Payns, carrying a walkie-talkie.

"You're on this deck tonight," said Ahmed, giving him a suspicious look. "But you're being paid to serve drinks, not to get chatty with the guests. Got it?"

De Payns nodded and turned to the bar.

"Champagne and vodka shots," said Otis, clicking his fingers and pointing at a silver tray.

"Where's Simone and Claire?" asked de Payns.

"VIPs couldn't control their hands," said Otis, shaking his head. "Susan sent them downstairs."

"What, there's not enough women to hit on?" asked de Payns, nodding at the dancefloor, which was thronged with shapely females in skimpy dresses.

"Some dudes only want what they can't have," said Otis. "Start with the champagne."

De Payns did the rounds, keeping the guests and the escorts topped up. He was on his way back to the bar when he was intercepted by Carrie, the striking American woman in the fuchsia dress.

"Fred, is it?" she asked, with a winning smile.

"Madame Carrie," he said, affecting a short bow. "How is your drink?"

"Tide is out," she said, holding up her glass. "Wanna hear the secret of my success?"

"Please tell me," said de Payns, pouring.

"When we're working, we're working," she said, steely but friendly. "We don't fuck the help."

De Payns smiled with relief. "I totally agree."

"Good," said Carrie. "I don't want my girls getting distracted, you understand me?"

De Payns nodded. "Sure."

"So, we're agreed." She smiled. "No more charming Frenchman."

De Payns stood on the aft part of the helicopter deck, the breeze off Sicily having died down to a cool but still night, the stars shining. *Azzam* was anchored off the western side of the island, and he imagined the view would wow the guests in the morning. He pulled a cigarette from the cigar tube and went to light it.

"Got one for me?" came a South African voice.

He turned and saw Josey, now out of his red coverall and wearing a gray tracksuit and sports slides.

They lit their cigarettes. "Amazing how geography is so important," said the South African. "Every empire has made a point of controlling Sicily because, from a maritime point of view, it divides the western and eastern Mediterranean."

De Payns nodded. He'd been on a class trip to Syracuse when he was at boarding school, and it was obvious that the Greeks thought a foothold on Sicily was important. As did the Phoenicians, Romans, Normans, Ottomans, and the various Catholic military orders, such as the Templar Knights, who'd held commanderies on the island.

"Never understood how the Italians held on to it," said Josey with a shrug. "Strikes me as the kind of place that a superpower would like, know what I mean?"

When the mechanic had departed, de Payns opened the cigar tube and dropped in the MicroSD card from his watch, then added the USB key that contained Boris's laptop hard drive. He screwed down the cap of the cigar tube and turned an inner cap a quarter turn, activating a tiny beacon that would only be visible to observers with night-vision goggles. He looked around briefly—double-checking he was in a zone not covered by security cameras—then threw the canister into the water. It sank slightly and then bobbed up. Drawing the key ring from his pocket, he activated the infrared torch and pointed it aft of *Azzam*, clicking a series of three long dashes into the darkness. This, too, would only be seen by people wearing night-vision goggles. It was now up to the dive team on the boat following the yacht to find the canister and get the prod back to Paris.

De Payns dragged on his smoke and looked over the transom of *Azzam*, clicking his laser torch three more times for good measure; then he turned and headed for his cabin. He felt lighter, knowing he no longer had compromising material on him and that the Cat would have everything he'd gathered, even if something happened to him between *Azzam* and Paris. He just wished he'd been able to find something in Faisal's room. All he had at the moment was an overheard conversation and the gossip of an escort; Briffaut would want more than that.

Lying in his bunk, he went over every step he'd made during the day, auditing himself for mistakes or oversights. He mentally stepped through the infiltration of Faisal al-Mismari's stateroom and the download of Boris's MacBook. Would Ahmed or Boris pick up on something? Would the Wagner Group security people? He had limited control over that. He'd stayed as clean as he could, but there were cameras all over *Azzam*, and he hoped that the fact he couldn't see any in the passageways and staterooms meant there were none to be seen.

As he drifted off, his mind wandered to Jacques. Susan had told the crew that he'd been flown back to Nice for a medical emergency. Given the people on this boat, de Payns knew that the medical emergency would be broken fingers and missing teeth, but it was just as likely the randy ski instructor was learning to swim with concrete flippers. Again, de Payns regretted that he'd had to use Jacques as a decoy—it wasn't fair. But he stopped the train of thought. As Carrie had said at the disco, when you're working, you're working.

CHAPTER
TWENTY-FIVE

Azzam berthed at Port Hercules at 4:00 p.m. The Hibiscus bus driver dropped de Payns at the Nice Ville station, and he just made the fast train to Paris, arriving at Gare de Lyon before midnight. He was driven to the Bunker after a pickup near the Marriott, and he'd gone straight to his office to write his report on his *Azzam* infiltration. He managed to grab some sleep in the employee lounge before being woken by Briffaut shortly after 6:00 a.m. Now he was in Briffaut's car, reading a document the boss had given him as they headed across Paris for a meeting with Marie Lafont. De Payns finished reading just as they moved into the Cat's security system.

"This arrived at our Rome embassy?" asked de Payns. "Why the embassy?"

Briffaut pointed at the file. "Look at the postmark."

De Payns flipped to the appendices behind the eight-page report and looked at the photocopied stamps on the envelope. It was postmarked Genoa, from the same day he and Lolo had followed Starkand.

"Did Starkand mail something?" asked Briffaut.

"He paused at a mailbox at the airport," conceded de Payns. "It wasn't conclusive that he mailed something."

"I don't believe in coincidences," said Briffaut, his leg jiggling for a smoke. "Let's talk to the brains trust."

The Operation Bellbird meeting was held in a SCIF on the fourth floor of the Cat, a large room with a twenty-seater oval conference table and a large screen on the far wall. Anthony Frasier, director of the Operations Directorate—the DO— convened. Also present were Christophe Sturt, director of the DR, Briffaut, Lafont, de Payns, and Lars Magnus.

"Let's look at the details," said Frasier, nodding to Marie Lafont.

She distributed files to the participants. De Payns briefly flipped through his, seeing cuts from his *Azzam* report and inclusions from the research on the woman in the orange top who had met with Starkand.

"Things are happening quickly, so let's run through the new prod, and then we'll get to the next steps," said Lafont, putting on her half-glasses. She pointed a remote control, and the screen at the front of the room lit up while the overhead lights faded.

The first image projected on the screen was a picture from de Payns's Garmin watch, taken in the owner's bar on *Azzam*.

Lafont pointed her laser. "We know about the Emiratis," she said. "They're supplying weapons to General Haftar, and they don't care where they source them." She moved the laser around the other men present. "We have four persons of interest on this boat. Boris Orlevski, Leonid Varnachev, and Faisal al-Mismari, and on the left is Jamal Hussein ul-Huq, who has a royal title but is an Emirati arms dealer. He also has a bank in Cyprus which provides vendor finance for illegal weapons purchases."

"Orlevski," said Frasier. "Where have we heard that name?"

"Boris Orlevski is a military commander in Wagner Group," said Lafont. "He's a former major in Russia's naval Spetsnaz, and we can connect him to actions in Chad, Sudan, and Syria. General Haftar likes Orlevski and takes his advice, which is dangerous because Wagner Group is a proxy for Putin."

"And Varnachev?" asked Frasier, pointing at the screen.

"He works in the corporate and political end of the business, dealing with the politicians and generals who are buying Wagner's services," said Lafont. "He's ex-GRU with a history in Somalia and Mali."

"Al-Mismari?" asked Sturt.

"He's General Haftar's nephew. Swiss boarding school, economics degree at Oxford, and business studies at INSEAD," said Lafont. "Al-Mismari's job is to remake the eastern side of Libya into a petroleum power. Russia is helping him do that."

Lars Magnus cleared his throat. "Vladimir Putin intends to expand Russia's military presence and reinforce it with economic power, oil, and gas predominantly. Libya is an economic power play for Putin."

"What are Haftar and Wagner Group cooking up?" asked Frasier.

"Look at page five of the file," said Lafont, turning the pages. "Aguilar accessed Orlevski's laptop. The hard drive is encrypted, and we haven't broken it yet, but we gained access to his emails, which go through remote servers."

Page five contained translated emails between Orlevski and Varnachev: Varnachev asking if al-Mismari has agreed to the Vulcan deal and Orlevski replying, *Haftar's people are locked in—I understand they'll use AKM*. Varnachev's next email addressed the importance of eliminating "Hammer and Anvil."

Orlevski assured him: *They understand the value of our continuing friendship—they won't fail.*

Frasier leaned back, staring at the report as if it might bite. "Vulcan, Hammer, and Anvil," he said. "What's our thinking?"

Lafont licked her thumb, turned another page. "Well, we understand that General Haftar has agreed to carry out Vulcan. He will use al-Kaniyat soldiers to execute it, and I doubt Haftar would use al-Kaniyat for a round of negotiations . . ."

"Al-Kaniyat?" asked Sturt.

"That's the AKM reference," said Lafont, looking over the tops of her glasses. "The British services labeled them the al-Kaniyat militia seven or eight years ago, and the acronym stuck."

Frasier made a face. "Al-Kaniyat—it rings a bell. Were they in Chad?"

Lafont nodded. "AKM is a jihadist militia that controls parts of northeastern Libya on behalf of Haftar, and we believe Haftar has used them on his southern border against a terror outfit that operates on the Chad side."

Frasier grimaced. "Fuck, and they're being deployed in Europe? Tell me: who or what is Hammer and Anvil?"

Lafont hit a key on her laptop; a familiar picture of a bearded man projected on the large screen. "Based on other product, and Eastern Europe chatter, we think Hammer is Igor Kolomoisky."

"The Ukrainian billionaire?" asked Frasier. "Russia wants Kolomoisky dead, and they're getting the Libyans to do it. Why?"

Magnus raised his voice. "Kolomoisky is a major player in Eastern Europe's energy system. He owns gas fields and power stations, and he controls a lot of the gas flows into countries west of Ukraine. Russia has tolerated Kolomoisky because everyone has been making money through the connectors that take Russian and Central Asian gas into Europe."

"But . . ." prompted Lafont.

"But Kolomoisky also wields military and political power, and the Kremlin now sees him as a proxy for American aggression in Ukraine."

Frasier squinted at Magnus. "Kolomoisky's relationship with the CIA has been known for years. What's changed?"

"Kolomoisky supports Ukraine president Volodymyr Zelenskyy, and Zelenskyy now wants to join NATO," said Magnus. "Getting rid of Kolomoisky means the Kremlin could install their own guy in Kiev and undo the CIA's control."

Frasier nodded slowly, not taking his eyes off Marie Lafont. "Our analysis is very close to how the Kremlin spins it."

"The CIA's use of Kolomoisky is acknowledged in the Western services," said Lafont, avoiding defensiveness. "Just because the Russians think Zelenskyy is an American puppet, doesn't mean it's untrue."

Briffaut shook his head with frustration.

Lafont continued. "Kolomoisky's company, Privat, is the dominant player in Ukrainian media. His network broadcasted a TV show in which Volodymyr Zelenskyy played the President of Ukraine, and during the 2019 election Kolomoisky's network played that show on loop. Kolomoisky funded the presidential campaign, and I don't believe Zelenskyy made one speech."

De Payns watched on in silence. He remembered the 2019 Ukraine elections, which Zelenskyy won in a landslide. The French posture had been neutrality on Ukraine, built around the Minsk II Agreement of 2015 concerning Ukraine's Russian-speaking regions of Donetsk and Lugansk. Minsk II was supposed to be mediated by France and Germany, with the aim of reaching a ceasefire. But protections for Russophones in the Donbas were not enforced because Ukraine threatened to shut its westbound gas pipelines if its sovereignty was impugned. De Payns could sense an unnamed force trying to shatter that neutrality and draw France into the quagmire of Ukraine.

"Okay," said Frasier. "If Putin takes Kolomoisky off the board, he can weaken the Americans, install his own president, and exert more control over the gas markets?"

Lafont nodded.

Frasier tapped the report. "If Kolomoisky's our Hammer, who's the Anvil?"

Lafont looked grim. "We're still working on that."

At the coffee break, Christophe Sturt wandered over to de Payns and sat on the board table so he was looking down. He was immaculate, his perfect suit and sleek haircut making him as smooth as a seal.

"Good to see you again, Alec," he smiled, stirring sugar into his coffee. "I wanted to thank you for accepting the arrangement with our new man in Moscow."

De Payns could feel Briffaut's gaze boring into him, but he kept his eyes on Sturt. "He's a good operator, Director. It's going to be fine."

"Sometimes, in this business we find ourselves making compromises, but we do it for France, yes?"

De Payns forced a smile, knowing Romy would rather he prioritize his family when traitors abducted her children. "Certainly, Director."

As Sturt walked away, de Payns smelled a waft of mandarin peel—Sturt's famous cure for the cigarette smell on his fingers that he had to keep from his wife. Everyone has a secret, thought de Payns, even Christophe Sturt.

When everyone had their coffee and biscuits, Frasier came back to the table and addressed the room. "Assuming we can stop this assassination, it would have to be clandestine, run from the Bunker. Can we make an argument to get involved?"

Lafont took a breath. "If Russia targets this man, they'll have a plan for filling the vacuum, and we can assume the alternative to Kolomoisky will not be good for the West."

Sturt nodded at Lars Magnus, who answered, "The Nord Stream Two pipeline into Germany reinforces Kremlin influence in Berlin, which is bad enough. But with Kolomoisky no longer there to support Zelenskyy, and a Russian presence in Kiev, Putin will control around sixty percent of the gas used in the EU."

"The Kremlin can hold our economies to ransom?" asked Frasier.

"Effectively, yes," said Magnus. "It's soft power. The power to do whatever they want without Occidental governments complaining about it."

"There must be other gas fields besides those controlled by Russia," said Frasier.

"There's a couple," said Magnus. "Algeria and Libya send gas to Europe."

"But Libya's in play," added Lafont. "Go to page four."

Frasier flipped and read an extract from de Payns's report, nodding. "Wagner Group is paid by Haftar, but it will also earn royalties on the captured gas fields in the west of Libya?"

"That was discussed on *Azzam*," said Lafont. "Joint control of Libyan oil-and-gas production, including Greenstream, which goes from Libya to Sicily. Control of Libya also gives Putin a stronger leverage over Niger's uranium mines."

Frasier looked at Magnus. "What about North Sea gas?"

"Running out, and only meeting British demand," said Magnus. "Europe gets gas from Norway, but it's unlikely Oslo will grant any more leases. And the Groningen gas field in the Netherlands will close before 2030."

Magnus looked back at his notes. "There's another reason Russia might want Kolomoisky out of the way. The EastMed project."

"What's EastMed?" asked Frasier.

Magnus tapped on his laptop and brought up a map of the Eastern Mediterranean. He shifted his laser pointer to the pocket defined by Turkey, Syria, Israel, and Egypt, with Cyprus in the middle. "The largest economically viable natural gas reserves in the world right now are on the seabed off the coast of Israel and Egypt."

Sturt said, "That explains why Putin is beefing up in Syria."

Lafont nodded. "And why he's made Egypt the world's largest importer of Russian wheat."

Magnus let the comments go. "Currently the gas runs through pipelines into Israel, Jordan, and Egypt. But there's a proposal by the East Mediterranean Gas Forum—of which France is a member—to pipe the gas into Europe via Cyprus, Greece, and Italy."

"Cutting Russia out of the European gas market?" asked Frasier.

"And bypassing Turkey—they're both opposed to it," said Magnus.

"The Russians have been trying to get ahead of EastMed," said Lafont. "They're supporting Hezbollah in Lebanon, they have military bases in Syria, they're supplying weapons and wheat to Egypt, they own politicians and banks in Cyprus, and they have Wagner Group in Libya. Turkey's TurkStream pipeline takes Russian gas into Europe—they won't break with Russia."

"So, EastMed is encircled by Russia?" asked Frasier.

"Yes, sir," said Magnus. "We should also note that Kolomoisky has equity in an undeveloped field off Israel, and he is a strong proponent of the EastMed pipeline. This alone puts Kolomoisky in direct confrontation with Putin."

Frasier's face took on a pained expression. "Kolomoisky is connected to EastMed?"

"Yes," said Magnus. "Perhaps more important, the Biden government withdrew US support for EastMed around three weeks ago."

Sturt sat up. "I didn't read that."

"Biden did it quietly, through the Greek and Israeli foreign ministries," said Magnus.

Sturt and Frasier stared at each other, perplexed.

"Perhaps Lars can give some context?" suggested Lafont, nodding to Magnus.

"The EastMed project hinged on the United States or Russia giving it safe passage," said Magnus. "Under Trump, the US passed a law that supported it, but in late January of this year the Biden Administration withdrew support, citing its aversion to new fossil fuel infrastructure."

Sturt shrugged. "Europe loses a cheap gas supply because the Americans say so?"

"We have our own problems in Europe," said Magnus. "Germany supports the US position on the EastMed pipeline, as do Turkey and Russia. Supporting the pipeline is France, along with Greece and Italy."

"Will the Americans support EastMed under a different president?" asked Frasier.

Magnus paused. "It's unlikely that the US or Russia will ever support EastMed—Europe imports around two hundred billion cubic meters of Russian gas per year, so it's a massive market, and EastMed potentially supplies to that market cheaply, bypassing

Russian piped gas and American LNG. Trump's support for EastMed was a practical alternative to Nord Stream Two, which Trump publicly opposed because of the leverage it gave Putin in Berlin."

Lafont thanked Magnus and, returning to her agenda, indicated to Briffaut that he had the floor.

Briffaut leaned forward. "Director, in the back of your file is some background on the mystery woman from the Starkand meeting. The yacht she boarded in Portofino is called *Melissa*. It's owned by Red Ocean Holdings, which is clearly a Cypriot corporate front . . ."

"Is this woman associated with the drop we received from Starkand?" asked Frasier.

Briffaut nodded. "We're still working on Starkand and the woman from the yacht, so we can't be definitive about what they're doing."

"Are we being provoked by Starkand?"

"Almost certainly," said Briffaut. "But we should remember that the reference to this apparent assassination did not come from Starkand and the yacht woman. It came from an Eastern European source."

"So, we're back to this assassination," said Sturt. "Any idea how we respond?"

Briffaut said, "If the Russians want to influence Europe with assassinations, we must act."

"How?" asked Sturt.

"I suggest we work on clandestine intelligence gathering and interdiction. Below the radar, nothing for the Élysée to worry about."

"Marie?" added Frasier.

"I agree. The narrow view is that if we know AKM is about to act in Europe, we have to shut it down."

Sturt looked suspicious. "And the broader view?"

Lafont paused and focused on the far wall, a woman carefully weighing her words. "Putin always has a plan B. If Kolomoisky remains as kingmaker in Ukraine, Putin goes to plan B . . ."

"Invasion?" asked Sturt.

"Most probably," said Lafont.

Sturt sat back, not convinced. "Surely Putin is too smart to take the CIA bait and invade a country the size of Ukraine? The Americans take all the upside, and the Russians have to destroy the place in order to own it. What's the English saying? '*Ashes in their mouths*'?"

Lafont stayed calm. "It doesn't matter if the Americans provoke an invasion, or if Putin just can't help himself. Our concern should be what that leads to."

"Which is?" asked Sturt.

"France and Britain will become involved because Germany's not up to it—too close to Russia," said Lafont. "Putin will bring Iran and China into the Black Sea, and the United States ends up with a major new LNG market in Europe."

"I think that's enough," said Sturt, who looked as if he'd swallowed an egg. "We can leave that kind of speculation for the Élysée, non? Right now, plan A is under our noses."

Lafont paused. "I agree with Dominic: we can't allow al-Kaniyat a foothold in Europe. If the connection to Russia is awkward, then we do it quietly—we don't poke the bear."

Frasier looked at Sturt, the room aware of the French president's preference for neutrality in Eastern European matters. "You okay with clandestine interdiction?"

Christophe Sturt looked around the table, weighing the presidential appetite for risk given France's eternal dance between the US, Russia, and the EU. He settled on Briffaut. "Define interdiction."

Briffaut deadpanned him. "We find, we assess, and if we can win, we engage."

Sturt chewed his lip. "You can do this without a trace?"

"Like a ghost," said Briffaut.

CHAPTER
TWENTY-SIX

The countermeasure to Vulcan was dubbed Operation Ellipse. It required a plan to be drawn up and authorized by Anthony Frasier, however it would first be constructed by the *chef de mission*, Alec de Payns, alongside Mattieu Garrat, the deputy to Briffaut who managed operational resourcing at the Bunker.

"Can you get me something tomorrow?" asked Briffaut as they sped across Paris in the black Viano transporter.

"Ask me after I've had a shower," said de Payns.

"Give me broad strokes," said Briffaut. "Mattieu can start a budget, and I'll have it signed off. I have to manage Frasier. You see what he's up against with Sturt. My God, so political. He should have been a minister."

De Payns laughed, the tension of the meeting leaving him. "Did you see how Sturt shut down Marie when she mentioned China and Iran?"

"Politicians find it easier to claim they didn't know about an outcome," said Briffaut. "Sturt will not be transmitting Marie's observations to the Élysée, you can bet on that."

"What's Sturt really worried about? When Magnus was explaining the EastMed commercial dealings . . ."

"I suspect France is working politically on EastMed, and Sturt doesn't want a bunch of knuckle-draggers like us frightening the horses. It puts Sturt in a position with us, but screw him—men who divide their loyalties multiply their enemies."

"Is that Julius Caesar?"

"No, it's my mother," said Briffaut. "Luckily, we work to Frasier."

"I'll get a plan together," said de Payns. "What are you thinking?"

"We need more intelligence. We have to squeeze Lotus and Keratine, even if they are owned and handled by the DR. Fortunately, Jim owes us . . ."

"And we have Starkand and Orange Top," said de Payns. "We can start with those four."

The Viano driver raised his voice at a windshield washer who wouldn't get out of his way when the light went green. Briffaut spun to eyeball the nuisance, and when he turned back his expression had changed. "What about that other matter?"

De Payns had been waiting for it. "I don't want to be put on medical leave."

"You won't," said Briffaut. "Do you trust me?"

"With my life, but not with your career."

Briffaut burst into laughter, clearly tickled by the insult.

De Payns didn't see the humor. "I'm not going on medical leave."

Briffaut leaned forward, facing de Payns. "I give you my personal guarantee. I just want you well, and I want Romy onside with the Company."

De Payns looked out the window. "I'll start with Starkand's phone, see if it's burned."

"Get the boys in the basement on it immediately," said Brif-faut, as the van entered the security box at the Bunker. "I want to see where he gets his product and why he's sending it to us."

De Payns rinsed plates and handed them to Patrick, who placed them in the dishwasher, a little too loudly.

"You object?" asked de Payns, handing his oldest son a rinsed bowl that had recently been filled with mussels.

"I'm tired. Why do I have to do this?"

De Payns smiled at him. His son was starting to grow tall and was using his body more on the soccer pitch. "So, you think your mother should have to do all the shopping, and then make a beautiful dinner for you and your brother, and then she should have to do the washing-up as well?"

Patrick shook his head, his sandy blond hair glinting in the kitchen lights. "No, I guess not."

"Maybe she should take out the garbage, too?" de Payns continued. "Although that would defeat the whole purpose of having sons."

Patrick managed a small smile. "Don't worry, Dad. I do it all when you're away."

De Payns handed him another plate. "I'm glad to hear it. So, what's up?"

Patrick peered through the servery gap in the kitchen to where his mother was looking through Oliver's school readers. Then he lowered his voice. "I want to get my hair cut at Tulips, and Mom won't let me."

"What's—" started de Payns, but Romy's voice cut through from the dining table.

"The answer's no, Patrick," she said. "Nothing you say to your father will change that."

"Mom!" whined Patrick. Then, turning to de Payns, "Dad!"

"I said no," yelled Romy from the other room. "And your father agrees."

De Payns looked through to the living area, where Romy's face was a mask of annoyance. "What's Tulips?"

"A barbershop where they do mullets," she snapped. "And he's not going there."

"Charles did," said Patrick.

"Yes, and Aunty Ana is furious," said Romy. "You're not getting your hair done by Blanche."

"Who's Blanche?" asked de Payns, lost.

"She's the barber at Tulips," said Patrick.

"And you want Blanche to give you a mullet? Why?"

Romy appeared in the kitchen. "Nice try," she said to her son. "But the answer's still no."

Patrick slumped. "Why not? The school allows it."

"Because *I* don't allow it," said Romy. "Now go and get your stuff ready for tomorrow."

When Patrick had left, Romy grabbed a bottle of Riesling from the fridge and poured two glasses. "Blanche is a cool Jamaican. The boys love her because she listens to what they want and she ignores the mothers. If you've noticed a whole lot of unauthorized mullets walking around, that's Blanche."

De Payns smiled and sipped the wine. "*Aunty* Ana?"

Romy shrugged. "The boys have been getting closer to her, and she started referring to herself as Aunty. It's a Syrian thing, apparently."

De Payns let it go. His own sister lived in New York and didn't have much to do with the family, and Romy only had a brother. If the boys were happy to call their mother's friend Aunty then he wouldn't argue.

"By the way," said Romy, "what's happening in Ukraine?"

"It's on the TV," said de Payns, noncommittal. "Putin

is threatening to go into Donetsk and Lugansk to protect Russian-speaking Ukrainians."

Romy gave him a look that said *don't bullshit me.* "You know what I mean, Alec: I'm talking about the energy part of it."

De Payns heard small alarm bells going off. "Why do you ask about energy?"

"I was at lunch with David today, and he said that no one cares about the Ukrainians. The Russians and Americans just want to control Europe's gas supply, that's all."

"Well," said de Payns, trying to keep it light, "I guess David is the expert, non?"

"Don't be like that," she snapped, leaning on the kitchen counter. "He created the energy program at Tirol Council, so he has some ideas about the politics of gas."

"Does he ask you about it?" asked de Payns, trying to keep suspicion out of his voice.

"No," said Romy, shifting her weight onto one leg. "I was talking about the potential shift in Western Europe if Putin annexes the Donbas, like he did Crimea, and David had another way of looking at it."

"Which was?" asked de Payns.

"David thinks Putin was relaxed when Poroshenko was in the presidential palace because Poroshenko was reluctant to push Ukraine membership of NATO. But when Zelenskyy became president in 2019, the whole NATO thing became too aggressive, and Russia could claim America was on the doorstep. He says Russia overplayed its control of Europe's gas and the Americans have overplayed their control of Ukraine."

"This David sounds quite smart," said de Payns, a modest amount of jealousy coming into play. "He's—what—former government, now retired?"

Romy looked at her feet. "No, he's our age. He was at

McKinsey after leaving the Sorbonne. He was made the program director at Tirol three years ago."

"I see," said de Payns, the trickle of jealousy gaining speed. "He's a pointy-head."

Romy smirked.

"What?" asked de Payns.

"Well, he's certainly an intellectual, but there's another side to him. He races in a thing called the Career Cup, or something like that."

"Races?" asked de Payns. "Like, running?"

"No, no," said Romy. "He races Porsches."

"Porsche Carrera Cup?" exclaimed de Payns, jealousy now running rampant.

"That's it," said Romy, smiling. "He's got a trophy in his office. Apparently, he came first."

CHAPTER
TWENTY-SEVEN

The security door pulled back in the basement area of Y-9, and Lolo let de Payns inside.

"How's Starkand's phone?" asked de Payns, as he walked toward Lolo's desk.

"Last activity was eleven thirty-four a.m., Munich," said Lolo, wiping his fingers with a food wrapper. "When he puts the battery back in the phone, we'll know pretty fast."

A Y-9 operator named Tranh looked up from a bank of four monitors, one of which had a large map of Europe on its screen. "He's using the same phone," said Tranh. "That's one thing in our favor."

"Let me know when we get the signal," said de Payns.

De Payns didn't tell Lolo that a team headed by Templar was also establishing an environment around Lotus, and Jim Valley had been tasked to draw in Keratine.

The security buzzer sounded, and the screen beside the door filled with Margot's face. Lolo leaped up to give entry to Briffaut's assistant.

"Boss wants to see you," said Margot, one arm full of files and nodding at de Payns. "He's in the park."

De Payns wandered out to find Briffaut on his favorite bench with a cigarette.

"The outline of Operation Ellipse looks good," said Briffaut, referring to de Payns's initial counter-assassination pitch. "What about the Starkand phone?"

"He used it this morning in Munich and then went dark."

Briffaut nodded. "This came through on the diplomatic wire twelve minutes ago," he said, handing over three pages of printouts.

De Payns looked at them: a military order giving the go-ahead for *Vulcanus*. It also referred to the "Europe operation" but gave no details.

De Payns flipped to the next page. It was a Turkish navy confirmation of clear passage for Russian navy missile cruisers and landing craft to pass through the Bosporus—the narrow neck of sea that divided the European part of Turkey from its Middle Eastern rump. It confirmed Russian navy vessels had moved from the Mediterranean to the Black Sea.

The third piece of paper established the movement into the Khmeimim Air Base of Russian receiver modules for downloads of data from the FSB drones operating out of the Syrian air base.

De Payns looked up from the printouts. "Genuine?"

Briffaut took back the papers. "Probably. They're being verified."

"Where did these documents come from?"

Briffaut tapped his ash. "They were in the mail at our Berlin embassy this morning, with a Munich postmark."

"Starkand," said de Payns. "Fuck!"

"It gets better," said Briffaut, sucking on his Camel. "DR have looked for similar mail at the embassies and found an earlier one at The Hague, postmark Amsterdam."

"When?" asked de Payns.

"Few days before Rome," said Briffaut. "By the way, the British want a Maypole."

"Why?" asked de Payns. A Maypole was a meeting of two intelligence agencies to assess information in common and see if there was any benefit to sharing information.

"They want an exchange," said Briffaut. "They have concerns about something that could happen in Europe."

"Vulcan?" asked de Payns.

"Our external liaison department believes the Brits received the same intel as us from an unknown source," said Briffaut. "That source might be even more unknown to them than it is to us. If the DR accepts the Maypole, we'll find out."

De Payns made to go, but his boss touched his forearm. "Have a look at these, tell me if you recognize anyone."

Briffaut produced an A4 envelope that contained three printed photographs in the eight-by-ten format used by intelligence agencies. The first photograph was a grainy blowup of security footage, featuring a man sitting in the back seat of a car. De Payns didn't recognize the face. The second photograph was of the same car, focused on the man in the front passenger seat; he had a thick neck and a soldier's haircut, and de Payns didn't recognize him either.

He paused on the last picture. It was grainy and it was a still taken from a video. But he knew the face of the man driving the Audi. His name was Mikhail, and he chewed the world's worst-tasting gum.

"Him," said de Payns, holding up the photograph. "One of the Wagner Group heavies on *Azzam*. Who is he?"

Briffaut took the picture, stashed it inside his jacket. "DGSI tracked a few suspicious sightings in the hours after Degarde's death, and they came up with a charter boat that journeyed up the Seine with three Russians on board. They got off at an industrial dockland and were picked up in a car. The security camera did the rest."

De Payns's skin crawled. Wagner Group was operating in Paris and killing the Company's officers.

"We'll get these pricks," said Briffaut. "It's just a question of when."

CHAPTER
TWENTY-EIGHT

Jim Valley walked the promenade that lined Baku's waterfront on the Caspian Sea. There was an outdoor café on his right, and he found a table where his back faced a tree and he had a view of pedestrians coming from both ends of the promenade. He ordered a coffee and checked his watch: 9:39 a.m. He avoided looking around; there were two overwatch operators from the Company surveilling him and readying for his 10:00 a.m. meeting with Lazar Suburov, the FSB officer based across the border in Grozny, Russia, who the Bunker had codenamed Keratine.

Valley stirred sugar into his coffee and assessed his surrounds. Keratine had not been properly transitioned into working for Paris, and the Company had an urgent request for information from him. Once Valley got to know his new charge, things might be different, but hitting him cold with requests for information was going to be interesting. It was a tough assignment, working in Russia and running traitors from the FSB, but he'd been thrown a lifeline by Dominic Briffaut, and he wasn't going to screw it up. The operation to abduct Aguilar's wife and children and make them think it was a training exercise for the Company was a despicable thing to do, and the fact it had been ordered by his superior, Philippe Manerie, only gave him legal cover, not a moral one. Now he had a chance to reestablish his credentials with the Company. And although he worked for the DR, it was Briffaut and the DO whom he owed. He would return the favor by walking into the wolf's mouth. He looked at his watch and drained the coffee. Then he stood and walked to his meeting.

Valley tapped three times on the door of the suite on the fourth floor of the Hotel Bristol, a tourist hotel that overlooked the Azerbaijani capital's seafront. Through the window at the end of the carpeted hall, he could see the Caspian stretching to the south, where a journey by ship would end at Iran's northern coast.

"Yes?" came a voice from behind the door, in English but with a heavy Russian accent.

"A friend from Geneva," said Valley, also in English, and the door opened.

The man was slightly shorter than Valley and twenty years older. But he was fit and had some fight in him.

"I made coffee," said Keratine, securing the door and then walking past Valley to the living area of the suite. "We're clean for now, but perhaps we could make this quick?"

Valley ignored the time pressure. French intelligence officers were trained to always control an asset and to set their own parameters.

"Coffee is good," said Valley. "I take mine black."

Keratine poured coffee from a plunger into mugs on a dining table. Valley took a seat and pulled a mug toward him.

"I'll give you a protocol before I leave," said Valley, keeping things civil but curt. "You'll be compensated, but before we go too far, let's talk about what you can provide."

"That depends on what France wants," said Keratine, crossing his legs and stirring sugar into the strong-smelling Azerbaijani coffee.

"No," said Valley, giving a soldier's smile, "that depends on what you can provide."

They looked at one another, and Keratine broke the contact. "I'm not playing games with you. I'm just unsure what I bring."

"What's happening in Ukraine?" asked Valley. "Russian missile cruisers moving into the Black Sea?"

The Russian shrugged. "Do you know why French submarines are loitering off the Andamans?"

"Do you know who's asking the questions in this conversation?" replied Valley.

Keratine nodded his acquiescence. "You know what I do in Chechnya? I do what you're doing now. I recruit and run traitors. Some of them make drops, and others talk. Some can even be convinced to put bugs under tables and plant trackers on cars, that sort of thing. Does France really want to know what a group of students are doing at Chechen State University?"

"You finished?" asked Valley.

Keratine let out a sigh. "I'm just saying—"

"You're just misdirecting, that's what you're just doing."

Now the Russian had an innocent face. "How can I—"

"Shut up," said Valley, making his large body more obvious. "The whining's over. Now we talk."

"About what?"

"Wagner Group," said Valley.

"What about them?"

Valley put his elbows on the table, making Keratine focus on him. "Wagner Group is controlled by Russia. We'd like insights."

"I have nothing to do with Wagner Group," said Keratine. "They don't operate out of Chechnya."

"They've been used in Transcaucasia," said Valley, referring to the oil-rich land bridge between the Black and Caspian seas. "Don't tell me you have nothing to do with them."

"Our paths have crossed," conceded Keratine. "But Wagner Group operates at arm's length from the services. They're limited to foreign activities. Grozny is Russia."

"That's not the answer Paris wants to hear."

"Look, I never asked to betray my country, and I never claimed to have product that would interest France."

"I'll give you a week," said Valley, making to stand. "You might remember something."

When Keratine saw Valley draining the coffee, he held up his hand. "Okay, wait a second," said the Russian. "Give me a clue. What are you really after?"

Valley laughed at the counterespionage maneuver. "You really just tried that on me? I think this is going to be a very short friendship."

Valley walked to the door and grabbed the handle.

A throat cleared behind him.

He turned, looked at Keratine's taut face.

"Okay," said the Russian. "There's a Wagner Group connection I can give you."

Valley let the door close. "Yes?"

"Leonid Varnachev, they call him Lenny."

Valley nodded. "Was he GRU, Spetsnaz?"

"GRU. He made lieutenant colonel," said Keratine. "He just started operating out of Tartus naval base in Syria. He's senior in Wagner, so he's being noticed."

"What's he doing?" asked Valley.

"It's only gossip."

"So, start gossiping," said Valley, hand reaching for the door handle.

"Lenny's organizing an assassination."

"And?" prompted Valley.

"It's in Europe."

"Gee, that narrows it down," said Valley.

"All I've heard is Europe," said Keratine.

"When?" asked Valley.

Keratine shrugged. "It's gossip, agents talking."

"Okay, final question and we'll formalize an arrangement. Who's being hit?"

"Where's my guarantee that I won't be thrown under the bus?"

Valley cocked an eyebrow but said nothing.

They looked at one another.

"Varnachev is running it directly," said Keratine, finally after breaking eye contact. "I can't just ask about that sort of operation because only a handful of people would know about it. There's an assassination in Europe, I can give you that."

"Political?"

Keratine nodded quickly.

"Okay," said Valley. "A political assassination in Europe, but no name? You're giving me nothing but paranoia."

Keratine sighed and looked at the ceiling. "Okay, I'll work on a name. But I can give you something that Paris might want to know."

Valley waited.

"We know there's a traitor on our side, feeding information to the Occidental services," said Keratine. "Get what you can from this person as quickly as possible because we will catch him."

CHAPTER
TWENTY-NINE

De Payns pushed the pin into the picture of Lenny Varnachev, so the Wagner man's face formed the center of a web on the "Ellipse" corkboard: Varnachev, surrounded by Orlevski and al-Mismari, and the Emirati prince Jamal. Vladimir Putin's picture sat over the top of the Wagner Group web, which was connected by red tape to Kolomoisky—labeled *Hammer*—and *Anvil*, with a question mark under the word. Sitting beside the Wagner web was a picture of Mikhail connected to a picture of Paul Degarde, and a photo of Lotus and the Russian embassy officer, Andrei Lermatov. At the other end of the long operations room, another corkboard labeled "Bellbird" carried pictures of Starkand, the woman they were calling Orange Top, and the yacht *Melissa*.

He couldn't stand to look at the trombinoscopes. They were too inconclusive and just reminded him of how much work there was to do.

He looked at his watch: one minute late for Mattieu Garrat's budget meeting. He scooted down the hallway, past Briffaut's office, and found Garrat staring at his screen in a west-facing office.

"Aguilar, I was about to call you," said Garrat, an OT in his late forties who had worked in the field before being made Briffaut's 2IC. "Talk me through a couple of these Operation Bellbird requests, and then I'll have this down to the boss to sign."

De Payns took a seat.

"You say we need two subs and six OTs, on standby for an unnamed city in Western Europe?" asked Garrat, not looking up from the screen. "That's not cheap. When they're on standby they can't be deployed elsewhere."

"We're waiting on a phone environment for Starkand," said de Payns. "We have to be ready to go."

"Two of the OTs are techs from Y-9, and they're costed at the top band," said Garrat, chewing his lip. "Don't be surprised if the boss pushes back on this."

"He told me to take what I need, and he'll sign it," said de Payns, smiling lightly. "And he's in a hurry."

Garrat sighed and shrugged, muttering about how he'd be the one explaining the blown budget when the department auditors made their rounds.

The scheduled Operation Ellipse update meeting comprised only de Payns, Briffaut, and Marie Lafont. Lafont went through the new product from Jim Valley. He had FSB confirmation of Wagner arranging a hit, and Lenny Varnachev was named as the one running it. No mention of Kolomoisky, no date, no venue, and no ideas on who "Anvil" might be.

Marie Lafont paused and tapped the arm of her spectacles on the report. "Keratine warned Jim that there's a traitor in the Russian services, selling prod to the Western services." She looked at de Payns. "Any ideas?"

"Try this," said Briffaut, sliding a sheet of paper to her.

She read quickly and peered over her half-glasses at Briffaut. "Andrei Lermatov? Remind me."

"The SVR officer at Russia's Tbilisi embassy. He made the drop to Lotus."

Lafont looked back at the report, her face hardening. "He's dead? Confirmed?"

Briffaut nodded. "A reliable source."

De Payns looked at the report when Lafont handed it to him. It said Andrei Lermatov had been found strangled in a public toilet in Vake Park, Tbilisi. *Evidence of a homosexual tryst gone wrong.*

"FSB," said de Payns, handing the report back to Briffaut.

Lafont shook her head. "What is it with the FSB and gays?"

"It destroys the family's prospects, along with killing the traitor," said Briffaut. "By the way, Lotus wants to come in."

"Why?" asked de Payns.

"First Lermatov went missing, now one of his sources—a Syrian air force officer—has dropped off the map. He's surmised the Russian services are cleaning up a leak, and Lotus is worried he's on the list."

"Has Lotus been blown?" asked Lafont.

"No evidence of it," said Briffaut, "but he says his sources are being caught."

"Do we want him alive?" asked de Payns.

"I haven't decided yet," said Briffaut. "First, we'll need to bring him out in one piece."

Lafont said, "We have the Maypole this afternoon. Tony wants me running our side. I need you there, Dominic, if you can make it."

"The British are in Paris?" asked Briffaut.

"Yes," said Lafont. "They're highly motivated."

When Briffaut was behind his own desk once more, he told de Payns to stay on Starkand. "Shrek can bring Lotus out."

"What about Jim?" asked de Payns. "He'd be closer."

"Jim is on Shrek's team, and so is Jéjé," said Briffaut, sitting back. "When Lotus arrives in Paris, I want you to bring him to the hotel. Alive—and that goes for you too."

De Payns looked at his boss. "You're expecting trouble in Paris?"

"Aren't you?"

De Payns didn't respond, but his mind went straight to Paul Degarde; he couldn't help it.

"You're impeccable about your last mile," said Briffaut, as if reading his mind. "Keep it that way."

Sensing a lecture coming, de Payns changed the subject. "About this Maypole—I might do a sidebar, if it's okay with you?"

Briffaut put his foot on the desk, grabbed his coffee. "I don't like sidebars, and the Cat hates them. Remember what they did to Burland?"

De Payns remembered: an OT who worked at the Cat, Drew Burland, conducted a sidebar with a CIA agent he knew personally, during a difficult operation involving a Mali general. Word of the meeting got back to Sturt, and Burland was accused of treason. He was last heard of working as an assistant librarian in Rouen.

"Name one advantage that France gains from you going under the table?" challenged Briffaut.

"If all the services are getting the same prod from Starkand, then we all get to offer the same thing and nothing more," said de Payns. "The Maypole could be fruitless and we waste time . . ."

Briffaut raised his eyebrows. "Or even more fruitless than usual. Okay," he said. "Do it."

De Payns waited at the Café Français, on the edge of the Place de la République. He had an outside table and watched the early afternoon tourists amble past, rugged up against the cold but still enjoying the clear Paris skies.

"This seat taken?" said a voice, and de Payns turned, saw a heavyset man in his late thirties looming over him.

"It's reserved for geniuses," said de Payns.

"Then what the fuck are you doing here?" replied the man.

De Payns stood, shook Mike Moran's hand, and let the Englishman give him a very fast hug.

"So, you knew I'd be on the Maypole?" asked Moran, who wore aviator sunglasses and a heavy woolen coat that looked as if it was made for the Royal Navy. "Anything else I should know about?"

The waitress approached, and de Payns asked for two Kronenbourgs. "I thought there'd be a good chance the Brits would want a sidebar, and they'd fly you in to lure me out."

Moran laughed. "There you go again, all that French overanalysis. You remind me of that bloke in *The Princess Bride*—you know, the one with the table and the shell game?"

"What does it say about the English that I was dead right?"

The beers arrived, and Moran raised his bottle. "To triple-reverse logic," he said.

"*À la tienne,*" said de Payns, and they clinked beers.

They went through what they wanted from one another without admitting anything.

"The external liaison people are going to do the Maypole dance," said de Payns, "but they'll probably withhold more than they say."

"Agreed," said Moran. "If you're wondering about the

information about Russian movements, it's coming as anonymous mail to our embassies in Europe."

"Rome, Berlin, and Amsterdam?" asked de Payns, thankful
for his woolen scarf as a cold Paris breeze ruffled the pigeons of
Place de la République.

"Those are the ones I know about," said Moran, "and it's all
snail mail. Old school, like a le Carré novel."

"Intelligence bases in Syria, missile cruisers through the
Straits into the Black Sea?" asked de Payns.

"Yes, and yes," said Moran, draining his beer. "The question
is, who's sending the same prod to our embassies?"

"And why?" added de Payns.

"My suspicious mind has been at work," said Moran.

"Mine too."

Moran looked around at the tourists and leaned forward.
"I don't want to appear too paranoid, mon pote, but it's like
someone wants to generate an anti-Russian feeling among us."

"Like someone wants a lot of focus on Ukraine," said de
Payns.

This established, they updated each other on their families, and then Moran looked at his watch. "Have to see a man
about a dog."

"Until next time," said de Payns.

"By the way," said Moran, as he stood and pushed his chair
under the table, "I heard you're a very nice nautical roommate."

As his friend walked through the scattering birdlife, de Payns
thought back to the steward named Simone and wondered what
she had retrieved for SIS.

CHAPTER
THIRTY

Sensei John took the dojo through a series of warm-down stretches and then performed his final protocols, which ended in the boys and girls making small bows to their sensei before walking to their parents.

De Payns waited, relaxing into the moment but anxious about Lolo and Tranh identifying activity on the Starkand phone.

"Hi Alec," said Ana, coming up beside him. "You have the boys tonight?"

"Yes, normal hours today," said de Payns, smiling. "Gives me some time with the kids."

"Lucky you, with a job where you can wear jeans and sneakers," she observed. "I spent half my career limping around in shoes that were killing me."

"You working now?" asked de Payns, keeping it light.

Ana wrinkled her nose. "Looking around, but nothing's taking my fancy."

Oliver walked up, handed his sports bag to de Payns, and drank from his water bottle.

"Hi, Ollie," said Ana, before de Payns could say anything.

"Hi, Aunty Ana," he replied. "Did you see Charlie on the pads?"

"Yes!" she said. "My son, the Bruce Lee of Montparnasse!"

"Kung fu is Chinese," said Oliver, suddenly serious. "Karate is Japanese."

"Oh, my mistake!" said Ana, laughing.

Patrick and Charlie joined them, having helped Sensei John put away the karate gear, and they walked to the door of the church hall, the boys running out into the early evening.

The TV news carried a story about Macron easing up on COVID masks, and it was followed by a short piece about Russian troops and armor massing on the border with Ukraine. There also seemed to be Russian troops on Ukraine's border with Belarus, part of a joint exercise but without much exercising. De Payns sipped on his Riesling, pondering the shorter-than-usual delay between an intelligence service knowing Putin's moves and the media reporting them. It felt structured.

In another part of the apartment, the boys were fighting over who had installed the dry towel outside the shower and who had the right to use it.

"The wet person gets the towel," yelled de Payns, "and they have to come back with a dry one for whoever is next in the shower."

There was silence.

"Confirm!" he shouted.

"Yes, Dad!" said Patrick, and he could hear snarling from the bathroom.

Romy emerged from her office and checked the oven. "Don't let them get dry towels all the time," she said, taking the glass of wine on the counter. "They should use the ones in their room."

"They're wet."

"Because they leave them on the floor," said Romy, with a small roll of the eyes. "They'll never learn to hang them up if they can always grab a new one. I'm sick of all the washing."

De Payns muted the TV. "Why doesn't Ana work?"

"Umm," said Romy, surprised by the question, "I guess she has Charlie, and Rafi earns enough. I think she has something going, though."

"So she does work?" asked de Payns.

"Not really, just bits and pieces," said Romy, stirring a sauce on the stovetop. "She used to be with one of those big American accounting firms. I think she'll go back to that."

"Ana the accountant, eh?"

"She was on the consulting side," said Romy. "She'll go back to it when she finds something she likes." She added some salt to the sauce, then said, "So, I've RSVP'd, for the energy gala night."

"Great," said de Payns, forcing a smile that he hoped didn't look like a grimace.

"You need a dinner suit."

"Okay," he said.

"We'll be on David's table, which could mean Tony Blair, maybe."

"I'm looking forward to meeting him," said de Payns. "And Bill?"

"Won't make it," she said, pausing to sip her Riesling. "You have to promise me something."

"Sure," he said, sitting up.

"Let this be a social night," she said. "No working, okay?"

"Sure, honey, I would never—"

"I mean, I don't want you *working* people. Not at this thing."

"Fair enough," said de Payns, sitting back. "I'll just enjoy it."

CHAPTER
THIRTY-ONE

The overnight Y-9 desk picked up Starkand's cell phone shortly before midnight. It was activated for nineteen minutes in Bern, Switzerland, during which time the duty OT, Tranh, texted Lolo, who contacted Aguilar.

De Payns was picked up by Paulin and Lolo from a street corner at 1:21 a.m. The vehicle was an Iveco trades van used by the Bunker as a sub. Paulin drove and Lolo sat in the back, preparing his spinner laptops. They headed south for the Swiss border on the A6 freeway, while the mission team—Templar, Danny, and Brent—headed for Bern in another sub.

They arrived on the outskirts of the Swiss capital at 7:44 a.m., driving across a bridge over the Aare River into the medieval city.

De Payns held the transmit button in his jeans pocket. "Y radio check."

The answers—"Copy Templar," "Danny," "Lolo," "Paulin," "Brent"—came back to de Payns's earpiece. As they drove up a hill into the city, the snow-covered mountains of the Bernese Alps loomed in the distance.

"Lolo, you got the tower details?" asked de Payns from his front seat perch, cracking a window and lighting a cigarette.

Lolo read out the tower that Starkand's call had been routed through.

"Only one tower?"

"Yes," said Lolo. "Nineteen minutes on one call, then he shut it down. There's only one hotel definitely in the range of this tower—and I guess he likes luxury?"

"He's staying at the Bellevue Palace, huh?" replied Paulin. "That's where you stay in Bern when someone else is paying."

De Payns got on the net and told Templar where they were headed, leaving his colleague to instruct the mission team.

They drove around a block, while Lolo accessed the hotel's online photo gallery. They parked at the end of a narrow road that ran along the eastern side of the hotel, a hundred-and-fifty-year-old sandstone edifice. Paulin and Lolo walked back to the main road—Kochergasse—to take seats at a café that overlooked the entry to the Bellevue, and de Payns entered the foyer of the hotel, grabbed a *Le Monde*, and took a seat in the visitors' lounge. From his armchair he could see the menu board for the restaurant breakfast and smell the bacon.

"Alert Templar," came Templar's voice in de Payns's earpiece. "We're at the rear of the Bellevue."

"Copy Aguilar," said de Payns. "The restaurant looks busy, let's get someone in there."

"Templar copy."

The first bump from Starkand's IMSI came at 8:28.

"Alert. Target has activated his phone," said Lolo on the radio net. "It's close by."

"Tell me if it moves," said de Payns from his seat in the hotel's lobby.

Six minutes after the phone powered up, the man they knew as Starkand walked down the red-carpeted steps of the hotel lobby, fifteen meters away from de Payns. He was dressed in a blue suit and taupe overcoat, a dark brown leather carryall over his shoulder.

De Payns let Starkand walk past him and looked for over-watch. When he judged it clear, he keyed his mic. "Y alert, alert. Target is wearing a taupe overcoat, a dark brown leather carryall over his shoulder. Target is exiting the hotel, turning east along Kochergasse."

"Danny copy," came the response, and Danny—dressed in jeans, a black woodsman's jacket, and a blue ski hat—stood from his table at the café and exited onto Kochergasse.

De Payns stayed calm, controlling his nervous energy. He didn't want to keep getting photographs of Starkand—he wanted material progress.

"Vehicle two, position yourself ahead of target," said de Payns. "Danny, you have the lead."

The response came back affirmative, and the van moved slowly into traffic.

De Payns walked to the valet at the front steps, holding out his dark green woolen scarf.

"I think one of your guests just dropped this," said de Payns, pointing after Starkand. "Over there—good-looking chap, nice suit and an overcoat."

The valet looked down the street. "Ah, yes, Mr. Vadasz. I can take that for him."

De Payns smiled. "It's no problem. I'm walking his way, so I may as well give it to him. He might be cold without it."

"Thank you, sir," said the doorman.

"Did you say Peter Vadasz?"

"No, it's Michael—Michael Vadasz."

As de Payns reached the second car, Danny's voice sounded in his earpiece. "Danny for Y, target walking east on Münstergasse, even numbers side."

De Payns saw Starkand to his left, moving eastward along the street, which was broad for a medieval European city. He found a zone about forty meters behind the target, blending with the morning commuters.

Starkand crossed the street to the riverside and then veered right into the square in front of the imposing Bern Minster that dominated the skyline of the Old City. There was a poster board in front of de Payns, and he paused at it, like a tourist looking for directions, and watched Starkand stop at one of Switzerland's bright yellow mailboxes; he produced four envelopes from his bag and slid them into the box.

"Aguilar for Y," said de Payns into his radio. "Target just mailed four large envelopes."

Starkand stood back from the mailbox and looked around casually, like a tourist. Then he retraced his steps across the square as the sun hit the street and walked west down the odd numbers side of Münstergasse.

De Payns held back. "Aguilar for Y, target walking west on Münstergasse, odd numbers side."

"Danny copy, I have the target."

De Payns could see Starkand eighty meters in front of him, taking his time. He paused beside a bakery and pretended to look at the pastry displays.

"Danny for Y," came the voice twenty seconds later. "Target is crossing the street to even numbers—entering a café on Münstergasse, beside a travel agency. Café name: Frohsinn."

"Copy," said de Payns. "Stand by."

He knew that Paulin would be positioning the sub on Münstergasse and that Templar had his sub on the parallel street.

De Payns blended with the pedestrian flow and walked toward the café.

In the entrance to the modern eatery, he almost bumped into a brunette woman. He allowed her to go first, and she flashed him a smile. Following her in, he decided that she looked better in her orange silk blouse, though she still looked quite stunning in a blue woolen coat over a white jumper.

"Aguilar for Y, target in contact. Contact is female—she is known to us. I want a picture. Templar, Brent, you stay on her after she leaves," said de Payns.

He took a seat in the half-full café and perused a menu, listening as the woman greeted Starkand. It was small talk, as far as he could make out, and they both spoke in English but with jumbled accents.

He ordered a coffee and *pain au chocolat* and gave up trying to hear their murmurings. The café had jazz playing, and he was only getting one in five words.

As he finished his coffee, the woman—who was clearly in charge—stood and left.

Four minutes later, so did Starkand.

De Payns gave him a minute's head start, and then he paid.

Out on the street, he saw Starkand to his left.

The radio activated in his ear. "Y alert—female target just got in a taxi," said Brent.

"Copy," said de Payns, zipping his jacket against the cold as he followed Starkand along the street. "Templar?"

"Templar copy."

Starkand led de Payns back to the Münsterplatz, where half an hour earlier he'd mailed his envelopes. This time the target walked directly across the square and disappeared from view down a public pathway. The square was on a plateau over-looking the Aare River, and when de Payns followed to where the target had disappeared, he saw that the pathway led down through a maze of roofs and vegetable gardens to the main riverside promenade.

"Aguilar for Y, visual on target," said de Payns into his radio. "He's on a pedestrian-only passage to the river road."

"Vehicle one copy," came Lolo's voice. "We're on our way."

De Payns pulled back, blending with Japanese tourists and local joggers, as he navigated the centuries-old descent to the river, some of it open and other parts covered and inducing of claustrophobia. He emerged out of one gallery of stairs and almost ran into Starkand, who was standing in the morning sunlight, looking over a vegetable garden and speaking into his phone. De Payns walked past him, clicking on the radio to confirm he had visual, before joining a family of Americans who were photographing the gardens.

"It's like a rabbit warren in here," said de Payns, holding up his phone to take a shot.

"The Fricktreppe," said the middle-aged American woman in a Chicago Bears hoodie.

"No need to swear," said de Payns, and the woman laughed and slapped his arm, before repeating the joke for her hard-of-hearing husband.

He used the social activity to swing slightly and take a shot of Starkand, who was still on the phone and did not seem interested in the Franco-American jokes.

De Payns wandered away from the Americans and pretended to be looking at his photos, but he was concentrating on the voice in his earpiece: Templar, letting him know that the woman in the café was heading in the direction of the airport.

Starkand walked past him, and de Payns followed, descending the Fricktreppe until they emerged in the shaded Badgasse, a cobbled narrow street between two rows of four-story townhouses. There was a taxi idling thirty meters away, where a woman was paying her fare. Starkand raised his hand, walking toward the red-and-yellow taxi.

"Target is taking a taxi. Vehicle one—position?" asked de Payns into the mic.

"Vehicle one, on the promenade."

"Stand by," said de Payns, and made for a passage that other tourists were walking through. Moving quickly, he came out in sunlight on the promenade, his team's Iveco van fifteen meters to his right. Climbing into the van, he pointed. "He's in a red-and-yellow cab, heading east."

Paulin hit the gas, and the van surged forward, but as they approached the crossroad, the taxi came out of the street and turned right, rather than left, so it was going in the opposite direction to the van.

"That's him," said de Payns, as the taxi passed him, Starkand in the rear seat.

Paulin pulled a U-turn so they were heading west on the promenade, but they'd lost the taxi.

"Lolo, anything?" asked de Payns.

"No, boss. He turned on the phone for two minutes, but it's off the network again."

"Anyone see the cab number?" asked de Payns, who hadn't.

"One zero six," said Paulin. "The company is Nova Taxi."

"Get me a number, Lolo," said de Payns, as the van accelerated through the traffic.

Lolo read out the number, and de Payns dialed. A dispatcher picked up immediately.

"Yes, look," said de Payns in French, "my wife left her wallet in one of your cabs . . ."

"When?"

"About five minutes ago. I'm in another cab now, and I was

hoping you might know where it's heading? It's quite urgent—
the wallet has all our credit cards."

"Do you remember the taxi number?" the woman asked in
good French delivered with Germanic harshness.

"Taxi one zero six," said de Payns. "It was my wife he was
dropping off. At the Badgasse."

"Please wait, caller," said the woman, and de Payns was put
on hold.

The dispatcher was back on the line within twenty seconds.
"They're headed to the Hauptbahnhof—the driver will wait at
the drop-off apron out the front."

"We're on our way, thank you so much," said de Payns, and
disconnected.

They arrived at the drop-off area at the front of the Bern railway station seven minutes later. De Payns got out of the van and
walked with the foot traffic into the concrete-and-steel squared-off
railway station, a contrast to the architecture of the Old City. He
moved quickly through the morning crowds and caught sight of
Starkand, heading for the downward escalators. De Payns slowed
and announced to the team he had recovered visual. The interior
of Bern's station had three levels of balconies. He couldn't detect
any eyes on him and followed his target to the lower level, where
Starkand stopped in front of the departures board, before walking
across the concourse. Then he paused at platform seven, beneath
the sign advising that the next train was going to Frankfurt, and
he stopped to look at his phone: a smartphone this time, not the
flip-top burner he'd used on the Fricktreppe. De Payns pretended
to be interested in the arrivals and departures board. He wished
Starkand would get a move on so de Payns could see where he
was headed. Worried about lingering too long, de Payns drifted
to a kiosk and keyed the radio. "Aguilar for Lolo, I need you at
the station entrance. Let me know if the target exits."

"Lolo copy," came the reply. "In place at the entrance."

De Payns looked at the chocolate bars, selected one, and stood at the counter, maintaining a line of sight with the target. As he paid for the chocolate, a rumble grew louder and a whoosh of air blew out as a Deutsche Bahn Intercity train roared into platform seven. Starkand walked away from de Payns as the train slowed. De Payns fumbled to pay for the chocolate bar and set off after the target, dodging the travelers who were getting up from their benches and milling around. As he tried to keep sight of the target, another train screeched into platform eight, causing more travelers to start moving.

He got caught behind a high-school hockey team, jockeyed past them, and now realized he'd lost Starkand; the train platform curved so that he could not see the far end, his vision further obstructed by the people now alighting from the newly arrived train and mingling with those boarding.

"Aguilar, lost visual on target—repeat, lost visual on target," he said into the mic, as he got to a position from where he could see the nose of the train, but no Starkand.

"Shit!"

De Payns walked swiftly to the end of the Frankfurt train, checking the large first-class windows and their luxury interiors, but no Starkand.

As if suddenly remembering he'd left something behind, he turned and walked back the way he'd come, as railway workers called to each other and a whistle echoed down the annoyingly curved platform. To his right he saw a set of stairs that disappeared downward into the platform; it was a midplatform underpass that linked the thirteen platforms and led to the main concourse, according to the sign. The Frankfurt train behind him hissed and the doors shut, and the train in front of him—at platform eight—was filling up, people moving into the fluoro-lit cabins. He walked down the underpass ramp, and ascended the stairs for platform nine, in time to see the SBB Swiss train for Basel easing out of the station. Through the window, on the far side of the first-class cabin, Starkand sat in an airline-style seat, pulling a magazine from his leather overnight bag. He appeared not to realize he was being observed.

As he walked back to the concourse, de Payns's mobile phone rang. "Templar visual on female target—arriving Bern airport."

"Copy Aguilar," said de Payns.

De Payns emerged from the warm station into the cold morning and climbed into the van. He turned to Lolo. "I lost him, but he's on his way to Basel."

The secondary cities of Europe had high-speed trains moving through them at a constant frequency, and a person like Starkand—or de Payns for that matter—could head anywhere in Western Europe in the space of a day, without followers being able to predict a destination.

"Find a list of connecting trains that leave Basel within thirty minutes of his arrival," said de Payns. "But first, let me have a go on your laptop."

De Payns opened his own encrypted channel to Briffaut on the laptop and sent him the photograph of Starkand taken in the Fricktreppe, and requested that Briffaut raise the name/pseudonym #MICHAEL VADASZ# with the SIS Maypole. Starkand had eluded de Payns, which was either a fluke or because he'd seen a follower and lost him. De Payns wanted to know which one it was.

Passing back the laptop, he realized he was hungry and suggested a bite to eat.

As Paulin drove them out of Bern and onto the road west to France, they found a midsize café and parked. De Payns's phone buzzed, and Templar's familiar voice sounded again. "Female target has left Bern airport on a private plane—repeat, private plane."

De Payns nodded to himself. The Starkand situation was starting to stink.

"Her destination?" asked de Payns.

"*Ouais mon pote*, destination is Larnaca."

De Payns let his breath go in a long exhale. Orange Top was in charge, and she was based in the same city as the yacht he'd seen her embark in Portofino. "Confirm Larnaca, Cyprus?"

"Confirm Cyprus," said Templar.

CHAPTER
THIRTY-TWO

Shrek grabbed the keys from the top of the driver's-side tire and unlocked the side door to the Georgian Water and Power van parked in the industrial wasteland south of Tbilisi. He and Jim Valley climbed in, slid the door shut behind them, and found the coveralls and caps waiting where the Company's local asset had promised they'd be.

They dressed quickly, and Jim checked his watch. "Fifty-four minutes until go."

"Let's hope Lotus is still in one piece," said Shrek.

He'd been concerned about Jim Valley's connection to the disgraced Philippe Manerie, but he had to admit that the OT was an efficient professional and it was never a bad thing to work with someone of his size and experience with violence.

They'd spent the previous day and night shifting Lotus around Tbilisi, and now they had him in a serviced apartment, chosen for its underground parking garage. Jéjé was guarding the Company's asset, but the team had gained the attention of a carload of heavies whose vehicle was owned by a Monaco shell, a typical FSB setup. Now they needed a way to extract Lotus from the heart of Tbilisi before the FSB could grab him.

They drove across the Georgian capital on the east side of the Kura River as dawn illuminated the spires and rooks of the city. The traffic was light compared to Paris's morning rush hour, and Shrek swung the van onto a main arterial road. After three minutes driving toward the massive reservoir that watered the city, he turned right into the wealthier suburbs.

They slowed as they approached the apartment block; unlike apartment blocks in Paris and London, that were built right to the footpath, Tbilisi's residential buildings usually had a street-fronting parking area and an apron to the main doors. They pulled into their safe house address, and Shrek drove toward the underground entrance, passing a black Chevrolet SUV sitting squarely in the middle of the parking zone. Two powerfully built men sat in the front seats of the SUV, pointedly looking up at the second-floor windows where they assumed Lotus was hiding. Shrek could sense Jim shifting his weight, alert to the danger in the Chevrolet but not intimidated.

Shrek made a show of stopping beside the tradesmen's ringer and pushed a button. From inside the building, Jéjé released the door to the underground, and the vehicle door folded upward on itself. Shrek and Jim drove into the underground, Jim pulling his CZ 9mm pistol from under the seat. They paused just inside the entry, waiting to see if the FSB thugs were going to follow them into the parking garage.

"I guess they bought it," said Shrek, staring in the van's side mirror.

The door unfolded itself to the ground, and they drove to the elevator station in the center of the garage. Shrek left Jim in the van and walked to the stairwell, making his way up the four flights of stairs to the second floor. He was panting by the time he reached the safe house door—not from exertion but from adrenaline. He, Jéjé, and Jim had spent twenty-four hours staying one step ahead of the FSB agents and he was ready for action.

He knocked three times and Jéjé opened quickly, his own handgun held at his side. "How we looking?"

"Clear, for now," said Shrek, entering the apartment. In front of him was a rolling view of modern and old rooftops, punctuated by trees, that descended slowly to the river. Standing in the living room was the man they called Lotus: freshly showered but grubby nonetheless.

"You ready?" asked Shrek.

Lotus shrugged. "Maybe I should ask you the same question?"

Shrek ignored him. "We have his bag?" he asked Jéjé.

"Here," said Jéjé, picking up a cabin bag from a small breakfast table.

Shrek grabbed Lotus's jacket, pushed aside the lapels, and shoved his hands inside the Georgian's turquoise silk shirt to check that the ballistic vest was properly secured.

"Hey, watch it," said Lotus, twisting away from Shrek's hands.

Shrek smiled. "Don't get all coy. Keeping you alive is my job."

Jéjé checked his pistol and walked to the door, which he cracked slightly. "We're clear," he murmured, and pulled the door fully open.

Shrek grabbed a handful of Lotus's jacket at the waist with his left hand and unholstered his handgun with his right hand. Then he walked Lotus to the door, peered out, and tucked Lotus in behind Jéjé as they made a caterpillar to the stairwell. Their rasped breathing echoed as they made their way down the first flight of stairs. A door creaked open and then slammed shut, making the three of them jump.

"Resident," said Jéjé softly as he raised his hand to pause their progress.

They listened to scuffed shoes on concrete, and then the basement door squeaked and slammed shut.

They moved again, slowly but smoothly, Jéjé leading and Shrek moving Lotus where he wanted him using his hold on the man's jacket.

They reached the basement door, and Shrek holstered his handgun under his left armpit. Jéjé pulled Lotus back so he couldn't be seen. They paused for half a minute, listening intently. A car started in the garage and moved past the door. Shrek wanted to keep moving. He said to Jéjé, "Keep him here, I'll call when it's clear."

Shrek pulled the door and stepped into the underground garage where there were three men: Jim leaning on the hood of the Georgian Water and Power van, with an FSB thug on either side of him. The garage door was still closing, suggesting that the Russians had slipped in when the resident in the stairwell had driven out.

Shrek saw it very quickly: the Russians were saying something in Georgian or Russian to Jim, who was smiling and trying to bluff his way through.

"*Privet, kak delat,*" said Shrek, putting on a big smile as he walked to the larger of the two heavies in a gray windbreaker.

The Russian smiled back. "*Privet priyatel,*" he started, and Jim punched him hard in the throat, crushed his instep with a stamp-kick; he clutched the Russian's right hand before it could grab a pistol, breaking the man's wrist in one fast twist and downward thrust. Shrek moved straight for the second FSB guy and kicked him hard in the solar plexus, doubling him over as the Russian slumped onto his arse. Shrek pounced on him, held the Russian by the hair, and drove a quick punch into the man's left temple, knocking him out.

Jim turned back to his prey as the man started to yell with pain. He kneeled and punched the man hard in the carotid artery, rendering him unconscious. Pulling the loom of zip ties from his back pocket, Jim hog-tied the Russian in the gray wind-breaker, and as he started tying the second Russian, Shrek took possession of the FSB firearms and walked them to a dumpster, where he actioned them, disassembled them, and disposed of the pieces. They stripped the radio transmitters and earpieces from the FSB agents and discarded these too.

"Come through, Jéjé," called Shrek to Jéjé and Lotus, as he tied off the other Russian. "We're clear."

Jéjé came through the door, and they stashed Lotus in the van. Then the three of them loaded the Russians into the back of the van, since Shrek didn't want them being found before the Frenchmen and their asset had left the country.

As they waited for the garage door to open, the tension palpable, Shrek checked his watch. "We could make that midday flight," he said.

"No point lingering in sunny Georgia," said Jéjé, from the rear of the van.

They drove out into the morning sunlight, past the black Chevy SUV. Now there was a blue SUV parked beside the black one and two men standing on the apron, looking around as if they'd lost something.

Shrek and Jim both smiled and gave brief waves as they drove past the FSB men. They paused at the curb, then pulled out and headed for the airport.

CHAPTER
THIRTY-THREE

The information board at Charles de Gaulle's Terminal 1 showed Lotus's flight from Istanbul had arrived twenty-one minutes ago, but still no Lotus. De Payns fought the instinct to check his watch and instead took an update from Claude—a former Army operator who had joined the Company two years earlier—who had identified two persons of interest milling around in front of the arrivals hall.

"They're standing off," came Claude's voice in his hidden earpiece. "But they're looking for someone, and it's not you."

"Copy that," said de Payns, reaching for his warm coffee which sat on a table in the concourse café. "They armed?"

"Claude copy," said his colleague. "Paulin overheard one of them; they're Russian, or something Eastern."

"You know what to do with the cars," said de Payns, referring to their standby plan should a hostile team show itself at the airport.

De Payns was more fidgety than normal; Lotus was being brought to France because the FSB was on to his network, but the Russians seemed to also have a welcome committee waiting in Paris.

Balancing the odds was de Payns's team, which was broken into groups: Templar and Thierry, waiting in a red BMW in the B1 car park; Paulin and Claude, in the arrivals area of Terminal 1, and Aline and Marc in a white Renault at B2. Danny was on a motorbike, ready to ride overwatch on the car that took Lotus into Paris from Charles de Gaulle. Their job was to deliver Lotus to the George V hotel in Paris without him being killed or snatched. They were all linked to de Payns's radio set, which transmitted from a small box in his pocket, linked to a tiny earpiece in his left ear.

At 3:06 p.m. Claude's voice crackled again. "Claude to Y—the package is moving toward you. Our POIs are moving toward the package."

De Payns turned slightly to his left and saw a middle-aged Georgian man in a dark pea jacket and tweed trilby, who he knew as Lotus.

"Greetings, Lado," said de Payns, rising and offering to take Lotus's large suitcase. "That's your only bag?"

"Yes," said Lotus, taking a seat at the table, his face grumpy. "I'd love a coffee."

Before de Payns could intercede, the Georgian had ordered a coffee. "Delayed flights," said Lotus softly. "It just kills the whole day."

"Nice to see you, Monsieur Devashvili," said de Payns, aware of potential danger. "We have some unwanted visitors around us, and I'd suggest we start walking. Just follow my directions, and when I ask you to accelerate, just do it, okay?"

Lotus's face pinched slightly. "When you say unwanted, does that mean Russian?"

"Yes," said de Payns. "They know you're here. Do not look around or try to make eye contact with anybody, okay?"

Lotus nodded slowly and pointedly did not look around. "Are we safe in Paris?"

"Probably," said de Payns, standing.

"They've already killed two of my associates," said Lotus, "so I'd prefer that you were a bit more certain."

De Payns grabbed the suitcase by its handle and urged Lotus onto his feet. "This way," he said, steering the Georgian away from the table and into the foot traffic of the dome-roofed concourse.

"Aguilar for Y," he said into his mic. "I have the package. How are we placed?"

"Both POIs are behind you; you have twenty-five meters on them."

"Aguilar copy, heading for the cars."

He steered Lotus along the western wall of the terminal concourse and hooked sideways toward the elevators that took travelers to the parking garages below.

As soon as they were out of the concourse and into the elevator area, de Payns said, "Now!"

He pushed Lotus past the elevator doors and directed him down the spiral concrete stairwells, aiming for level B2. De Payns was quietly surprised by how fast his charge could move. They reached the B1 landing and could clearly hear feet entering the stairwell above him and running down the stairs. They reached the B2 door and burst through, finding the white Renault idling.

"In you get," said de Payns, opening the rear door and showing Lotus where to lie, as Aline held a blanket aloft. "Stay down and do as you're told," said de Payns, and he slammed the door as the car sped away.

De Payns turned and reentered the stairwell, hearing the telltale chatter of people spotting their prey. He listened, and once de Payns was certain his followers had given up on B1 and were coming down to B2, he let them catch a glimpse of him before descending further to B3. Jogging across the B3 car park, he headed for a secondary set of fire stairs that would take him back up to the main concourse. When he got to the secondary stairwell, he could see the Russians giving chase, and he knew his exfiltration plan was working: the white Renault would have stopped at B1, and Lotus was being shifted into a red BMW. The BMW would be driven to the furthest exit of the parking building, while the white Renault exited through the main gate.

Reaching the main concourse again, de Payns hurried along the middle of the walkways, so the Russians could see him. When he was sure he was being followed, he made a filature, a sudden ninety-degree exit out a side door and onto a traffic apron, where he could see a shuttle bus taking on passengers. He jumped on the bus and moved to the back with the other travelers, watching out the window as the bus accelerated toward the next terminal. The two Russian followers stepped into the Paris sunlight and looked around like two lost puppies. Lotus was on his way to the George V, and de Payns got off his bus at the RER station between Terminal 2C and E and caught a train into Paris.

CHAPTER
THIRTY-FOUR

De Payns put his COVID mask in his pocket and lit a cigarette at the café he'd found across the road from the George V.
Although masks were no longer mandatory, de Payns found
them useful for daytime operations. He used the smoking action
to scan the street, seeing Danny's motorbike parked at his ten
o'clock, and knew that the team's backup man from the Lotus
operation was sitting in a café and watching the hotel, freaking
out at the cost of a cup of coffee in this part of the city.

He keyed the radio. "Aguilar to Danny. Package is secure?"

"Danny copy. We're clear. Standing by."

He sat back and relaxed with his cigarette and coffee, having
just used three trains to get from CDG to this part of Paris.
Now he was waiting to be called in by Briffaut, who was debriefing Lotus upstairs. The café played news radio rather than the
customary jazz, and de Payns listened to the bulletins that talked
about the Russian buildup in Ukraine's east. It felt like a very
controlled media rollout, and he was cynical about such "news."
Accurate numbers on troop deployments and inside knowledge

of joint military exercises in Belarus did not appear in the news because of excellent journalism; they appeared because someone like Sturt or Frasier wanted them there.

De Payns was on his second coffee when he received the call to tell him he was needed. He rose to his feet and crossed the road to the Hotel George V. The sun had set, and cold was settling on Paris.

On the fifth floor, the DGSE guard opened the suite door. De Payns walked through to where Briffaut stood in the living area, looking through the glass at Gustav Eiffel's "temporary" structure which was lighting up for its nightly show.

"He's having a shower," said Briffaut, now in his shirtsleeves, no tie.

"How did it go?" asked de Payns.

"He had a lot to drink," said Briffaut, looking intently at the window frame in front of him. "We had a heart-to-heart, and he really talked. He's expecting us to hide him and his money."

"He thinks he's in Switzerland?" asked de Payns.

"He says the Russians are aware of leaks to the European services, and the prod anticipates everything they're planning. The Russians think Lotus is the leak."

"Does Lotus suspect there's another source?"

Briffaut shook his head slowly. "He didn't mention it, but the important thing for us is that the prod is authentic—authentic enough that the Russians are killing off the Lotus network to shut it down."

"Does he know which specific piece of information is really annoying the Russians?"

Briffaut looked at de Payns. "I tried to edge him into *Azzam*, Wagner, and possible assassinations, and he couldn't help me," said Briffaut. "If he was going to start singing, now would be the time, but he didn't. So I'm thinking the source the Russians are really looking for is the Starkand group. What do you think?"

De Payns realized his boss had been trying to unhitch the window, and he finally succeeded.

"But the *Azzam* prod was brought in by Degarde, from Lotus," said de Payns. "He's claiming no knowledge of that whole side of it?"

"Our friend is mainly worried because he's been spreading himself around the services," said Briffaut, fishing one of his Camels from the pack.

"How thin?" asked de Payns.

"Germans won't take his calls, and the Americans said no to a meeting," said Briffaut. "It turns out he's also been talking to the British and the Israelis . . . and God knows who else."

"I guess polygamy has its risks," said de Payns, accepting a cigarette.

"The man's a whore," said Briffaut, lighting up and holding the flame for de Payns. "He suited us while it suited us. But now he's admitting to having talked to us more than the others, we can't have anything more to do with him."

De Payns agreed. "Spoiled meat?"

Briffaut looked down on the street. "No one must know that we had him. The risk of embarrassment is too high."

They exhaled their smoke through the opened window, aware it was illegal to smoke in a French hotel.

"Had him?" asked de Payns. "That sounds terminal. What happens now?"

"We'll give him that," said Briffaut, pointing to a metal brief-case on the table. "That's his one million euro, which should buy him a room like this for a week."

"One million?" echoed de Payns, grimacing.

"Yes, he gets his money," said Briffaut. "France honors its promises."

De Payns laughed. "Where do I drop him?"

Briffaut shrugged. "Anywhere in Paris, so long as it's safe for you and Danny."

"And that's it?" asked de Payns.

"We can't use him anymore, and we can't have him associated with France. Drop him off somewhere, go home, and see the family."

De Payns dragged on his smoke. "What about *his* family?"

"He's cut them loose," said Briffaut, shaking his head and making a face. "He demanded an exfiltration just for himself. His wife and kids are probably in a basement right now."

"For a million euro?"

"And a French passport and a new identity." The director of Y Division allowed himself a rare smile. "A deal's a deal."

Lotus held the briefcase close to his chest, like a child who doesn't want to surrender their teddy bear. As they descended to the parking garage in the elevator, Lotus was chipper, even pleased with himself, despite the attentions of the FSB.

De Payns kept silent, lest he make a comment about the man's family and their fate. He keyed the radio and told Danny they'd be emerging in a couple of minutes, heading north.

They got in the DGSE car, and Lotus couldn't help himself. "Where are we going?"

"Can't say," said de Payns. "You'll see when we get there."

"Your boss told me it's in the fifth arrondissement," said Lotus. "That was the deal."

De Payns drove north up the Avenue George V, bathed in neon signs that beckoned people for a drink and a meal. They crossed the Champs-Élysée into a precinct of smaller hotels and expensive bars.

"I do love this city," said Lotus, smiling now.

They took a left-hand turn, followed a one-way street system, and ended up outside the Hôtel Balzac, where de Payns pulled the car to a stop.

"The Balzac?" said Lotus, peering through the side window with disappointment. "Not what I expected."

"You're not booked into the Balzac," said de Payns.

Lotus hugged the briefcase closer. "Then why are we here?"

"This is where you get out."

Lotus stared at him. "I can't get out here, on the street."

"Where else would you get out of this car?" replied de Payns, deadpanning him.

Lotus's Adam's apple bobbed. "On the streets of Paris, I'm a dead man! The FSB are following me, remember?!"

De Payns nodded. If the FSB didn't pick him up, the Russian mob certainly would.

"I demand to speak with Monsieur de Murat," said Lotus, referring to Briffaut. "We had a deal!"

"The deal is that briefcase," said de Payns. Glancing in the rearview mirror, he saw Danny had stopped forty meters behind him. "You've been paid a million euro. Time to go."

"Go? I can't go anywhere," spluttered Lotus, his usually sleazy voice now whiny and needy. "They'll find me and kill me, have you thought about that?"

"Have you thought about where your family is right now?" asked de Payns, leaning across the man's chest and opening the passenger door from the inside. "Because I have."

"Leave my family out of it."

"Like you did?" replied de Payns. He waited for a woman with a pram to walk past, then he reached under his seat and presented a CZ 9mm handgun, which he held low at Lotus's bladder.

"You can't do this," said Lotus.

"You either get out and walk with your money, or I shoot you and keep the briefcase. Your call."

Lotus's face froze in fear, his eyes wide in understanding. He slowly reached down, unclicked his seatbelt, and inched sideways, putting one foot and then the other on the pavement, as if in a trance.

"Don't forget this," said de Payns, grabbing the wheelie suitcase from the back seat and throwing it out the door after Lotus.

"You—you can't do this," Lotus pleaded.

"And yet, there you are," said de Payns, reaching for the door.

"You damn French," said Lotus, rage replacing fear. "You make a deal and then you fuck me!"

"Don't spend it all at once," said de Payns, accelerating into the traffic of Rue Balzac.

His last vision of Lotus was of a confused man, hugging his money.

CHAPTER
THIRTY-FIVE

Romy added an extra squirt of Arpège and assessed herself in the mirror. There weren't too many lines around her eyes, and her blonde hair was naturally thick. Her figure was still trim, even after two natural births in her thirties.

The smell of pancakes was wafting under the door of the bathroom, and she heard the yelps of competitive male conversation about soccer and action scenes in movies, her boys trying to outdo each other in front of their beloved father. She smiled to herself; they were both slightly flat when he went away, and yet all he had to do was turn up for breakfast and Oliver and Patrick would come alive like flowers turning to the sun.

She felt torn about the boys—they knew there was something special about their father, and they tried to play to it when they could, even if they knew her reticence about her husband's macho side. She'd gone along with the karate lessons, although she wasn't totally comfortable about Sensei John's nostrums for life. But she had succeeded in persuading Alec to sell his motorbike before Patrick was born, and she'd warned her sons off rugby, even though they were fascinated with the game their father had played at boarding school.

She applied lipstick, staring at herself and wondering what she was going to do about this family. Her eruption on the beach at Deauville had taken her by surprise as much as it had hurt Alec. She'd known a reckoning was coming as her PhD had drawn to its conclusion and Oliver had started school. But she hadn't grappled with how much bitterness she felt until she was sitting on that beach destroying him. She'd gone too far, said too much. But she was alone, and angry with Alec for making her feel so weak. Becoming immersed in her dream job hadn't helped. And neither had her attraction to her boss, David. It wasn't just his looks and his easy sense of humor. He was an intellectual with plans to improve the world. He shared his thoughts with Romy, while her own husband kept everything to himself, occasionally creeping around the apartment at night or breaking into paranoia as he challenged her about conversations she'd had. Romy needed to speak about her husband—as every woman did—and in Ana she'd found someone who understood what she was going through and offered her unconditional support.

"Coffee's ready," Alec called from the kitchen.

Romy stood straight, flattened her blouse against her belly, and smacked her lips at the mirror.

She turned to go, then looked back. Then she added one more squirt of Arpège to her décolletage, before walking out to join her men.

The WIP meeting finished at 10:29 sharp, the Tirol Council think-tankers being mindful of David's edict that no meeting should last longer than half an hour.

Romy took a photo of the whiteboard that contained her green energy financing plan, before wiping it clean.

"Excellent presentation, Romy," came a male voice from behind her, as the participants left the meeting room. "I hope Gerard took notes; he might learn how to stop sending us all to sleep."

Romy turned with a smile to face David. He was an athletic, handsome man in his early forties who wore expensive suits and no tie.

"Gerard needs to have PowerPoint taken away from him," she joked. "It's become his security blanket."

"I need to remind people that we're not Americans," said David, with a flash of good dentistry. "Not everything has to be a slideshow."

He pushed his hands into his pockets as Romy collected her laptop from the conference table. "Your matrix of how the energy transition will be financed?" continued David. "It's going to be an influential white paper, but I'd like the OECD to see it first."

Romy looked at him, aware she was holding her laptop between them as if it were a barrier. "I'd like that."

"When I mentioned it to Klaus last week, he was excited and thought he'd like to prioritize it into the OECD agenda," said David. "I think this is something we can get into a briefing format for him before we publish it."

"Sounds great," said Romy.

David nodded and smiled. "I'd like you to present to Klaus, perhaps at the end of the week? If he finds it as impressive as I do, we might get an OECD mandate for our energy projects."

"Okay," she said, slightly bashful. She'd been out of the workforce long enough to have lost her youthful confidence, and now she found it hard to take praise. Ana had chided her for it, reminding her that a PhD from the Sorbonne put her in a select group of people who were expected to be thought leaders.

"I think we should go over it together," said David, with a full-beam smile. "How about dinner?"

CHAPTER
THIRTY-SIX

Jim Valley eyed the second round of vodkas being placed on the table in front of him and considered his position. He was at a sensitive point with the Russian FSB asset they were calling Keratine. The man was reluctant to give himself totally to the Company, even as he knew Paris had compromising information: Keratine's son was gay, and Keratine was concealing it. The fact that the Russian hadn't reported the DGSE approach to his masters was a jailable offense. Keratine was screwed, but he was pushing back.

"A second round?" Jim asked Keratine.

They were in the main bar of the Baku Marriott, looking over the Caspian Sea, having enjoyed a lunch that had finished with a shot of vodka. The meeting had failed to progress their arrangement. Paris wanted Keratine to start producing, while Keratine was still weighing up two evils: he could be hanged by Russia for spying for the French, or the French could expose his son, who would then be subject to the military's brutal "conversion therapy" if the Russians could catch him.

Keratine smiled wryly. "You're going to lure me into some dangerous and treacherous places," he said, raising a shot glass. "I need to trust you."

"So, we drink vodka for lunch, and then I'm okay?" replied Valley. "Sounds very Russian to me."

Keratine laughed and pushed the other shot glass toward the Frenchman. "You have placed me and my family in a terrible situation. I'm sure a few drinks won't alter your dominant position."

"You made a cryptic comment to me the last time we met," said Valley, picking up the glass. "You said the Russian services knew about a traitor and you were on to him."

"Yes, I did," said Keratine, throwing down the vodka. "That situation has largely been cleaned up. The rats have been caught."

Valley drained his glass, and Keratine raised his hand for the waitress.

"What about that other matter?" asked Valley. "You were going to get me more details."

Keratine issued a request to the waitress, and they watched her line up glasses on a tray and commence pouring.

"I have an extra detail, but we have to agree on the depth of our trust," said Keratine, his eyes boring into Valley's. "You see, the Russian services have rules and procedures, but Lenny Varnachev can act any way he sees fit."

Valley nodded as the waitress arrived with the vodkas.

"Given that several European services are aware of a possible assassination," said Valley, as the waitress left, "I'd say Wagner Group is a bit leaky about the plot."

"Certainly," said Keratine, lifting a shot glass and nodding for Valley to do the same. "But none of those services has the name Lazar Suburov attached to its intel, and I'd like it to stay that way."

Valley raised his glass, and they both drank.

"And what of you, Monsieur Guy?" asked Keratine, eying another vodka. "Who else are you dealing with in my corner of the world?"

Valley smiled. "It's better if you talk and I listen."

"I mean," said Keratine, reaching for another glass, "we've just shut down a ring of traitors who were supplying to the West, so I wonder who else you might be running?"

Valley chuckled as he too reached for a glass. "You were saying? About the assassination?"

They drank.

"You tell me something about yourself, Guy, and then we talk," said Keratine. "I can't talk to a ghost."

"You've probably already worked it out," said Valley. "You FSB guys are pretty smart."

"Okay," said Keratine, taking another vodka. "I guess you're French special forces, served in Africa or the Middle East, and you've also got some brains so they pushed you sideways into the Company before you started failing your Marines physicals."

Valley roared with laughter and grabbed a shot glass. "You're a funny guy, Lazar," he said, and downed the vodka. "Pity you're not a chatty guy."

Keratine took his final glass and raised it at Valley, who picked up his own. "Libyans," said Keratine, sculling the vodka, and raising his hand to summon the waitress. "The thing will be carried out by Libyans. That's all I have."

"Wagner's hitters are from Libya?" asked Valley.

Keratine shrugged. "Varnachev recently met with Haftar's people on a superyacht, I'm told. I'm assuming he's tied up with Libya."

"That'll do for now," said Valley. "And by the way, I've never failed a physical."

Valley finally got away from Keratine at around 8:00 p.m. and headed for his suite. He could outdrink most people, but he was close to passing out as he hit the bed. He'd managed to vomit a couple of times in the restaurant toilets, to maintain some sobriety, but he was still very drunk. As his face sunk into the pillow, a knock came at the door. He staggered over to it, his head swirling. He wasn't armed, and he wondered if Keratine had been spinning him along, his FSB henchmen just waiting until he was alone in a room. Through the peephole he saw a beautiful woman in the hallway. He opened the door and saw she was tall and blonde and wearing a black fur coat. When she opened the coat, she was wearing nothing but her high heels.

"Lazar sent me," she said, with a smile. "May I come in?"

Valley immediately sensed a trap, but he had no choice. If he said no, he risked alienating his new friend, but to sleep with her could lead to blackmail, since the major hotels in this part of the world were infiltrated by the Russian services and the room was most certainly filled with FSB cameras.

Valley put on a smile, called her in, gave her a kiss, and asked if she could have a shower first. When the woman had left for the bathroom, Valley leaned into the sofa back so the cameras could not see what came next: he put his fingers down his throat and vomited, a painful experience given his throat was already raw from the vomits he'd forced during the afternoon. When the naked woman emerged five minutes later, she found the Frenchman lying in a pool of vomit, asleep on the sofa, and when she couldn't wake him, she left.

Keratine found Valley at the breakfast buffet the following morning and laughed at the Frenchie who couldn't handle his drink.

"And I thought about making you an honorary Russian," said Keratine, handing Valley a foil of Advils. "If you can't rally for a woman like that, you're no countryman of mine."

As Valley nursed a hangover and sipped strong coffee, he wondered what the Company was going to do with Lazar Suburov.

CHAPTER
THIRTY-SEVEN

"Dr. Marlene is in the building," said Briffaut, stirring three sugars into his morning coffee.

De Payns tensed. "How nice for her."

He'd only dropped into the boss's office to see if Jim Valley was getting anywhere with Keratine.

Briffaut gestured for de Payns to sit. "We had an agreement about Dr. Marlene."

"I'll do it," snapped de Payns, almost reflexively, "but not right now—I can't risk being put on medical in the middle of Operation Ellipse."

Briffaut sipped at his coffee. "This is about duty of care. I didn't want to say it, mon cher, but you're making me."

"No," said de Payns, shaking his head and unable to look at Briffaut. "Just give me—"

"She's waiting for you in interview room six," said Briffaut. "Go talk to her."

De Payns stood slowly, feeling like a condemned man. He

lingered, hoping Briffaut might change his mind, but the boss turned his focus to a pile of reports on his desk. "Go," he said again, without looking up.

De Payns left the office and stalked to the second-floor kitchenette. Taking a deep breath, he thought about how he would deal with Dr. Marlene. He'd be amenable and open, enough to please Briffaut, while not allowing the session to go too deep.

The only pods left in the canister beside the coffee machine were mint-flavored. He cursed but then, spying what he thought was a normal espresso at the bottom of the container, he shoved his hand in and dug around for it.

"Caught with your hand in the jar again," said a voice behind him. "Might have to report this."

De Payns turned and saw Shrek. "You're always creeping up on people. We need to get you some squeaky shoes."

They shook hands, gave each other a slap on the arm. "What brings you in?" asked de Payns, setting up the coffee pod.

"Then I'd have to kill you," said Shrek. "And you may not like that."

"If you did, I'd have to unfriend you—in a nonviolent way, of course."

"*Évidemment*," said Shrek, smirking. "At least now I know who's stealing the real coffee."

De Payns shook his head as the machine chugged out coffee into his mug. "Who buys this flavored shit?"

"Thought that was you," said Shrek. "The orange ones, last week?"

"I blame you for the Turkish delight—it's like a cup of incense."

Shrek looked around to see who was close. "Lotus arrive okay?"

"Yes," said de Payns, putting sugar in his coffee. "The FSB kept an eye on everything."

"More than seven hours and less than eight," said de Payns, as evenly as he could. Dr. Marlene was on to the same thing his doctor usually harassed him about: his sleep patterns.

"Is that uninterrupted sleep?" she asked.

De Payns paused and observed the woman. Fine-featured, her dark hair was cut in a bob, and she wore expensive but understated clothes: cashmere cardigan, pleated skirt, mid-heel shoes with no hint of toenail. She was very smart and refined, and de Payns fought the urge to manipulate her.

"I wake up a bit, I guess," he said.

"What happens when you wake up?" she asked.

Marlene had dragged the chairs away from the interview table and arranged them in the open, facing each other, with little space between them. Certainly not enough to get away with lying.

"Well, that depends if my wife is awake," he started with a raised eyebrow, but held up his hand. "I'm sorry, let me . . ."

Marlene smirked and crossed her legs on the other side, a sure female sign of a conversation having grabbed her interest. "You were going to misdirect me," she said, smiling.

De Payns laughed. "Yes, but I stopped myself. How strange is that?"

"It's excellent," she said. "Let's talk."

They went through the stress of the job, the fears he lived with, and even delved into his Anglo-French background.

"I remember seeing in your file," she said, contemplative, "that you were at Cambridge for a while?"

De Payns paused, wondering if they were going to have the "Moran" chat. He'd been living with the Morans after leaving school and had been accepted as a foreign intake at their college, Magdalene at Cambridge. It wasn't until he was halfway through his first year that he felt the pull of his family heritage and its Templar lineage, and he'd left Cambridge to join the French air force.

"Perhaps an English institution made me realize my inherent Frenchness," said de Payns. "Or maybe I just hated university."

"Tell me about the young Alec," Marlene said. "Alec the fighter pilot. Were you happy, serious, ambitious?"

De Payns breathed out. "I was a young man who'd found something he was really good at, and it gave me a sense of purpose. Yes, there were parties and motorbikes and lots of bad behavior when we were off base, but there was focus too. I was twenty-one, twenty-two, and flying missions over the Balkans. It was stressful, dangerous, high-adrenaline stuff, and I loved it."

"You met your wife during these years?"

De Payns paused. He wanted to tell her to mind her own business but stopped himself. "Yes, that's the Alec she fell in love with. The dashing pilot who liked a laugh and a drink."

"Past tense?"

"She asked me to sell my motorbike before our first son was born . . ."

"And you complied?"

"Well," he said with a smile, "she asked nicely."

Marlene got him talking about their courtship, the wedding, and his English mother. But as hard as he tried to steer her away, Marlene kept bringing him back to his job with the DGSE and what it was doing to his relationship. He admitted that it was hard to be married to a strong, educated woman and expect her to ask no questions about where he was or what he was doing.

"She can't call me or text me for days sometimes," he said. "She has to pretend that this is all normal, to the kids and her friends. Her closest friend has noticed something's off, and she's getting nosy."

"Women do that," said Marlene.

"Clearly," said de Payns. "It's doing Romy's head in, and she's told me that she's over it."

"How do you communicate when you're home?"

De Payns felt embarrassed. "We fight, or it's tense and we avoid talking."

"Physical fights?"

"No," said de Payns. "Never that."

"Do you scare her?"

"Yes," said de Payns, feeling uncomfortable. "Some of my actions frighten her."

"Like?"

"Like a couple of drunks were hassling her, so I stopped them."

"Where?" asked Marlene.

"The Metro," he admitted. "The boys were there. I'm not proud of it."

"Do you have other women?" she asked.

"*No!*" he said, sitting up abruptly, not so cool anymore. "God, no—that's not even . . . I mean, shit, *no.*"

"And her?"

De Payns shifted in his seat. "No. I don't think so. I mean, I trust this woman with my life. I see the way men look at her, but she doesn't play around."

"No new friends, new colleagues that she talks about?"

De Payns shook his head, then paused. "Actually, she's really impressed by her new boss—David—but I think that's more of an ideological thing, you know?"

"Tell me."

He shrugged. "Climate change and so on."

"Yes?"

"Well, they agree on everything, I guess."

"I see," she said, eyes twinkling. "Is there a problem between you and Romy on this issue?"

"Not really," said de Payns. "I think clean energy is a great idea, but when a group of smart people just *agree* on everything all the time, then you don't have theories tested by reality."

"She pushes back on your opinion?"

"We can laugh at our different views of the world, but lately she's acting like her think tank is the savior of the planet while my work uses violence to solve problems."

"But violence is a big part of your work, yes?" Marlene stated matter-of-factly. "Do you think that affects your behavior outside work? You mentioned the drunks, for example. Is there anything else?"

De Payns closed his eyes. Should he risk going deeper? Well, he was in it now. "Yes," he admitted. "I have these dreams." He described being woken by nightmares that he couldn't remember. The only trace that remained, after he was fully conscious, was pure terror.

"I see," said Marlene, nodding thoughtfully. "I've heard around the Company that we lost a colleague recently," she said. "Were you close?"

"No, not close, but I knew him."

"Is he in your nightmares?"

De Payns sighed and looked out the window. "My nightmare is not what happens when I'm asleep—it's a reality. The colleague you're talking about? The bad guys came to his house, and they killed him in front of his family. *That's* the nightmare."

"I get it," said Marlene, grimacing.

"What a normal person would call paranoia is my reality," said de Payns. "It's a reality for our colleague's wife and daughter; it happened in their home. They still live with that."

"That makes you feel unsafe?"

"It makes us all feel unsafe," he said, waving his hand to encompass the building they were sitting in. "We do a very tough job, but our weak spot is our families."

"You feel responsible for something you can't really control?"

De Payns nodded. He could sense something welling up in him. "If anything terrible happened to my family, it would be my fault. I can't let that happen."

Dr. Marlene's face changed slightly. "What do you do when you wake in fright?"

De Payns could feel himself heading for the cliff. "I'm not ready to retire, you know that, right?"

Marlene smiled. "Your boss doesn't want to see you retired."

"And yet here we are."

Dr. Marlene maintained eye contact and dropped her notepad onto the carpet. "I wasn't here. We didn't talk. You're not in my diary. I'm here to see Dominic," she said.

De Payns took a deep breath and tried to exhale slowly, but the air came out in a whoosh. "Okay, so a few nights ago, I had the nightmare."

"What did you do?"

De Payns shrugged. "Walked around in the dark, listened for sounds, checked the boys, tested the locks, looked for bad guys on the street . . ."

"What time of night are we talking about?"

"Around two."

"Fully awake?"

De Payns laughed. "Oh, yeah. Heart pumping, ready to fight."

"You wake up in that state?"

"Yes," said de Payns. "I wake up panting."

"So, you checked on the house and the kids, and then . . ."

"I sat on the sofa in front of the TV. Waiting."

"Waiting for what?"

De Payns shook his head. "Whatever is coming."

"What would you do to the threat?"

"Shoot it, most probably," said de Payns.

"With what?"

"The handgun."

Dr. Marlene looked at him. "You have a gun at home?"

"Yes, I do my rounds of the house with my pistol."

"How long did you wait?"

"I was on the sofa for—I don't know—five or six minutes."

"And then?"

"My wife came and got me," he said, immediately realizing how childish that sounded.

"How did she react to the gun?"

"She took it away from me."

"Was she scared?"

"She was crying."

"Why?"

De Payns looked at the floor, a dampness at the corner of his eyes. "You know why."

"Tell me, Alec."

De Payns shook his head. "She thought I might kill myself."

They sat in silence for a few seconds.

"She just misread the situation," said de Payns, having recovered from the slip.

"The situation was right in front of her," said Dr. Marlene. "Maybe she saw what she saw?"

De Payns smiled. "No, I was having a bad night, that's all," he spoke firmly, for his own benefit as much as the doctor's. "There was nothing to see."

CHAPTER
THIRTY-EIGHT

Briffaut shoved a packet of papers across his desk. "That's the maildrop you witnessed in Bern yesterday. It arrived at our consulate in Geneva this morning."

De Payns looked at the five pages: each one was a reconnaissance report raised for Russia's "Syria Directorate," the Kremlin's code for FSB. The reconnaissance material covered Libya's major oil-and-gas production locations, its export terminals, and the Italian terminus for the Greenstream gas pipeline that brought gas from Libya and pumped it into Europe.

"Aside from Gela," said Briffaut, "all of the Russian recon sites are in western Libya, under the control of the GNA."

The Government of National Accord was the US-backed government that General Haftar was so determined to overthrow with the help of the Russians.

"It's not news that the Kremlin has its eyes on Libyan gas, but I still want to know who's feeding it to us," said Briffaut, pushing a file toward de Payns. "Now you're here, have a look at what we learned from the Brits."

De Payns went back to his office and sorted through the Maypole material. The British had received the same documents that Starkand had dropped to the French, and SIS had concluded they were being steered toward a view of Russia's intentions generally, and more specifically a Wagner-supported energy strategy. The British were wary, said the external liaison officer's notes. There was also pressure from the Foreign Office warning SIS not to concern itself with Russia's cornering of European gas given the UK's intention to move to green energy.

It was clear the Company had moved faster than SIS on Starkand, capturing him on camera, along with the woman he'd been seen with in Portofino and Bern; she was thought to be his handler. It put the Company in the ascendant when it came to information sharing, except for one small detail: SIS believed a person who looked like Starkand had been in the official party of a photo opportunity organized by the South African energy minister's office two years earlier, to publicize a commitment to offshore wind turbines on their southern coast. The man in the photo was Raymond Quinette, a Belgian clean-energy consultant with a mandate from some of the biggest investment banks in Europe.

De Payns flipped the page in Briffaut's file and found a photograph lifted from a newspaper. It wasn't exactly a crisp image, and de Payns fished in his second drawer for his magnifying glass. In the foreground of the picture were two smiling South African politicians and two Danish engineers; in the background was a windswept headland, overlooking the Southern Ocean. At the back of the group stood a middle-aged man wearing a cap and sunglasses. His jaw and mouth looked familiar. Could be Starkand, but inconclusive.

De Payns looked at his watch: just past four, giving him an hour before he was supposed to clock off. He reached for his secure landline phone and hit two buttons.

"Lars," he said, when the BER–E Lars Magnus picked up on the other end. "Is someone working on this Raymond Quinette name?"

"Yes, but it doesn't lead anywhere."

"Is he from a service? Is it industrial espionage?"

Magnus paused. "Hard to tell. The South Africans are trying to attract a billion US dollars of investment into their green energy program, and we think there was Russian money in the wind turbines."

"Was?"

"Some negative press was leaked about Putin's designs on Africa's energy system, and the use of Wagner mercenaries in Sudan and Mali. Suddenly, the banks were pulling out."

"Quinette is Belgian apparently, from an energy consultancy. What was the firm called?"

"Neptune Energy, incorporated in Brussels but no longer around."

"If this is our guy, he's dropping energy prod that implicates Putin," said de Payns. "Have we considered that he works for a company that competes with the Russian energy companies Gazprom and Rosneft?"

"We're considering everything, but we need a name. The material he's dropping is very serious, and while it's unlikely that Putin will invade Ukraine, if he does we're looking at a real stranglehold on gas into Europe. We're assuming that's what these drops hint at."

De Payns thanked him. "I know you're answering to the boss, but can you at least let me know if you find a name or any known aliases for Quinette?"

"Sure thing," said Magnus.

De Payns was preparing to leave for the day, stacking his files in his safe and twirling the combination wheel, when there was a rap at the door.

"Yes?"

He turned and found Shrek in the doorway. "Boss is waiting for us at Levallois," said Shrek, referring to the headquarters of the DGSI, the internal intelligence service, also known as the Cousins.

Shrek and de Payns made good time considering it was the beginning of the rush hour and to get to Levallois in the west of Paris meant using the commuter freeways and crossing the Boulevard Périphérique that encircled the city.

"What's this all about?" asked de Payns, blowing cigarette smoke out the window as Shrek drove.

"I'm thinking we have a breakthrough on the Degarde situation," said Shrek, as cagey as ever.

"The boss had you working on that?"

"Yep," said Shrek. "I worked on a video of the Russians, but that's about it."

"I identified one of them," said de Payns. "His name was Mikhail, a bodyguard on the superyacht."

"Wagner Group?" asked Shrek.

"He was guarding a senior Wagner guy," said de Payns, "so I assume yes."

They stopped at the DGSI security gates and were directed to the intelligence section. Inside the secure area of the building, Briffaut was sitting beside Marie Lafont at a kitchen table, talking into a phone.

Marie Lafont stood. "DGSI picked him up in Saint-Denis," she said.

"Who?" asked de Payns.

"Mikhail Manturov," she said. "You spoke to him on *Azzam* apparently."

They waited for Briffaut to finish on the phone, then the four of them walked the hallway to a guarded checkpoint and descended a flight of stairs that led them to a set of doors. "I'll go in with Aguilar," said Briffaut, handing an earpiece to de Payns before turning to Shrek and Lafont. "You two observe and feed us if anything occurs to you."

The interrogation cell featured a steel table and a bolted-down chair on one side, two normal chairs on the other. Mikhail Manturov was wearing a pale green tracksuit, his muscular frame squeezing out through the shoulders and arms of his sweatshirt. His feet were bare.

"Quite the night," said Briffaut, sitting.

"Who are you?" snarled the Russian, in good French.

"I'm not confused," said Briffaut, his tone light. "But I believe you were when the cops picked you up staggering around in Square Alex-Biscarre?"

The Russian shrugged. "I'd had a few drinks. Not like a Frenchman to worry about that."

"When you threaten a cop, we take notice," said Briffaut. "Even more so when you suggest that bad luck will come to the police officer's family unless you're released."

Manturov raised an eyebrow and nodded, but he was looking at de Payns. "I know you?"

"I doubt it," said de Payns. "What's your occupation, Mikhail?"

"Backpacker," he said. "From Rostov."

"That's a good haircut for a backpacker," de Payns commented, nodding at the army crew cut. "What happened to the man bun?"

Manturov shook his head, confused by the term. "What is that?"

"What do you do in Rostov, Mikhail?"

Manturov chewed on the inside of his mouth. "I'm a barman, work on fishing boats, that sort of thing."

"What are you doing in Paris?" asked Briffaut.

"Just living on savings, staying in the hostels. You know: going to bars, doing Paris."

Lafont's voice crackled in de Payns's ear: "He doesn't live in a hostel—it's a Russian-owned private hotel. We've found paramilitary clothes in his room."

Briffaut pulled a Camel from his coat. "Rostov . . ." he mused, lighting the smoke. "Means you speak Ukrainian, as well as Russian."

Manturov's face hardened, his pale eyes squinting. "I guess you're not a cop."

"I guess you're not a backpacker," said Briffaut, looking around for an ashtray. "Backpackers don't need paramilitary clothing or stupid haircuts."

"In that case, I guess you're not a backpacker either," said Manturov, smiling.

"No," said Briffaut, going along with the joke. "I'm not. Where were you on February second?"

"I've been in Paris for a month," said Manturov, shifting his weight.

"Which part of Paris were you in on that date?" asked de Payns.

Manturov shrugged. "Who did you say you were?"

"I didn't," said de Payns. "You don't remember that night?"

Manturov turned up his palms. "Maybe I was drinking. Remind me."

"You'd remember raping a woman, non? Especially if it was in front of her young daughter?"

Manturov transformed, the backpacker smirk giving way to a military stone face. "That's a very specific detail."

"It was a very specific night," said de Payns.

"I guess I need a lawyer."

"I guess you're out of luck," said Briffaut.

"This is France," said Manturov, trying to engage in a staring contest with Briffaut. "I have my rights."

"Who said we're in France?" replied Briffaut, winning the contest.

"You have to charge me," said the Russian, still heavy but with a slight whine in his voice.

"With what?" asked Briffaut, sucking on his smoke.

"This murder . . ."

"I didn't accuse you of murder."

"I mean rape," said Manturov, slightly too quickly. "Excuse my French."

"You haven't admitted to anything," said Briffaut, "so who's talking about a crime?"

Manturov nodded slowly. "Can I have a smoke?"

"No," said Briffaut. "Perhaps we can move on from the crime and talk about other things."

Manturov's nostrils flared, and de Payns could see him trying to breathe without using his mouth, a technique used by military people to stay mentally acute. "Other things? We back to being drunk in a park?"

"You seem to be a fan of French law, so you'd be aware of how we treat mercenaries?" said Briffaut.

Manturov gulped. "Mercenaries?"

"If you're a soldier being paid by anyone except a government, you have no legal protections in France," said Briffaut. "You're not a combatant, and you're not a prisoner of war. You aware of that?"

Manturov tried to stay defiant, but his pupils dilated.

"Under French law, you're a hostile military alien, meaning no trial, no rights, no Geneva Convention. You're just a nonperson locked up in a French internal security cell."

Manturov held up his right hand, the manacle chain clanking. "Let's stop for a second."

"I doubt the embassy is coming for you," said Briffaut. "Because the whole point of mercenaries is that the embassy is never invoked."

Manturov looked at his hands.

"And I can assure you," said Briffaut, "that our location is the last place your employers will ever attack."

"I can make a phone call," spluttered the Russian.

"Your hearing is good," said Briffaut, standing. "But your comprehension is shit."

"Wait," said Manturov, struggling for something more to say. "Look, I—"

"I'll tell you what I'll do," said Briffaut, leaning on the table, balanced on two sets of boxer's knuckles. "There's been a misunderstanding, obviously, so what I might do is have a chat to some Russians I know . . ."

"Don't do that," said Manturov hastily. "There's no need."

Briffaut turned to de Payns, affecting concern. "I think we know someone at that private military group . . . What are they called again?"

"Wagner Group, I think," said de Payns. "And you're right: there was that really nice fellow who asked us to call if we ever needed help."

"Yes," said Briffaut. "Boris, I think."

"Boris Orlevski," said de Payns, clicking his fingers.

"We should contact him—what do you say, Mikhail?"

Manturov's large, squarish head sagged slightly, and he fixed his gaze on the wall. "I don't know who you're talking about," he said mechanically.

"Not to worry," said Briffaut. "We'll see if he knows you."

Manturov turned to him. "Maybe you shouldn't."

"Don't be modest. Boris should hear how helpful you've been to the French services, and I want you to get the credit."

Manturov stretched his neck and looked at the ceiling. "This is France, and I have my rights, even in a cell."

"Okay," said Briffaut, heading for the door. "I'll get Boris down here. Might even release you into his custody."

As the Russian stood and struggled against his chains, Briffaut and de Payns left the room.

CHAPTER
THIRTY-NINE

De Payns and Lafont sat next to each other, facing Briffaut and Shrek in the back of the Viano.

"We have another Maypole tonight," said Briffaut. "With the Russians this time."

Night had fallen on Paris, and de Payns could see that yet again he would be missing the family meal and bath time. Romy would be stewing when he got home.

"The Russians?" he asked. "Who called the meeting?"

"Novak," said Lafont, meaning Tatyana Novak, SVR head of station at Russia's embassy in Paris. "She was quite urgent about it."

"That's Putin-urgent," said Briffaut. "The Russian services only move that fast if the order comes from the Kremlin."

De Payns nodded, picking up on the way his colleagues were staring at him. "You two cooking up something?"

"Keratine is not producing as he should," said Lafont. "Our man in the East managed to get a detail on the Vulcan assassination. Keratine says Wagner will use Libyans to do it, which we already know to be true. But Keratine is not reliable."

Briffaut cut in. "He told Jim they'd cleaned up a major traitor ring that was feeding the West, but he wanted to know who else Jim is running."

"Acknowledging Lotus but wanting us to talk about Starkand?" asked de Payns.

"Yes," said Briffaut. "That's our interpretation. But he also tried a blackmail trap on Jim, so I think we'll burn him."

"What did Keratine do?"

"Insisted on drinking vodka with Jim all afternoon and then sent a prostitute to his room."

"Was it set up by the FSB?"

"No way to tell," said Lafont. "We're thinking of dropping some bait to the Russians at the Maypole, and we'll see if they were monitoring Keratine the whole time."

The Maypole was conducted in an old hearing room on the ground floor of the Cat. Leading the French team was Richard Larmes, head of the Company's external liaison department. His counterpart was a Russian embassy officer who looked like Marlon Brando, before the actor needed elastic waistbands: Sergei Valkov, a suave SVR man. Aside from Lafont and Larmes, the French contingent was bolstered by Briffaut and de Payns, who sat at a DGSE listening post in the room next door.

Tatyana Novak sat opposite Richard Larmes, her signature helmet of immaculate blonde hair refusing to budge even when she looked around for her pen. The Russian team was rounded out by the embassy longtimer Konstantin Osterman, who pretended to be doodling on a piece of paper in front of him.

Tatyana Novak kicked off after Richard Larmes had called the meeting to order. She told the French that a manipulated leak on their side was spreading false intelligence among other services, and that this represented a national security breach for Russia. It was crucial that they discover the identity of the leaker.

Novak paused from her introduction and looked straight through Larmes. "If the DGSE is not willing to help," she said bluntly, "we'd consider this destabilization operation against Russia to be coming from the French, which would create serious tension between our two countries."

Larmes, who had experience with Russian tactics, responded with a charming smile. "We'd be more than happy to help. But may I ask, how did you identify this leak?"

Novak met the French charm with professional hardness. "We know that this person we call Dragonfly is sending false information against us to various European embassies."

"Were those packages sent to Russian embassies?" asked Lafont, playing dumb.

"No," said Novak, face like a doll and heart like a hammer. "We were given the Dragonfly product by a friendly service."

"By which you mean BND?" prompted Lafont. "The Germans?"

"Well . . ." said Novak.

"Come on, Tatyana," said Richard. "This is a Maypole that *you* asked for. We have to know who is receiving this misinformation product if you want our cooperation."

"Okay, Germany," said Novak. "But you knew that already."

"I'd still rather be told."

Novak tapped her pen. "Let's start with the basics: every piece of product in these drops is about Russian military movements and top-secret correspondence with other nations. This is not the sort of leak that is conducive to stability in Europe, and it's naive to think a single individual is behind it."

Lafont laughed inwardly. Russia preferred European instability because it was seen as promoting Russian strength.

"We're aware," said Lafont.

"It would be greatly appreciated if Russia had the support of our French friends on this," replied Tatyana with a fake smile, knowing the DGSE would already be working on it.

Larmes nodded slowly, as if taking the Russian request seriously. "But your Dragonfly won't be easy to find, and it would monopolize a lot of our resources."

Novak pursed her lips. "As I said, a lack of interest on the part of the DGSE would be construed as hostile to Moscow. Surely you wouldn't want that?"

Lafont eyeballed the Russian, furious, but Larmes remained calm. "We have something that might be of interest to you," he said, handing over a large envelope that hinted at intelligence leaks from Russian officials in the Transcaucasia region. "That's a measure of our good faith," continued Larmes. "Perhaps you could share the latest status of your research. From what I understand, we're assuming Dragonfly is Russian or at least very well connected, right?"

Novak leaned away as if smelling something bad. "This person is not Russian."

"How do you know?" asked Lafont.

Konstantin Osterman finally raised his head from his doodling. "There is nothing in here that is alarming to a Russian," he said, deadpan. "The selection of leaks betrays a Western paranoia about Russian aggression."

Lafont nodded. "So, let's hear the Russian view. Any insights, given the prod?"

Novak and Osterman swapped a look, then Novak spoke. "Someone is being paid to leak material that destroys peace between Russia and the West. And when a person is paid for information, we all know what happens to the quality."

"You're saying this is false product?" asked Richard.

"No," said Novak. "I'm saying that a perfectly routine request to navigate through the Dardanelles can be made to look heinous in the context of it being stolen by a spy and trafficked into other services. The DSGE knows it better than most, non?"

Lafont allowed herself a small smile.

"So," continued Novak, "I'm concerned that France is encouraging this enterprise, rather than unmasking it . . ."

"Okay, enough," said Lafont, leaning across the table and looking Novak in the eye. "We don't know Dragonfly, or what is supposed to be achieved with these drops. We'd like to find the source, ourselves . . ."

"You're not doing a good job."

"Well, what can we help *you* with Tatyana?" asked Lafont, an edge in her voice. "Maybe there's something we can provide?"

Novak sat back, crossed her arms, and looked quickly at Osterman, who nodded slightly. "Perhaps you could verify a name?"

"Try me."

"Probably working for the Americans," she said. "Her name is Brenda."

Lafont shrugged. The name meant nothing to her, but even if she did recognize it, her response would be the same. "The name is not familiar, but I will check. Is there anything more you can tell us?"

Novak scoffed. "This isn't a fishing expedition, Marie."

Sergei Valkov raised his hand for silence and directed his gaze at Lafont. "I can tell you, Madame Lafont, that this 'Brenda' is not Dragonfly. Perhaps more senior, but not the same person."

"Okay," Lafont said, scribbling the name on a pad. "Anything else?"

Valkov was obviously the power in the room, because the

Russians looked at him while he made up his mind. He stared at Lafont, still as a sphinx. "We believe Brenda operates in Paris, and possibly Ukraine," said Valkov finally. "Perhaps this jogs the Company's memory?"

CHAPTER
FORTY

Lafont stayed at the Cat, and Briffaut offered de Payns a lift in his Viano. "So," said Briffaut as they headed south, "ever heard of Brenda?"

"No," said de Payns. "But I'd like to know who they're talking about."

"Paris and Ukraine!" said Briffaut. "We'll run the names, but you can chase it up."

Briffaut's phone buzzed. He grimaced and mumbled at the voice on the other end, and when he hung up, he looked at de Payns. "Mikhail wants to talk."

They arrived at Levallois just before 9:00 p.m. Mikhail Manturov was brought out of his cell and ushered into the interview room.

"I'll talk, but what do I get?" asked the Russian without preamble. "The Russians will harass my family and hunt me for the rest of my life."

"Or you can take your chances with the French military justice system, but that still means your family is exposed," said Briffaut. "And as soon as the mercenary prosecution is done, you'll be in a civilian court for murdering a government employee and raping his wife."

"I did neither of those things," said Mikhail, deflating slightly. "I'm a good soldier, but I'm not a bad person."

"Who did it?" asked Briffaut.

"What are you offering?"

"You won't hang," said Briffaut. "If you convince me it wasn't you who did the rape and murder that night, I can talk to the prosecutor, but you'll be my asset."

"A French asset?" replied Manturov, shaking his head.

"You'll get paid, but you'll work for it. It's better than what you'll get from Boris Orlevski."

"Okay," said Manturov. "But I need a story that I'm dead, killed by the French. I have to protect my mother and my sister."

Briffaut turned to de Payns, who nodded.

"Okay," said Briffaut. "We can do that. Who was the leader that night?"

"His name is Victor," said the Russian. "I don't know his last name; we all work with pseudonyms."

"What was he trying to discover?"

"I don't know, I wasn't briefed. I'm just the muscle."

"What was the conversation?"

"Victor wanted to know what the Frenchman had read in the files he brought back from Prague," said Manturov. "The target said to Victor, '*I don't really read them, I just look over them to check there's something there.*'"

"How did Victor know there was product coming into Paris, and at that time?"

Manturov shook his head. "He has a boss. That's where he gets his orders. He had a picture of the target, and we were told he was flying into Paris in a certain window of time."

"Victor's boss is Russian?"

"I assume so, but I never asked him."

"So," said Briffaut. "You followed him to his apartment?"

"Yes, Victor didn't want to go straight into the apartment the night the Frenchman returned in case he had a gun."

"So, you wait until he's at work, break in, and rape the wife, then wait for the man of the house to come home?"

"That's about it."

"What was Victor asking about specifically?"

"Victor asked the target if he'd seen any names in the prod," said Manturov, forehead creased in recollection. "And the Frenchman said he remembered something like *Azzam*. So then there's lots of yelling about *Azzam* and the Frenchman saying, '*I don't know about* Azzam.'"

"What did Victor want to know?"

Manturov made a face. "I think he wanted to know who gave him the information, and the Frenchman said he didn't know."

"He said, '*I don't know*'?" asked de Payns.

"He said words like, '*I don't know how it got there, it wasn't in the drop.*' Something like that."

Briffaut sneered. "That doesn't make sense, Mikhail. We have a deal, remember?"

Manturov paused. "The Frenchman was confused, Victor was angry."

"And then Victor killed him?"

Manturov sighed. "It went on too long, and Victor hit him once too often with his sidearm, and the Frenchman didn't wake up. Victor didn't want to kill him. At one point, he was talking about abducting him, taking him back to Marseille."

"Marseille?" asked de Payns. "That's Vieux Port, right?"

Manturov eyed him.

"Which yacht are you living on?"

"I don't remember the name," said Manturov. "It's Spanish and it never really stuck. I have a photo in my phone."

De Payns walked to the door and asked the security guard to bring in Manturov's bag.

"How many of you are living on the boat?" asked de Payns.

"Five," said Manturov, as the guard came in with the bag.

"You planning something?" de Payns asked, rummaging in a gym bag filled with clothes.

"Not really."

"Sounds like something," said Briffaut. "Five Wagner mercenaries on a yacht in Marseille, coming up to Paris to do jobs. What's next?"

"You have to speak to Victor."

"Can you arrange that?"

Manturov laughed. "Anything else you want?"

"How do you communicate with Victor?" asked Briffaut.

"In person, and on jobs we have the radio, just like DGSE."

"Not by phone?" asked Briffaut.

"Not allowed," said the Russian.

De Payns looked at Manturov's iPhone and put it in the Russian's hands. "Let's see a picture of that yacht."

Manturov's hands crawled over the phone, finding the picture. But as de Payns watched, he saw the man's fingers pinch on the side of the black protective cover, pulling out a small plastic plug from the case.

"*No!*" said de Payns, leaping forward, Briffaut seeing it at the same time.

They grabbed at his hand, Briffaut pushing the pill away from the Russian's mouth and de Payns using his left forearm to push the mercenary's head away from the suicide capsule. The Russian was strong, and de Payns grunted against Manturov's neck muscles until Briffaut shook the pill from his fingers, and they watched it bounce across the lino floor.

The three of them panted, de Payns's throat dry and rasping as he stood and looked at the soldier, amazed that the man was now cracking a smile.

"What are you smiling about?" demanded Briffaut, dropping the Russian's hand. "You just tried to end it."

The Russian looked at the ceiling and laughed, his manacles jangling. "You really are desperate to keep me around. So now we get to make a bargain about my family before you hear what I have to say. It's nice to be wanted."

"Jesus," said Briffaut, shaking his head. "What is it with Russians?"

CHAPTER
FORTY-ONE

The restaurant was situated just east of the Square Louis XIII and catered more for Parisians than tourists in every way except the opening hours. Romy had agreed to a dinner meeting with David if she could be out of there by 7:45 p.m., allowing her to get to Ana's and pick up the boys post-karate.

She felt guilty, despite telling herself that this was a business meeting and she was doing nothing wrong.

"So, your husband—Alec, is it?" asked David, pushing away the work files as their grilled sole arrived. "Did you say he worked for the government?"

"Yes, he's a bureaucrat at the Defense Ministry," she said, complying with Alec's cover story. "He's in logistics and procurement."

"Ah," said David, tearing his bread. "He's close to the purse strings. Is he interested in any of your public–private funding structures? Getting Defense into renewables would be a great influence on industry."

Romy chuckled and reached for her wine. At the neighboring table was a couple who looked like an executive with

his secretary, and Romy realized this was a place that opened
early deliberately to capture the illicit workplace-lover market.

"Alec is not interested in renewable energy?" David asked,
disingenuous.

"Oh, he's interested," Romy assured him. She held her poker
face for two seconds, then laughed, looking away.

David's smile was slightly condescending. "You don't sound
sure about that."

"Look, he gets it, he understands the issues and the
science . . ."

"But?"

"But he . . ." Romy paused as she thought about how to
put it. "His job is defense—protecting France—and he's serious about it."

"But so are we," said David, leaning in. "Two degrees of
warming is catastrophic for France, not to mention Europe."

Romy nodded. "Yes, that's true, but the French military's
mission is rather more immediate. Generals don't have a choice
to switch to intermittent energy sources."

David opened his mouth in a silent O. "I see. I haven't heard
that argument for a decade."

Romy wanted to make a smart retort, but she held back.
"At Tirol we're finding ways to transform the economy, but our
armed forces need the means to defend the country. Different
missions, both of them worthwhile."

David leaned back, out of the intimate zone, and reached
for his wine. "Some truths don't need to be aired, Romy, okay?"

"What do you mean?" she asked, taking a mouthful of the
excellent fish.

"I mean, when you meet Klaus, dazzle him with this stuff,"
he said, tapping a folder of her work. "Perhaps leave out the
military commentary."

Romy was relieved she'd avoided a romantic trajectory, and without sabotaging her career. "Is that a sore point for him?"

David shrugged and looked around the room. "Klaus is too busy saving the world to worry about securing the country."

Oliver had lost a shoe, but before de Payns could go and look for it, Romy told her youngest son to go and find his shoe for himself.

"You can't do everything for them," she chided, munching on a corner of toast, her briefcase sitting on the table where de Payns was nursing his coffee. "They'll never grow up."

He smiled. "I hope not."

"Did you see your suit?"

De Payns could see the suit bag from a hire shop hanging near the TV set. "I haven't seen this one, but I know what a dinner suit looks like."

"Can you try it on?" she asked, sipping her coffee. "If it's not right, I'll change it today."

"Shit," he murmured, walking over to fetch the suit bag. "I've just got dressed."

"I've never asked you to be my plus-one, ever," she said, primed for the fight. "You're going to make me feel bad about this one time?"

"No, I'm excited about it," he said, unzipping the bag and pulling out the pants.

"Those are a thirty-six," she said, watching like a hawk as he took off his jeans and pulled on the suit pants. "Try the jacket too."

De Payns slipped on the jacket, and Romy looked him up and down. "It'll do," she said. "The tie's in there, and I got you a new shirt."

"Just like James Bond," he said, giving her a wink.

"Bond doesn't fall asleep watching *SpongeBob*," she said, checking her watch and suddenly tensing. "You all set for

tomorrow? You'll leave plenty of time to get to the Palais?" The
gala was to be held in the giant Palais des Congrès convention
center west of the Arc de Triomphe.

"Sure," he said.

"Nothing looming from Dominic?" She stood and reached
for her briefcase.

"He knows better than to tell me what to do."

"Bullshitter," she said, shaking her head.

Oliver wandered into the room with a schoolbag, wearing
one shoe, and looked at his father. "Are you going to a funeral?"

"Maybe my own," said de Payns, laughing but trying to
hide it.

De Payns was thinking about the mysterious Brenda as he
climbed out of the République Metro, and he was also wondering how the Wagner Group mercenaries knew to target Paul
Degarde for a piece of information he didn't know he had. Did
the Russians already have their eye on the person who was leak-
ing product to Lotus, as suggested by Keratine?

As he walked into dull sunshine, a text pinged on his phone,
and after reading it, he turned and went back to the Metro, made
two changes of train, and emerged at the Champ-de-Mars station
twenty minutes later. He bought coffee at a vendor and crossed the
street into the Champ de Mars, moving to his right and walking for
two minutes until he saw Mike Moran, sitting on their usual meeting bench in one of the leafy glades, away from the tourist circuit.

"Still in town?" asked de Payns, taking a seat but not looking at his friend.

"Wanted another chat," said the Englishman.

"You mean, your bosses weren't happy with the Maypole
and wanted to get more?"

"Not a bad guess," said Moran. "Don't *you* want more?"

"Well, given we have credible intelligence about an assassination in Europe—and France is in Europe—I'd say, yes, I'd like to know more about all of this."

A small gust of wind ripped through the park, which Moran reacted to by pulling up the zip on his winter jacket so the collar surrounded his jaw. "I was building a map of which prod came from where, and something didn't really fit."

"Which part?"

Moran shook his head, his eyes inscrutable behind aviator sunglasses. "Okay, follow the ball," he said, as an elderly woman walked a small dog on the other side of the glade. "We did a Maypole with the Germans."

"Lucky you."

"They had everything we had from those embassy drops, and there wasn't much to go on. I mean, the Russians want to ring-fence Europe with petro-extortion, and they'll use whatever means to do that. Some of those documents are jaw-dropping, but they're not an unknown Russian pattern."

"So, what's out of the pattern?" asked de Payns, fishing a cigarette from his jacket pocket.

"*Azzam*," said Moran.

"Tell me," said de Payns.

"*Azzam* seemed to be part of the embassy series of prod, but it didn't come from there, did it?"

"No," said de Payns, dragging on his smoke. "*Azzam* wasn't part of it. That was just our sidebar."

"This is important," said Moran, turning his body toward his friend. "I mean, *Azzam* is where we got the assassination information, so establishing who sent us to the yacht could resolve a few things."

De Payns laughed. "You have me intrigued. Why don't you kick off?"

"Okay," the Englishman said, "listen to this. Our man in the East was coming back to England a couple of weeks ago with a Ukrainian army file. He scanned it in his hotel room and sent it on the secure connection."

"Okay," said de Payns, sipping his coffee.

"So, he gets back to London, but he's brought the originals hidden in his briefcase. They contained lots of written comments in the margins from a general, and he wanted them analyzed."

"Okay."

"So, he's putting together a report, and then he goes to the debriefing, and the bosses are saying, '*Why is there prod missing from our debriefing packs?*'"

"What was missing?" asked de Payns.

"They have a pack put together from the electronic files he sent, but when he started going through his version of the prod, the hard-copy file has one extra page in it."

"I see," said de Payns, smoking.

"Our man looks at the extra paper in the hard-copy file of originals, and says, '*Well I don't remember this being in the prod.*'"

"The added paper was about *Azzam*?" asked de Payns.

"Yes," said Moran, "which got us started on the same trail that you hopped on."

"It was slipped in?"

"Our colleague remembered a woman in the business center of the hotel who was very helpful and friendly."

"Anything memorable?"

"Well, she was very attractive and smart, but our colleague recalls her being a redhead with nonmatching eyebrows," said Moran, "and our friend pondered that she might have been wearing a wig."

"She slipped some prod into your friend's collection," said

de Payns, "hoping it would be taken to London and included in the briefings?"

"And it was, and it checked out, and we got someone on that yacht."

De Payns smiled, realizing his friend wanted him to run the same checks on the material Paul Degarde had brought in from Lotus. Given Manturov's revelations that Paul Degarde wasn't totally sure how the *Azzam* mentions landed in his product, it was worth investigating.

"I'll look into it," said de Payns. "Any pictures of the mystery woman?"

"A still from the hotel lobby security footage," said Moran, pushing a small envelope across the park bench.

De Payns stood, flicked his cigarette. "I'm interested, but I want to hear your theory before I go frightening the horses."

"I think another service put us up to it," said Moran, looking up at his friend. "Someone wants the French and British to engage with Russia, confront them on what's happening in Europe."

"So they don't have to do the confronting themselves?"

Moran looked back at him. "I hope it's that simple. Anything for me?"

De Payns hesitated but decided to risk it. "Any insights on the name Brenda? Probably a pseudonym."

Moran stayed impassive. "Linked to the Russian prod?"

"That's the assumption," said de Payns. "We can't see much."

"I'll ask around," said Moran, standing to go. "Happy hunting."

CHAPTER
FORTY-TWO

Maahi steered the old Mitsubishi Pajero across the dirt track that wended through the interior wadi country of central Libya. The air was dry, and the desert shimmered with heat, the occasional blast of road dust entering from a hole in the floor pan of the vehicle.

He'd left his coastal town of El Agheila almost an hour earlier to drive to a meeting that filled him with dread. Beside him, his younger brother, Demir, pretended to drum along to the beat of an Arabic song on the radio, a station that broadcast from Cairo.

"How much further?" asked Demir, taking his feet down from the dashboard.

"It's just ahead," said Maahi, nodding. "But look up. That's who we're meeting."

Demir peered at the sky, where a silvery aircraft glinted in the desert sun. "Let's race them," he said, excited.

"No one's racing in this old thing," said Maahi, smiling at his fourteen-year-old brother and remembering happier times, when their whole family performed for weddings and birthday parties. Now he ran errands for the al-Kaniyat militia, which stole land and wealth from Libyans on behalf of General Haftar.

"Come on," said Demir. "The faster we can do this for Parzan, the better we look."

Maahi slowly shook his head. Parzan al-Sharif was one of the al-Kaniyat commanders who had elevated himself to leadership status when Mohammed al-Kaniyat had been killed by an American bomb. Parzan had concluded that the al-Kaniyat militia's appearance on Western war crimes lists necessitated a new strategy, whereby normal townsfolk were coopted into the local warlord's schemes. One afternoon, Parzan summoned Maahi and his father to a disused mining camp inland from El Agheila. It was the kind of invitation one couldn't refuse. Maahi remembered the meeting vividly: the wafting camouflage netting that was strung across the compound; the cheap barracks and makeshift kitchens; the expensive satellite communications equipment that looked suspiciously as if it were supplied from the West.

Parzan had been sitting under the camouflage netting on a director's chair, peeling an orange. He was dressed in desert cam military fatigues with a shemagh worn loosely around his neck rather than his head.

"Who do you work for?" asked the al-Kaniyat commander.

Maahi's father replied, "I'm a musician."

Parzan stood and shot the musician in the head. Before the son could even scream or cry out, the warlord had asked Maahi the same question.

In shock and shaking with fear, Maahi responded, "You. I work for you."

And that had been the last day of freedom for seventeen-year-old Maahi. The al-Kaniyat militia paid him, which enabled him to provide for his mother and brother, but

he was now a slave to one of the most bloodthirsty warlords
on earth.

He approached the small airfield that had been bulldozed
by an oil-and-gas company ten years earlier. A small shed sat
alongside the runway, and the genset that had once powered
the airfield lighting system now sat derelict, stripped of its solar
panels and batteries. It looked to Maahi like the story of Libya:
a once-wealthy nation reduced to a rabble of thieves.

Maahi parked the Pajero beside the shed, and it plinked
as it cooled. To the south, the twin-engine plane lined up and
came in low, kicking up white dust and pebbles as it motored
across the desert, losing speed.

The plane rolled to a stop in front of Maahi and Demir and
depowered. The airstairs were pushed out and folded down to
the ground. Two men descended. The older of the two had a
noticeable hunchback and wore a dark suit that suggested he
usually worked in a town or city. He carried a conspicuous black
9mm handgun in a hip holster. The smaller of the pair was
younger and dressed in black jeans and a black windbreaker, a
shoulder holster visible under his jacket.

"You're it?" asked the man in black, when he was standing
in front of Maahi. "They sent me a kid?"

Maahi nodded. "I'm here to pick up a package?"

The man in black chuckled and looked around through
dark sunglasses. "Where's Parzan?"

Maahi shook his head; he wasn't allowed to say.

The hunchback returned to the plane and almost immediately came back down the stairs, a satellite phone to his ear,
followed by two large soldiers without uniform. The soldiers
carried what Maahi knew to be submachine guns, although
they weren't the American or German models favored in the
desert—they looked like Russian Makarovs.

The hunchback paused at the foot of the airstairs, terminated his phone call, and spoke to his companion in Arabic. "Faisal! We're clear."

Faisal looked around the desert airfield and then up at the sky, suspicious. "Let's go," he said finally, pointing to Maahi's car.

"Go where?" asked Maahi.

"To Parzan," said Faisal. "He's expecting us."

The soldiers took two metal cases from the fuselage luggage hold and put them in the back of the Pajero. Maahi got in the car, and Faisal climbed in beside him.

"Got any aircon in this thing?" he asked.

"No, it's broken," said Maahi.

"Your brother will stay here with my friend, okay?" said Faisal, with a winning smile. "I guarantee he'll be safe."

They made good time across the desert, Maahi chatting with Faisal while the soldiers stayed silent in the back.

"So, are you one of the musicians that Parzan has told me about?" said Faisal.

"I play when it's possible," Maahi said. "The wars make it hard."

"What's your ambition?" asked Faisal, lighting a cigarette and offering one to Maahi, which he took.

"Peace," he said, as they passed a massif that rose out of the desert like an animal's back. "No more fighting in Libya."

In the wadi off the main road, a yellow Toyota van was almost hidden from view. Maahi knew it as Parzan al-Sharif's drop zone for weapons and explosives. There was an aquifer close to the surface, so there was some foliage around the wadi, and the militia considered it relatively obscured from the drones that flew over the desert.

Parzan al-Sharif put on a big smile when he greeted Faisal,

and together they walked away from the van, the soldiers standing off. Maahi sat in the Pajero, worrying about his brother.

Faisal and Parzan parted less than ten minutes later. Faisal spoke to his soldiers before peeling off to the cab of the van to deal with the paperwork. One soldier approached the Pajero. "Can you give me a hand?" he asked Maahi.

They went to the back of the Pajero and grabbed one handle each of a large metal ammo box, and they walked it to the load space of the yellow van. Maahi then helped with the second, larger box, which was so heavy his fingers almost gave way as they lifted it. As he deposited the box in the van, he heard its contents shift with a dull metallic clank.

Maahi's eyes widened—he couldn't help it—and he stole a glance at the soldier on the other side of the box.

"*Dhahab*," said the soldier, with a conspiratorial smile. Gold.

Maahi gulped, wondering what he was witnessing.

The soldier put a finger to his lips in the international sign for, *Keep your mouth shut.*

On the drive back to the plane, Faisal was pensive, and Maahi worried that he'd said something wrong.

"You're the Europe group, right?" Faisal finally broke the silence. "You're in the drumming troupe?"

"A drummer, yes," said Maahi, wondering if this meant he was going to Europe. "Also some dancing and singing."

Faisal nodded to himself, blowing smoke out the slightly cracked window. "I have some advice for you, Maahi."

"Yes?"

"If you ever find yourself in a strange country, and things are not going well, go to the embassy of America or France or Britain—one of those countries—and ask for asylum."

Maahi was confused. "This word?"

"Asylum," Faisal said. "Say it."

Maahi repeated it several times—"A-*sy*-lum"—slightly intimidated by his passenger's serious face.

"You know the LNA?" asked Faisal.

"Yes."

"You know Haftar?"

"Of course."

"And you understand the al-Kaniyat militia?"

Maahi nodded and, still confused, asked, "What is asylum?"

"A safe place," said the older man. "Don't forget my advice," he said, and flicked his cigarette out the window.

CHAPTER
FORTY-THREE

Before de Payns could sit down at his desk and check the picture Mike Moran had slipped to him, Margot appeared at his door. He presumed she was going to summon him to a meeting with the boss, as she usually did, but instead she said, "Aguilar, I am going to book another session between the boss and Dr. Marlene." Her expression was the softest he'd seen on her. "What date do you think would work for him?"

De Payns breathed deeply and kept his face neutral. "The boss usually gets the most out of the doctor when he has a month between sessions."

"You're right, of course," said Margot, with a brief smile, "but in this case, he wanted a week."

De Payns sighed and then gave in graciously. "The boss knows best . . ."

"Yes, he does." Margot turned to leave. "And he wants to see you."

De Payns restored the Moran envelope to his pocket and went to see Dominic Briffaut.

"Where were you?" asked the boss, when de Payns walked in.

"Sidebar with Mike Moran," said de Payns, taking a seat as Margot closed the door behind him. "He wanted more."

Briffaut considered an apple he was holding, then pointed to a thin blue folder on his desk. "Present from DR. Take a look."

Opening the file, de Payns found two pages: the first was a requisition sheet acknowledging the research tasking; the second page stated that there was no match in the sources and pseud-onym database for #BRENDA#.

"Valkov was serious about that name, so stay on it," said Briffaut. "You were at the Champ de Mars?"

"You a spy or something?" replied de Payns.

"One of my lesser faults," the boss said, biting into the apple. "The Russians didn't go for Keratine. That prod we gave them at the Maypole? No response from the FSB."

"So, he's ours?" asked de Payns.

"Well, the FSB thinks he's theirs, and that's the main point."

De Payns knew the early days of a new source could be uncertain. "That thing at the hotel?"

"I didn't like the prostitute trick, but our new source could be trying to even the scales, which is to be expected. You'd do something like that yourself . . ."

"Is Keratine producing yet?"

"Reluctantly," said Briffaut. "But with Lotus out of the game, we need a source in the East, and this one works in the FSB. I don't want to lose him."

"You want some carrot, along with the stick?"

"How would you cement a source?" asked Briffaut.

De Payns sat back and thought. "Well, for a start, I'd need some authority over him, so Jim would have to be managed by me, not the DR."

"Let's assume that's already happened," said Briffaut.

"Okay, I'd show him the carrot—money, a job, French passports."

"And perhaps get him talking about what he wants to talk about?" suggested Briffaut. "He doesn't want to turn on his FSB buddies, but he might not be so delicate about the GRU . . ."

"Or Wagner Group," said de Payns.

"Precisely," said Briffaut. "I don't like to rush these things, but with Lotus gone, we need Keratine on board and delivering."

"And he answers to me?"

"Of course. I'll get those French ID packs ordered, for Keratine and his family. But you'll be managing Jim—between the two of you, we can bring Keratine over."

Changing the subject, de Payns asked that he be allowed to knock off by five the next day. "Romy's work is holding some big gala dinner," he explained.

"You know the score," said the boss. "The answer's yes until it's no. Now tell me, what did Moran want?"

De Payns took him through the SIS theory of an interloper dropping teasers about *Azzam* into prod that was destined for the British or French services. The Brits wanted the French to find the person who made the secret drops about *Azzam*, he explained, so they could confirm it was the same person.

"Who have SIS found?" asked Briffaut, tossing the apple core in his wastepaper bin.

"Mike gave me a photograph," de Payns said, pulling the envelope from his jacket and passing it to Briffaut. "I haven't had a chance to look at it yet. It's from a hotel. They think she got friendly with their man in the hotel business center, and that's where she dropped in the product."

Briffaut opened the envelope and pulled from it an eight-by-ten color print.

"Fuck," he said softly, handing over the picture.

De Payns took the photograph, eyes widening as he recognized the woman in the picture. She was wearing a red wig and a pair of spectacles, but de Payns would always know her as the woman in the orange silk top.

When Aguilar had left, Briffaut leaned back in his chair and put his feet on the windowsill. The SIS theory was interesting, and Briffaut assumed his counterpart in London had implanted it in Mike Moran's ear before sending him to France, knowing it would end up in Briffaut's mind.

He let the cogs turn, thought about which other service wanted the Brits and French to uncover a Russian assassination plot and then try to stop it. Such an action would put that nation firmly in the opposite corner to Russia. He was jolted from his reverie by Margot knocking on his door and leaning in to ask if he needed anything before she left for the day.

"A copy of this," he said, handing her the picture.

She reappeared a few minutes later with the picture, then said goodnight.

"Goodnight, Margot." Once she had gone, he locked his office door from the inside and resumed his seat. Did this really go back to the Minsk Agreements, or was he stretching too far? The second Minsk Agreement had ended the war in the Russian-speaking southeast of Ukraine—the Donbas—but had left France and Germany to administer the peace. The two countries had pleaded neutrality as the Ukrainian Azov Battalion militarized the Donbas region and committed atrocities, which had drawn in Russia and the Wagner Group. The President's advisers gambled that France could be best friends with everyone, but failing to enforce the Minsk Agreement had spawned many enemies. Chaos in the Donbas had encouraged the rise of Kolomoisky's Azov Battalion, the expansion of Wagner Group and the entanglement of the Americans, in the guise of NATO.

Rising, he pulled the Glenfiddich bottle from the map drawer of his bookcase and selected an American shot glass. He poured a dram, drank it, then unlocked his safe and pulled out an old address book and burner phone. He found the number he wanted quickly and dialed.

"Yes?" answered a woman's voice.

"Monsieur de Murat, at your service," said Briffaut.

"I'll be at my usual place, usual time," she said, and hung up.

Briffaut walked into the Canard Vert restaurant in the Marais district at 6:30 p.m. and followed the narrow passageways through the decrepit series of connected buildings, past a mahjong club, to the rear bar. It was dark, poorly lit, one of those Paris bars that the government's tourism board would never let a visitor see.

"Monsieur de Murat," the woman said, as Briffaut walked up to her corner table.

"Gabrielle," he replied, removing his woolen overcoat. "Scotch, neat," he said to the barmaid, and took a seat.

She smiled. "It's been a while." In her late forties, Gabby Castigan worked for the BND, Germany's foreign intelligence agency. She had operated in Madrid, Moscow, Santiago, Mexico City, and London, but the Germans' default posting for this woman was Paris. She'd also been Briffaut's lover—in two separate and equally disastrous affairs—but now they kept things professional with an occasional drink.

"Always nice to get a call from you," she said, sipping on her vodka tonic. "But I suspect this'll be about work."

The Scotch arrived, and Briffaut asked for another vodka.

"We've had some curious drops through our embassies lately," he began.

"Hence the Maypole," said Castigan, draining her glass and pulling her smokes from the jacket slung over her chairback.

"Yes, and it went nowhere," said Briffaut. "Because we're all getting the same prod, the services have an opportunity to pretend they're being open, but they're not."

"Someone is playing with the services," she said, lighting her cigarette as the new vodka arrived. "And then the services play with one another. Don't you love this business?"

"I do, which is why I want a sidebar."

Sidebars required the swapping of information with another service in a non-official capacity, making the participants vulnerable to charges of treachery. A sidebar could only be conducted between people who trusted one another implicitly.

"You go first," she said, with a soft-eyed smile that had been used to great effect on many targets over the years.

"Tell me about *Azzam*."

Castigan tapped the ash from her cigarette and gave a quick glance around the room. "Well, Monsieur de Murat. That's quite an opening."

"The Brits and us, we both had prod planted in material that was otherwise being brought out of Eastern Europe," said Briffaut. "The planted information steered both services toward *Azzam*."

She stirred her vodka with the blue tiki stick. "This is when I show that I know what *Azzam* is?"

"It would help to verify that you know what I'm talking about."

She put the tiki stick in her mouth and looked at him. Her eyes were green, and although the thick honey-blonde hair now sported streaks of gray, she was still a beautiful woman. "And why would I want to verify that?"

"Because the events that flow from *Azzam*, the Brits believe,

are an attempt to get France, Britain, or Germany to enter into
a conflict with Russia—unambiguously."

"And why is it currently ambiguous?"

Briffaut paused. "Because France and Germany sat back and
ignored their Minsk Agreement responsibilities in the Donbas,
and the UK gave us diplomatic cover to do so. And now the
Russian wolf is at the Ukrainian border, huffing and puffing,
and no one wants to argue about it because the Kremlin can
crush our gas supply."

"And someone is dropping material into intelligence files that
will force one of us to declare themselves for or against Russia?"

Briffaut let this dangle. "What do you know about *Azzam*?"

"What do *you* know?"

"We were on board," said Briffaut. "And so were the Brits."

Her pupils dilated. She was experienced enough to know it
and looked away. "Well, that's one of those things which might
have been raised at the Maypole, don't you think?"

"Not if Germany wasn't in a giving mood that day."

"Touché," she nodded slowly and stubbed out her cigarette.
"I'm not deep in the details; it's being run out of Berlin."

"But you clearly know about it."

"What can you give me that makes this sidebar bear fruit?"

Briffaut slipped an envelope out of his jacket pocket and
slid it across the table. Castigan picked it up without losing
eye contact and opened it on her lap. She looked down at the
picture then looked up again, shaking her head.

"You bastard," she muttered.

"Interested?" asked Briffaut.

"How did you find her?"

"I wasn't looking," said Briffaut. "I missed it in the first
photo I saw, but this one made me look closer, and I thought
it was Zeitz."

"The first photo? Thought you weren't looking?"

"She turned up in another operation," said Briffaut. "I've never met her, remember; she just seemed familiar because of your problems with her."

"Can I keep this?"

"Your turn to give."

Castigan leaned back slightly. "We tried to get on *Azzam* but failed. You're saying the Brits and the French got that inserted prod, too?"

"You acknowledge it was inserted?"

"That's the working assumption."

"We agree," said Briffaut. He pointed at the photo. "It was planted—by Christine."

"Where's the photo from?" she asked.

"A hotel in Eastern Europe," said Briffaut. "I'm guessing the Marriott in Bucharest."

"All that Saddam marble," she said. "What's she doing there?"

"I can't talk about that," Briffaut replied. "Let's just say a friendly service thought they were being played with the *Azzam* prod and worked it back."

Castigan shook her head. "I thought she'd gone to America after the Damascus thing."

"Just tell me one thing: is she working for Germany?"

"Hard no," said Castigan, nostrils flaring. "Berlin wouldn't let her mop a floor after Syria."

"Keep the photo, but if you find her, call a Maypole, okay?"

"I'll do that," she said, and her face changed. "Your timing is shitty."

"I do my best."

"I thought you might be looking for company tonight?"

Briffaut let himself get drawn into her gaze. "What happened to the Norwegian?"

"I have a thing for right-wing men, as you know, but Herr Klos was a bridge too far."

"He had a lot of fruit salad on his chest for a man who never left the office."

Castigan laughed, throaty and worldly. "And he had a swastika in his basement."

"Nice Nazis, those Norwegians," said Briffaut. "Always the great teeth."

She picked up her drink. "I said to him, '*That's a pretty flag, but my Jewish grandmother would not approve.*' And he said, '*Don't be embarrassed—there are ways to cover up your genetics.*'"

Now Briffaut laughed. "He sounds like my kind of racist. I'd put him in blackface and get him tap-dancing. He can call me *massah*."

"He'd take one look at you and shit himself," she said, chuckling.

"I'm working on being nice, but I reserve the right to hurt people I don't like."

Castigan's laughter died. "I miss you, monsieur."

"You've got a night ahead of you," he said, finishing his drink. "And you owe me."

CHAPTER
FORTY-FOUR

De Payns yawned and asked Lolo to start the third video file. It was 10:00 p.m., and he'd been looking through video since he'd been dragged back into the Bunker by Briffaut and set to work on finding Christine Zeitz, the former BND agent who seemed to be operating against the Company. They were in the Y-9 basement of the Bunker, a bank of screens in front of them, Lolo and Tranh doing the tech work on the security camera footage from Paul Degarde's Prague hotel, sent over by the DGSE chief of post in the Czech Republic. De Payns had assumed that because Paul Degarde was a courier of product from Lotus, he only spent twenty-four hours in a city—sometimes less—before returning to Paris. However, on his final job for the Company, Paul Degarde had spent a second night in Prague. The product inserted into the Lotus files would have had to occur after the source meeting in Prague and—he assumed—before getting into the taxi at CDG. The taxi company had confirmed one passenger. Given de Payns's experience of fieldwork, he considered the most likely place for the insertion was Degarde's hotel in Prague, with a human contact. It was certainly how de Payns would do it.

"Okay," said Tranh, shuffling his mouse and indicating three screens. "I've got our person of interest tracked."

De Payns scraped forward in his chair and watched over Tranh's shoulder.

Lolo pointed at the leftmost screen. "This is the Old Royal Post's main bar—it's twenty seventeen Prague time when our man walks in from the restaurant."

They watched Paul Degarde order a whisky and sit at a table against the far wall, his eyes wandering to a wall-mounted TV screen that played a news service.

"At twenty thirty-one, our POI enters the bar," said Lolo, as Tranh jumped the video to the new time code.

De Payns leaned forward. The person of interest was a blonde woman in her early thirties, dressed in expensive jeans and a green woolen jumper with a half-zip. De Payns knew the face—Christine Zeitz. On the security video, she ordered a glass of white wine at the bar and turned to inspect the room.

"She takes the table beside our man," said Lolo, signaling for Tranh to switch the video feeds. The angle showed Zeitz taking a seat at a neighboring table, so Degarde was ninety degrees to her right. She put her small tourist backpack on the table and rummaged in it, uninterested in the neighboring French tourist.

"Here's the approach," said Tranh, and they watched Zeitz unfold a map on her table, sip at her wine, make a confused face, and then look around before settling her gaze on Paul Degarde, who—rather than look at the pretty woman—watched the TV news. Degarde turned to face her, and they seemed to talk about the map. Zeitz then moved to Degarde's table, with her map and backpack.

De Payns allowed himself a chuckle: even without having

an audio track, he knew exactly what she was saying to Paul
Degarde, and how Degarde would be agreeing that some of the
Czech words bore no relation to what the French or English
translation would look like.

"They're having a great old laugh," said Lolo, "but after
twenty-three minutes, our man is on his feet and going to the bar.

Tranh jumped to the next time code, and they watched
Degarde stand. As he moved to the bar, Zeitz grabbed his room
swipe key—in its Royal Post cardboard wallet—and put it in
her backpack. De Payns watched the blonde spy leave her hand
in the backpack for seven seconds before removing the room
card and placing it back on the table.

"Bitch," he murmured. "She scanned the room card."

"It gets better," said Tranh.

"I have no doubt," said de Payns, as the video showed
Degarde arriving back at the table with a whisky in one hand
and a glass of wine in the other, his arrival causing Zeitz to stand,
obviously excusing herself to go to the bathroom.

"Let's go to person of interest number two," said Lolo, indicating the middle screen where the time was 21:07. It showed
the hotel lobby, where several people sat in the lounge area. As
Christine Zeitz emerged into view, walking to the restrooms, a
middle-aged man in a blue windbreaker who'd been reading a
magazine in the lounge stood and followed. Zeitz emerged two
minutes later and returned to the bar.

"No cameras in the restroom approaches," said Lolo. "But
look."

The man in the blue windbreaker reappeared a minute later
and headed for the elevators. "Our man's room is on the third
floor, over here," said Lolo, pointing to the screen on the right.

The man in the blue windbreaker left the elevator at 21:12,
now wearing a baseball cap pulled low on his face. He walked

toward the security camera and used a white swipe card to open
room 312, the card he'd constructed using data stolen from
Degarde's room key.

"This is our man's room," said Lolo. "And this guy is fast.
Watch this."

The time code showed the man in the blue windbreaker
spent eighty-two seconds in Paul Degarde's room.

Yes, thought de Payns, it was fast, but plenty of time to find
Degarde's camera, photograph new prod, and delete it from
the card.

Christine Zeitz had stayed at the Old Royal Post hotel, and the
Company's Prague team was able to access the hotel system and
confirm that she'd used the name Giselle Hess. They ran credit
card and airline cross-checks on "Giselle Hess," looking for her
movements after infiltrating Paul Degarde in Prague. They found
an Air France booking in her name, traveling Prague–Paris the
morning after she'd met Degarde. She boarded the flight, and
it landed at 11:22 a.m. The photographs they had from her
meetings with Starkand and Zeitz's field operation at the Old
Royal Post showed two different looks: one with brunette hair,
the other blonde. Briffaut's briefing on Zeitz was that she used
disguises and could turn up as anything.

In Portofino, Lolo had captured IMSI and IMEI data when
Zeitz used her phone—or what they concluded was her phone
by the spinner's tracking of the number when the German
transferred from the Portofino quay to the superyacht *Melissa*.
There were no guarantees that she'd be using the same phone in
Paris, but if she was—or if the phone was sitting in her hand-
bag switched off but still pinging to find the closest tower—it
would show up.

The search for phone activity on cell towers had to be done

with the cooperation of the phone companies, and the speed with which they responded was inconsistent. However, Tranh had developed a relationship inside France's cell-phone regulator, and he had the data eighteen minutes after de Payns asked for it.

They crouched around Tranh's screen, and he searched the spreadsheet attachment for the day that Paul Degarde flew into Paris. There was no activity.

"Okay," said de Payns. "Try the next day."

Tranh searched, and there were three entries.

The first started at 9:51 a.m. on a cell tower listed as 610552.

Lolo searched the cell-tower map on his laptop and found it, near the Champs-Élysée, just west of the Arc. The connection lasted one minute forty-eight seconds and then passed to a tower labeled 610496.

Lolo entered it in his map software, and it showed further west on the Champs-Élysée, and this tower connection held for one minute eight seconds before it passed to the third cell tower, 612330. The phone disconnected at 9:55 a.m.

Lolo entered the third tower number, got its location, and allowed the Venn diagrams from the three towers to overlap and graphically tell the team what they already knew: the day after planting material in Paul Degarde's camera, Christine Zeitz had been in a vehicle moving westward along the Champs-Élysée.

"Sitting in a cab?" asked Lolo.

"It's possible," said de Payns. "I guess it depends on the call. This is a burner phone, so she's talking to someone who's in the game, and she may or may not do that in front of a taxi driver."

"So, she's with someone else in Paris?"

"Or she's driving the car?"

De Payns tried to put himself in her shoes. "It's heading up to ten o'clock, so I'm thinking she's on her way to a rendez-vous of some sort."

De Payns took the still prints of Christine Zeitz from the Royal Post and added them to the trombinoscope for Operation Ellipse. He attached the name and her alias and stood back from the board: he had Zeitz occurring on both the Ellipse and Bellbird boards, since Zeitz was connected to the *Azzam*-assassination material, as well as being connected to Starkand. Something wasn't clear: was Zeitz giving source material to Starkand? If that was the case, why would she have to drop prod into Lotus's files? It was most likely that Zeitz was giving one set of material to Starkand to send to the Occidental services by mail, but she had another game: to make fake prod look like it came from trusted Russian sources of the type cultivated by Lotus. It was a clear tactic of "confuse by informing": not just delivering many shards of prod into a service's catchment but dropping them in different channels to hide the source of them.

So Zeitz and Starkand had their roles, but what of Brenda? He grabbed a piece of paper, wrote *Brenda* on it, and pinned the paper between the two corkboards. He didn't know how they connected, except that the Russians had asked about Brenda in the context of Starkand and the *Azzam* prod. He was fairly sure Starkand was the delivery agent and Zeitz was running him. They'd seen her in Portofino and Bern, and she was in charge. So where did that leave Brenda? Was she Zeitz? Or was Brenda another person, deciding what went in the mail and what was slipped into the services product that was walked out of Eastern Europe? If Brenda was a Paris-based operative being hunted by the Kremlin, the Company needed to find her before the Russians did.

De Payns looked at the clock on the wall. It was just after 11:00 p.m., and he was tired. He stood and heard a knock at the door: Lolo.

"Thought I told you to go home?" said de Payns.

"Tranh asked me if you wanted the other tower connections for Zeitz's phone?"

"There were others?"

"Yes," said Lolo. "Today."

De Payns descended to the Y-9 basement with Lolo and leaned over Tranh's shoulder to look at the telecom spreadsheet. The Zeitz burner phone had been activated and connected to tower 1931 for twenty-one seconds at 11:19 a.m.

"Twenty-one seconds," said Lolo. "Quick conversation."

"She turned on the phone, got an incoming text message, and then typed an answer and sent it," said de Payns, who was well versed in such liaison management. "Twenty-one seconds is doing well. Where's the tower?"

Lolo opened up his cell-tower map and inserted *1931*. It dropped a red digital pin on an area de Payns knew too well.

"Southern edge of Jardin du Luxembourg," said Lolo, looking up and smiling. "Right in the middle of the Bobos. What's she looking for? An open marriage?"

De Payns couldn't help a smile, but his paranoia was rising. "That's our job for tomorrow," he said. "Why is Christine Zeitz in the heart of Paris?"

CHAPTER
FORTY-FIVE

Maahi nodded, his throat so constricted that he couldn't trust himself to speak. The operation had been sprung on him, and while his first reaction was to say no, he knew he had a younger brother and a widowed mother to think of.

Parzan al-Sharif sat on the edge of his desk in a shallow dugout at the back of his desert compound. The camp had been inherited from the previous al-Kaniyat commander, who had lost his powerbase when militia founder Mohammed al-Kaniyat was killed in a Turkish missile strike, using an American weapon. The rumor persisted that Parzan had provided the coordinates to the Turks, a move not unheard of among the militia commanders who generated great wealth through their connections to General Haftar.

"This action is of personal importance to me," said Parzan, dressed in his signature desert cams and scarf. "Your loyalty will be noted."

The man's appearance reminded Maahi of a picture torn from an old *Newsweek* magazine and pinned to the kitchen wall of the trucking company his father once drove for. The picture was of PLO commander Yasser Arafat, and Maahi wondered if Parzan—a primary-school teacher by profession—had seen the image and decided it was a look of authority.

Libya had become that way since the end of Gaddafi. Schoolteachers commanding militias, mayors making bombs, pilots flying gold to Switzerland; farmers' sons turned into armed thugs, and former IT engineers running slave markets.

Drummers making courier runs for warlords.

Maahi had drummed in his family troupe, playing for weddings, homecomings, and other celebrations. Maahi had almost forgotten the joy of performing with his father and uncles. What he was being asked to do now made him sick to the stomach.

"You remember your training with the machine pistol?" asked Parzan, looking at one of his small cigars.

"Yes," Maahi whispered. In his first months in Parzan's cadre, he had been trained to use an MP5 machine pistol which had its stock removed, so it was easy to conceal. It was easily slung under an armpit and was not visible if the carrier wore a baggy shirt or jacket over the top.

"You were accurate with that weapon," said Parzan, lighting up. "I need you to be accurate again, under great pressure."

Maahi nodded.

"This is your reward for success," Parzan said, resting his hand on a stack of American dollar bills. "That's one thousand US dollars. I'm sure your mother would appreciate that."

Maahi wondered how long his mother would retain possession of such an amount if her oldest son was not around to protect her.

The commander smiled. "I have faith in you, Maahi," he said. "In fact, my belief in you is so strong that I will keep Demir here with me."

Maahi looked into Parzan's eyes and knew in his heart that if the opportunity ever came, he would kill this man. "Why does Demir have to stay here? He's not part of anything."

"Yes, I know this," said Parzan. "So, we're agreed, then? There's no reason to make your brother a part of this operation?"

Maahi breathed in deeply through his nose. "We'll keep Demir out of it," he said. "You can rely on me."

"Good," said Parzan, smacking the tops of his thighs. "You're going to play music in Europe—you should be excited."

CHAPTER
FORTY-SIX

Briffaut's Viano van stopped and started through the Paris morning commuter traffic. De Payns watched the director of Y Division reacting with annoyance and fatigue as he jumped from one phone call to the next.

"We have to get in front of what the Libyans are planning," said de Payns, as his boss ended a call. "I can't believe we've had no hits on something as big as an assassination in Europe by al-Kaniyat."

Briffaut's phone rang again, and he answered. "No, Marie, I'm coming to the Cat," he snapped. "See you in thirty minutes, reserve a SCIF. Thanks, goodbye."

He hung up and turned back to de Payns in the facing seat. "I want you on Zeitz, and I want answers about Vulcan and what exactly we're dealing with."

Briffaut keyed his phone. "Mattieu," he said to his 2IC, Mattieu Garrat, "Aguilar is escalating Operation Ellipse, on my authority. I want the budget and the approvals signed in advance. Whatever he needs, he gets, and I'll deal with the Cat when they complain. Got it?"

There was a pause, and Briffaut's face hardened. "Tell them there's no slow-walking on Keratine's new ID, and yes, there's three of them: father, mother, son."

The Châtelet Metro loomed, and when the van stopped, de Payns got out and trained and bussed to Noisy, where Tranh and Lolo had just taken over from the night shift duty techs. When de Payns sat down in the Y-9 security area, he could see several screens were being monitored.

"Starkand," said Lolo, pointing at one screen, "and Zeitz," he said, pointing to the second. "Starkand's phone pinged twice in the last few hours. It's in Paris."

"Still pinging?" asked de Payns.

"No," said Lolo. "And we picked up activity on Zeitz's phone last night. Brent and Thierry are on IMSI alert in the spinner vans, either side of the river."

De Payns nodded, knowing that a fresh hit from the phones would allow the spinner vans to get there quickly, perhaps establish a big bubble and then attempt to isolate the users down to a small bubble created by the phone's IEMI. He spied a third set of laptops sitting on Tranh's desk, running graphic programs. "What's that?"

"An associated number for Zeitz," said Lolo. "The activity logs show a number that's been called from her phone. We thought we'd do a phone environment on this one too."

"Excellent," said de Payns. "Let me know when we get something."

CHAPTER
FORTY-SEVEN

Gabby Castigan used two train lines and emerged from the Bastille Metro station shortly before 8:00 a.m. She walked northeast, into the secondary streets, and used her training to ensure there were no followers. She found the Red Lion, which still functioned as a hotel, although some of the rooms doubled as safe houses for the CIA. She climbed the two-hundred-year-old wraparound staircase to the second floor and walked to suite 208—chosen, she surmised, because it had ready access to two internal stairwells and was connected to the rear fire escape. Taking a deep breath she, rapped out the agreed knock—three shorts and a long—and waited.

The woman who opened the door smiled and waved her in.

"Hi, stranger," said the woman whom Castigan knew only as Brenda. "I got coffee and *pains au chocolat*. You hungry?"

Castigan nodded and took a seat in one of the expensive armchairs. She could see the Gare de Lyon from where she sat, and it gave her a flash of nostalgia as she remembered tumultuous but unforgettable times with Dominic Briffaut, stealing away on a train to Marseille, drinking all the way, and staggering into their hotel at the other end. She felt terrible about what she was doing, but in her world very few decisions were regret-free.

"What's up?" asked Brenda, pouring coffees from a French press.

"I was contacted by Dominic Briffaut last night," Castigan said.

Brenda's eyebrows rose as she lifted her coffee to her lips. "I see. How do you know him?"

"Damascus," Castigan said, with a pang at the memory. "And Paris."

"What did he want?"

"They're on to Christine."

"How?"

"They have a photo of her in a hotel lobby—Bucharest, they think—where she apparently dropped something into another service's pouch."

Brenda's face remained impassive. "Are they guessing, or do they know?"

"They know it's her. They're certain she's inserting prod into Occidental intelligence—information that doesn't come from official sources."

"What do they conclude?"

"That someone is steering the Western services to focus on Russian wrongdoing."

They looked at each other for a beat, and Castigan marveled at the stillness of the woman in front of her. So beautiful, so smart, and yet something so suburban and stable about her. If Castigan was running her, she'd have paired her with a military or diplomatic "husband" and let her draw the details out of her social interactions.

"And where do they think she is operating?" asked Brenda.

"Briffaut contacted me to see if I knew," said Castigan. "I didn't."

"Dominic Briffaut wouldn't ask a BND officer a question like that unless he knew more than the person he was asking," said the CIA woman. "But you're aware of that."

"He wanted to know why Germany held back at the Maypole, and I said that as far as I knew we didn't; it's just that we didn't have much to give. And he admitted that the British supplied the picture, not the DGSE. He wouldn't let me keep the photo."

"So, he was fishing?" asked Brenda.

"Yes, but he said he had another photo of her, and in that image he hadn't recognized her."

Brenda nodded. "You're courageous, turning up here and just teasing me with this."

"I'm not teasing."

"Well, let me remind you that Christine Zeitz lost her job and narrowly avoided prison, and here you are walking around Paris, a free woman."

Castigan shook off the memories of Damascus, a crazy period in which stress and alcohol had marred her judgment. "Chris was hardly blameless . . ."

"Yet it was you who allowed the Hezbollah agent into the file room and then threw Christine under the bus to save your own career."

"It wasn't exactly like that," said Castigan, flustered.

"The video I have tells a different story," said Brenda. "Now let's go back to the beginning. What does Briffaut want from the Germans?"

"He wants to know what we got from *Azzam*."

"And you said?"

"I said we couldn't get on to *Azzam*, but I gather that the French and British succeeded."

"That's it?"

"All he's got is a photograph from Bucharest, and one from somewhere else."

"Any idea of the somewhere else?" she asked.

"No, he didn't say," said Castigan, feeling nauseous from her betrayal.

Brenda produced a movie-star beam. "You think perhaps the Company is at a loose end?"

Castigan nodded in agreement, but she was thinking that Dominic Briffaut was at his most dangerous when the answers were no longer easy.

Jéjé read his *L'Équipe* magazine and kept his eye off the target while also monitoring her. He had let her get well ahead of him after she left the hotel and kept an eye on her as she descended into the halls of Gare de Lyon. It wasn't a hard job given her height and head of dark blonde hair, held in place with tortoise-shell clips. Now he rode in her carriage, curious about why this person was a target.

After thirteen minutes and ten stops, the woman stood in anticipation as the train squealed and slowed at Porte Maillot. She was well dressed and sexy, if not a little mature for Jéjé's tastes. She walked to the doors at the other end of the car, and Jéjé keyed his radio. "From Jéjé—alert. Target alighting at Porte Maillot."

"Aline copy, I'm standing by," came the response, and Jéjé could see his colleague standing in front of a snack vending machine in the concourse, dressed like a university student.

The doors shut, and the train accelerated toward Les Sablons, with Jéjé still in the carriage.

"Aline to all," said his colleague. "Visual on target."

Jéjé relaxed, knowing that the primary following had been handed to Aline. Halfway to the Sablons station, the radio crackled again, its reception becoming weak.

"Aline to all," said his teammate. "I've lost visual—target is in the nest."

The train stopped at Sablons, and Jéjé stepped onto the platform, waiting for the train to come the other way. He texted a secure update message that would be relayed to the boss. It was a strange gig, thought Jéjé, following this woman from a sordid Vietnamese restaurant to her apartment building, then to a private hotel, and on to the German embassy. There was now a sub at the Red Lion hotel, waiting to take photographs of whoever exited. He checked the arrival board for the next train and wondered what the hell Dominic Briffaut was up to.

CHAPTER
FORTY-EIGHT

The first hit on the Starkand burner phone occurred just after 10:00 a.m. Lolo got the call from the phone company, and the spreadsheet was sent through, showing a twenty-second burst through a tower numbered 610491, in Les Halles. The associated number received the call through tower 1539. They displayed the tower locations on Lolo's graphic simulator, and it suggested Starkand had communicated with someone close to the Gare de Lyon.

"Hang on," said de Payns, looking at the number Starkand had contacted. "That isn't Zeitz's phone?"

"No, it's one of the numbers Zeitz has called," said Tranh. "It's an associated number, and now that number has called Starkand."

"We have a trio, and they're in Paris," said de Payns. "Send it to the spinner teams, and ask for a complete phone environment for each of them."

Lolo got on the phone to Brent and Thierry, telling them the locations, while Tranh sent the information.

De Payns returned to his trombinoscope in the operations room and connected the phone number that was once associated with Zeitz to Starkand too.

Briffaut wandered into the room, coffee mug in hand.

"What do we know about this mystery phone number?" asked Briffaut, after he'd pondered the trombinoscope for a few seconds.

"It was an associated number from the phone environment we had on Zeitz's phone," said de Payns. "Now it's being contacted by Starkand, and it's in Paris."

"There's three of them, not two?"

De Payns said, "At least three."

"Where?" asked Briffaut. "Show me."

De Payns handed over the printed phone-tower maps.

"This is the mystery phone?" asked Briffaut, pointing to the area around Gare de Lyon.

"Yes," said de Payns.

"Could be the Red Lion hotel," said Briffaut.

De Payns looked at him. "That's a fairly specific guess, boss."

"It was the Americans' Paris antenna, ten years ago," said Briffaut, referring to a non-official HQ for the CIA, which they used as a safe house and meeting place. "They could be using it again."

De Payns stared at his boss.

"Okay, I have something to tell you," said Briffaut. "Walk with me."

They walked to Briffaut's bench in the park outside the Bunker and lit their smokes.

"I had a meeting last night," said Briffaut. "Sidebar with an agent I know from BND. She worked with Christine Zeitz in the old days, before Zeitz was dumped by the German services."

"The Damascus thing?"

"Yeah, that," said Briffaut. "I wanted to see the German reaction to the photo."

"And?" asked de Payns.

"Fifty-fifty," said Briffaut, ducking into his coat collar as a cold breeze drifted across the lawn. "My contact was surprised that we had the photo, but not surprised that we'd taken an interest in Zeitz."

"So how did we get to the Red Lion?"

"I had her followed," said Briffaut.

"Fuck, boss," said de Payns. The general rule of sidebar meetings was no tradecraft, no surveillance.

Briffaut shrugged. "I'm a spy, not a priest."

"And she went to the Red Lion?"

"First thing this morning. And now I have Shrek on it, getting us images of everyone who walks out of that hotel."

"What's your theory?" asked de Payns, knowing that Briffaut wouldn't assign a team without good reason.

Briffaut sucked on the smoke and looked across the walls of the old fort. "We might have the CIA tickling our balls. We'll see what Shrek brings back."

"Interesting," said de Payns. "The Americans are the only service that hasn't asked for a Maypole."

"I'm not jumping to that conclusion," said Briffaut. "The Red Lion is an old antenna. Could be that someone is misdirecting us."

"We okay for that five o'clock finish today?" asked de Payns, determined to make the gala night a success for Romy.

"You picked up those Keratine passports from Mattieu? You onboarded Jim?"

De Payns swore silently.

"You get that sorted before five," said Briffaut, flicking his cigarette into the grass, "and you're a free man."

"Can I get that in writing, for Romy?"

"Of course not," said Briffaut, buttoning his coat and turning for the Bunker. "What would this job be without constant disappointment?"

De Payns's feet hurt. He collapsed onto the sofa as the noise levels rose. Given that he was going to the gala dinner with Romy, and it was a Friday night, Oliver and Patrick were having a sleepover at the Homsis' place, and the apartment rang with happy cries as the kids got their bags ready. Romy and Ana seemed oblivious to the racket, but de Payns felt beaten by the week. He was now chasing a misinformation ring that was luring the Occidental services into conflict with Russia. The Company was unable to ignore an assassination attempt, even if it was obvious that the information was a manipulation, possibly by the Americans. He was stressed by how much there was at stake, although at least he had the comfort of knowing that the DR had smoothly transmitted Jim Valley to de Payns's management, and the passports and other French IDs were being prepared.

He lacked the energy for a cocktail party or a seated dinner with a politician or CEO. An anticipatory migraine threatened at the prospect of being lectured about the sins of carbon emissions or meat-eating.

"Give Dad a hug," said Romy, and Oliver made a flying leap onto his father's stomach, causing de Payns to flinch at the impact. He wrestled his six-year-old to the side and could feel him vibrating with joy; this was his youngest son's first sleepover.

As he lifted his boy sideways, he noticed Ana handing a plastic bag to Romy.

"Okay, you be good tonight," said de Payns, wondering at the bag. "Both of you."

He headed to the shower, thinking about Ollie's excitement

and wondering how many of his kids' milestones he was missing. He dried off and tried talking himself into a higher level of energy and away from his gnawing anxiety about al-Kaniyat and the Wagner Group, assassinations, and information wars. This was Romy's night, and he wanted her to be proud when she presented her husband to the Tirol folks.

Romy hurried into the bedroom in her underwear, looking flustered.

"What was in the bag Ana gave you?" he asked, brushing his damp hair.

She paused. "Ollie's jacket."

"Oh," he said.

"Um, yes. He—he left it at Ana's."

"Really?" de Payns asked. "He was wearing it yesterday morning."

"Yes, he was," she said. "But she took the boys yesterday after school—I had an evening meeting."

"Your office must stay open late . . ."

"No," she said, "I grabbed a bite to eat after work—with David."

There was silence between them. De Payns let it hang.

"We were going over a white paper I have to do for the OECD," she said, sounding defiant.

"Okay," he said, with a smile. "I thought you were doing lunches."

She looked at her feet and then attempted a smile in response. "It was a convenient time to talk over my paper."

"I understand," said de Payns, keeping his tone light despite the jealousy gnawing at him. "I have dinner with all sorts of people; it doesn't mean anything. Anyway, I'm looking forward to tonight. It'll be great."

Romy left the room, and de Payns felt terrible for her. He

spent his life in restaurants and bars, with people he had no intention of declaring to his wife, and yet he'd cornered her into admitting something just because he could. He'd used silence as a weapon on his own wife, a professional technique—something he'd vowed he'd never do.

He found the dinner suit on the bed along with a new shirt, still in its box.

"Honey," he said over his shoulder, as Romy reappeared in the bedroom. "Um . . . about the shirt."

"Yes?" she prompted.

"It's blue, and it's got a frilly front."

"So?" He could see her stiffen.

"I'm sorry, but I don't—"

"Stop the military family bullshit," she snapped. "This is my night, and this is what the men wear at these events."

"Blue?" he repeated, incredulous. "I'm a guest tonight, not the waiter."

"Fuck, Alec!" She stormed from the room, returning several seconds later with her phone in hand.

"There," she said, thrusting it at him. "That's David on the left, at the OECD symposium three weeks ago. Look at his shirt!"

De Payns squinted at the screen and saw a group of three people: on the left was Romy's boss, the slightly too-good-looking David, who indeed wore a blue frilled shirt with his dinner suit.

"Okay for David, the racing-car driver," said de Payns. "But I'm sure Tony Blair wears white, no frill."

"That's not the point," Romy said, but de Payns was no longer listening. He took the phone from her hand and looked at the photo more closely. Beside David was Romy, looking fantastic in a burgundy strapless dress. But it was the third person in the photograph who had caught de Payns's eye.

"Who's that on your other side?"

She peered at the fifty-something, well-groomed man he was pointing to. "That's Henry—Henry Krause."

"Ah," said de Payns. "Is he a colleague from the Tirol Council?"

"Henry's our energy expert," she said, like he was an idiot. "I've told you about him. He's amazing. He helped me put together the fiscal equalization work we're doing on the energy transition. You know: the project with the IMF?"

"Interesting," said de Payns, looking at the picture again and seeing a cigarette in Starkand's hand. "Will he be there tonight?"

"Yes, but not on our table."

"That's a shame."

"He'll be looking after our VIP," said Romy, smirking.

"Sounds intriguing," said de Payns.

"It was confirmed this afternoon. I was helping David with his speech notes, and he told me."

"Who is it?"

"Bill Gates," said Romy proudly.

De Payns whistled. "What's a computer magnate doing at a European clean-energy conference?"

"Bill's really into renewables and hydrogen," said Romy. "He's focused on the future. Henry has been working with him."

"Oh, really?" replied de Payns.

"Yes, they've become very close. It's quite a coup to have him at the dinner and involved in our programs."

As Romy headed for the shower, de Payns took a picture of her phone screen with his burner phone and sent it to Briffaut. He typed out an accompanying message: *STARKAND identified—man at right of group. Works at Tirol Council. Will be at tonight's clean-energy dinner.*

CHAPTER
FORTY-NINE

He had to hand it to the wonderful David: the man could talk. De Payns watched him on the stage and found himself laughing at the man's jokes.

A senior economist from the IMF took to the podium next and spoke about doing "more," before introducing Tony Blair and inviting him to speak.

De Payns wondered at some of the blue-sky claims for renewable energy that were thrown around the room, and whether anyone was going to make a speech about the security risk of allowing Russia to control most of the gas into Europe. With coal-fired power being eliminated, national power grids needed gas to smooth out the volatility of wind and solar, and where were these countries going to get it if Russia cut them off? De Payns was fascinated by the certainty of the people in Romy's world; for them, there wasn't a sliver of doubt that solar panels and EVs were the future, yet there seemed to be no strategy for the alternatives if gas pipelines from Libya, the Middle East, and Transcaucasia were controlled by Putin and his proxies.

That work took place in SCIFs across Europe, the intelligence folks trying to plug gaps in the policy solutions.

"You okay?" Romy asked him. He nodded, taking in her glamor. She combined brains and looks, and he understood why David might be showing too much interest. Didn't forgive him, but certainly understood.

He glanced at his watch: 7:58 p.m. He excused himself, giving Romy's hand a quick squeeze as he kissed her cheek and walked to the toilets of the vast main hall of the Palais des Congrès. He'd been in the Palais once before, during a training exercise run by the Company, but it was more impressive when filled with a thousand drinking, talking people.

He headed down a service hallway and used a blank key on the security door at the end of the hall. Jamming his foot in the door to stop it slamming, he found two men standing behind a trade van, dressed in black, their balaclavas pushed up their faces.

"Like the shirt, mon pote," said Templar, the taller of the two men.

"You trying out to be a gendarme?" asked Danny, feigning concern. "Or you got a job on *The Love Boat*?"

"Shut it," said de Payns. "Starkand is a smoker. Tony Blair will speak for ten minutes, then we eat, and I'm going to get him outside for a smoke around nine. There's a smokers' terrace on the ground floor, facing west. It has vehicle access."

Templar handed de Payns a radio set. He strapped the battery transmitter to his ankle, pulled the wire up to his pocket, and slipped the tiny earpiece into his pocket, where it would stay until he activated the system. "Stand by—it might be earlier or later than nine."

De Payns returned to the dinner and took his seat, clapping hard when Tony Blair told the conference, '*It's up to us*', without clarifying who was the "us" or what was the "it."

The waiters started moving around with food. The lights came up, and de Payns made pleasant small talk with a Big Four accounting firm consultant, who assured him that there were trillions of dollars on offer from renewables. "It's not an energy transition," the consultant said, as if he knew where the pirate's treasure was buried. "It's a wealth transfer."

De Payns nodded politely, his grasp of money ending at around the two billion mark. He kept his eye on Henry Krause—Starkand—who was at the next table and was indeed seated beside Bill Gates. He accepted a top-up of wine, but barely touched it. A second course was served—seared salmon with a sauce—and when the accountant moved away, the too-perfect David dropped himself into the vacated chair and held out his hand.

"David. I work with Romy," he said, friendly and confident.

"Alec. I live with Romy," and David laughed as de Payns shook his hand.

"Oh, I know," said David, running a hand through his Hugh Grant mop of hair. "You turned up as *galante compagnie*. It has been noted."

De Payns relaxed slightly. Some French men honored the man by complimenting the wife. "Clearly, she is out of my league and also too intelligent."

"She is a special person," agreed David, "and so smart. She is unraveling some of the social costs of the transition. It's complex stuff, and we're lucky to have her."

"I'm glad you enjoy her company," said de Payns, smiling with an edge.

"It's more than her company," said David, reaching for the accountant's uneaten bread. "Her work has caught the attention of the OECD. It's good news for all of us."

De Payns decided to let his irritation with David slide a

little, and he took a sip of the above-average wine. "So, Romy tells me you're a racer?"

"Ha!" the man said, slapping his leg. "If I could keep the car on the track, you could call me a racer. I spend too much time in the kitty litter, I'm afraid."

If not for the man having taken his wife to dinner, de Payns might have liked him. "Tell me, she talks a lot about David and Henry. Who does what?"

"I'm the director," said David, touching his chest modestly. "I allocate the priorities and ensure the research programs are doing what they're supposed to do."

"And Henry?"

"He's our energy director, but he's also a roving ambassador," said David. "He's well connected with governments, big pharma, and the oil-and-gas industry. He got Bill Gates here tonight—he's that kind of operator."

"Fascinating," said de Payns.

"Let's go meet him," said David, standing and moving toward the adjacent table before de Payns could respond.

De Payns followed and found himself being introduced to Henry Krause.

"Well," said Krause, standing and offering a short bow and a handshake. "I've heard a lot about you, Monsieur de Payns, and all of it good."

De Payns detected a Germanic harshness to the man's French. "Likewise, Herr Krause," said de Payns. "A pleasure."

"Alec is at the Defense Ministry," said David. "Have I got that right?"

"Yes, the logistics side," said de Payns.

"Oh, of course," said Krause with a smile. "It takes an army of managers to keep one Mirage in the sky."

"That's my line," said de Payns, and they all laughed. "My

wife told me you were a smoker; is there a place we can have a smoke? I've been dying for one since the speeches started."

"You read my mind, Alec," said Krause.

"I'll join you," said David, to de Payns's annoyance.

"Over here," said Krause, leading the group to a side terrace.

De Payns inserted the micro earpiece in his right ear and keyed the radio with the button in his pocket as they moved through the crowd. "From Aguilar—alert, alert," he murmured. "I have the target plus a witness. We are moving out. Proceed as planned. I'll look after the witness."

"Templar copy."

He followed David and Henry down a flight of stairs and through two large glass doors to a street-level enclosure. An Italian man was standing too close to an attractive woman who had personal space issues. The Italian took one look at the band of males invading the smokers' area and ushered the woman back inside.

De Payns accepted a smoke from David and wished he'd brought a coat with him as he caught a puff of chill wind from the north.

"Brisk," said Krause, putting a cigarette between his teeth and lifting his lighter to the other men's smokes. "Every time they say it's a mild winter, I say wait for February, and then tell me . . ."

The black hood was slipped over his head in one smooth motion, and then black-clad arms were around his neck and under his arms, and another masked man dressed in black was lifting Herr Krause by the legs and ankles. Before anyone could utter a sound, Henry Krause was being carried like a roll of carpet to a van that had pulled up.

"Hey!" said David, as Henry Krause was bundled into the side door of the van, and the vehicle accelerated into the night. "What . . . what *was* that?"

David turned to de Payns, his mouth gaping. "Did you see that, Alec? What the hell just happened?"

"Perhaps he pissed someone off?" de Payns suggested mildly. "There are a lot of jealous husbands around."

CHAPTER
FIFTY

On their way home in a taxi, de Payns let Romy snuggle into his chest.

"Thank you for being charming," she said into his shirt. "It makes a difference when you're like that. It lifts the room."

"It went well?" asked de Payns.

"It was perfect," she said. "The speeches, the guest list . . ."

"The frilly shirt," de Payns teased.

She sat up, hit him in the chest. "You looked great, Alec."

"That's what the guests said when they asked me to fetch more wine."

She laughed and looked him in the eye. "I really appreciate the effort you made tonight."

"I was glad to be there," he said. "Your colleagues are nice people."

She leaned on him again. "What did you say to David?"

De Payns forced a smile. "We had a nice chat about his racing cars."

"What about when you went for a smoke?" she added. "Did

you say something to him out there? He came in looking as white as a sheet and didn't look at me for the rest of the night."

De Payns shrugged. "I have no idea. He was fine when I left him with Henry. Apparently they needed to have a talk about something, so I made myself scarce."

"That's weird," she said. "He looked so worried."

Shrek walked north from the Seine, and across the Place Vendôme. Behind one of the buildings that fronted the square was a trade entrance to an old building. One of the loading bays was down a ramp, in the basement level. Shrek input a passcode and walked into a holding area with two wide freight elevators in front of him. To the left was a warehouse with the Company's white sub parked inside the roller door, Lolo leaning on it.

"Over here," said Templar, who stood in the doorway of an administration office.

Henry Krause was inside, chained to an interview desk. Briffaut stood in front of him, smoking, and Danny sat on a sofa on the northern side of the office.

Briffaut met Shrek at the door. "I want you to question our guy," he said under his breath, as Templar jogged to the sub. "Templar's got something he needs to do."

"He's talking?" asked Shrek, as the sub's engine started.

"Says he's CIA. I want you to shake him out before we have to check that officially."

Shrek looked at Krause: saw an educated man, good head of salt-and-pepper hair, some money behind him. Now reduced to answering questions in a basement.

Shrek took the chair in front of Krause. "Did you enjoy the conference?"

"Cut the crap," said Krause, a disgusted look on his face. "Jesus, you French take the cake."

"You're welcome," said Shrek.

"In the middle of a dinner, with Tony Blair and Bill Gates not fifty meters away, you put a hood over my head and throw me in a van? Are you out of your mind?"

"We take spying seriously, especially if it has something to do with our energy system."

"Screw you and screw the DGSI," Krause said, trying for some authority. "Check my bona fides, and let me out of here."

"You're spying for a foreign government, and you think you're walking out of here?" replied Shrek, smiling. He was pleased that Starkand had the wrong agency. "I think you've seen too many movies."

"I work for the CIA."

"No one from the CIA ever says they work for the CIA," said Shrek. "That's not how it works."

Krause slumped. "I'm an agent of influence. Ask them."

"Are you paid?"

"Yes," said Krause.

"To do what?" asked Shrek.

Krause looked around the room. "Can I have a smoke?"

Shrek gave him a cigarette, and Briffaut fetched an ashtray. "You were saying?"

"I influence people," said Krause, shrugging. "I tell people my opinion about certain matters, and because of my position and background, people who also have influence start to see things my way."

"And people fall for this?"

Krause smirked. "Many do."

"What do the Americans want you to say?"

"You know," he said, sucking on his cigarette. "You got the mail."

"I want to hear what *you* know, not what *I* know," said Shrek.

"Okay, lately it's been the Russian buildup in the Eastern Med and the Black Sea, Russia's aggressive moves in Libya, Russia controlling gas pipelines into Europe, Putin choking Europe. That kind of thing."

"You say *lately*," Shrek noted. "What about previously, when you were Raymond Quinette?"

"That was another time, another job," said Krause.

"The Belgian consultancy—Neptune Energy—that you worked for in South Africa?"

Krause shrugged eloquently.

"So, you work at the Tirol Council, Neptune Energy, and the Ligurian Institute?" asked Shrek. "Sounds like interesting work, and maybe even worthwhile. So why sell out to the Americans?"

Krause paused, seeming confused, then chuckled to himself. "Oh, I see—you really don't get it."

"What?"

"These organizations *are* the Americans," said Krause, winking. "The Americans own the think tanks, and the clean-energy consultancies, and those organizations pay me. They are all cover structures."

Shrek slowly shook his head. "Tirol is owned by your employer?"

"I assume so; I've never asked for the paperwork."

"So, you spout opinions to shift policy? You're a provocateur?"

"Well, the Russians started Greenpeace, and they fund the anti-fracking activists, so I guess that makes it a level playing field. I don't feel ashamed, if that's what this is."

"So, you go down to South Africa, pretend you're an expert adviser, and talk them out of a wind farm . . ."

"A wind farm financed by the Russians," said Krause. "The more wind and solar you install, the more you need gas. Get it?"

"The Americans are putting a lot of work into other countries' energy systems," Shrek remarked.

Krause smiled. "The Russians and Americans agree on one thing: energy is destiny."

Shrek swapped a quick look with Briffaut. "So, this is about American energy?"

Krause nodded. "Well, LNG from the United States is more reliable and cheaper than gas from the East," he said. "In certain circles, the Americans are fairly open about this."

"Which circles?" asked Shrek.

"The IEA," said Krause. "Heard of them?"

Shrek didn't like the condescension. "I don't remember the IEA calling for American LNG in Europe."

"They have a ten-point plan to disconnect Europe from Russian gas," said Krause. "The American Petroleum Institute forecasts that by 2030, there'll be *no* piped Russian gas being used west of Ukraine."

Shrek looked at Briffaut, who took up the interview. "Sounds like American disinformation to me. That's what you're paid to spread, right, Henry?"

Krause shrugged. "It's not my fault that journalists and government advisers ignore this material. The API and IEA are both prolific publishers."

"Who is your handler?" asked Shrek, tiring of the energy talk.

"I don't know," said Krause, looking at his hands.

"Would a week in the cells jog your memory?"

Krause sighed, exasperated. "Giselle. That's the only name I've heard."

"Giselle Hess?" asked Shrek, referring to the ID Zeitz had used in Bucharest.

"That's her."

"What's her nationality?"

Krause said, "German American, I think. She speaks both languages like a native."

"What does she do?"

"Gives me materials. Sometimes I just mail them to embassies and consulates, other times I slip them into papers I'm writing, as if it's my own research. Or I can just walk them into meetings."

"What kind of meetings?"

Krause smiled. "With journalists, politicians, advisers working on energy strategy. You should really let me go; it would be better for you."

Briffaut shook his head. "You've been caught spying in France. You should start thinking about what's good for you."

Shrek and Briffaut moved to another office in the basement, while Danny guarded Krause. Briffaut admitted that at some point he'd have to let the Americans know their agent had been caught, but there was a grace period during which a service got to question their detainee about operational matters.

"He's claiming to be a fool who traffics documents and narratives, no questions asked," said Briffaut. "I think we can test that."

"Where do you want me to push?" asked Shrek.

Briffaut looked at the ceiling. "Vulcan. We got that information from *Azzam*, not Starkand. Let's see what he knows about it."

Shrek pulled up a chair and sat in front of Krause once more, offered the man a cigarette.

"This is very Gestapo," said Krause.

"Are you German, Henry?" asked Shrek, leaning forward with his lighter.

"Austrian, with a French mother."

"You're painting yourself as no one in particular, but the

Americans have you in the middle of something very serious with the Russians," said Shrek.

"I know nothing about . . ." He stopped.

"What do you know nothing about?"

Krause slid down in his seat, so his neck was on the chairback. "You'll have to contact the Americans. Just let me go."

"Let me make this clear: even if you were an agent of a foreign government, we would never hand you over if you were involved in an act of terror or sedition."

Krause sat up. "That doesn't apply to me. I'm an agent of influence, that's all."

"Assassination falls under both."

"What?!" Krause exclaimed, the veneer of cool melting. "I have nothing to do with assassination."

"You know about one, and you haven't divulged it to the French security services," said Shrek.

Krause put his hands on the interview desk like a man trying to stabilize himself on a rocking ship. His eyes darted to the corners of the room, as liars often did when they were looking for a credible way through.

"You see, Henry, when we catch Giselle, she'll be bailed out in half an hour because she's the real thing, but you'll be sitting in a basement trying to organize a lawyer. That's how it goes."

"You're bluffing."

"And yet you were snatched from under the noses of your US intelligence masters, and they didn't lift a finger."

Krause shook his head.

Shrek smiled. "It was actually an American who told me that there's no such thing as an agent of influence, only a pawn on a chessboard."

"Fuck off," said the Austrian.

Shrek kept it conversational. "Your handler, or her handler, is dropping Henry Krause in a burn pile right now. The Americans are not coming for you."

Krause's eyes sought focus.

"Shall I leave?" asked Shrek.

"No," said Krause, holding up a manacled hand. "Look, I have nothing to do with that assassination."

Shrek said nothing.

"What do I have to do to get out of here?" asked the Austrian.

"Tell me what you know."

"Okay," said Krause, gesturing for another smoke. "The only material I've seen that relates to assassination was originally included in a drop I did in the Netherlands. I checked what I was sending, and I objected."

"Why?"

"For the reasons you just outlined," said Krause. "I didn't want to be associated with that kind of activity. It wasn't economic or strategic; it looked more like criminal."

"And what happened?"

"I heard nothing more about it until you brought it up just now."

"What did the material say?"

Krause sucked on his cigarette. "There was a meeting on a superyacht—in Monte Carlo, I think. There was an operation called . . . I don't know—Vulcan, I think it was."

"What is Vulcan?"

"Something to do with Hammer and Anvil."

"That's not helpful. Who's Hammer?"

"I'm pretty sure Hammer is Igor Kolomoisky, the Ukrainian gas oligarch," said Krause.

"And Anvil?" asked Shrek, keeping emotion out of his voice.

Krause shook his head. "I don't know."

Shrek let it go. "Where will they try to kill Kolomoisky?"

Krause was flustered. "There's a big event called the Eastern Gas Conference, in Istanbul. Kolomoisky will be a surprise guest speaker."

"Why?"

"I believe he's an investor in the EastMed gas pipeline and the gas fields between Israel and Cyprus. If Kolomoisky is backing EastMed, he'll bring his politician with him, parade him around all the bankers and oil executives."

"*His* politician?" echoed Shrek. "Who would that be?"

Krause gestured for another cigarette, and Briffaut stepped forward to oblige.

"None of this was said to me explicitly," he began.

"Just tell us," said Shrek.

"My guess is Volodymyr Zelenskyy," said Krause, avoiding eye contact.

"You mean *President* Zelenskyy?"

"Sure," said Krause. "Zelenskyy owes everything to Kolomoisky, even his television career."

Shrek paused, the meaning of it sinking in. "Zelenskyy is Anvil? He's the second target?"

Krause shrugged and tapped the ash from his smoke. "I honestly don't know. If Kolomoisky is at the Eastern Gas Conference, he'll be there to persuade the bankers and politicians supporting EastMed and to test whether there's an appetite for it, now that the Americans no longer support it."

"When's this conference in Istanbul?" Shrek asked.

Krause breathed out. "Next week. Can I go now?"

Briffaut sat on the table, putting Krause in shadow. "One more thing you can do for me."

"Yes?" replied Krause.

"When's the next contact with your handler?"

Krause's eyes widened, and then he gulped.

CHAPTER
FIFTY-ONE

Maahi felt the plane tilt forward, and his stomach went with it. The flight out of Benghazi had filled him with nervous anticipation, but what he had not been prepared for was the motion sickness he'd experienced all the way across the Mediterranean to what they assumed was Turkey or Greece. Around him were five other members of the drumming troupe that had once centered on his father and Uncle Omar. Now his father was dead, and so was Uncle Omar. The "Uncle Omar" on this flight was one of Parzan's lieutenants—Akeem—a former fruit-and-vegetable wholesaler who now commanded his own militia cell within the al-Kaniyat organization and took delight in stealing folks' money and raping the women. The people of El Agheila had joked that the age of the warlords had allowed ordinary men to have anything they wanted, and yet they were imprisoned by their own low expectations. "*Steal money and rape women?*" his mother's former boss had once said of Akeem. "*He could have just become a policeman, and at least he'd have a decent uniform.*"

Maahi's stomach griped with the descent of the aircraft, but there was nothing left in him to vomit.

Two rows in front, Akeem stood and turned to face the musicians. He glowered at the group, his long teeth bared like an animal's.

"Remember, you are the Libyan Drumming Troupe from El Agheila," he said, a smile splitting his face. "You do what you're told, and you'll be back with your loved ones before you know it."

Akeem looked around the musicians, some of them in their best clothing for their first-ever visit to a foreign country and all of them scared for the welfare of their families. "If you disappoint Parzan . . ." He let silence tell the rest of the story.

The plane touched down, Maahi's hands clutching at the armrests. When he opened his eyes and let out his breath, he could see the floodlights of a vast area, populated with airplanes and buildings. As they taxied, he saw a large structure with a sign he couldn't read. They were ushered off the plane and into the building, where Akeem produced passports for the troupe—a passport Maahi hadn't known he possessed—and then they picked up their drums and other instruments from the oversized luggage section and were whisked onto a bus.

When the troupe arrived at the hotel, Maahi was placed in a room by himself and told not to leave. He looked through the fourth-floor window at the bright lights of the huge city and wondered what he would be required to do.

He sat at a small sofa and picked up the magazine on the coffee table. He flipped through pages of photographs of the Bosporus and the huge bridge linking Asia Minor to Europe. He recognized these landmarks from his brief schooling.

He put the magazine down again. He thought of his little brother, Demir, sitting in Parzan's compound in the desert, waiting to learn his fate. He considered his own predicament. And he pondered the advice of the man he'd picked up at the airfield a week before, the Westernized one. What was the word he insisted Maahi learn?

He returned to the window and looked out on what he now knew was Istanbul.

Asylum, he thought to himself. Faisal had told him to find an embassy and ask for asylum.

CHAPTER
FIFTY-TWO

Templar drove quickly but smoothly into the heart of the sixth arrondissement via the Boulevard Saint-Germain, Danny beside him in the passenger seat and Lolo perched in the rear seat with his IMSI-detecting spinner laptop. It was 10:52 p.m. In eight minutes from now, Starkand was expected to contact his handler, Christine Zeitz. On the other side of the Seine—somewhere in the ninth arrondissement—Jéjé's team was also poised, waiting for Zeitz's phone call, with Tranh on the spinner and Paulin riding shotgun.

Templar calculated there was a fifty-fifty chance that the Americans had seen Starkand's abduction from the clean-energy conference, and Zeitz was aware that her agent of influence was now controlled by the DGSE. If they had been detected, Zeitz's burner phone would now be in pieces in various garbage bins, probably around a busy Metro station. But if the Starkand snatch had gone undetected, they might have a chance to find Zeitz through her phone activity.

They found a park at the north end of Montparnasse

Cemetery and waited. At 11:01, Lolo muttered that they had
a connection on Zeitz's phone. It opened a connection for the
twenty seconds required for a text message, from somewhere
off the Boulevard Raspail, east of the Rennes Metro station.
They drove to Lolo's instructions, and the connection opened
up again, for twenty seconds. She'd responded to her agent of
influence and confirmed her location.

"Get a location?" asked Templar.

"Just up ahead," said Lolo, pointing. "It's in behind the
shopping *galerie*, right there."

Templar pulled into the curb fifty meters from the Metro
and saw a grouping of older buildings with a narrow alley disappearing among them.

"In there?" asked Templar. "Where does it lead?"

"The map shows an internal courtyard, one of those used
for parking," said Danny. "She could be in a car?"

Templar grabbed a handgun from under his seat and put a
small but powerful camera inside his lined jacket. "I'm having
a look," he said, pulling down the brim of his cap and slipping
out the van door.

It was a traditional part of Paris, the five-story buildings
of the Haussmann period dominating. He walked across the
road, hands jammed in his jacket pockets, and keyed his radio
to check the connection with Danny and Lolo.

He walked down the alley and reached a square that formed
the rear parking area for three buildings. It was here that Lolo
had identified as the most likely location of Zeitz's IMSI and
IMEI signal. The air was still; passive light fell from a few apartment windows and an entrance foyer. He stood still, listening
hard but hearing mostly TV sound echoing across the square.

There was a flash of light so brief he almost missed it. He froze,
waiting, and then saw it again. Someone lighting a cigarette, in

a car, then sharing it with another person? He strolled forward, assuming it was innocent yet also being careful. He kept his gait casual and untrained. As he approached the car hidden in the darkness, an engine revved—a motorbike—and suddenly it was coming at him. He moved to his right, but his hip hit a car's hood, and the front wheel of the bike collided with his left kneecap, twisting him sideways and throwing him to the ground.

He rolled a couple of times on the wet tarmac, the shock of the impact worse than the pain.

"I'm down," said Templar into the radio, trying to regain his feet. "Hit by a motorbike now heading toward you."

"Danny copy," came the reply.

As he tried to put weight on his leg, a car revved to life and squealed out of its parking spot, accelerating in the opposite direction. Templar squinted and caught the registration plate.

"From Templar," he said into the radio again. "I have visual on a car—it's moving in the opposite direction. I make it a silver BMW—five series, I think."

"Danny copy—I have visual on the bike. We're following."

Templar asked Lolo to write down the license plate of the car and get it to the Paris police. "Call the Bunker first, and get them to trigger the support protocol," he said.

Templar steadied himself on his injured leg and limped toward where the car and motorbike had been parked. Turning on his phone torch, he looked around. The tarmac was damp as a result of rainfall earlier in the night. But there was nothing left on the ground. He felt his knee shaking and lowered himself to sit on the curb. An elderly man walking a dog approached Templar with caution. "Are you okay, monsieur?" he asked, his face a mix of pity and disgust.

"I'm fine," said Templar, wiping the street dirt off his jacket. "I'm just really sober."

The man smiled broadly. "Well, there's always a cure for that, non?"

"Believe me," said Templar, "I'm going to be working on it."

She kept to the speed limit but stayed off the main boulevards, until she could find a side street that contained no surveillance cameras. She found a series of narrow streets off the Boulevard de Magenta, north of Place de la République, and parked beside a restaurant dumpster in a service lane. Removing the Paris license plates, she swapped them for a "56" plate from Brittany. Both plates were compliant and legal, registered to a 2021 silver BMW 530i. She placed the Paris plates in the spare tire well and then broke down her burner phone and disposed of it in the dumpster. Next, she drove south into the thirteenth arrondissement, where she descended to the B2 level of a private car storage facility, parked the BMW in one of the lock-up garages, and left the building via the stairwell.

She walked four blocks, feeling nervy, and found a bar. In the corner was a spare table, which she took, ordering a black coffee and a glass of amaretto. She cycled her breathing and thought about the events of the evening. What were the loose ends? What had she missed? What was her exposure? She'd been sitting in the BMW, in their usual liaison. Christine had arrived and debriefed, clarified the final product drops in the concluded operation, and explained how she would keep her asset on ice until he was needed again. They were about to go their separate ways when a dark mass had moved out of the night and into the square behind the apartment buildings. Chris had glanced at him first, as she lit a cigarette, and then on taking a closer look had sat bolt upright, scared. The person moving toward them was a large but athletic man who also moved carefully. Obviously trained and clearly dangerous.

"Go!" she'd said, and Christine had slipped out of the car and onto her motorbike. As she'd started the machine, the man had focused on the rider the way a tiger brings its entire body to concentrate on a deer. She'd pulled out and ridden the bike at the man, who, astonishingly, didn't jump out of the way but seemed to lean away from the bike, as if accepting the pain in advance and already planning his next move. The reactions of a professional.

She drank half of the amaretto and chased it with coffee. It felt good, and she drank the rest of the liqueur and sipped at her coffee, annoyed that France didn't allow smoking in its bars.

She'd left the scene in the other direction, giving the man the opportunity to see her license plate: it didn't matter that he was sprawled on the ground; if he was from a service then he'd have captured the registration number, which was why she'd switched plates and hidden the car. Having her number plate logged by an adversary could result in grave consequences. But her main concern was the fact that the man was in the square at all. Had he followed either of the two women?

She signaled for another amaretto and thought some more about her exposure. Besides being tailed, there were two other risks. First, Christine could be caught, and she might talk. If that was the case, they would have her right now, and there'd be no way to neutralize the threat, except that Chris didn't know the name of her handler and probably didn't have a photograph. The other problem was the burner phone. She'd followed every protocol on the phone, only ever using it with one person, as recommended by the CIA, and the phone was never left switched on. She would assemble it, use it quickly for voice or text communication, and then depower and disassemble it again, leaving the pieces in the lockbox under the driver's seat of the BMW, where she also kept her SIG Sauer 9mm.

The second amaretto arrived. She picked it up, gazed into its mysterious color, and inhaled the fragrance. It calmed her. There was a wrinkle in her phone protocol: one short call, one evening, when she was running late and her personal iPhone had no charge. She'd made the call for family reasons, but the person at the other end was so random, with so little connection to her world, that she'd deemed it low risk. Very low risk.

She smiled to herself and drank the amaretto in one hit. The DGSE were good, but not that good.

CHAPTER
FIFTY-THREE

"Marie is coming over to brief us on this gas conference at eight," said Briffaut, looking into his early morning coffee. "Lars Magnus will be with her."

De Payns nodded as he scanned the one-page summary report from the previous night's interview with Henry Krause. It was shortly before 6:00 a.m., and de Payns—who'd been texted at 5:00 a.m. by his boss—was getting up to speed on the Krause revelations.

"Zelenskyy?" asked de Payns, still amazed. "That's extreme . . . but Kolomoisky and Zelenskyy are not on the official guest list?"

"That's right," said Briffaut, examining a biscuit. "And before you ask, yes I have considered that the Americans fed Krause the rumor about Zelenskyy being a target, but I think his opinions are his own."

De Payns looked up from the one-pager. "Where is Starkand now?"

"We have him in a nice hotel room, and we're monitoring

his phone and internet," said Briffaut. "We don't think he's blown. It could be useful to see where the Americans send him next."

"He's cooperative?"

Briffaut winced. "A cornered animal can be cooperative. Let's just say he's very focused on the threat of espionage charges. And besides, he's going to this gas conference in Turkey."

De Payns knew he was about to be told to mind his own business, but he asked anyway. "Have you turned him?"

"Watching and waiting is what I'm doing," the boss said. "The reason I wanted you here early is to alert you to something."

"Yes?"

"The Tirol Council. It's a front for our American friends."

De Payns felt the blood drain from his face. "Fuck!"

"Luckily, that wasn't Shrek's reaction when Krause revealed it. We're clear on your level; Romy's not in danger."

"Am I?"

Briffaut shook his head. "These think tanks traffic in political and corporate opinion. They build consensus so journalists start to spout opinions as if they're facts."

Scenarios roared through de Payns's mind. "Jesus Christ."

"Tirol is being monitored," said Briffaut, pointing de Payns back to the report from the Krause interview. "I'll let you know more if you need to know."

De Payns turned his attention back to the document in his hand. "You think the Russians will come after Zelenskyy and Kolomoisky?"

Briffaut sipped. "If Putin thinks Zelenskyy and his benefactor are tools of the CIA, then he might justify it. It might even be a least-worst outcome for Europe. If Putin can change the regime in Ukraine, perhaps he won't invade?"

They locked eyes.

"Let's see what the brains trust has to say," said Briffaut finally, looking at his watch. "They'll be here soon."

Marie Lafont opened the Operation Ellipse meeting in the second-floor SCIF by reminding the team that the President's office was still not prepared to raise the assassination with the Kremlin or with Kiev. "France will not abrogate its neutral stance on Ukraine, or its economic interests in Russian gas, which means there won't be a political engagement. This will be a job for the DO."

She looked over her half-glasses at Briffaut, who gave the mildest of shrugs. "By the way, how's your OT?" she asked. "The one who was hit by the motorbike?"

Briffaut smiled. "He's tough. His ego sustained the most damage."

Lafont asked for details on the vehicles, and Briffaut told her the motorbike had proved elusive in the Paris traffic. He showed her the printout on the BMW 5-series: a 75 number, meaning it was registered at a Paris address, which was a fleet-leasing company. The lessee was a nonsense shell company with a serviced-office corporate address and nominees run through the Caymans.

Briffaut said, "We've been able to look at the handler's associated phone numbers and their phone activity. Just about all of it is in Paris, in very short bursts, which suggests he's based in Paris and operating with texts."

She took off her glasses. "What's the theory?"

Briffaut tapped a finger on the conference table. "The Americans steered us to look into *Azzam*, and that revealed an assassination plan by Wagner and the LNA. It feels like we're being nudged into something we can't walk away from."

"Which brings us to this," murmured Lafont, referring to

a file which also sat in front of de Payns, Briffaut, and Lars Magnus. "The information on Vulcan you have acquired, thanks to the American agent of influence. He alleges that Hammer is Igor Kolomoisky, and Anvil could be Ukraine's President Zelenskyy."

She clicked on her remote, and a picture of Volodymyr Zelenskyy emerged.

"Kolomoisky and Zelenskyy no longer really appear together in public, but if it happens it's expected to be at the Eastern Gas Conference in Istanbul next Friday and Saturday."

She pointed a remote, and the screen came alive as the room's lights dimmed. A large conference hall appeared on the screen. Lafont paused at an interior shot of an enormous auditorium. "This is the main hall, where the opening gala dinner night will be held on the Friday night. The MiT expects Kolomoisky to give the keynote on Saturday night."

They went through the mechanics of the Company's cooperation with Turkey's main intelligence agency—the MiT—with an outreach that would include credible intelligence about a terror threat at the event, but no mention of Zelenskyy, Kolomoisky, or Ukraine. The cooperation would not mention Russia or the United States.

"We're giving the Americans a wide berth in all of our discussions," said Briffaut, looking at Magnus. "You think the Americans are running Ukraine?"

Magnus dodged the question. "The Americans made Zelenskyy think he can join NATO, and they installed missiles at the Russian border, knowing that those two things alone would poke the bear. This is Putin we're talking about—not Gandhi."

"And if they succeed in killing Kolomoisky and Zelenskyy?" asked Briffaut.

"Their first step would be to try to put their own guy in the

President's palace. If they can't achieve regime change, they'll try an invasion—which also aids the Americans economically."

"How so?" asked Briffaut.

"The US has become the world's largest producer of gas in the past few years, even surpassing Qatar," said Magnus. "Europe is their target market. They expect European demand for imported LNG will increase a hundred and fifty percent by 2040."

Briffaut rolled his eyes. "This is all economics?"

Magnus allowed a rare smile. "Perhaps all economics is really energy?"

CHAPTER
FIFTY-FOUR

The plane banked and lined up for a landing at Samandira Air Base, twenty kilometers east of Istanbul. There was a uniformed detail waiting at the floodlit apron in front of a medium-size hangar, and de Payns led Danny, Shrek, and Jéjé down the stairs and into a Mercedes van. They drove along the apron and arrived at a building with a low, flat profile and large antennas on the roof which reached hundreds of feet into the air.

A guard stopped de Payns and his team at the vestibule and searched them for weapons before they were allowed in.

"Captain Marak," said the soldier who met them at the door of a large interview room, introducing himself. He was built like a middleweight, despite the disguise of the good suit. "Monsieur Droulez?"

De Payns stepped forward and shook his hand, and the Turk ushered him into the room, closing the door behind them. They sat at a table that looked over the nighttime activities of the Turkish army air base.

"This is not unheard of," said Captain Marak, "but it's new to me."

De Payns did as Briffaut had instructed and listened. Captain Marak was a Turkish intelligence officer from the MiT who, according to Briffaut, had been ordered to support the DGSE mission.

"If I understand this correctly," said Marak, "your service has clear intelligence that a Libyan militia linked to the LNA is planning a terror attack at tonight's Eastern Gas Conference?"

De Payns smiled, knowing that Turkey was a major backer of Haftar's enemy in western Libya, the GNA. "That's correct."

"May I ask how you retrieved that information?" asked the captain.

"I can't tell you because I don't know," said de Payns.

Marak nodded. "The instruction from my government is that this conference must go ahead as planned. My government is very sensitive about perceptions that we are vulnerable to terrorism, and they have economic arrangements with half the participants at this conference, representing billions of dollars. The government hosts this conference every year to make Turkey look stable and . . ." He clicked his fingers, searching for the word.

"Investible?" de Payns suggested.

"Yes," said Marak. "So, we have to do it this way, but it will be my call. You can assist and observe, but there will be no bang-bang. This is all beneath the radar. Understood?"

De Payns nodded. "Got it," he said.

Shrek checked in to the Bridge Hotel as the sun came up in Istanbul. He was sharing with Danny, and Aguilar was rooming with Jéjé. The call to prayer echoed around the vast city, and he made his habitual checks of the room, which was on the fourth floor. He could find no transmission devices, so he moved to investigate the hallway and the fire stairs, as well as determining how many levels the elevators could access. Even in the security-obsessed Company he was known as "thorough," which he preferred to "paranoid." Paranoid was a pathological condition; being thorough kept him alive.

They met at the restaurant on the ground floor of the hotel for breakfast, which in the usual Turkish way matched perfect coffee with over-sugared pastries.

Aguilar talked them through the evening's operation. Captain Marak from the MiT was going to let the French observe, but they would only be armed with 9mm handguns and vests once they were inside the Istanbul Congress Center, and they would be under Marak's command.

"He used that word, '*observe*'?" asked Shrek, as Aguilar spelled it out.

"Those are the rules," said Aguilar. "And he also specified that there's to be no bang-bang."

"Just as well I'm a pacifist," said Jéjé, which made the group laugh; the only person in the Company who loved fighting more than Templar was Jéjé.

Shrek left the crew and walked into the foyer, looking around the newsagent kiosk that was situated where the hotel met the footpath. He stood behind a postcard rack and observed the street, assuming there was an even chance of the MiT being nosy. Shrek wasn't going to make a thing of it, but he liked to know who was where.

It was a mild morning, people starting to move down the street, and across the road he could see another hotel lobby, with the word "Budget" in its name. A group of people milled near the sidewalk in front of it. They looked slightly out of place, maybe provincial or rural judging by their poor dress sense and cheap fabrics. He touched a postcard on a revolving rack but kept his eye on the other hotel, wondering what aberrant movement had drawn his eye. He was about to turn away and investigate the loading docks out the back of his hotel, when he saw a young man—perhaps more Tunisian or Berber than Turkish—step away from the group and walk swiftly along the street. He was conspicuous by his red jacket and baggy taupe pants, and he was followed quickly by an older man, perhaps thirty-five, who had noticeably big teeth, like a horse. Horsey swooped on the escapee, grabbed him by the left bicep, and hauled the Berber in the red jacket back into the hotel lobby.

It happened very quickly, and Shrek pulled back into the shadows of the kiosk, bought a pack of chewing gum with loose change, and scanned the street for more action. It didn't look like MiT—not professional enough—and Turkey's organized criminals were an altogether better-dressed bunch than the thug with the teeth who'd descended on the Berber.

After a few minutes, satisfied there were no followers on the French crew, Shrek slid away to investigate a potential rear exfiltration route.

CHAPTER
FIFTY-FIVE

After an hour walking around the Istanbul Congress Center, de Payns was already tired. The Congress Center was a large, sprawling, easily accessible sieve of a venue, and by the time he'd been introduced to most of it, de Payns felt as if he'd walked fifty miles. He didn't have much choice in the matter; his job was to fit in with MiT's operation, and, as instructed, he'd adopted a professional look with a suit and office shoes.

The Eastern Gas Conference had started on Friday evening, and there'd been a brief Saturday morning session. Now the afternoon was drifting along in plenaries until the closing-night dinner at which Kolomoisky was going to speak. De Payns walked the vast Harbiye Auditorium with Captain Marak, noting its layout: the entrances and exits, and the latticework of service passageways that connected the main hall to the back-stage area.

He followed Marak onto the stage, and they looked over a room large enough to accommodate several basketball courts. "I'm advised Kolomoisky's table is there," said the captain, pointing to an area twenty meters from the lip of the stage. "The main corporate and political tables are either side."

De Payns scanned the sea of big round dining tables, then the tiered seating rising at the back of the hall. The room could be accessed from more than one level of the building, he realized. "Entry from two levels?" he asked.

"Actually, three," said Marak. "There's service access from a mezzanine level below."

The backstage area was a system of green rooms, changing rooms, kitchens, and administration offices for the theater management. They walked down some service stairs and came out in the mezzanine, from where the car parks below could be accessed. In front of the escalators that took delegates up to the halls and auditoriums was a bank of security gates that matched the ones at the top of the building.

De Payns wasn't comfortable with the setup, but he noticed a lot of uniformed security around the building, and Marak assured him there were intelligence agents and cops in plainclothes.

"We have four hours before this evening's event," said Marak, looking at de Payns. "You may as well get some rest, because these gas people will send you to sleep, I promise."

The bus stopped in the covered drop-off area at the side of the Congress Center, and Maahi filed out with his troupe. The building was enormous, rising up like God's spacecraft and visible for miles. He'd never seen anything like this city, and it had grabbed his curiosity. But when he'd tried to have a look around after the breakfast in the hotel, Akeem had grabbed him off the street and dragged him inside, where he'd held up his phone and threatened to call Parzan.

Akeem led them in through the service entry and up an

escalator, something Maahi had used only once before, at Istanbul Airport. Maahi's throat was dry, and his palms were already sweaty. He wondered how well he'd be able to hit the drums in this nervous state.

They reached the top of the escalator and saw the security gates, manned by guards, ahead of them. A conference official with a blazer and a walkie-talkie led them to a service door, and one of the security guards came over with a detection wand and cleared each of the troupe one by one. Inside the service door, they walked up a flight of stairs until they were in the backstage area of the huge auditorium. Maahi could hear voices booming over the loudspeaker system and lots of laughter. It was so noisy; it sounded like there must be a thousand people out there.

The man in the blazer showed them into their dressing room, then hurried away, leaving the door open behind him. Several porters brought in the drum cases, flutes, and guitars from the bus and left them in a pile on the carpet. Akeem opened two large gear bags and dispensed costumes to the players, and as the troupe pulled on their long, loose white robes, a wave of sadness overwhelmed Maahi. Donning the robe brought back memories of traveling and playing with his father, uncle, and cousins, and he felt homesick for that life, for that era of Libya.

When they were dressed, Akeem checked his watch.

"An hour before we go on," he said. "Let's warm up the drums and flutes."

He pointed to Maahi and Kabil, a large member of the troupe who'd also been forced into the service of Parzan and the al-Kaniyat militia. As the rest of the players tuned their instruments, the two of them followed Akeem into a short hallway that connected two changing rooms.

"Stand here," said Akeem, beckoning them toward a

Coca-Cola vending machine. "There are no cameras covering this spot."

Akeem took a key from his pocket, unlocked the door of the machine, and swung it open. He dragged out a black sports bag and kneeled, unzipping the bag.

"One each," he said, handing Maahi a Heckler & Koch MP5. It was a weapon he knew well. Maahi weighed it in his hands and instinctively checked for safety and load. The black submachine gun had the small fifteen-round magazine, and it had been shortened by removing the stock, so it ended in a pistol grip. A looped shoulder strap was attached to the back of the pistol grip assembly, which had an exposed loop where the stock had been removed. It was a standard setup for the al-Kaniyat militia.

"Like this," said Akeem, and he raised his robe, hooked the MP5 strap over his shoulder, and let the weapon drop so it was hanging under his armpit. When he put the robe down again, there was no sign of the weapon, thanks to the small magazine, which didn't protrude.

Maahi and Kabil followed his lead, adjusting their straps to their own liking and then securing their guns so they didn't show.

When they were done, Akeem drew them in and gave the youths their assignments. "You have your targets," he said, looking them each in the eye. "And remember: it does not offend Allah if you kill a Jew."

Too scared to talk, Maahi just nodded. He had never even met a Jew.

"We're going to make history," said Akeem, his long white teeth pushing into a smile. "Europe has never met the al-Kaniyat militia. But after tonight, they will never forget us."

CHAPTER
FIFTY-SIX

Briffaut took the meeting at the Cat through the events of the previous twenty-four hours: the Maypole with the Turks, the reticence about talking publicly of the risk of a terrorist attack, and the agreement with the Turkish services to deal with it below the radar. Since the Turks would never interfere with a Russian operation, the French had told the Turks the attack had been planned by their enemy General Haftar but would be carried out under the false flag of a Libyan militia.

"Turkey is always careful with the bear," said Briffaut, "but they also hate terrorists."

Christophe Sturt frowned. "Will the two of them—Zelenskyy and Kolomoisky—be at this gas conference?"

Briffaut shrugged. "It could go that way. They've appeared together before, and the Tirol Council consultant believes they might have something to announce."

The DR director was under pressure; Briffaut could tell by the way he chewed his bottom lip. Sturt would be required to advise the Director General of the DGSE, whose office would impart the day's intelligence to the President's office at the Élysée. While such a position gave Sturt standing within the Company, it also put him in the headlights. If the French services were interrupting a Russian operation, then the fiction of French neutrality toward Russia started to look thin.

Sturt asked, "If Ukraine makes so much money from hosting Russian gas pipelines into Europe, why would they invest in the EastMed pipeline?"

"They'd do it for money," said Magnus, "but they'd also do it as a hedge against Putin switching off the gas through Ukraine. The United States has withdrawn support for EastMed, so Kolomoisky has an opportunity to take leadership and ensure his investment is successful."

Back at the Bunker, Briffaut sat at his desk and brooded. It wasn't unusual for politics and national security to collide at a SCIF meeting, but the inclusion of gas was making him nervous. When the Élysée had been lobbying the Merkel government to drop its plans for Nord Stream 2, the French Ministry of Economics and Finance had concluded that a sudden switching-off of Russian gas—if Germany was relying on Nord Stream 2—would have catastrophic effects on Western Europe. Energy would quickly become too expensive for households and businesses, and the real winners would be LNG exporters, the United States and Qatar, who would charge the spot price, pushing up the price of gas and electricity even further. The efforts of the French government to stop Germany going ahead with Nord Stream 2 had been unsuccessful and had been complicated by Berlin's campaign to have France's nuclear power excluded from Europe's green energy framework.

Briffaut felt responsible for cracking the information racket that was luring France into a position on Russia. He stared at a blue file that sat on his desk. It contained the printed still shots from Shrek's surveillance of the Red Lion hotel. The pictures had already been run through France's database of "faces," but there had been no matches. The images had also been disseminated in the DR section, with no luck there either. Perhaps the Red Lion really had ceased to be the CIA's antenna in Paris, and Gabby Castigan had a genuine reason to be there?

He was about to put the folder into his safe but decided the pictures could be of use on the Operation Ellipse or Operation Bellbird trombinoscopes. He walked into op room four and found Templar there.

"How's the leg?" asked Briffaut, taking a seat beside him at the table.

"Not broken, but it's swollen," said Templar. "At least I've still got my looks."

"Did you see the note from the techs?" asked Briffaut, indicating a white ring binder labeled *Operation Bellbird—Handler Calls.*

Templar looked: a Post-it stuck on the hard cover noted that in eighteen days of phone logs from the handler's phone, only one looked genuine and had not been verified.

"I want all the boxes ticked on this Krause–Zeitz ring," said Briffaut. "Short of finding them, let's work out who they were talking to."

Templar flipped to the marked page and saw the pink highlighter underlining the unverified number. It was registered in the name of Jabir Okimba, with an address in the eastern Paris suburb of Gagny.

"I'll get Paulin on it, leave it with me."

"Go easy on the Percodan," said Briffaut as he left the room. "I need you sharp."

CHAPTER
FIFTY-SEVEN

De Payns and Shrek heard the MiT radio system click on their Turkish walkie-talkies: Captain Marak was on the net.

"A VIP guest has just been announced," said Marak. "President Zelenskyy—confirm President Zelenskyy of Ukraine."

"Copy that," said de Payns, and turned to Shrek. They were standing on the marble floor of the mezzanine, watching the guests and delegates arriving from the car parks downstairs and being herded through the security stations before being channeled into the auditorium.

"I guess it was a badly guarded secret," said Shrek. "Let's go to work."

They were dressed in suits with ballistic vests under their jackets and Glock 9mm handguns, supplied by the Turks, in shoulder holsters.

De Payns clicked the Y confidential frequency. "Aguilar to all, looks like we have Zelenskyy coming in as the VIP."

"Jéjé copy, all clear up the top."

De Payns and Shrek let themselves into the service stairwell and climbed it to the backstage area of the auditorium. There they split up, Shrek going to the left-hand side of the stage and de Payns to the right. From his position in the wing, de Payns could see Jéjé on one side of the hall and Danny on the other. The noise was intense, the conference a rowdy convergence of capital and politics, an unholy alliance in some people's eyes but also the lifeblood of the oil-and-gas industry. De Payns looked out at the spread of tables, hosting perhaps a thousand people, with waiters milling between them serving food and alcohol. The table in the middle of the front row had a few empty chairs, though Igor Kolomoisky was already seated, along with his entourage. Sharking around Kolomoisky were two obviously military security people, wearing dark gray ripstop hiking gear, with black bum bags at the front serving as holsters. De Payns thought they were soldiers by the way they held themselves, and he assumed they were from Kolomoisky's private unit of the Azov Battalion, the Black Corps.

The thwomp of helicopter rotors was faintly audible as an MC readied herself in the backstage area, a man with a walkie-talkie giving her instructions in Turkish which sounded like a request to hold off on beginning the proceedings.

"From Marak," came the call over the Turkish walkie-talkie. "VIP has his own security team. They're coming down from the helicopter pad, everyone hold their stations."

The room buzzed as the Zelenskyy group came in the side entrance to the auditorium. The Ukraine president was dressed in his usual activewear, and his grooming was immaculate, totally in keeping with his acting background. As he was escorted to the center-front table, well-wishers reached out for handshakes as he passed. De Payns counted four presidential bodyguards, all looking heavy and efficient.

The man with the walkie-talkie handed the MC a slip of

paper. She read it, made a face, then walked out onto the stage with her microphone and greeted the room in English. "Good evening, delegates. We have some very special guests in the house tonight."

De Payns clicked his radio. "Aguilar to Jéjé—what's it like on the floor?"

"Jéjé to Aguilar," said the former navy diver. "There's a lot of booze making the rounds, and the show hasn't even started yet."

"Aguilar copy," said de Payns. "Keep visual on Zelenskyy."

According to the Eastern Gas Conference program, the main course would be served and then the keynote speaker—which the crowd now knew was Igor Kolomoisky—would address the room for twenty minutes, after which a Bedouin drumming troupe would be giving a brief performance. De Payns looked up from the program and peered through the gap in the stage curtain at the conference floor. The center-front table was becoming a train-switching yard, with grandees of all sorts coming over to kiss the ring and make themselves known to Kolomoisky and Zelenskyy, who were both seated facing the stage. Concentric circles of security folded around the table, the closest being the bodyguard who had a chair placed directly behind Zelenskyy, and various people fanning out around them. The security was intense, with no attempt to blend in.

The delegates ate their meals and drank their booze, and de Payns felt a rising sense of irritation at the spectacle. Too many people, too many guns, too much at stake. Istanbul was a crossroads of east and west, and also Europe and Asia Minor, and every banker, engineering executive, and drilling consultant from both continents seemed to be in attendance.

The MC announced that Igor Kolomoisky was going to address the conference, and de Payns locked eyes with

Kolomoisky's senior security person as he walked his boss to the stage. The man's paranoid gaze reflected de Payns's own feelings.

Kolomoisky spoke in fairly good English about the cooperation required to get the EastMed pipeline working and the importance of the four main seabed gas fields between Cyprus and Israel for Europe's future energy security. Then he paused and smiled. Behind him, a huge screen played video footage of a gas rig on the ocean; de Payns could see it from the feedback monitors in the backstage area. The footage featured a helicopter panning shot of the rig, which had the name Pontus on the sides. "We've been drilling in an area off the coast of Israel, between Leviathan and Tamar, in what is known as the Pantheon field. We expect to extract ten billion cubic meters of natural gas each year from Pantheon, which—along with the other gas field on this seabed—will supply Israel, Jordan, and Europe with affordable gas for decades to come."

The applause began, but Kolomoisky wasn't done. "We heard the disappointing news several weeks ago that the Biden Administration had withdrawn its support for the EastMed pipeline"—there were scattered boos, and Kolomoisky held up his hand—"but the European Commission still supports it, and so do I!"

The crowd cheered.

"Tonight, I can say that we are very close to announcing that the EastMed pipeline through Cyprus, Greece, and Italy will soon be in a position to confirm a consortium of investors and bankers. When we do that, I look forward to telling you that we are starting construction—stay tuned, folks."

The cheers grew, and Kolomoisky smiled and again held up his hand, the consummate showman.

"But before we can connect directly into Europe, next week we will be moving our first consignments of Pantheon gas onto a floating processing and storage ship."

Even without the threat of an assassination, Kolomoisky's words made de Payns stiffen: the Kremlin was unlikely to let EastMed progress without Russian involvement.

Kolomoisky finished by praising the Israelis, the Cypriots, the Egyptians, Italians, Greeks, and French, to rapturous applause. As the noise of the crowd rose, a small army of security assembled on the stage, surrounding Kolomoisky, with no one bothering to conceal their firearms.

When the Ukrainian oligarch finally returned to his table, acknowledging the plaudits like a Roman emperor, the backstage area came alive with the venue managers telling the drummers they had a one-minute call. Technicians readied lights and clipped microphones to the drummers' robes. As the musicians were about to go on, de Payns asked Jéjé and Danny to keep an eye on things, while he motioned to Shrek in the other wing.

"Let's have a look around," said de Payns when his colleague joined him. He wanted a better look at the rabbit warren of rooms and corridors behind the auditorium.

"Everyone in here was searched," Shrek reminded him.

"I know," said de Payns. "I can see everyone out the front, but I can't see anything twenty meters that way." He pointed to the backstage area.

They walked the main backstage corridor with all the changing rooms opening off it. There were a lot of people in the confined area, more so when the drummers filed out of a doorway in their flowing white robes and Bedouin headwear. As they walked past the Frenchmen in the direction of the stage, de Payns noted that their toothy leader seemed intense, and there was some lingering eye contact from him. A younger man—perhaps eighteen years old—walked beside his leader, and as the troupe passed, de Payns wondered if he'd seen the leader's left hand clasped around the younger man's bicep, as if pulling him along.

Pausing, de Payns made to alert Shrek, but his colleague was already focused on the leader.

"Outside the hotel this morning?" murmured Shrek. "That's them."

De Payns turned and followed Shrek, and as they did the leader of the troupe looked over his shoulder, eyes focusing on Shrek, and released the young man he'd been shepherding. The leader's right hand gripped at something beneath his billowing robe, and he raised it toward Shrek, revealing a rifle shape as it came horizontal. Shrek pushed aside the barrel with a soft left hand and threw a hard straight right into the leader's right shoulder joint, popping it. In a single movement, Shrek's left hand gripped the rifle and yanked backward, pulling the leader's right arm out of its socket. The leader started to scream but was stopped short by a punch in the throat and then a stamp-kick to the left patella that hyperextended the leg, leaving him in a crumpled state of agony at Shrek's feet.

The backstage people started yelling, technicians clambering over one another at the sight of a machine pistol, and the crowd stampeded.

The youngster who'd been manhandled turned and ran down the hall past de Payns as the troupe stepped back from the fray amid yells of panic. De Payns turned to follow the youngster but came face to face with a larger, stronger man who had his own rifle now horizontal under the Bedouin robes and pointing. The gun fired as de Payns crouched into it to his right and drove up with his legs, throwing a left hand onto the rifle barrel and driving the heel of his right hand into the point of the shooter's nose. The shooter's head jerked backward in a spray of blood, and de Payns kicked the man in the solar plexus, getting both hands on the rifle as his assailant sagged to the ground. In a fast, trained action he twisted the barrel backward and smashed the rifle stock into the man's teeth, tore the rifle free, and drove the stock downward into the man's nose, hard. Beside him, Shrek had taken possession of the leader's weapon; it looked like a chopped-down MP5, weapon of choice for the terror cells of North Africa.

The gunfire drew more panic, and from the stage area Captain Marak appeared, handgun leveled and MiT agents tucked in behind him.

"You go," said Shrek, nodding at the fleeing young drummer. "I'll deal with Marak."

Standing, de Payns dropped the submachine gun and drew his handgun. He turned and saw the young drummer at the end of the hall, going through the service door that led down to the mezzanine. De Payns sprinted after him, keying the radio as he ran. "Aguilar pursuing Tango to the mezzanine."

He reached the spring-loaded door and paused, wondering if the terrorist was waiting on the other side. De Payns could hear his footfalls receding down the stairs and burst through the service door. At the bottom of the stairs, the terrorist's robes billowed as he reached out and pushed through the door. De Payns pursued, staying rhythmic on the steps rather than rushing. He reached the service door before the lock fully clicked, and he shoved through with his shoulder, pistol raised and sweeping the room in a two-handed weaver stance. A middle-aged couple with name badges recoiled in horror, and a group of women tried to hide behind one another. One of them pointed to the escalators that led down to the parking levels.

De Payns reached the escalator in five strides across the marble and saw the runner at the bottom of the moving stairs, throwing off his Bedouin robe and revealing a shortened MP5 slung under his right armpit in the style made famous by Yasser Arafat's bodyguards. De Payns skipped down the escalator three steps at a time and could see the youngster—now dressed in jeans and an FC Barcelona shirt—running for the second escalator. Hurried shouts and the footfalls of security followed de Payns as he reached the top of the next escalator, which would take them to the lowest level of the complex. He was closing on the kid and had to make the decision: shoot him in the back or take him alive and let Captain Marak extract the truth. He had to balance that against his safety. The machine pistol the kid carried could shred de Payns to ribbons.

The Tango reached the bottom of the escalator when de Payns was halfway down. He raised his handgun, but the runner sprinted into the car park.

De Payns reached the lowest level of the parking building and looked out, saw the kid's head bobbing fifteen cars away, his eyes wide and scared. A security guard emerged from an office beside one set of elevator doors, armed with a 9mm pistol, and quickly assessed that the panting Frenchman was not the threat. De Payns pointed at the kid, and they split, the guard running for the western side of the parking building, where a green exit sign glowed, while de Payns continued down the middle, keeping his eye on the runner, who showed no signs of slowing. De Payns wondered how much longer he could maintain his own speed. He'd worn a pair of black Salomon hiking boots with his chinos and sports jacket, rather than the office shoes he'd worn for the walk-through of the Congress Center earlier in the day, but his fitness was not good, and his lungs were starting to burn.

The runner jagged to his right suddenly, cutting across de Payns's trajectory at a right angle and making for the eastern exit sign. De Payns put in an extra effort, realizing that the would-be assassin was just seven cars away now, having given up his advantage in order to avoid the Turkish guard. The exit sign loomed over an apron that was free of cars, and the runner got to the fire door beside another set of elevators. But instead of pushing through the door, the terrorist stopped and turned to face de Payns who also came to a halt, his Glock raised. De Payns panted, his throat rasping, and the kid slowly brought up his MP5 level with de Payns's stomach, looking him in the eye.

"Take it easy," said de Payns, gasping for breath but not shooting. "Don't touch the trigger."

Behind him de Payns could hear the shouting of the MiT agents and security coming closer, but the kid and the Frenchman kept their eyes on each other. Sweat dripped between de Payns's shoulder blades, and he held steady, no sudden movements.

"Put it down, kid," said the Frenchman, gulping for breath. "Let me help you."

The kid seemed to take forever, his eyes darting toward the stampede of Turkish security officers. But slowly he clasped the gun by its barrel, unhooked it from his shoulder, and threw it onto the concrete, where it clattered and bounced. De Payns moved forward, handgun trained on the kid's face, wondering if there was a bomb vest. As he got a foot to the MP5 and kicked it away, a cacophony of threats and orders blasted from the MiT officers who'd just come around the corner behind him.

He gave the terrorist one last chance. "Please."

The kid's hands went up in the air.

"Asylum," said the kid, eyes wide but somehow trusting. "*Asylum.*"

CHAPTER
FIFTY-EIGHT

De Payns sat in one of the visitors' rooms of the MiT in downtown Istanbul. A television mounted on the wall showed footage of the Istanbul Congress Center taken from a helicopter, the area surrounded by flashing lights of police vehicles and ambulances, journalists breathless and excited about what they were reporting on. De Payns couldn't understand a word but he got the gist: terrorists had attempted a mass shooting, with Ukraine's President Zelenskyy and billionaire Igor Kolomoisky as the targets. The primary point of the bulletin seemed to be that the shooters were foreign terrorists, judging by the ISIS training footage cut into the news reports, and the intended victims were Jewish, evidenced by the file footage of the putative victims wearing kippahs.

De Payns was exhausted, and his feet hurt from running on concrete. The night's outcome could have been worse: no one was dead, only two people in hospital, and the Turkish government was able to say it had stopped a terror attack by Haftar's Libyan terrorists thanks to European intelligence-sharing—all without the Turks knowing they'd stopped a Russian operation . . .

But the Russians would know, de Payns realized, as he thought about the shot from the burly shooter's machine pistol. It had passed his leg and embedded in the corridor wall, according to Marak. He wondered if he was too old for this and if Romy's instinct that the job had run its course was correct. If he'd died in a conference hall in Istanbul, what succor would Patrick and Oliver be able to take from their loss? They wouldn't read about their dad in the newspapers, and when France awarded him the Légion d'Honneur posthumously, it would be at a secret ceremony in the same place where they'd just memorialized Paul Degarde. The family would be told to not discuss it, his own boys would be encouraged not to ask questions. What fulfilled him so significantly, he realized abruptly, meant only emptiness and absence for his family.

The door opened, and Captain Marak walked in. "My service has just spoken with Monsieur Larmes," said the Turk, referring to the DGSE's head of external liaison. "You can have five minutes with Maahi—he's the young fellow you caught."

De Payns stood. "Five minutes? Don't you mean five hours?"

"You wouldn't let me anywhere near him if we were in Paris," the captain pointed out. "I'm allowing this in recognition of your cooperation in thwarting the attack. Thanks to your intelligence, we avoided the worst-case scenario."

"There were other shooters. Do I get time with them?"

Marak gave him a knowing smile. "They are not in a state for visitors, I'm afraid."

As they walked to the cells, Marak asked: "A hit on the Ukrainian president, by a Libyan militia—will this be a Haftar trend?"

De Payns shrugged. "Al-Kaniyat soldiers are guns for hire. I'd be surprised if these shooters know why they're here."

The kid was in leg-irons and manacles, a chain holding his hands close to a U-bolt on the table in front of him. He'd been crying and looked very scared. He also looked intelligent and sensitive, not like the Maghreb terrorists and thugs de Payns had dealt with in the past.

"*Français?*" asked de Payns, and the kid—Maahi—shook his head.

"English?"

"A bit, sometimes," said Maahi. "Are you French?"

De Payns ignored the question, took a seat, and offered Maahi a cigarette. Then he lit their smokes. "You ran away from the auditorium. Why?"

Maahi looked at him with honest eyes. "I didn't want to do what they wanted me to do."

"Who's they?"

Maahi looked away. "They'll kill my family if I say."

"I'm guessing al-Kaniyat militia," said de Payns. "If you don't argue, then I'll assume you agree."

Maahi smoked and looked away.

"Okay, so they have your family?" asked de Payns.

"My brother," said Maahi. "He's fourteen. And they know where my mother lives."

De Payns nodded. "What did they ask you to do?"

"I had to kill a man," said Maahi.

"Who's the man?"

"I don't know his name," said Maahi.

"An overweight guy, with a beard?" asked de Payns, describing Kolomoisky.

"No, he's thin, and the hair . . ." Maahi searched for the word. "Like a movie star."

De Payns nodded. "Your job was to shoot this man?"

"Yes," said Maahi, nodding. "Akeem told us that there'd be two men. Gray hair and dark hair. I had to shoot the one with dark hair."

"What about the other shooters?"

"Akeem said the dark man was my target," said Maahi, no hint of lying. "I don't know about the others."

De Payns took a deep breath, trying to alter his thinking on the run. "Why you?"

"I'm a good shot," he said. "When they killed my father, they said I had to work for them because I used to hunt and I could handle a rifle."

"MP5?" asked de Payns.

"And AK47, G3, M4, and fifty-cal machine gun."

De Payns nodded. "Those are not for hunting."

"No, mister."

"Who trained you on those weapons?"

"Al-Kaniyat," said Maahi.

De Payns was aware of the clock ticking. "What's your commander's name?"

Maahi looked away. "I can't . . ."

"They've already got your brother," said de Payns. "You could do worse than helping me."

"Who are you?"

"I can help you if you help me."

Maahi gave up, slumped in the chair. "Parzan. Parzan al-Sharif."

"Does he work for General Haftar?" asked de Payns.

Maahi nodded. "He's the al-Kaniyat commander around El Agheila."

"When I cornered you, you said 'asylum.' Why did you say that?"

Maahi paused. "A man told me to."

"Who's the man?"

"Faisal. He came to see the commander in Libya."

"Faisal told you to seek asylum?"

"Yes. A week ago, I had to pick him up from the airfield and take him to meet Parzan."

"Where was Faisal from?"

"American accent, but Libyan," said Maahi. "He had money for Parzan. He asked me if I was in the Europe group."

De Payns frowned. "Europe group?"

"Yes," said Maahi. "That's what he called us, the ones going to Turkey."

"So there was another group?" asked de Payns.

Maahi shrugged. "He said we drummers were the Europe group."

The door opened, and Captain Marak walked in.

"Time's up," said Marak.

Marak held the door, and de Payns paused on his way out. "The kid asked about asylum, is that possible?"

Marak smiled. "It's being done."

"They have his brother," said de Payns.

Marak pulled the door shut as they walked into the corridor. "These terror outfits are holding thousands of kids—can't save them all."

CHAPTER
FIFTY-NINE

Lenny Varnachev hit the button on his secure landline, killing the call.

"We're on," he said to the bullnecked man who sat on the couch on the other side of his office. "We have a meeting this Friday. I'll go, you manage the loading."

"Agreed," said Boris Orlevski. "You're better with Salah; I'll get those missiles on the ship."

Varnachev nodded as he lit a cigarette. After the failed assassination attempt on Zelenskyy in Istanbul, they wouldn't get another shot at the Ukrainian president. The next mission—the Anvil—was more daring, but it had to succeed. The planning leveraged the Wagner Group's connections in Syria, especially in the Hezbollah militia known as the al-Ridha Forces. The Homs-based militia had been trained and equipped by Wagner Group for several years, and Boris Orlevski had personally overseen some of the specialist navy commando training. The Wagner approach to regional dominance had been to work with private militias, giving them what they needed in return for services rendered in the future—services that created distance between Kremlin policy and so-called autonomous local actions. The al-Ridha arrangement was now coming to fruition, but Lenny knew his Director of Military Operations, Boris Orlevski, was not totally comfortable with the erratic and emotional commander, Salah.

"I think I'll bring a small inducement to our meeting," said Varnachev, with a smirk.

"Salah likes an inducement, as long as we're not kidnapping his daughter," said Orlevski, chuckling.

"Shit, no," said Varnachev. "God, this isn't fucking *Africa*. I was thinking of a cash bonus—something to make his eyes bug out."

Lenny noted Orlevski's agreement and swiveled in his chair so he was looking over the Tartus naval base on Syria's Mediterranean coast. The ships were Russian, and so were most of the buildings and people, and while Europe's intelligence services kept a close watch on the base, no government had raised a serious concern about it. Which suited Lenny Varnachev; his office was in the defense contractors' annex of the base, on the first floor of a building called Pacific Holdings Co. To anyone who asked, he was just a naval chandler, fulfilling his contract with the Russian navy to maintain their HVAC systems or ensure the video-on-demand system worked.

"What about our friend and his machine?" asked Orlevski. "If that doesn't work, the whole mission falls apart."

Lenny swung back and looked at his colleague. Boris was an old-school special-forces warrior who should have had a glorious career in the Naval Special Recon Unit, except the recon frogmen were under the command of the military-intelligence directorate, the GRU, at a time when the FSB gained favor in Putin's inner circle. That was how Lenny—the GRU intelligence officer—and

Boris Orlevski had ended up in Wagner Group. They'd both hit FSB-created roadblocks in their advancement, and now they made a great team, thought Lenny: Boris planned and executed military shenanigans, and Lenny connected at a corporate and political level with those who needed Wagner Group soldiers and firepower.

"Our friend says the machine works," said Lenny. "It was developed in Sarov in the 1970s—it's predictable."

"I've heard that kind of assurance before," said Orlevski. "But still, anything out of Sarov is usually as dangerous to us as it is to our enemies."

"Manfred is reliable," said Lenny. "Besides, the machine is on its way to Haifa. It's leaving Sarov this morning."

Orlevski reached for his coffee mug. "Okay, so your electrical crew receives the machine and installs it on the rig? And the Syrians come in from the sea?"

"The Syrians will have some firepower," said Lenny. "That's your end. Will Javelins do the job?" he asked, referring to the American anti-tank missile system.

"Yes," said Orlevski. "They're easy to use, and we've been training these al-Ridha creeps on target acquisition and firing. Once you lock on to a target, it's fire-and-forget, from a range of over two kilometers."

Lenny laughed. "Trust the Americans to build something so dangerous that can be operated by a monkey."

Orlevski chuckled. "I know. The operator's screen looks like a video game. A fifteen-year-old Chechen could fire this more effectively than she could give a blow job."

Lenny sniggered. "The Javelins are simple, and they have great range, but do they give us enough bang? Our job is to make prime time."

"The Javelins are perfect," said Orlevski. "The first part of the warhead pierces steel, and the second part is high explosive."

"We'll get ignition?"

"Oh yeah," said Orlevski, lighting his own cigarette. "The warheads we're using will blast the entire gas system with two thousand degrees of heat. It's going to look great on television."

CHAPTER
SIXTY

Paulin caught sight of Jabir Okimba shortly before eight o'clock on Sunday morning. It was cold and drizzling, typical of Paris in February.

Paulin had checked Okimba's address against the file developed by the DR and then spent the night watching from behind a line of dumpsters, on an angle that gave him a view of Okimba's apartment door on the second floor of a 1980s low-cost apartment building. Now the mystery man was moving through the gray morning mist toward Gagny station. Paulin took a seat at the opposite end of the carriage to Okimba and stifled a few yawns as they sped into Paris, his job made easier by the bright red down jacket that Okimba wore over jeans and lace-up boots. He assessed Okimba as his sheet showed him: ex-military, still fit, and liked to walk as if he had a purpose. The fact that he worked at La Poste was not of interest to Paulin. Many migrants worked at Europe's largest postal service, but that didn't mean it was all they did.

Okimba alighted at Saint-Lazare station and made for

another platform, a large black sports bag slung across his left shoulder. It was now 8:30 a.m., and there were more people around, allowing his visual signature to be lost in the endless crowds of the Paris train system. Okimba joined a train on the number 12 line heading south across the Seine, and Paulin watched him help a woman with a pram onto the train and then eyeball a couple of lounging youths until they gave up their seat for the lady with the baby.

Monsieur Okimba was not a man to take crap.

Paulin stayed near the back of the carriage and alighted when Okimba did, at Notre-Dame des Champs, a Metro station on the west side of the Jardin du Luxembourg. By then, Paulin had decided that Okimba was not in the game, but he was something.

Okimba walked two blocks northeast of the station and turned down a small side street where a church hall was set back from the road. A couple of parents waited outside the hall with their children, and Paulin could see that one of the children—a boy of around ten—had his white *gi* leggings on under his coat and tucked into his boots.

Okimba greeted the parents and kids, opened the church-hall doors, and let them walk in ahead of him. A gentleman, thought Paulin. He emerged from his hide beside a bus stop and fell into step with a woman walking toward the church hall with a boy and a girl, both of whom wore their white gi under cold-weather clothing.

"Excuse me?" he said to the woman, as they neared the hall. "Is this the martial-arts school?"

"Yes," said the woman. "The Karate for Life dojo. That man who just unlocked the door is Sensei John."

"Okay," said Paulin. "I have a nine-year-old who wants to do karate. How do you rate this dojo?"

She beamed. "Sensei John is the best. He teaches respect

and mental strength. And he hates devices, tells kids to engage in life, not to become addicted to an iPhone."

More parents and children were arriving. Paulin pulled back to the curb, took a quick photograph of the hall, and slipped his phone back in his pocket. A woman glared at him, perhaps wondering if she was in the photograph. He smiled at her and headed back to the Bunker.

De Payns hammered out his reports as best he could. His head buzzed with fatigue, and he used coffee to maintain his focus. The events of the previous thirty-six hours were a blur, but Briffaut was waiting on the reports from de Payns, Shrek, Danny, and Jéjé before the official debriefings.

Having filed his R report, de Payns hastily constructed the O report, with its subjective observations: Maahi's intelligence about there probably being more than one group operating under "Vulcan" and Marak's remarks that the Turks' main focus was on keeping their country "investible." Then de Payns shut down his computer, checked his safe, and was about to kill the lights when Aline appeared at his door.

"Boss wants to see you, Aguilar."

Trying to keep a smile on his face, de Payns peered in Briffaut's door, his backpack over his right shoulder. "You called?"

"Reuters story from Cannes," said Briffaut, pushing a one-pager across his desk.

De Payns read the two-paragraph news story issued that morning: a Georgian businessman, Lado Devashvili, had been found dead in his room at the Hotel Splendid in Cannes. He had been shot twice in the head. Police were investigating. Monsieur Devashvili was the former deputy-secretary of the Department of Agriculture in the Soviet Socialist Republic of Georgia. He was survived by his wife and three children.

De Payns pushed the report away. "And what about the family?"

"It's not your fault," said Briffaut, slipping the report into an opened file. "You did your job, Lotus did his."

De Payns nodded. But he felt nauseous.

"I see you filed your reports from Istanbul," said Briffaut. "Tell me what I need to know."

De Payns pinched the bridge of his nose. "The shooters were from Libya, run by al-Kaniyat, but they were just musicians who were being coerced. The weapons were chopped-down MP5s. The Turks think the guns were hidden in a Coke vending machine a week ago, which is why the security screening was useless."

Briffaut nodded. He'd already received the basics from MiT, which had included photographs and biographical information about the Libyan hit squad. "You don't sound convinced."

De Payns sighed and looked out the office window. "The youngest of the hitters was a teenager, Maahi, and the Turks gave me five minutes with him . . ."

"And?"

"He was forced into the mission by an al-Kaniyat commander named Parzan. They're holding Maahi's younger brother in Libya. And he said Faisal—I assume al-Mismari—had landed in the area with money for Parzan. They were making small talk, and he asked if Maahi was in the Europe group."

"Europe group?" Briffaut's brow creased, the implication sinking in. "Meaning there's another group?"

"That's how I understood it," said de Payns. "Maahi also assumed there was another group."

"So if they missed Zelenskyy and Kolomoisky, there's another group ready to complete?"

"Or," said de Payns, "it could mean there's another group with a different mission."

Briffaut made a face. "Tell me what you're thinking."

De Payns shifted in his seat. He hadn't organized his thoughts properly, and he'd been trained not to be too creative in his theories. "What do we know about the EastMed pipeline, and the Pantheon field?"

Briffaut shrugged. "What Lars and Marie told us. Massive gas field off Israel, and the gas is going to Egypt and Jordan."

"And Europe, if Kolomoisky has his way."

Briffaut and de Payns stared at one another.

"We've been very focused on Wagner and Libya, the Americans, and this information network that's been manipulating us," said de Payns, "but the speech Kolomoisky gave to the conference was about his ownership of the Pantheon field. With the US withdrawing support for EastMed, Kolomoisky wants to complete the pipeline into Europe, via Cyprus, Greece, and Italy."

Briffaut leaned back in his chair. "And who would hate to see that?"

"The same people who want Kolomoisky dead."

Briffaut leaned forward suddenly and looked at his watch. "The Lotus material, about the Tartus buildup and the Russian drones . . ."

"It fits with Putin's embrace of Hezbollah and Syria, and his cornering of the Egyptian wheat trade," said de Payns. "Lars also mentioned that the gas fields off Israel currently don't send gas to Europe. Maybe the Kremlin wants to keep it that way?"

"I'll get Marie and Lars to build out the file on Pantheon and EastMed."

De Payns suppressed a yawn.

"This is great timing," said Briffaut, standing and looking out his window on Paris as night fell. "Jim Valley is meeting with our Russian friend on Tuesday."

De Payns massaged his temples. "Grozny?"

"Azerbaijan," said Briffaut. "Keratine seems busy over there. Take a look at this."

De Payns took the thin file that Briffaut handed him. It was a backgrounder from the DR on Russian intelligence dynamics. It was a regular update that covered seven or eight of the Russian services, highlighting new appointments, deployments, and gossip.

"The FSB section," said Briffaut. "Page eleven."

De Payns glanced over the half-page brief, a short paragraph catching his attention:

The FSB is in conflict with the GUSP [Directorate of Special Programs of the President of the Russian Federation]. The conflict arises from Putin's Special Programs that either cut across FSB operations or detract from its budgets. Senior FSB directors in Moscow complain that the President's Special Programs create confusion among foreign services with whom the FSB might otherwise cooperate and create diplomatic questions where the FSB wishes none to be raised. Senior FSB people are concerned about Wagner Group's influence in the Kremlin via the GUSP. The founder of Wagner Group, Yevgeny Prigozhin, was recently seen inside the Grand Kremlin Palace, accompanied by Leonid Varnachev, a Wagner Group executive currently located at Tartus, Syria.

De Payns looked up. "Lenny Varnachev is meeting directly with Putin?"

Briffaut shrugged. "If he's walking around in the Grand Palace with Prigozhin, I'd say he's got access to the President's office, and the FSB hate him for it."

"You think that Keratine and his FSB buddies are keeping an eye on Wagner Group?"

Briffaut raised an eyebrow. "I'd bet they're all over Varnachev, waiting for him to fuck up so they can push him off the train."

"That's what we'd do," said de Payns.

"Damn right," said Briffaut, picking up his cigarettes but not opening the window. "I want you there with Jim. Let's really squeeze Keratine, see what he knows about Lenny Varnachev."

CHAPTER
SIXTY-ONE

The 9:00 a.m. meeting was held in the main SCIF on the DR floor of the Cat. Christophe Sturt was there, in his three-thousand-euro suit, allegedly made by Macron's tailor. So was the DO director, Anthony Frasier, who looked at his watch as if he had a more important place to be. Marie Lafont, Lars Magnus, Dominic Briffaut, and Alec de Payns rounded out the group, with Charlotte Rocard—Sturt's 2IC—operating as a serial head nodder whenever her boss spoke.

Lafont talked through a brief version of the Istanbul events. When she'd concluded her precis, Sturt leaned on the oval table, making a steeple with his fingers. "The Russians missed, so where are we now?"

Lafont said, "Russia is massing on the Ukraine border and it's exerting—"

"I mean, where are we now in relation to what you put to us two weeks ago?" Sturt broke in. "The Kremlin uses assassinations to effect regime change in Ukraine, and if that fails, Putin invades?"

Lafont deferred to Anthony Frasier, who took the question.

"We had no choice but to stop the assassination attempt in Istanbul," he said. "The Kolomoisky equation isn't just Ukraine—it's also about Europe's future gas supply and what it means for the French economy."

"What about the Americans?" snapped Sturt. "Where do they fit in?"

"We have a watch on them," said Briffaut. "Henry Krause has been released to the wild, and he's now our source. His story about the think tanks checks out. The Americans seem to have founded the Tirol Council and the Ligurian Institute, but it's much harder to prove that they run the output."

"Now we know where the Chinese got the idea," said Frasier.

"Yes, Director," said Briffaut. "We've identified Krause's handler—Christine Zeitz—but we can't find her. And Zeitz has a handler who we can't ID."

"If Krause is now working for us, why can't we find Zeitz or the handler?" Sturt demanded.

"Krause is more like a delivery mechanism," said Marie Lafont. "He gets his messaging from a Proton Mail account, which he disseminates through his reports and meetings. The mail drops to the embassies were not a regular thing, according to him. We're monitoring his comms, but our disruption of the meeting in Paris has certainly burned that connection. It won't be revived."

"Zeitz's handler is in Paris," said Sturt, tapping the report with his index finger. "And attempting to manipulate us. Aren't the Americans supposed to be allies?"

Lafont said, "The Americans have a plan for Europe's energy and a plan for NATO and Ukraine. They have a right to pursue their interests, just as we do."

Sturt nodded his agreement. "And the Kremlin?"

"By now the Russians know we frustrated their attempt in Istanbul."

"So, they go to plan B?"

Frasier rolled his pen between his hands. "Have you seen the news about Russia on the Ukraine border?"

Lafont said, "Yes—our American friends are now going directly to the media rather than shopping it through the services and the embassies."

"So, Putin invades?" Sturt asked.

Lafont caught a quick look from Frasier. "We've been looking at another scenario."

"Yes?" prompted Sturt.

"One of the al-Kaniyat shooters in Istanbul referred to his team as the '*Europe group*,'" she explained. "We're going back over the prod on Vulcan, and we're open to the idea that 'Hammer' might refer to a first action by Wagner Group, and 'Anvil' might be a second."

Sturt stared at Lafont as if looking upon a child's poor report card. "A *second* action?"

"Shit, Marie," said Frasier, leaning back in his chair and throwing his pen on the table.

Lafont looked over her half-glasses at the faces watching her intently. "We are looking in two directions. Western Libya was mentioned on *Azzam*, and especially Wagner Group's support for General Haftar seizing the GNA gas infrastructure, notably Bouri and al Sharara."

"Makes sense," said Frasier. "That would mean Putin controls the pipeline into Italy."

"What's the other scenario?" asked Sturt.

"Kolomoisky's speech in Istanbul addressed the EastMed pipeline, which could take Israeli and Egyptian gas into Europe without going through the expensive LNG process. He mentioned the Pantheon gas field—it's achieving first offtake this weekend."

She clicked her remote. The lights dimmed as an offshore gas rig filled the screen at the northern end of the SCIF. "Lars, please talk us through it."

"The rig is called Pontus," said Magnus. "When producing at full capacity, it will be maybe the world's sixth- or seventh-largest gas production facility, and a competitor to its next-door neighbor, the Israel-owned Leviathan."

Lafont clicked to a picture of a rig and a floating processing facility, and then to one of a red gas-processing vessel, the *IceMAX*, that was going take gas off the Pontus rig.

"Why would Putin allow Israel to develop Leviathan?" asked Briffaut. "It ruins his gas racket."

"The gas is piped to Egypt and Israel; it's not in the Europe market," said Magnus. "And the Russians are invested in Leviathan. Putin signed an agreement with Israel in 2015 for Gazprom to develop the field."

Frasier grimaced. "Smart move. Like having the mafia invest in your restaurant."

"What about Pantheon?" asked Sturt, scribbling notes on his pad. "What are the interests?"

"Mainly Igor Kolomoisky," said Magnus. "He's aligned with the Cypriot government, where he has citizenship. There's American and French capital and a Canadian operator. They'll use a floating production storage and offloading ship to take the gas to Italy or Israel, until the EastMed pipeline is operational."

"I'm guessing Putin doesn't want Kolomoisky piping cheap Israeli gas to Europe?"

"That's about it," said Lafont. "Hence, a Libyan and Israeli scenario. It's in the hands of the DO."

All eyes turned to Briffaut, who nodded wearily, like a man who was accustomed to the ball bouncing back to him. "We're on it. We'll know when we know."

CHAPTER
SIXTY-TWO

De Payns opened a bottle of Riesling from the fridge and from the corner of his eye watched Patrick shut the dishwasher door.

"Forget something?" he asked his oldest son, nodding at a pile of dishes in the sink.

Patrick shrugged. "Dishwasher's full."

Putting down the wine bottle, de Payns opened the dishwasher and saw a chaotic jumble of plates and glasses. "Plenty of room in there, *mon fils*. Just stack them closer together."

Patrick sighed. "Do I have to?"

"It'll only take you a minute, and then you're free."

Patrick's mutterings followed de Payns as he picked up the wine bottle and walked into the living room and sat on the sofa with Romy.

"You were saying," she said, as he poured them each a glass of wine. "The doctor?"

"It's going really well," he said, affecting a sincere smile. "I'm booked into monthly sessions, and I'm really happy with the progress."

She looked at him slightly too long. "What happened to *'the shrink can end my career'?*"

He sipped the wine. "She can also help me to get well. I'm focusing on that part."

Romy made a face that said she needed some convincing. "What did you talk about?"

"I'm not supposed to go into details . . ."

"In general terms."

"Well, you know, my stress levels and sleeping. A chat about fatigue and paranoia and how those two can feed one another."

"Any advice about how to stop the paranoia?"

De Payns stayed serene. "Everything you know about. Avoid becoming fatigued, get good sleep, immerse myself in non-work-related things."

"What about your marriage?"

De Payns took a breath. The last time they'd traversed this terrain, in Deauville, he'd been ambushed and had reacted poorly. "Yes, we went over that."

"And?"

"And it's really great to be able to talk about my feelings . . ."

"Screw your feelings," she snapped. "Everyone's got feelings. Not everyone's in *this* marriage."

De Payns nodded and took another sip. "I told her that things don't work so well when I have to go away and you can't contact me, and I can't tell you what I'm doing."

"That won't change," she said. "Does she have advice for when my husband stalks around the house at three in the morning, looking for terrorists?"

"Look, Romy—"

"Or perhaps a safety word for when he decides to beat someone half to death in front of his kids?"

De Payns nodded. He wasn't going to be defensive. "That was terrible. I'm so sorry I did that . . ."

"The gun, Alec," she whispered, as if he hadn't spoken. "It's not the first time you've carried it around in the middle of the night, but it's the first time that I thought you might . . . you know."

"That will never happen," he said, feeling some deep emotions. "I couldn't do that to you, to the boys."

"What does the doctor say?"

De Payns paused, instinctively wanting to dissemble. But he knew he couldn't. "She says you saw what you saw and you were scared, and I can't ignore that."

"You think?"

"Look, I've been stressed—really tired and paranoid—but I'm working on it," he said, trying to hold back the tide of emotion and reluctant to raise Degarde's death. "One thing you could do is maybe refrain from talking about me with Ana, until I'm well."

"Ana is like a sister to me," Romy said, voice flat and uncompromising. "If not for her, you and I . . ." She shrugged.

De Payns gulped. "Just pull it back a little?"

"Has it occurred to you that secrecy only makes it worse?" she said. "My God, have you ever heard women talk about their husbands? The whole thing is details."

De Payns rubbed his face with his hand. He was worn out and worried about having to go to Azerbaijan. He couldn't operate professionally in the field if he thought his home life was a leaky boat. "Give me two months," he said, aware that his eyes were damp. "I'm going to turn this around, but I need to know that I'm solid at home. Can you give me that?"

She nodded once, short and sharp. "There's only one alternative to you getting yourself well, and I'm not there yet."

De Payns exhaled. That would do for now.

CHAPTER
SIXTY-THREE

The view from the storeroom of Caspian Commercial Laundry did not include Baku's famous coastline, but it was a secure location for meetings thanks to Jim's local contact, who was paid enough to see nothing.

De Payns watched Jim Valley walk across the car park at the rear of the laundry, and when Valley was in the first-floor room at his allotted time of 11:00 a.m., they made coffee and waited for Keratine to show at 11:30.

"We're going to squeeze him," said de Payns, when Valley asked about de Payns' unexpected visit.

"For anything in particular?" asked Valley, stirring sugar into his dark local brew.

"Boss thinks we need carrot and stick," said de Payns. "The prostitute business means he's panicking a bit, looking for some leverage on you."

"It was very Russian," said Valley, with a smile. "I didn't take it personally."

"Of course not," said de Payns. "You brought the citizenship packs?"

Valley patted his woolen coat. "They're here. It was a nice
touch, including the son."

"No problems at the drop?"

Valley shook his head. "The embassy is good in this part
of the world."

"We're under some time pressure, so we need Keratine working with us, and giving rather than us chasing."

"Suits me," said Valley, his fist enormous as it grabbed the
mug handle. "What's the time pressure?"

"We think Wagner Group has something planned—maybe
by the weekend, if the analysts are correct," said de Payns. "We
think it'll be an infrastructure strike, probably natural gas, which
means they'll outsource it to a terror outfit."

Valley nodded. "You mean like al-Kaniyat in Istanbul? That
was Wagner, right?"

"Yes," said de Payns. "There's a second target, and Keratine
probably knows more about Wagner Group than he's letting on."

"Okay," said Valley. "I'll follow your lead."

Lazar Suburov, the man they called Keratine at the Bunker, was
not happy to see de Payns.

"I came to meet the gravedigger, but instead Paris sends me
the executioner," he said, nodding when Valley offered him coffee.
"The French certainly know how to make a man feel comfortable."

"Comfortable?" replied de Payns with a smile. "You mean
like a hooker in a mink coat?"

"Ah," said Keratine, as the coffee mug was placed in front
of him. "I would not call Sonja a hooker, but point taken."

De Payns signaled for the materials that Jim Valley was
carrying.

"I sensed some reluctance from you, Lazar," said de Payns, "and it occurred to me that perhaps we could reach a professional compromise, even given the obvious power imbalance in our relationship."

Keratine laughed briefly. "When the French use their manners, you know you're fucked. What are you proposing?"

De Payns took the manila envelope from Valley and pushed it across the table to the Russian.

Keratine's eyes widened as he opened the envelope. "French passports and new identities." The Russian examined them with an expert eye. All FSB officers were trained in validating documents, and de Payns noticed he paid particular attention to the French drivers' licenses and the health-insurance cards.

"It's the four-star package," said de Payns.

"It's good to feel appreciated," said Keratine. "Why not the five stars?"

"Because that would include a million euros, and I don't have a million euros for you," said de Payns. "New identities, French passports, and free health care is as good as it gets for a full colonel in the FSB."

"And what's the catch?"

De Payns shrugged. "If you don't want to work with us, then perhaps we drop the material about Nikolai to the Russian services?"

Keratine tapped the documents. "I'd have to verify these."

"You have already," said de Payns, smirking at a ruse he would have attempted himself. "Besides, we both know that those documents could be invalidated as soon as you've inquired. We've taken an incredible risk to bring these documents here, so you can sight them. You can see that the documents are real."

Keratine leaned back in his chair and seemed to deflate. "You're right, they're real, and they'll get us both killed. You can't leave them with me."

"Okay," said de Payns, gesturing for Valley to return the documents to the envelope. "They'll live in my safe or a place you nominate. Are you ready to work with us?"

Keratine shut his eyes. "The spy trusting the spy? Sounds like a comedy."

"You could just as easily screw me," said de Payns. "One click of your fingers and I'm in the back of an FSB van."

They stared at each other. De Payns could hear the Baku traffic outside.

Keratine finally sat forward and shoved his hands in his coat pockets. "Where do we start?"

"Wagner Group," said de Payns.

Keratine widened his eyes; the pale eyes of a man who'd been trained in stillness. "That's quite an opener."

"I was hoping you'd say that."

De Payns allowed Keratine to talk without interruption. The Russian described the creeping influence of Wagner Group via the President's Special Programs Directorate, the GUSP.

"Your colleague here—Guy—asked me about Varnachev two weeks ago, and I really couldn't go into it," said Keratine, lighting his fourth smoke. "It's too dangerous. This is not a subject that many of us in the services will talk about, let alone discuss with outsiders."

"Are you scared for yourself or for your son?" asked de Payns.

"Both," said Keratine. "It's the presidential intelligence directorate, with its own budget and private troops. It's like the Nazis with their SS that answered only to Hitler. It's very dangerous, and the FSB has been opposed to the arrangement since Wagner mercenaries were first deployed in Crimea in 2014."

"What was the problem?" asked de Payns.

"Wagner Group are just private soldiers," said Keratine. "It was annoying and confusing when they were deployed to the Donbas, but that was a tit for tat . . ."

"You mean because Kiev was using Azov Battalion private troops?"

"They were called Black Corps back then, and most of us in the services accepted the Kremlin's logic: to fight a deranged private militia, send one of your own."

"What happened?" asked de Payns.

"We had a very delicate situation in Syria, which was effectively a civil war engineered by a foreign power, and an extremist caliphate growing in the vacuum," said Keratine. "Moscow sends in Wagner Group, and they descended like a pack of dogs on one bone. Ridiculous stuff that made it almost impossible to get good prod out of Syria and for us to do our jobs."

"What about the GRU?" asked de Payns, referring to Russia's military intelligence and rival to the FSB.

"GRU are not in the Wagner loop," said Keratine. "They're as unhappy as we are."

"So, what are you doing about it? If the GRU and FSB both want to eliminate a pest, they don't usually miss."

Keratine sat back and observed de Payns. "If you're suggesting you'll piggyback on what we're doing with Varnachev, that gets all of us killed, including my family and maybe yours."

De Payns shifted in his seat, trying not to show how hard this last comment hit him. "What are you doing with Varnachev?"

Keratine raised his hand. "This conversation is suicide."

De Payns leaned forward slightly. "It's the only conversation which can actually save you and your son."

Keratine steeled himself. "We've been following Lenny Varnachev for weeks, ever since he arrived in Tartus. He's been having meetings at the Four Seasons in Baku with some very bad people."

"How bad?"

"The Homs Hezbollah militia," said Keratine, eyebrows raised. "They call themselves the al-Ridha Forces, and they're led by a maniac named Salah."

De Payns knew the name. Salah had been a Marxist at university in Paris and was now a born-again Islamist.

"Homs?" echoed de Payns. "He was part of that ISIS insanity?"

"Yes," said Keratine. "One of those devout Arabs with a bank account in the Caymans."

"What is Varnachev talking with them about?" asked de Payns.

"We're trying to find out. We also have chatter about a Russian scientist delivering a 'machine.'"

"You haven't listened in on these meetings directly?"

"It took us a while to find the meeting place, and when we did there wasn't enough time to get the listening post in place. But the next time, we'll be ready."

"When is that?"

"You can't be there."

"*When?*"

"Friday, ten a.m."

De Payns eyeballed the Russian, who glared back.

"You can't be anywhere near this. You may as well give me a t-shirt that says *traitor*. I'm giving you all I can, but be realistic—Varnachev is protected by the Kremlin."

"Okay," said de Payns, understanding the problem. "Then I strongly suggest you get creative."

Keratine reached for another smoke but didn't light it. "All I can give you is the room number. What you do with it is none of my business."

CHAPTER
SIXTY-FOUR

Dominic Briffaut received Aguilar's message, sent from a burner phone in the field, just before midday, when he was in his office talking with Marie Lafont. It was brief but to the point: Keratine was conducting surveillance of Lenny Varnachev at the Baku Four Seasons on Friday morning.

Briffaut looked up from his screen as Lafont assured him there was no chatter out of Libya concerning military actions on the GNA's gas infrastructure.

"The system that connects Libyan gas to Sicily is a huge target. We'd be hearing something through our communication channels if a strike was planned."

"We have a source in the LNA," said Briffaut, referring to General Haftar's government, "but nothing from there. The only prod from Benghazi is that Wagner Group is shitty with al-Kaniyat for failing in Istanbul, but Haftar supports al-Kaniyat because those lunatics control large areas of desert for the general. He won't turn on them."

"So we're back to the Israel scenario?" asked Lafont.

"We're back to keeping open minds and seeing where Wagner Group leads us," said Briffaut. "We're tapping a Russian source."

"I hope it's not the Pantheon field and this whole Kolomoisky mess," said Lafont, standing and collecting her files. "Sturt is jumping around like his handmade shoes are on fire. French involvement in Pantheon and the EastMed pipeline is paramount for the President. But at the same time, we can't muscle up like we did with the Turks last year because when it comes to Mediterranean gas, the Élysée reads Turkish actions as a proxy for Moscow."

"Okay," said Briffaut, raising his hands in mock surrender. "We're totally clandestine. And I guess we need gas as a backup plan if the Germans manage to take nuclear power out of the EU's net-zero pathway?"

Lafont smiled as she turned for the door. "If gas is good enough for the Germans, it must be good enough for the French, right?"

Briffaut bade her farewell and mused on Germany's net-zero energy plan which curiously allowed the emissions of natural gas but penalized the zero emissions of nuclear. When gas became the economic currency of Europe, France would want ownership in the cheapest supply of it, which was Pantheon and the EastMed pipeline. The French navy had recently been in standoffs with Turkish warships in the eastern Mediterranean over gas drilling in disputed waters. The Turks were obviously being goaded by Moscow into drilling outside their economic zone, but with Putin still controlling more than half of Europe's gas supply, this was not the time to call it out.

He turned back to the Aguilar message and typed a response: *Message received. Stay in place, cavalry coming to you.*

Briffaut hit send, then raised his voice toward the door. "Margot! Get me Templar, please."

The mission team comprised four people: Templar, Shrek, Danny, and Jéjé. They each attended to last-minute gardening of their fake ID legends in Paris, then took separate routes into Azerbaijan.

In Baku, de Payns checked into the Sea View Hotel and immediately checked the room. He was not happy with an assignment on the run, and he usually pushed back against DR taskings that came with small budgets and tight timeframes. But this one was ordered by Briffaut, and he understood the need to stay in Baku. He made a perfunctory check for microphones and cameras. The place looked clean, so he went outside and walked the street for half an hour, satisfied himself that he wasn't being followed, and ate at a cheap café. Templar was procuring a vehicle and listening equipment, and Shrek, who had dealt with the Four Seasons' concierge—making him an offer he couldn't refuse—was charged with finding a room adjacent to the Varnachev room, where the meeting would be held.

The next day, Wednesday, de Payns did a bit of sightseeing, like a tourist, waiting for the late afternoon. At a bus stop on a road that led down to the waterfront and Azneft Square, he found four white *gommettes* on the advertising board, meaning the mission team was primed and in place. He added his own white sticker to indicate he was present and ready.

At 11:45 p.m. he awoke to his alarm, dressed, and walked through the darkness to a small park with kids' swings and a water fountain. He waited by a tree, in shadow, and at 12:01 a.m., a battered Fiat van pulled up.

"Nice wheels," said de Payns, jumping in. The van smelled of spilled paint and rotten cabbage.

"I'm all class," said Templar, as he drove them across town.

In the hills above Baku, Templar parked in a scrubby layby. He gave de Payns a new burner phone and showed him two twenty-year-old Beretta 9mm pistols he'd acquired.

They both lit up cigarettes.

"Do we have the listening gear?" asked de Payns.

"It's a little older than we're used to, but I'm assured it works," said Templar, reaching into the van behind them and bringing forward a black Cordura sports bag. "It's got either plug-in or battery, and it can also transmit."

De Payns pulled an object the size of a coffee can out of the bag. It was five times the size of the wall microphones the Y Division used. "Wonder if Maxwell Smart ever used this?"

"It's the amplifier that counts, and ours is Danish, top of the line," said Templar. "I got us a directional microphone too," he added, lifting out a parabolic dish with a handgrip attached.

In its own bag was a set of mission radios that had seen better days, but they had micro earpieces and the system seemed to work.

De Payns nodded. "How are we with the Four Seasons?"

"Shrek's concierge friend has got us a room beside Varnachev's," said Templar. "We're pretty sure he's traveling as Ivan Borovich."

"This Hezbollah creep and his bodyguard," said de Payns. "Any sight of him?"

"No—the team have gone over the file photographs of Salah, and they're on the lookout. Shrek is calling him 'the Weasel.'"

"Let's not underestimate him or his backup. What about Wagner Group heavies? Seen anyone around?"

"No, and I understand that Varnachev travels alone, an old spy habit."

"What about Danny and Jéjé?" asked de Payns.

"Danny's keeping an eye on the hotel, and Jéjé's at the airport to give us the heads-up when Varnachev or Salah arrives."

"You seen Keratine?" asked de Payns.

"No," said Templar. "He could be up there living on room service."

"We'll need pics of Lenny and whoever is with him," said de Payns.

Templar smiled and pointed at the glove box. "Brought the Canon, but also got a pen camera if we feel the need to loiter in the foyer."

"I can handle the Canon from long range," said de Payns, "but I don't know about up close with the pen. He could recognize me from *Azzam*. Besides, I'd rather be in the sub monitoring the Varnachev meeting."

"Once Varnachev arrives at the hotel, Jéjé can take photos in the foyer," said Templar. "Otherwise we're in the sub. All set?"

"I'll let you know in twenty-four hours."

CHAPTER
SIXTY-FIVE

The call from Jéjé came through just after lunch on Thursday. Varnachev had walked through arrivals with a cabin suitcase—no checked luggage—and had jumped in a taxi, heading for town. The entrance to the Four Seasons looked like an old palace with not a lot of hides available to de Payns, so he stood at a pedestrian crossing looking down a cross street and took pictures of Varnachev getting out of the cab, with the Canon resting across his forearm and pointing at right angles to his body.

Varnachev walked into the hotel, checked in and went up to his room on the fourth floor, and de Payns circled back to the sub, climbed into the passenger seat where Templar was playing with the digital receiver and picking up music.

"What's that?" asked de Payns, as Templar tuned the receiver and clarified the sound being captured by Shrek's wall microphone on the hotel-room wall he shared with Varnachev.

"That's the in-house music channel," said Templar, with a smile. "Our Wagner man likes jazz."

They listened for more than an hour as Varnachev alternated between television news channels and a channel that played jazz. Then Varnachev had a shower before calling room service and ordering a cheeseburger and fries. Judging by the sounds of the door opening and a cap being popped, the Russian had a beer with his burger.

It was cold in Baku when the sun set, and Templar turned on the engine to get the heater working. De Payns went on the radio at 8:21 p.m. to check the airport status with Jéjé. Salah still hadn't shown, and the last arrival for the day was scheduled to land at 10 p.m.

"We need our sleep," said de Payns, when the TV was switched off and they could hear Varnachev brushing his teeth.

"Zero six hundred at the RV?" asked Templar.

"I'll be there," said de Payns.

The audio quality was not perfect, but it was pretty good for a mic that was pulling words through concrete. De Payns had a hard drive plugged into the receiver, recording everything, and Templar was running another receiver for the directional parabolic mic that Shrek pointed at Varnachev's wall.

They munched on pastries and drank black coffee as the sun threatened to rise, and at 7:02 a.m., Danny—sitting in an armchair in the foyer—keyed his radio mic and said, "Salah just entered by a side door with two thugs. Gone up in the elevator. Stand by."

They waited, and after forty-five seconds Danny came back on the net: "Fourth floor."

"Salah's early," said de Payns, to Templar. "So he arrived by road or he has a private aircraft."

"Or he's been in Baku for a few days and he's been hiding in a hotel," said Templar.

Danny told the mission team: "Going to fourth floor," which meant he was going to check that Salah's heavies weren't harassing people in rooms around Varnachev's.

Three minutes later, Danny came on the radio again: "They made one pass of the third floor but all good."

The wall microphone audio started with a knock on Varnachev's door, and the Russian taking control of his meeting. "They're not coming in," he said—pointing at Salah's heavies, presumably. "The breakfast is good here. We'll call them when we need them."

Speaking in English, Salah argued, but Varnachev won the point. "If anything from this conversation ever leaks out, I prefer that there's only one person I have to visit, and that's you, my friend," he said, with a big Russian chuckle.

The door clicked shut, and the Russian offered Salah coffee and told him where to sit.

Headphones on, Templar and de Payns listened intently. The Cat would not have time to go over possibly hours of conversation, so the message de Payns sent to Briffaut at the conclusion of this meeting would have to get to the heart of it.

The pleasantries ended, and they could hear Varnachev offering Salah a gift. "How much is there?" asked Salah, after he'd opened the latches of a briefcase.

"That's five hundred thousand euro for you personally."

"Personally?"

"As I said, it's between you and me," said Varnachev. "I don't deal with ideas, and al-Ridha or Hamas or Islamic Jihad are simply ideas. I deal with people. You and I have the relationship, that's how it works."

"Okay, so we have a relationship," said Salah, with a heavy accent but pretty good English. "Wagner shows us friendship, and al-Ridha returns the friendship."

"I'm glad we see it the same way," said Varnachev.

"I understand that we're going to hit a gas rig, but when do I get the Javelins?"

"First things first," said Varnachev. "You have the team?"

"Yes, they were trained by this Boris."

"He trained five—you only need three. You have them ready to go?"

"I don't have a target, and I don't have the Javelins."

"Are they ready to go?" Varnachev repeated. There was a pause—Salah nodding, perhaps—then the Russian continued: "As agreed, they board a boat in Hadera, between Haifa and Tel Aviv, and rendezvous with a ship. I have the papers for your people. They're logged in the Israeli security system, and the boat's skipper is one of ours."

"Yes," said Salah. "They take two Javelins off this ship, and the ship makes for Latakia and delivers one hundred and twenty Javelin systems to my people—"

"Deliverable on completion of your mission," interrupted Varnachev.

"The men will strike the rig with the Javelins. They are ready for this," snapped Salah. "But if I am to claim the responsibility and get the credit, I need to know where I'm hitting and have the footage ready for dissemination. You know this. This is the point of al-Ridha working with Wagner."

"The point of al-Ridha working with Wagner is that an unknown bunch of Hezbollah puppets in Homs get to strike out on their own account and not be constantly taking direction from Tehran or Beirut. *That's* the point. Clear?"

In the van, they could hear the heavy sigh from Salah. "Yes, we're clear. But still, I need to know that this ship is real and loaded with our Javelins."

"It's very real, my friend. In fact, it's being loaded today.

The ship will set out for Latakia on Sunday morning, and you will meet it just after midday."

"Where do we meet the ship? And what are we striking?"

Templar and de Payns could hear a piece of paper being unfolded, and Varnachev spoke again. "That's the RV coordinates, and your targets: the well bore itself and the rig-side system that the processing ship connects to. Commit them to memory, because that piece of paper is not leaving this room."

"There'll be some activity on Sunday because it's the first gas offtake at this rig," said Salah. "Lots of media?"

"I'd expect so," said Varnachev. "There's a chance that your people will get away in all the confusion."

Salah chuckled. "The Europeans and Israelis are not going to be happy about this one. But I have a question: we can hit the gas platform when it connects to the processing ship and probably make a big explosion. But they have all those safety valves that trigger as soon as there's a problem. I don't know that we can set the field on fire . . ."

"You're talking about the blowout preventers?" replied Varnachev. "You're right. They contain gas pressure and fire. But a BOP won't work if there's no electricity, no sensors or monitors to trigger it."

There was a brief silence, then Salah asked, "You can do that?"

"Yes, I can," said Varnachev. "You just put those Javelins where I tell you, and it will be like fireworks night."

De Payns hurriedly sent the sound files to Briffaut on his encrypted system, along with a message.

V & S hitting gas rig off Hadera with two Javelin rockets. Rig is likely to be Pontus since they'll be attacking a new rig making first gas offtake on Sunday. Hitters will have Israeli security registration. They will pick up two Javelin systems from a ship en route to delivering 120 Javelins to al-Ridha in Latakia. They will hit the well bore and the system on the rig that transfers gas to the ship. Salah remarked that Europeans will not be happy. V claims he will disable the blowout preventers on the rig by removing all power, sensors, and monitors.

De Payns split the teams: he and Templar would follow Varnachev, and Danny and Jéjé would tail Salah, a skinny rodent of a man. The Syrian and his thugs moved out of the hotel first, followed by the DGSE duo in a cab. Varnachev left ninety minutes later, and de Payns and Templar tailed him to a corporate helipad in the south of Baku, where he stepped onto an H145 helicopter. They watched the aircraft take off, turn, and set a course. It was heading west.

As they drove to the airport, de Payns took a call from Danny on the burner phone. "S and friends got on a flight for Amman. There's a connecting flight to Haifa."

De Payns stood in the Europcar car park of Baku International Airport and called a number in France. He was asked for an ID code to identify himself and then a response code that verified the office he was allowed to call. The operator confirmed and hung up. The burner phone rang three minutes later, Dominic Briffaut on a secure line.

"I got your message—where are you?"

"Still in-country," said de Payns. "Varnachev and Salah have decamped. They're heading for Haifa and Hadera."

"If the timing is for Sunday, we only have

Saturday—tomorrow—to sort this out," said Briffaut. "Any further details on this ship with the Javelins?"

"Only that the hitters will rendezvous with it on its way to Syria, so that means it's coming from Egypt or the Suez," said de Payns.

"Or Libya?"

"The only market that could supply one hundred and twenty Javelins to Wagner Group would be the UAE," said de Payns. "These weapons have probably come from the Gulf."

"If it's UAE, they'll be using Oman," said Briffaut. "Muscat?"

"Or Sohar?"

"I'll get Marie's team on it," said Briffaut. "I'll call the Israelis when I have more to say. This has to go to them, but I want you there anyway. You're at Baku Airport?"

"Yes."

"Stand by for a lift."

The French government Falcon 50 landed one hour and forty-eight minutes later, and an official from the airport collected de Payns and his team and shuttled them across to the military annex, where they boarded the small business jet. Once they were airborne for Haifa, the pilot patched through a call from Dominic Briffaut.

"You'll be met at Haifa by an Israeli security person. His name is Ben Adinsky, and you're Manu," said Briffaut. "He's your rank at the Shin Bet."

"Are we observing?"

"They'll let you operate in Israel so long as you're in Adinsky's chain of command," said Briffaut. "They've been tracking Salah for months—they're motivated and will take your input where they can."

"Okay, I'll stay in touch," said de Payns.

"And, just so I've said it," said Briffaut, "nothing to embarrass the Élysée, okay? Frasier is nervous. He's been told this Pantheon field and the EastMed pipeline is a part of the French plans for our future energy."

"Nice of them to tell us," said de Payns.

"Well, we know now," said Briffaut.

"Got it," said de Payns, signing off.

CHAPTER
SIXTY-SIX

Lenny Varnachev paid the taxi driver in cash and walked into the Haifa Sands Hotel, where he checked in as Ivan Borovich. In his second-floor room, which looked over the famous harbor and bay, he opened one of the two cheap cell phones he'd bought in Baku before flying to Haifa. Having switched it on, he made a quick call. After exchanging no more than fifteen words, he ended the call and made for the door.

The Anchor Holdings building was a light industrial two-story property in a rundown area of the Mifratz commercial zone attached to the Haifa port. Varnachev let himself in and made himself a coffee in the upstairs section of the warehouse and administration building while he waited for his associate to appear. From here he could look down on the parking area that formed the center of the commercial subdivision. As he sipped his coffee, vans and trucks came and went, loud beeps sounded when a forklift reversed, and overworked men in coveralls and hi-vis shirts went about their work. It was a perfect cover for Lenny Varnachev: while the combat side of Wagner Group was loud and obvious—and on CNN—Lenny's work entailed client management and the planning of operations that clients didn't want to be associated with. It meant a reversion to his old habits from the GRU, where fake identities, front companies, and "safe" buildings kept his trail cold.

Below him, a ten-ton truck pulled up outside the building, and the broad figure of Avi Aaron leaped out of the driver's seat. He was wearing jeans and a blue worker's shirt that sported a white logo.

"Come in," Lenny yelled when the front door creaked open, and he heard Avi stomp up the stairs like an ape.

"Coffee?" he asked, as Avi entered.

"You can't pull me away with no notice," he barked at Lenny. "I've got three men rewiring an entire transformer loom, and it's on a ship tomorrow morning."

"I'll take that as a yes," said Lenny, ignoring the man's anger, as he'd been trained to do in the GRU. "Two sugars, no milk?"

Avi whipped off his cap and sat at the kitchenette table. "Can we make it fast? When you get a maintenance contract for a gas project, the money's okay, but the turnaround times are virtually impossible." The Israeli, realizing he was getting no sympathy from the Russian, asked, "We all good?"

Lenny smiled. "I told you we'd have to be prepared to respond quickly, and you'll have to be ready tomorrow."

"Tomorrow?" exclaimed Avi, who had a neck that started under his ears. "What's happening tomorrow?"

"You'll be contacted urgently to replace an electrical control panel on the Pontus gas rig. It'll be on D deck, and they'll be in a hurry because that ECP controls the power to the rig," said Lenny. "And they can't take the gas off the rig and onto the process ship on Sunday without the ECP."

"And why won't they call DVJ at Hadera?" asked Avi, referring to the electrical contractors with the mandate for the rig.

"Because DVJ doesn't have the Siemens electrical control panel that Pontus needs and you do," said Lenny.

Avi leaned forward. "I don't carry a Siemens ECP, let alone one that controls a network of thousand-KVA transformers. DVJ will have it. It'd be part of their contract."

"Normally they would," said Lenny. "But not as of tonight."

Avi shook his head slowly. "Look, Ivan . . ."

"Perhaps I should explain the facts of our relationship to you," said Lenny, crossing his legs as he sipped on his coffee. "I could go to the Shin Bet, show them the dossier I have on Claudette Aaron, and let them decide whether Seabed Electrical retains its security clearance to work on Israel's energy infrastructure."

Avi looked at his hands.

"I mean, she is your wife and a director of your company, right?" continued Lenny, keeping his tone friendly. "And I believe that the security services would be fascinated to know that, before she became your wife, Claudette Aaron was known as Leila al-Dayad, part of Fatah's al-Dayad faction in Gaza."

"She was a kid, caught up in a pile of shit created by her father and uncles," Avi snarled. "If an Israeli Jew can forgive her, it should be none of your business."

"Oh, I agree, it's none of my business," said Lenny, nodding. "But the Shin Bet? They have different priorities."

Avi slumped in defeat. "We'll be ready to go tomorrow, but getting an ECP of that size at short notice will not be possible."

"Follow me," said Lenny, and he led the Israeli down the stairs into the building's ground-level warehouse. In the middle of a concrete floor sat a large cream-colored steel cabinet with five vertical doors. The word Siemens was stamped on the left-hand door.

"That's the ECP?" asked Avi, perplexed.

"Yes," said Lenny. "All you have to do is install it. And best of all, you get to send an invoice. Back your truck in here. I'll fire up the forklift and help you get it loaded."

Lenny watched Avi's truck leave the industrial park pause at the intersection with the main road. What the Israeli contractor understood to be a replacement Electrical Control Panel for the Pontus rig was actually an electromagnetic pulse machine—precision engineering that used explosive charges and a steel vacuum tube to send a sudden burst of electromagnetic energy through the atmosphere. If triggered at the right time, the EMP machine would fry and disable any electronic or wired circuitry within a hundred-meter radius. It didn't have to be the end-of-days machine that American preppers warned about on social media; it only had to disable the circuit boards, chips, and sensors that comprised a gas rig's blowout preventer. If the BOP could not stop the flow of gas during an emergency event, fire could flow unrestricted through the rig, destroying it.

He crushed his burner phone under foot and flushed the pieces down the staff toilet. He had one last coffee, then left the building, walking for several blocks to see if he was being followed. Once satisfied he was not, he took a taxi back to the Haifa Sands Hotel and opened the second burner phone. On the other end, Boris Orlevski picked up quickly.

"You still in Muscat?" asked Lenny.

"Yes," said Boris.

"Are we on time?"

"Yes," said Boris. "The package is halfway to Port Said."

CHAPTER
SIXTY-SEVEN

Briffaut and Marie Lafont arrived at the DGSI headquarters in Levallois just before 10:00 a.m.

"What if Manturov won't talk?" asked Lafont, as they passed through security. "What if he doesn't know?"

"Then we'll try something else," said Briffaut. "But for now, our Wagner mercenary is the best bet."

The DGSI guards dragged the Russian up to the same interview room where they'd last met. The Wagner mercenary didn't look as cocky or as physically fit as he had a week earlier. "You here to let me out?" he asked Briffaut. "You got a deal for my family, right?"

"I'm here to talk," Briffaut replied. "But you're reaching the end of your useful life to me."

Manturov tried to snarl, but it looked desperate. "The deal has to be that you get my mother out of Russia, with French papers—I want papers too."

"Really?" replied Briffaut, placing a file on the tabletop.

"Here's another view of the same situation. That's a file on you, your family, and nine of your military colleagues."

Manturov shrugged. "So what?"

"So that's going to Tartus base in Syria in a few minutes, addressed to Lenny Varnachev and Boris Orlevski. I will inform them that you have switched sides and that you are now working for the French government."

The Russian paled. "You can't do that."

"I can do what I want," said Briffaut. "Remember our chat about the legal status of mercenaries in France?"

"I already told you I don't know anything about anything. I was just a soldier when that lady was raped."

"You might know something. You're just unaware."

"Ask me," said Manturov.

"Have you ever operated in Israel?"

"Yes, but I never bombed nobody."

"Good for you," said Briffaut. "Where did you work?"

"Out of Haifa," said Manturov.

"The port?" asked Lafont, opening a window on her laptop.

"Yes," said Manturov. "They have a building there. I think it was better to be doing some things from Israel than from Syria."

"Can you describe the building?" asked Briffaut.

"Um, I think it was something to do with the sea, the ocean . . ." He frowned for a moment, then his face cleared. "Anchor!" he said. "Anchor Holdings."

Lafont's fingers rattled across her laptop keyboard. "It's in the Mifratz commercial center, an industrial park beside Haifa Port. That's it?"

"Yes," said Manturov. "That's it."

"What did you do there?" asked Briffaut.

"It was a place to sleep and to store things," said Manturov. "Weapons, money, vehicles."

"What is Varnachev doing there right now?"

"I don't know," said Manturov. "Varnachev is like a boss of bosses."

"I'm aware of who he is," snapped Briffaut. "Why is he in Haifa?"

Manturov shrugged. "I only know that we were going there next."

"We?"

"The crew down in Marseille. I told you about them."

"They'd gone when we went to the marina to find them. What was taking you to Haifa?"

"They don't tell us details," said Manturov, apologetic. "But the rumor was they were bringing a special machine in from Russia, and my friend Arky—who used to be an engineer in the Russian navy—he was going to make it into something."

"Something?" Briffaut repeated, annoyed.

"I think he said it had to look like a control box."

"I don't know what that means," said Briffaut. "What is the machine?"

Manturov shrugged. "Perhaps it turns out all the lights? Maybe you can't drive your car or use your phone? I don't know exactly; like I said, it was just a rumor."

"Fuck," said Briffaut under his breath.

Manturov was oblivious. "I think he said it had to look like Siemens."

Briffaut exchanged a look with Lafont, saw his own sense of alarm mirrored on her face; the Russian was describing an electromagnetic pulse machine. He rose abruptly; he had to call de Payns.

The Falcon 50 landed at Haifa Airport at 2:33 p.m. De Payns, Jéjé, Danny, and Templar we`re met by Ben Adinsky and his Shin Bet crew. Adinsky was midthirties, six foot tall, and athletic-looking.

They adjourned to an administration office.

"You guys armed?" asked Adinsky.

"No," said de Payns.

"Luka will fix you up."

A heavyset bald man in ripstop pants and a hiking shirt nodded.

"I suggest we split up," said de Payns. "We're looking at a crew in Hadera and one in Haifa, we think."

"Where does Salah fit into this?" asked Adinsky.

De Payns disclosed most of what he knew but stayed vague on the shipment of Javelins. If the UAE were selling them, they could easily be stolen French inventory, and he'd been warned by the Bunker not to embarrass France.

Adinsky looked at de Payns. "Manu, you can come with me to Haifa. Luka will lead the Hadera group."

"Okay," said de Payns, nodding at Templar and Danny to accompany Luka.

As Jéjé and de Payns walked toward the Shin Bet's Toyota Land Cruiser, their new Jericho 9mm pistols on their belts, Briffaut called on de Payns's burner.

"Varnachev's Haifa address is Anchor Holdings, repeat Anchor," said Briffaut. "It's in the Mifratz commercial zone. Our Wagner mercenary friend believes an EMP machine from Russia was brought there and then disguised as some sort of electrical box, maybe Siemens. You getting this?"

"Yes, boss," said de Payns.

"The tech people here say the EMP can disable every circuit on that rig, which means the safety systems won't work and a gas explosion can't be contained—a device called the blowout preventer will be disabled."

"Don't they have mechanical safety nets for that system?" asked de Payns, who had done a training exercise on a North Sea rig.

"Yes, but our engineers here say that those mechanical overrides still need sensors and monitors to trigger them. If the circuits are dead, the safety system doesn't activate."

They sped to the Mifratz commercial area, excited Hebrew spewing from the Shin Bet comms system.

"Tel Aviv wants to dispatch an IDF helicopter overhead," said Adinsky, from the front seat, "but I've said no. Let's use our brains before we start shooting, yes?"

"That suits me," said de Payns, adrenaline rising and the weight of fatigue and expectation resting heavily on him.

They swept into a lane with warehouses and light industrial buildings on either side, the driver of the Land Cruiser dodging trucks and vans before pulling to a stop in front of a large white roller door, above which was a sign that read Anchor Holdings.

They slipped from the car and advanced toward the building; de Payns noticed that the driver was toting a black submachine gun with a short barrel. The place looked deserted, and a few kicks at the main door revealed a steel-reinforced frame.

"Let's have a look," said Adinsky.

De Payns was about to put his lock-picking skills to work, but Adinsky gestured to the Shin Bet driver, who returned to the Toyota, revved the engine, and charged at the roller door, which flew off its guides and was left flapping like a sail in the breeze.

They walked in, guns raised, as workers from the neighboring businesses formed a nosy mob on the concrete apron. The drive-in warehouse area was empty, except for steel filings and loose screws lying on the concrete. Two wooden pallets lay empty, and a Nissan forklift was parked against the far wall.

"What are we looking for?" asked Adinsky.

"An EMP machine," said de Payns. "The size of a small fridge but disguised inside electrical controller hardware. I believe the cabinet will be Siemens—it's five or six meters long and two meters high."

They moved upstairs and looked around the abandoned administration suites.

"Nothing in the fridge," said Jéjé.

Adinsky walked to the kitchenette and eyed the coffee machine, putting his hand on it. "Still warm. Someone's been here maybe half an hour ago."

They spread around the subdivision, asking questions about who had been at the Anchor Holdings building, and the consensus was that a white ten-ton truck with a covered bed had backed in maybe forty-five minutes earlier and driven off shortly after. There were no markings on the truck, they said, but the driver had a logo on a blue shirt.

De Payns sensed that Varnachev was only half an hour in front of them, but he hoped it wasn't the head start the Russian needed.

CHAPTER
SIXTY-EIGHT

Templar sat beside Danny in the back seat of the Shin Bet Land Cruiser as the man in the front passenger seat—Luka—conversed with the analysts in Tel Aviv.

"What are they saying?" Templar asked, when there was a lull.

"I've explained that we have a crew of al-Ridha terrorists who'll be heading for Pontus on Sunday," said Luka. "They must have a way to get out there, so I've asked if there's a list of boats and ships that are allowed access."

"Any luck?" asked Templar.

"Not so far," chuckled Luka. "It can't be that hard."

"We could do it the other way," Templar suggested, looking out at the blue waters of the Mediterranean as they sped south toward Hadera. "Show some pictures of Salah to some of your favorite faces and see who freaks out."

"What if Salah isn't showing up in person?" asked Luka. "He could be hiding out and managing the operation. Do we have photos of the three Hezbollah shooters?"

Templar thought about that. "You got an informer in

Hadera? Someone who knows Hezbollah and doesn't like being roughed up?"

Luka smiled at his colleague behind the wheel. "I think we have just the person, don't we, Simon?"

Twenty minutes later, Luka and Templar walked down an alley ten blocks back from the docks at Port Hadera. They stopped beside a stinking dumpster and stepped through an open door into a tiny kitchen and emerged behind a counter in a café, surprising a skinny middle-aged Arab who was watching a TV fixed to the wall.

"What do you want?" growled the man, as a young woman in a hijab moved to his side. "You can't just turn up here, like this."

"Nice to see you too, Cheesy," said Luka. "Could we have a chat?"

"I have nothing to say to the Israeli services," the man snapped.

"Five minutes, then I'm gone."

Cheesy said something to the woman—probably his daughter, thought Templar—and then the three men adjourned to the kitchen.

"You want to scare all my customers away?" demanded the man, tearing off his apron.

"Salah," said Luka, as if Cheesy hadn't spoken. "You seen your buddy Salah lately?"

"No," said Cheesy. "He's too busy making money out of the Russians and Iranians. Why would he be in Hadera?"

"Do you know?"

"What can I say to you?" replied the café owner, and Templar saw a liar's eyes. "There's no al-Ridha here—that's all up north, Syria."

Luka said, "You know everyone, Cheesy. And I think Salah is in town. Would you like to help me find him?"

Through the fly curtain, Templar could see the daughter leaning in so she could overhear the conversation.

"I don't know Salah," said Cheesy.

"You used to," said Luka, stepping closer to the shorter man. "You used to shift his money around, so I'm sure you still say hello, that sort of thing?"

Cheesy shrugged. "I can't help you," he repeated. "I'm not in Syria—thank Allah—and I don't have to know anyone like Salah. No more!"

Leaving through the front door, they strolled down the street to a coffee shop that gave them a good view of Cheesy's café, while Danny and Simon kept an eye on the rear entrance. The café closed at 6:00 p.m., and Cheesy's daughter came out through the front door at 6:17, locking it behind her. Templar and Luka followed her for several blocks, into an area of Hadera that was more Arab than Jewish, the light growing dim as the sun went down.

"Interesting," said Luka under his breath to Templar, as the daughter hurried through a series of back streets to a small private hotel. "Her father's house is a mile that way." He gestured to the north.

They watched as the woman knocked on the door that fronted the street and, after some twenty seconds, was admitted. They couldn't see who let her in.

She left the hotel five minutes later, crossed the road, and boarded a northbound bus.

"I want to wait," said Templar.

Luka nodded. He keyed his radio and told Simon that they were going to watch the hotel.

Six hours later, they were still watching. The two Israelis were in the Land Cruiser around the front of the hotel, and Danny and Templar were standing in the shadows at the rear of the building, where there was a tiny car park. Templar had done a lot of waiting in his life. It didn't bother him. He wished he'd grabbed some more food when he had the chance and would have loved a glass of wine, but otherwise his eyes were fixed on a second-floor curtain that he'd seen pull back an hour ago. Someone checking to see who was out there? Someone who'd been warned that the Israeli services were sniffing around?

There was a landing on the same floor that opened onto a rear fire escape, which had a light glowing above it. Another hour passed, in which Templar didn't shift his eyes from the fire escape. Just after 3:00 a.m., his vigilance was rewarded when the door on the landing eased open and a man stepped onto the rear balcony. His hand covered by a t-shirt, he reached up to remove the light bulb, and in the instant before the light was killed, Templar saw the thin face and bald head of the man they called Salah. There was another brief illumination as Salah lit a cigarette. Templar had to laugh: the man who would blow up the largest rig in the Mediterranean obeyed the no-smoking rules in a hotel.

Templar remained motionless until Salah had butted out his smoke and went back into the hotel, then he whispered to Danny to stay put while he reported to Luka.

He crept around the side of the hotel to the Land Cruiser, where he briefed Luka on his find.

"I'll call in a response team," said Luka, lifting his radio.

"No," said Templar, who preferred to operate in the dark. "The girl gave them a warning, and they're probably spooked. Salah removed the light bulb just to have a smoke."

"You want to hit them now?" asked Simon. "There could be a lot of guns in there."

"We can't let them go," whispered Templar. "These

neighborhoods are crawling with spotters; the cavalry will just trigger them."

"What's your plan?" asked Luka.

Templar's adrenaline was running cold, the way he liked it. "You got any NVGs?" he asked.

Luka led them to the top of the rear fire escape, the four of them moving slowly, like cats. The steel framework of the fire escape was fairly new, and there were few creaks. Templar kneeled at the rear door Salah had come through and picked the lock in the door with a set of levers borrowed from the Shin Bet glove box. His heart was pounding, and his throat was dry. There were no foolproof ways to enter a building, but a lot of ways to screw it up and get dead. He forced the lock with only the slightest sound and held his breath as he pushed it in. They stealthed into the dark, their night-vision goggles showing up an interior landing with only two doors opening onto it. Templar pointed at one and touched his chest, and Luka nodded at the other. The two groups separated, and Templar crouched at the door he nominated and very carefully picked the lock. The clicking barrel of the mechanism seemed to roar in his ears, and when the pins fell properly and the lock released, he pushed the door slowly, his ears alert for any sound in the room behind it.

Danny aimed his pistol over Templar's shoulder as Templar stood in the doorway. He saw two beds, two men sleeping. He edged toward the first bed; the sleeping man's eyes opened, his head turning toward the door. Templar covered the man's mouth with his hand as he dived for the throat. Beside him, the second man made a small waking-up sound, and then Danny was on him.

The first man struggled until Templar put a neck hold on him with his forearm and introduced his pistol to the man's eyeball. At that point, the man went limp and surrendered.

"Not a sound," whispered Templar into the man's ear, "or I *will* kill you. Do you understand?"

The man moved his head to indicate that he did.

Templar and Danny and their two captives waited in the dark while a small scuffle broke out in the other room. When it seemed to have concluded, Templar dragged his prey to his feet and walked him through the darkness into the other room.

"Okay?" he asked, and Luka's voice came back: "Goggles off, lights on."

Minutes later, Templar regarded the four al-Ridha men who sat cross-legged on the floor of the hotel room, their wrists zip-tied behind their backs. The oldest, Salah, was around forty, while the youngest looked about nineteen.

"What kind of country is it where a man is assaulted like this in the middle of the night?" Salah demanded, defiant and half-naked. "Who do you think you are?"

Luka nodded to Templar, who took up the challenge. "Game's up, Salah. There'll be no rocket attack on Pontus tomorrow."

"I don't know what you're talking about."

Templar asked, "Who's taking this EMP machine out to the rig?"

"My God, you're French," sneered Salah, his eyes filled with hatred. "The French and the Israelis—you're as bad as one another."

"There's an EMP machine going out to the rig tomorrow," Templar repeated calmly. "Who's doing it?"

"I don't know," said Salah, smiling.

Templar punched him in the face, hard. Blood and mucus flew, and the man's nose flattened in a blue mess. Salah opened his mouth to scream, but Templar sealed it with his hand. "Who's the Haifa crew? Who's taking this machine out to the rig? Where are the Javelins?"

Salah shook his head. "I don't know," he said, voice muffled through Templar's bloodied hand.

Templar pulled his hand back as Salah gasped for breath.

"We're a crew for hire," spluttered the terrorist. "I don't know about the EMP machine, except that it will be set off."

"I don't believe you," said Templar.

"It's true," said Salah. "The Russians don't trust us—they trust nobody. They've got a way to shut down the safety systems on the rig with this machine, and then we're putting two Javelin rockets into the rig. We have no other job."

"And the Javelins?" asked Templar. "Where are they?"

"I have coordinates and a time, that's all," he said. "It's a sea rendezvous with a ship."

"How were you getting out to the RV?"

Salah laughed.

"That's not an answer," said Templar.

"Well," said Salah, chuckling, "the Russians got us jobs on a fire tug."

"You think it's funny, eh?" asked Luka. "There's, what, two hundred workers on that rig? Maybe fifty on the processing ship? You burn those people alive for what? A video on YouTube? Was that the plan?"

Salah shook his head. "Palestine will be free—you can't stop it."

Luka raised his pistol, and Templar gestured for him to desist.

"Which ship were you meeting?" asked Templar.

"*Golden Lady*," said Salah, spitting as the blood from his nose ran into his mouth. "I don't know where it's coming from."

"Where's Lenny Varnachev?"

Salah smiled. "In hell, I hope."

CHAPTER
SIXTY-NINE

De Payns woke to the sound of heated conversation coming through the wall. They were staying in a cheap motel in Haifa's south, and he could hear Adinsky in the next room, yelling into a phone. De Payns checked his watch: 6:49 a.m. He pulled on his pants and went into the Israelis' room, followed by Jéjé.

As the Frenchmen were ushered in by Simon, Adinsky ended the call.

"Everything okay?" asked de Payns.

"Luka and your boys have grabbed Salah's team," said Adinsky. "But they don't know anything about the EMP machine, only that it's going to be installed on Pontus."

"Installed?" replied de Payns. "It's going on a rig, so surely that means a rig has to ask for one?"

"No word yet from Pontus," said Adinsky. "But my boss said we can't wait for it to be delivered. If this thing were to be set off, the economic damage would be substantial; it has the capacity to destroy every circuit board in its vicinity. Can you imagine if every computer, every vehicle, every data connection in Haifa, our largest port, was fried? The gas industry might be protected by Faraday cages, but this city isn't."

"Faraday cages?" said de Payns.

"They provide protection from electromagnetic pulses," the Israeli explained. "The gas rigs have them."

"If the Israeli rigs have Faraday cages," said de Payns, "won't Pontus be protected from an EMP attack?"

"I asked about that," said Adinsky. "Our tech people think that if the EMP machine is disguised as a control panel, they'll install it inside the Faraday cages that would normally surround the electronics and safety systems."

"Attack from the inside?" asked de Payns.

Adinsky nodded. "That's what the Russians developed these things for. They're fairly portable, and they can be brought right inside the wire."

"Do we need more troops?" asked de Payns.

"We've already been given them," said Adinsky. "The IDF has a counter-proliferation team that deals with this stuff."

The phone trilled and Adinsky picked up. "Okay," he said, grabbing a pen and notepad from his bedside table. He wrote quickly, then ended the call.

"We have a plate number for the truck," he said to de Payns, standing. "So we have an address. Let's go."

They drove fast toward the port, passed the security checks at the precinct gates, and veered to the north, where a series of docks were supported by businesses. They parked behind a stack of containers, and Adinsky stood at the corner of one and pointed out a building to de Payns.

"There," he said. "Seabed Electrical Contracting, the white building."

De Payns saw a freestanding warehouse with 'Seabed-Electrical' emblazoned across tall drive-in entry doors. The structure was eighty meters across the concrete apron.

"That's where the truck is registered to," said Adinsky, binoculars to his eyes. "Seabed does electrical contracting for the gas industry. It's owned by Avi and Claudette Aaron."

"Looks like someone's home," de Payns observed, noticing a silver Chevrolet SUV parked beside a doorway. "How do you want to do this?"

Adinsky keyed his radio mic and spoke quickly in Hebrew. He turned back to de Payns. "IDF are on the perimeter, and they're standing off with the helicopters," said Adinsky. "They don't want the Tangos getting spooked and setting off the EMP."

"Who detonates it?" asked de Payns. "You wouldn't want to be standing next to it."

"No, it's effectively a bomb with a flux compression system at its heart. There's a lot of explosion, so I'd expect the trigger to be remote."

"Meaning the owners of Seabed Electrical are not going to set it off in their own warehouse."

"I wouldn't think so," said Adinsky. "Except that Claudette Aaron used to be Leila al-Dayad . . ."

"The Fatah al-Dayads?" asked de Payns. "You mean the hardliners of Gaza politics?"

Adinsky nodded. "That's why we have the IDF on the other side of that fence and a gunship ready to go."

"Fatah isn't Hezbollah-aligned, is it?"

Adinsky shrugged. "Bombers are bombers. I don't care what's on their bumper sticker."

"Can we talk to them first?" asked de Payns. "Can we jam the radio signals and see what's what?"

Adinsky chuckled. "You're a pure intelligence guy, right?

You just see these people as a source of information; I see a threat to my country."

De Payns inclined his head. "Yes, sure—that's my training. But think about it this way, Ben: you can blast that building with a missile, but how do you ensure the EMP doesn't go off?"

"That's what Tel Aviv and the IDF are squabbling about right now," said Adinsky, with a smile. "I bought us time by coming down here."

"Shall we?"

Adinsky made a face. "Shall we what? You want me to go in there? We have no idea who or what is inside."

"I'm a pure intelligence guy, remember," said de Payns. "I want to know."

They walked across the apron toward the warehouse, arms out, away from their firearms. De Payns was only eighty percent sure of what he was doing; there was no question it was a risk, but he needed to understand what was in that building and who was involved.

They were ten meters from the door in the side of the building when someone stepped out. Adinsky immediately went for his weapon, but the man's arms were in the air.

"Please," he said, his face a picture of anguish. "Please take this thing away."

Adinsky gestured with his handgun for the man to move away from the door. "Who's in there, Avi?" he demanded.

"No one," said Avi, his hands still in the air. "It's just me."

"Get on your knees, then lie on your stomach," snapped Adinsky. "Hands where I can see them."

De Payns moved toward the door and stepped inside, gun raised. A ten-ton truck sat in the center of the warehouse, surrounded by workbenches, lathes, and welding gear. Looking around, de Payns saw that Aaron had been telling the truth: the place was empty. He walked to the rear of the truck and looked inside. He saw a large Siemens cabinet with five vertical doors.

He moved back outside, where Adinsky had cuffed Avi Aaron. The Shin Bet Land Cruiser was heading for them.

"The machine is massive," said de Payns, as the vehicle pulled up.

Adinsky stood over Avi Aaron. "How were you going to trigger this thing?"

Avi turned his head so his right cheek was on the concrete. "I have nothing to do with it," he said, tears on his face. "The Russian blackmailed me."

"What Russian?" asked Adinsky.

"I don't know," said Avi. "He turned up about a month ago, he showed me . . . some things . . . about someone close to me . . . and said if I didn't install this ECP, the information would go to the security services."

"We already know about Claudette," said Adinsky. "You want me to believe she isn't in on this?"

"That's what the Russian wanted you to think," said Avi. "Claudette was rescued from all that crap when she was sixteen years old. She has no association with her family or with Fatah politics. She hates Fatah, she hates Hezbollah and Hamas. She went to university, she runs this company, and she has two fantastic kids. She's not a terrorist—she's an Israeli!"

De Payns sensed honesty. "Can you trigger this thing, Avi?"

"Trigger it?" the man asked. "I don't even know what it is. I just want it out of here."

"You haven't been given a detonation device?" asked Adinsky.

"No!" Aaron cried. "My job is to wait for a call from Pontus Operations. They'll need a new ECP for tomorrow's first gas offtake, and their contractors—DVJ—won't have one. But I do; it's sitting in there."

"In that case, who was going to detonate it once it's installed?"

"Why are you asking me about detonation? I'm an electrical contractor—I was supposed to install it, not detonate it."

"You have no idea who this Russian is?"

"No, but I think he's close by."

"Why do you think that?"

"Because there's never a car at his warehouse, and one time I had to meet him, I arrived early and sat in my car. He arrived on foot."

"Okay," said de Payns. "And?"

"And there're two hotels near his warehouse, the Sands and the Port View. Can you please get me out of here? What if he's watching us?"

Adinsky and de Payns swapped looks, then dragged Avi Aaron to his feet and ushered him toward the Land Cruiser.

When they were outside the port precinct, Adinsky got out of the car and made a call.

Getting back in the car, he turned to de Payns and Jéjé. "I'm taking you to the airport."

"And the EMP?" asked de Payns.

"The IDF have taken over," said Adinsky, shrugging. "They have a plan."

"What about me?" asked Aaron, who was sitting between Jéjé and de Payns.

"You're off to see the wizard," said Adinsky. "Thanks for the tip on the hotels."

"I told you the truth," said Avi, eyes red with tears.

"If we didn't catch you, you would have told us nothing," said Adinsky. "You'll get mercy from a judge, but not from me."

CHAPTER
SEVENTY

Briffaut was exhausted as he approached his office. Too many sleepless nights were eroding his sharpness, and he hoped he wouldn't miss a small but crucial detail.

He was reaching for his door when Mattieu Garrat, his 2IC, stepped into his path.

"Dominic, can I grab you for a second?" asked Garrat, looking around furtively.

They adjourned to op room four, where the trombinoscopes of two operations loomed on the far wall and a long trestle table contained files and mounds of paper in various states of organization. It was an operation still in progress, not at conclusion.

"The picture file from the SIS Maypole was in my office," said Garrat, "so I brought it down for Aguilar to file."

"Okay," said Briffaut, stifling a yawn.

"Aline was in here stacking the prod," his deputy continued, "so I gave her the file, and we had a quick look through it. It wasn't considered of interest the first time around, since the British had what we had, but this time I saw something . . ."

"Yes?" prompted Briffaut, almost swooning with fatigue.

Garrat flipped to a page with a photograph of a good-looking woman in her midthirties, dark hair. The image was not good, reflecting the fact it was probably grabbed from CCTV footage, and made more indistinct by the sunglasses the woman wore.

"Who's that?" asked Briffaut, pulling the file toward him. He squinted. "Shit, is that Christine Zeitz?"

"Yes, it is," said Garrat. "It's just a file picture that the SIS uses for Zeitz. It was taken in Larnaca a year ago. It's not considered important to our operation."

"Okay," said Briffaut, getting impatient. "So why are you showing it to me?"

"Look closely at the picture," said Garratt. "It's been blown up to get Zeitz's face, but there's someone else's hair in the background. I don't know why, I just had a feeling about it, so I called the SIS and asked for the original frame."

"And they sent it?"

"I was owed a favor for that time when—"

"Don't tell me."

"So, this is the original frame," said Garrat, producing another print. In it, a woman was standing beside Christine Zeitz at the foot of the gangway onto a yacht.

"Do we know the boat?" asked Briffaut, interested now.

"It's the *Melissa*," said Garrat, smiling broadly. "Our British friends have access to the security cameras at its home port of Larnaca."

"Who's the woman beside Zeitz? Is she anyone?"

"She's this person," said Garrat, presenting him with a glossy eight-by-ten print. "I did a *demande de criblage* on her a year ago."

Briffaut stared at him. "We *checked* this woman?!"

"Yes, full security clearance, and DGS came back negative."

"Who asked for the DDC?" asked Briffaut.

Garrat flipped to the note from the DGS, the internal security division of the DGSE.

Briffaut read it, and his breath caught in his throat. "Holy shit. Don't tell a soul about this—that's an order!"

CHAPTER
SEVENTY-ONE

De Payns sat in the departure lounge of Haifa's airport, keeping his distance from Danny, who sat in another row of seats. Jéjé and Templar had caught buses to Tel Aviv and were flying from there. It was part of the Company's security protocols that, having operated in-country as a team, the OTs traveled back to Paris separately, playing out their individual legends.

He'd slept very little. He was exhausted and confused. It was only right to let the Israelis deal with a threat in their own territory, as the French would always insist on doing in France, and being pulled away from the conclusion of his work was the nature of the job. But he liked it to be done right, and he preferred to be there at the finish.

As he waited for the 2:00 p.m. flight, he noticed the airport had three news services on different television screens. Al Jazeera carried a story about tomorrow's commissioning of the first gas from the Pontus rig and the Pantheon gas field. There were sweeping helicopter shots of the massive gas-processing ship, the *IceMAX*, standing off from the gas rig: the journalist explained that the ship would take off gas and ship it to Egypt, but one day that gas could be piped directly into Europe via Greece and Italy. De Payns drank coffee and winced, fearing that at any moment a Javelin rocket would shimmy through the air like a sliver of death and turn Pontus into a fireball. It made him nervous, even though he knew the threat was extinguished—for now.

The BBC screen carried a short piece about a section of Haifa losing power and residents complaining that their cars and computers no longer worked. He couldn't hear the sound, so he followed the English subtitles: the power company was calling it an "anomaly," and the government had "no comment" about the rumor that an EMP had been set off. The BBC interviewed a person who claimed that the oil-and-gas operators in the port area had not been affected because oil-and-gas operators in Israel protected their critical ITC infrastructure with Faraday cages, a claim the government person called a "conspiracy theory."

De Payns needed a drink. He went to the bar and ordered a beer, and while paying he saw another TV behind the bar. CNN was playing a news segment with a "Breaking" chyron across the bottom of the screen. A ship named *Golden Lady*—from Muscat, sailing for Port Said—had sunk in the Gulf of Aden as it tried to pass into the Red Sea. The report said French frigates had secured the area and were hunting for survivors. The TV footage showed what looked like dive boats and frogmen between the two warships. A local man was talking to a reporter, and CNN had provided a voice-over translation: "*The French navy opened fire on the ship—we could see it from the beach where we were fishing—they sailed up to the freighter and sank it.*" The French navy had issued a statement explaining that the frigates were conducting humanitarian operations in the wake of the maritime tragedy and disinformation about French aggression was emanating from terror cells in Yemen.

De Payns raised his beer and grinned. Wagner Group had just lost one hundred and twenty Javelins, which would be better recovered by French naval divers than left in the hands of Hezbollah's Homs militia. He also reflected on the fact that a bunch of sailors had lost their lives in the process.

He looked out the window as he sipped his cold beer. He thought about Romy and the boys, his marriage, and his own mental condition. Then he shoved the thoughts aside and concentrated on coming back from the moon and getting his final mile totally correct. He went to take another sip and realized he'd been holding his breath.

CHAPTER
SEVENTY-TWO

Dominic Briffaut sat in the passenger seat of the Renault Koleos, parked in a side street off the Quai des Grand Augustins, which gave him a small glimpse of the Saint-Michel bridge. He smoked his cigarette down to the end and flicked the butt out the cracked window, feeling the light splatter of rain on his hand as he did.

Beside him, Aline sat at the wheel and took radio updates from the six-person mission team placed around and inside the Cochinchine, a small bistro that overlooked the Seine.

"You're good to go, boss," she said, after they'd waited for seventeen minutes. "Bistro is empty. Target at the end table."

Briffaut emerged from the Renault and walked onto the quai, passing two subs that were bristling with OTs from the Bunker.

He walked for twelve seconds, then turned left into the bistro. It was just after 11:00 a.m., so the lunchtime rush hadn't yet begun. Briffaut unbuttoned his overcoat as he walked toward a table at the end of the narrow room. A woman eyed him as he drew near, and he noted that Templar was at the neighboring table and Jéjé was at the table beside the front door.

Briffaut sat opposite the table's occupant, a beautiful Syrian woman in her late thirties with a head of black hair, a high forehead, and very good dress sense.

"Hello, Brenda," said Briffaut. "We finally meet."

Her pupils dilated but she kept calm. "I don't know a Brenda. You have the wrong person."

Briffaut continued as if she hadn't spoken. "You're a CIA handler who operates out of the Red Lion, running an information network that includes Christine Zeitz and Henry Krause? I don't think I have the wrong person."

"Perhaps the wrong name?"

"Okay, I can call you Ana," smiled Briffaut. "I've confirmed your photograph with two services, and we can connect you with the *Melissa*."

Ana let the point go. "Well, I'm honored. This must be important."

"I won't take up your time," said Briffaut.

"Then why is your guy bolting the door?"

Briffaut didn't take his eyes off her. "I have a situation you could help me with."

"I doubt it," she said, sipping on her coffee. "But try me."

"I have a dangerous impasse that could be resolved in two ways."

"Sounds like a dilemma," she said, reaching for a glass of hazelnut-colored liquid. Briffaut guessed amaretto.

"The person trapped in this situation was used in a game, but she's not in the game."

"I see," said Ana, looking away.

Briffaut continued, "If I resolve the problem formally, the person in question has her life turned upside down. There'll be months of surveillance and interviews, and computer and phone audits—and, of course, there are two children caught up in this. Not to mention the embarrassment for two friendly services."

"Or?"

"I'm glad you asked me that, Brenda," said Briffaut, holding up his hand to stave off the bistro owner when she looked like she was going to approach him for an order. "Or we resolve this informally, professional to professional. I give you twenty-four hours to remove yourself and your family from France, and we can all get on with our lives. Romy de Payns won't be subjected to hundreds of hours of interviews in which she has to recall exactly what you asked and how she replied, and you won't have to worry about being hunted down by Alec's colleagues—who, I can assure you, will not tolerate a family being infiltrated."

Ana looked into her drink, and Briffaut thought he saw her back heave slightly. When she looked up, there was dampness at the corner of her left eye.

"Don't make me do this," she said. "I'm asking you, as a courtesy . . ."

"And as a courtesy to Romy, I'd never put her or her children through the official meat grinder, if I can help it," said Briffaut, in a flat voice. "So either you go, or I hand this to Alec's colleagues."

"Do you have to do this?" she pleaded. "Our families have become close. Those boys feel like my sons."

"Of course I have to do it," said Briffaut, annoyed by the emotional appeal. "You saw to that. You know where this goes."

She shook her head and looked into her drink. Her sorrow looked genuine. "You know, I didn't approach Romy. It was a friendship that grew naturally out of the preschool."

"And yet here we are."

"You don't understand: if I'd known who she was married to, I would never have suggested her for the Tirol Council. I wanted a friend, that's all. I wanted to put down roots in Paris. Please don't do this to us."

"You shouldn't have pulled her in," said Briffaut. "You know the rules."

"I was only told about her husband when it was too late," said Ana, tears welling. "You know, I'm a mother now—I'm getting out of the game and going back to consulting, I just hadn't made it official . . ."

She sniffed, and Briffaut could see an attempt to control her emotions.

"Twenty-four hours," said Briffaut, standing. "That's the best I can offer."

Ana nodded slowly, defeated. "I'll take the deal," she said. She looked up at Briffaut and then around the café at Templar and Jéjé, who stared back like two stone statues. "What guarantee do I have that I won't be killed when I walk out of here?"

"There'll be no guarantee if you don't honor our agreement."

Ana nodded and stood, grabbed her overcoat. "Romy will not forgive you for this."

"Romy will never know, and neither will Alec."

She wrapped her scarf around her throat. "Don't worry. I could never tell her."

She stopped at the door and paused, looking back at her coffee and amaretto.

"Don't worry about your coffee," said Briffaut. "I'll take care of it. We know how to treat our friends in France."

Briffaut watched her walk through the door and followed her outside, where light rain speckled the Seine. Templar joined him, and they watched as Brenda started to jog along the footpath.

"Ah, Paris, the city of love," said Briffaut, lighting a cigarette but not taking his eyes off the American spy. "I'm pretty sure she won't miss her flight."

CHAPTER
SEVENTY-THREE

De Payns chuckled at the antics of SpongeBob as he chewed on an apple. Oliver was curled up on the sofa beside him, and Patrick lay virtually horizontal on a beanbag. He was relaxed, having come straight from the airport, through his safe house, and back to the apartment. His weekends felt like a sanctuary, and he was putting Baku and Israel and the events of the past week behind him. He was even looking forward to the next session with Dr. Marlene—it wasn't comfortable, but it was helping.

The door opened down the hall, and de Payns told the boys to go and help their mother with the shopping. He heard the boys arguing about who would open the chocolate biscuits, then running down the hall to their room. Romy emerged and sank onto the sofa beside him, and he gave her a kiss on the lips.

"Can we get the news on?" she asked, preoccupied. "Something's happening in Ukraine."

De Payns changed the channel to France 24 and saw video footage of Russian tanks rolling down country roads and troops getting on transporter helicopters. According to the voice-over, Russian troops that were supposed to be doing exercises with the Belarusian army had crossed the northern border into Ukraine, and the Russian Black Sea fleet was on a combat footing after an alleged missile attack on the Russian navy at Sevastopol.

"It's started," said Romy, kicking off her shoes and pouring herself a wine. "With all the buildup, you'd think we could find another way to resolve it."

"Sure," said de Payns, not wanting to mention that the alternative was assassinations and regime change.

He heard her sigh heavily.

"You okay?"

"Not really," she said.

"What's up?"

"Well," she said, and de Payns heard a quiver in her voice, "the Homsis are leaving."

"Leaving?" asked de Payns. "Montparnasse?"

"No," she said, looking into her wine. "I bumped into Ana at the market just now . . ."

"And?" de Payns prompted.

"And she was very upset. The family has been urgently called to New York, something to do with Rafi's job. I couldn't follow it properly."

"That's a shame," said de Payns. "I guess that's the global economy now—we go where we have to go?"

"Sure," she said. "But I mean—well, they're going *tonight*. No goodbye dinners, nothing. It feels so sudden."

"That's weird," he agreed.

"We should have them over before they go," she said, sounding tremulous. "The boys are so close, and Ana and I . . ."

"Maybe they're too busy," said de Payns. "They probably have things to do if they're in a rush?"

"And maybe they're hungry," Romy retorted, pulling out her phone. "Let's get them over for lunch, at least."

Romy hit a saved number, then immediately made a face, looked at the screen.

"What's wrong?" asked de Payns.

"The number has been disconnected," she said, incredulous. She tried again, with the same result. "What the hell?"

"I don't understand," said de Payns, feeling awful for her. As much as the friendship had bothered him, he knew how important it was to Romy.

"Neither do I," said Romy, scrolling through her iPhone and hitting another number. Again she made a face. "Their landline has been shut off too."

She opened WhatsApp. "Ana has left our WhatsApp group." Her face fell. "Do you think she's dropped me?"

"No, I don't think that's it," said de Payns. "Let me try Rafi." He took his phone from the coffee table and dialed. Like Ana's, Rafi's phone had been disconnected. "Well, shit," he said. "I don't get it."

Romy threw her phone onto the sofa beside her and stood, so she was looking down on him. "Is this something to do with your work?" she demanded.

"No," he said, surprised. "This is news to me."

Her face hardened. "Would you tell me if it was?"

De Payns's heart went out to her because in that instant he assumed that yes, it did have something to do with him, and no, he'd never tell her. Every time he had to burn one of his fake IDs, the people he'd lured into his pretend life were faced with what Romy was encountering now: confusion, abandonment, sadness.

"Yes, I would absolutely tell you," he said. "And yes, this sounds like something that happens in my world, but I promise you I have no idea what's going on."

He stood too, and she gazed into his eyes for a few seconds, and then she crumpled. "I just wish I knew," she said quietly. "Ana's like a sister to me."

He held her as she cried.

"I have a terrible feeling that I'll never see her again," said Romy, sobbing. "I've been so alone, I have no friends, no one I can talk to, and now . . ."

"I'm sorry," he said helplessly.

"Please," she said into his shoulder. "Don't let this be the government—they can't take everything from us. Please tell me it's not the government doing this."

"It's not the government," said de Payns, unable to say anything else. "There'll be an explanation. There's always an explanation."

De Payns arrived at the Bunker early on Monday morning. Briffaut was in his office when de Payns entered, holding the coffee he'd made.

"You saw the stories in the papers?" asked Briffaut. "Ship sank off Djibouti."

"I saw that on TV," said de Payns. "Those sunken ships make for great diving."

"Yes, it's amazing what you can find down there."

De Payns sipped his coffee. "I heard in Haifa that an electromagnetic pulse machine had been set off. Apparently, all the civilian electronics were screwed, but the oil-and-gas people were okay because they have Faraday cages?"

"Sounds like a conspiracy theory to me," said Briffaut. "You hear about Salah and his gang?"

"Were they down in Hadera?"

"Yes, the Shin Bet got them. Caught them in a private hotel."

"That just leaves us with Brenda and the Starkand network," said de Payns.

"Gone to the DGSI," said Briffaut.

"Why?" asked de Payns. "The prod was being funneled through the embassies—that makes it ours."

Briffaut shrugged. "Sturt wanted it off our plate, and so did Frasier. Who am I to complain? Besides, we know the story, don't we?"

"I'd like to identify Brenda," said de Payns. "If she's operating in Paris, manipulating our foreign policy and our military responses, I'd like to know who she is."

"By the time the Cousins have bumbled and fumbled all over it, she'd have seen their surveillance from two miles away and gone to ground," said Briffaut, shaking his head. "Forget Brenda. We have bigger fish to fry now that Russia has gone into Ukraine."

"Well, Marie was right all along," said de Payns. "Plan B for Putin is invasion."

"Yes, and the only winners are Washington and Moscow."

De Payns was about to leave, then he turned to look at his boss. "Any ideas about Brenda?"

Briffaut looked at him, expressionless. "CIA but not one of the stupid ones."

"We almost had her, but as soon as Templar got close, she was in the wind."

Briffaut nodded. "She was well camouflaged."

"Maybe in plain sight?" asked de Payns, staring at him.

Briffaut smiled. "The best always are."

De Payns made to leave but Briffaut called him back. "I need you down in Niamey."

"What's going on in Niger?" asked de Payns.

"Take a seat," said Briffaut. "There's something I need you to do."

"An operation?" asked de Payns.

"No," said the boss. "There's no file on this, and you won't take any notes."

"You want me dressed as a waiter again?" asked de Payns, with a smile.

Briffaut shook his head. "We're finishing what we started."

CHAPTER
SEVENTY-FOUR

They flew in from Chad on a twenty-year-old helicopter and landed on the outskirts of Maradah in southern Libya just before 10:00 p.m. The man who met them at the airfield provided them with a white Nissan Patrol with the Sirte Oil Company logo on its doors. They changed into blue Sirte coveralls, and Templar checked the maps with the man, who also showed them the four jerry cans of gasoline on the roof racks and the cooler box loaded with food and drink for four people. A blanket in the load space contained Beretta handguns, NVGs, silencers, and M4 carbines, which Jéjé checked quickly and expertly under a headlamp on his forehead.

The load space also contained a box of grenades, spare magazines, and bullets. The radio comms gear was in its own bag, and in a black case Templar found a Vintorez sniper rifle, a collapsible Russian firearm that worked particularly well with a suppressor. Templar double-checked the supplies and loaded his UAV control module into the Patrol. It looked like a slightly fatter version of a laptop bag and did not give a hint of the destruction it could unleash.

The team of four drove through the night, arriving at a point five kilometers south of the target, just off the El Agheila–Maradah road that cut north–south through Libya like a surgical scar. The moon was waning but bright enough to throw some light on the desert trail. Templar, Danny, and Jéjé set off on foot; Shrek stayed with the Nissan and returned to the road.

After forty minutes of walking, they arrived at a ridge that overlooked the al-Kaniyat camp, where they sat down to avoid presenting a silhouette to those on the other side. Templar brought out his rangefinder binoculars and assessed the compound, which consisted of three shipping containers, a CAT generator on skids, and four relocatable buildings. A clearing in the center of the camp was covered with a large camouflage net of the type that artillery units hid under in World War II, with a small dugout on the side containing a desk and chairs. Three beaten-up Japanese pickups were parked on the outer rim of the compound. Templar lifted the binos slightly to see what lay beyond the living and working area of the camp and sighted a white shipping container fifty meters from the southern edge with the word COSCO in black. He could see a five-hundred-liter plastic water barrel outside the container doors and a ladle on the top of it. This was the container where prisoners were kept, according to his briefing pack.

He panned the binos and counted two sentries on the perimeter of the camp: one to the right, guarding the road into the camp, and one sitting in the cab of an old truck, facing the French team.

"Sentry at our twelve o'clock," said Templar, looking through the binoculars.

Templar, putting down the binoculars, asked Danny for the Vintorez, and he silently removed the pieces from the carry case

and put them together to form the rifle, screwing the suppressor down, not too tightly.

"I mark a hundred and eighty meters," Templar whispered.

He handed the rifle to Jéjé, who removed a night sight from his webbing and screwed it in place on the rifle. The former navy commando flipped down the bipod on the end of the Vintorez barrel, adjusted the scope for range, and lay flat on the ground, spreading his legs for stability. Templar picked up the binos and put them to his face. He focused on the guard in the truck cab, and as he watched there was a low whacking sound, and the guard fell forward in the cab seat, his head bouncing on the dashboard.

"Let's make it fast," said Templar, and they pulled night-vision goggles down across their eyes, stood, and walked down a ravine toward the camp. They waited at the truck cab, where Jéjé checked the dead sentry and came up with a ring of keys, handing them to Templar. Danny and Templar stealthed around the perimeter of the sleeping camp and finished off the sentry at the gate using a suppressed Beretta handgun.

"From Templar, sentry two is down," said Templar over the radio.

Jéjé moved in from the truck cab, the M4 carbine to his shoulder, and stopped at the corner of a demountable which they believed was the barracks for the al-Kaniyat shooters. Jéjé looked in one of the windows, observed the interior with his night-vision goggles, and pulled back.

"Jéjé at the barracks," he whispered. "I count nine fighting-age males."

"Templar copy," said Templar, as he jogged across the central square of the compound with Danny to a dingy old container with a dirty tarpaulin across its roof. Templar found the right key and unlocked the container door. Looking inside

with his NVGs, he could see only diesel and firearms and a box of grenades.

"Templar at central container. It's a weapons store. No kids."

He turned back to the compound and now knew that the final demountable was the al-Kaniyat commander's quarters, belonging to the man they called Parzan. He watched Jéjé move through the shadows to the quarters and open the front door very carefully.

"Jéjé at the commander's quarters," he said, having pulled back. "Confirm one male, sleeping. No kids."

"Copy that," said Templar.

He brought them together, and they moved back to their first vantage point, from where they'd made the sniper shots. Templar could have released the prisoners first, but his experience in Africa told him that when captive humans were released—kids in particular—they could do unpredictable things and jeopardize the operation. He would deal with the al-Kaniyat militia first and release the prisoners when they had clear air.

He took off the backpack he'd been carrying and brought out a laptop-sized plastic device, connecting a burner phone to it with a USB cord. The box was a spinner that could pretend to be a cellular base tower for any phone in the vicinity and was also a French military command-and-control system. He switched it on and watched the small screen on the box light up. Then he input the cell-phone number he'd been given by the DR in Paris. With the number in the box, he plugged earphones into the device and keyed the encrypted radio system.

He checked his watch: it was 4:23 a.m. "Black Crow on station. Confirm 'go' for the package."

Templar waited as a voice he knew well confirmed Templar's identity and authority.

"Copy that, Black Crow," said the voice. "Blue Nest standing by for trigger."

Templar nodded to the man beside him. "Danny, time for a wake-up call."

Danny moved down to the compound, picked up two empty steel drums by their handles, and flung them into the clearing in the center of the camp, where they bounced over one another, shattering the stillness of the night. Through his NVGs, Templar could see Danny pick up another steel drum and fling it after the first two, where it made even more noise as it banged and bounced its way across the compound.

Lights came up, and a demountable door opened as Danny scrambled up the bank, back to the team's vantage point. Two soldiers appeared on their barracks' front porch, squinting into the dark and jabbering in confusion as they aimed their rifles into the night. A third and fourth soldier pushed through the first two, looking for the threat.

Someone yelled a command, and the floodlights around the clearing lit up, the CAT generator roaring into life as the electrical load kicked in.

The team removed their NVGs, and Templar waited for Parzan, who emerged onto his front porch, bare-chested. The al-Kaniyat commander immediately started yelling at his troops, who spilled out onto the dirt, trying to find the source of the disruption.

It suited Templar—the longer they left their lights on, the harder it would be to see the French team in the darkness. Carefully, looking up into the clear sky, Parzan stepped off the porch, at which point Templar hit the green button on his burner phone. They watched Parzan freeze and look down at his pants pocket. Slowly, as if drawing a scorpion from his underwear, the feared militia commander reached for his phone.

"Come on, answer it," mumbled Templar. "You know you want to."

Finally, Parzan extended a reluctant finger to the screen and hit the receive button.

A mile above them was a circling French MQ-9 Reaper drone aircraft that carried a two-hundred-and-fifty-kilogram guided bomb—the GBU-12. The bomb had a receiver in its nose, which was now locked onto the IMSI in Parzan's phone.

Templar waited silently as Parzan listened. Neither of them spoke. It was French protocol to confirm a second mode of identity beyond the primary identification of the target's IMSI. Many terror commanders did not handle their own phones or laptops.

Finally, Templar said in English, "Is that you, Parzan? I've been trying to reach you."

"Who is this?" demanded Parzan, his face panicked, his eyes searching the darkness of the camp's perimeter for clues. "Who is this?"

"What time is it there?" asked Templar. "It should be almost eight-thirty, right?"

"*Who is this?*" shouted Parzan, his voice ringing out over the noise of the generator.

The voice analyzer in Templar's control box verified a match: the voice belonged to Parzan al-Sharif, one-time schoolteacher and now Libyan militia commander subject to a long list of allegations of human rights abuses.

Templar keyed the radio: "Voice identification confirmed. Clear to shoot."

Templar signaled his team to take cover, and they ducked into the crest of the dune they were occupying. Five seconds later, there was a faint whooshing sound, followed by a huge explosion which shook the ground and the air. As Templar and the team let the shock wave pass over their dune, chunks of earth and pieces of clothing began falling on them. Beyond them in the desert, they heard the tinkling sound of glass raining on dirt.

"Black Crow for Blue Nest," said Templar into the comms. "Package has arrived."

"Blue Nest out," came the voice. "Have a great morning."

"Get Shrek to pick us up," said Templar to Jéjé, shutting down the comms box. He stood carefully, assessing the camp. "I'll see you at the car."

There were pieces of bodies lying around the camp and a crater three meters deep where Parzan had stood a minute earlier. It was dark as Templar entered the terrorist camp, the floodlights having been blown out along with every window. Dust settled slowly, like a shroud of death, covering the camp with the distinctive smell of post-combustion bomb chemicals. Templar had become acquainted with that smell in Chad and Sudan, but he'd never been comfortable with it. It wasn't the smell of victory, as it was represented in the movies: it was the telltale odor of death, dismemberment, and civil dislocation. To release such power was not something to be done lightly.

He walked through the camp, around the smoking crater, and out the other side, to the container being used as a prison. It was peaceful out in the scrub, the waning moon casting an aura of calm. The sound of yelling children became louder as Templar approached the white container. One voice called out above the rest—a boy brave enough to be defiant and yet still sounding scared and defeated. The human spirit was a hell of a thing, he thought as he ladled a fresh tub of water from the plastic drum and placed it in front of the door. He found the right key from the guard's key ring and released the padlock.

A hundred meters away, the team's Nissan Patrol descended the approach road into the camp, its headlights killed. Shrek's voice hissed in Templar's radio earpiece. "Your ride's here, monsieur."

Templar threw the padlock into the desert and unclamped

the vertical locking bars on the container. The kids' voices died down; they were obviously worried about who was outside. In a calm and natural movement, Templar let the door swing open with a creak and turned for the Patrol.

The lieutenant in the remote drone cockpit went through his post-operation checks, confirming the aircraft's status with his female flight officer. The quarter-ton GBU-12 had been released on target, but they still had a Reaper to fly back to Diori Hamani International Airport in Niger, the site of France's main military presence for operations in Sahel.

As he set the navigation system for the drone's flight home, the nameless man from the government who had stood behind them during the operation walked to the flight screens in front of two pilot chairs inside the command center.

"Erase the flight data," said the tall, fit man. "And delete the ordnance logs for the bomb."

The lieutenant was about to argue, but when he looked up, he saw a person whose gaze was both charming and terrifying.

"Well," said the lieutenant, stealing a quick glance at the flight officer, "I can scrub the flight records, but we just dropped hardware worth two hundred thousand euros and—"

"Do you want me to show you how to do it?" asked the man, a small smile on his face.

"I can do it, but . . ."

The lieutenant knew from the previous four hours that this man not only knew how to fly but he had an intimate knowledge of the digital systems that enabled the remote drone cockpits. Now the lieutenant was unsure who he was more scared of: this man from Paris and his demands, or his commanding officer, who would eventually want to know why a two-hundred-and-fifty-kilogram guided bomb had been eradicated from the system and therefore from his annual audit.

He looked sideways at his flight officer, who shrugged as if to say, *What can we do?* The lieutenant reached for the computer mouse, clicked deep into the command-and-control system, and deleted the barcoded serial number for the GBU-12, along with the telemetry for its recent deployment—data that showed where it was released, at what time, and by whom.

The government man pointed to another screen, and the lieutenant entered that system and deleted the flight data of the Reaper drone.

"Nice," said the man, when the system confirmed the deletion. "And, of course, best you both forget this operation."

"What operation?" replied the lieutenant.

"Good answer," responded Alec de Payns. Turning, he pushed through the security door of the drone's Block 50 Ground Control Station. His eyes reacted to the dramatic African dawn as he left the semi-dark of the cockpit, and he paused on the tarmac in front of what looked like a forty-foot container with wheels attached at the corners. Then he lit a cigarette and turned east, reaching for his sunglasses as the sunrise hit his face. For a second, he felt very still, and in that moment, he recalled the Company's motto: *Nox Generat Lumen*—the night brings the light.